PRAISE FOR

THE HIDDEN LETTERS OF VELTA B.

**Finalist for the Oregon Book Award's
Ken Kesey Award for Fiction**

"Intimate, vibrant, and richly colored . . . [A] touchingly fabulist story."
— *Portland Monthly*

"A beautiful, tragic, and mesmerizing account of a fascinating place and people."
— *Eleven PDX Magazine*

"For readers who love historical fiction and magical realism, *The Hidden Letters of Velta B.* is a gift on par with Joanne Harris's *Chocolat* . . . Quirky, ethereal, hilarious, and sorrowful, Ochsner's intimate portrait of a group of people who must survive with each other's help, whether they like it or not, perfectly highlights the connections between the everyday and the transcendental elements of being human."
— *Shelf Awareness*

"[A] beautifully spun tale . . . Ochsner bewitches the reader with layer upon layer of spellbinding storytelling . . . An astonishing alchemy of history, romance, and fable."
— *Kirkus Reviews,* starred review

"Strange, vivid . . . Bizarre, often hilarious vignettes [feature] a cast of colorful characters and slapstick moments . . . Humor, mythology, and an immersive setting, as well as a few poignant and visceral moments as family secrets are revealed, render this a memorable tale."
— *Publishers Weekly*

"A captivating novel of secrets, love, and memory, *The Hidden Letters of Velta B.* revels in the tragicomedy that is life itself, binding the poignancy of human dreams to accidents of circumstance. Ochsner weaves magic from muddy roads and financially strapped dreamers, plotters, eccentrics, gypsies, failed dancers, chess masters, and philosophers — who, despite cell phones and bus service, could have lived in eons past. When an outsider threatens to move the town's cemetery, the excavation becomes the perfect metaphor of buried memories in a history-haunted land. This terrific novel knocked me out."

—Janet Fitch, author of *Paint It Black* and *White Oleander*

"In Gina Ochsner's extraordinary feat of storytelling, a dying mother seeks to armor her son with the power of myth and the strength of family history. The stories she tells are as rich as roasted eel from the river, but the ugly truth of their Latvian town's history keeps poking through like rocks in the hard cemetery ground. A spellbinding novel as tough as it is beautiful." —Helen Simonson, author of *Major Pettigrew's Last Stand*

PRAISE FOR GINA OCHSNER AND HER WRITING

"[Ochsner has] luminous writing, affection for her characters, and, especially, faith in language's humanizing power."

—*New York Times Book Review*

"[Ochsner has] a lean, poetic style whose fatalism brings to mind Flannery O'Connor's." —*Los Angeles Times*

"Chagall must have waved a magic wand over Ochsner."

—*Town & Country*

"[Ochsner] has her own power to transport." —*New York Times*

"Fluid, poetic storytelling, conveying dry wit and imaginative meta-phors." — *Minneapolis Star Tribune*

"[Ochsner is] a powerful artist. Her ability to lace words together in ways that are new, creating peculiar clarity, is formidable . . . One of the most delightful things about reading Ochsner is that she doesn't seem to be-lieve that boring people exist . . . [She] is an earnest, gentle, and funny writer." — *Salem Monthly*

"Ochsner's originality lies in her ability to make the unknown tangible by taking what we do know for definite and twisting it." — *Time Out*

"With her distinct voice, her knack for finding fresh images, and the ben-efit of what Robert Olen Butler dubbed the 'Big Gift,' Ochsner is ready for the big time." — *Writer's Digest*

"Ochsner moves deftly between the real and the imagined, and between the absurd and the profound, the comical and the terrible." — *Image Journal*

"[Ochsner] writes about real people doing their best to survive in unreal times . . . [Her] prose sparkles with wit and originality at every turn, while the characters' inner worlds glow with humanity." — *Guardian* (UK)

"Ochsner balances surreal and real with a light touch . . . [She] has a tal-ent for striking images, and she's quirkily funny." — *Independent* (London)

"Ochsner is a true artist." — *Times* (London)

THE
HIDDEN LETTERS
OF VELTA B.

THE
HIDDEN LETTERS
OF VELTA B.

Gina Ochsner

MARINER BOOKS

HOUGHTON MIFFLIN HARCOURT

BOSTON NEW YORK

First Mariner Books edition 2017

Copyright © 2016 by Gina Ochsner

Reading Group Guide copyright © 2017
by Houghton Mifflin Harcourt Publishing Company

Q&A with the author copyright © 2017 by Gina Ochsner

www.hmhco.com

Library of Congress Cataloging-in-Publication Data
Names: Ochsner, Gina, date, author.
Title: The hidden letters of Velta B. / Gina Ochsner.
Description: Boston : Houghton Mifflin Harcourt Publishing, 2016.
Identifiers: LCCN 2015037466 | ISBN 9780544253216 (hardback) |
ISBN 9780544703049 (trade paper) | ISBN 9780544253124 (ebook)
Subjects: LCSH: Mothers and sons — Fiction. | Spiritual healing — Fiction. |
Great-grandmothers — Fiction. | Family secrets — Fiction. |
Letters — Fiction. | City and town life — Fiction. | Blessing and
cursing — Fiction. | BISAC: FICTION / Literary. | FICTION / General.
Classification: LCC PS3615.C48 H53 2016 | DDC 813/.6 — dc23
LC record available at http://lccn.loc.gov/2015037466

Book design by Eugenie Delaney

Printed in the United States of America
DOC 10 9 8 7 6 5 4 3 2 1

A portion of this novel first appeared, in different form, in *The New Yorker.*

The author is grateful for permission to reprint lines from Muriel Rukeyser's
"The Speed of Darkness," from *The Collected Poems of Muriel
Rukeyser.* Copyright © 2006 by Muriel Rukeyser. Reprinted by
permission of International Creative Management.

The author is grateful for permission to reprint the *daina* on page 8, from
Albert B. Lord's essay "Theories of Oral Literature and the Latvian *Dainas,*"
and the *daina* on page 65, from Lalita Muižniece's essay
"The Poetic 'I' in Latvian Folk Songs"; both essays appear in
Linguistics and Poetics of Latvian Songs. Montreal: MQUP, 1989.

The *dainas* that appear on pages 86, 164, 170, 210, 263, and 266 are from
The Daina: An Anthology of Lithuanian and Latvian Folk-Songs, edited by
Uriah Katzenelenbogen. Chicago: Lithuanian News Pub. Co., 1935.

For Dace Berzins

The universe is made of stories, not of atoms.

—Muriel Rukeyser, "The Speed of Darkness"

THE
HIDDEN LETTERS
OF VELTA B.

CHAPTER ONE

YOUR FIRST DAY OF THIRD GRADE. The leaves crisped on the trees, curling orange, red, yellow. They crunched like brittle paper beneath our feet as we walked down our lane. The closer we drew to the school, the slower you moved. We spied other kids galloping toward the schoolhouse, their mothers in tow, juggling book bags, purses, and mandatory first-day gifts for the new teacher: yellow apples, embroidered handkerchiefs, chocolates. You had no book bag. I had no gifts. This was our third attempt in as many years to get through the dreaded first day. I had a pair of extra-large aviator muffs and these I slipped over your extra-large ears. As much to protect the tender cartilage as to dampen the colossal noise of the school yard.

Outside the wooden school doors, you grabbed my sleeve, turned to me. "I know I am peculiar," you said. "But am I *too* peculiar?"

The verbal torment at the hands of schoolmates, the pain inflicted by well-intentioned neighbors. That's what I heard in your voice. What I said, my hand on each of your narrow shoulders, "Maris, you are fearfully and wonderfully made."

It's a verse from Psalms, one of my favorites. I said it because I know the power words have. I've read Genesis. I've read how God spoke every blade of grass into being with the three little words *let there be.* The words: all potential, all possibility. Speaking a story makes it happen, and so I told you a story, told you it was yours.

> *A long time ago, so long ago no one remembers when, Bear-Slayer Boy rose out of the river's mud. His ears, enormous. Trimmed with fur and as large as meat pies. With those ears he could hear the stirrings of field mice three countries away. His gifts of discernment were unparalleled. Bear Slayer could hear how the heartbeat changes, how the voice tightens when someone tells a lie. He could hear the sweet caroling of the songbirds and knew what the fish in the river were thinking. Smart and wise, Bear Slayer, though a boy, was also strong and courageous. Once, when he was walking in the woods, a bear ambushed him. Without hesitation Bear Slayer, using only his hands, slew that bear, ripping it apart at the jaws.*

This story is a door opening. A door closing. The words are hinges, self-oiling through the act of repeated recitation. Repetition being a form of love, I told you the story every night during those magical, swift years of your childhood. *How big were those ears?* you often asked, your voice small in the growing darkness. *Bigger than mine?* You needed to know you were not alone in your oddity, that your outsize ears were not a mistake but a marvel. I leaned over you, turning chant to parable. These words being like the interlocking teeth of a zipper, you unzipped the teeth of the story, crawled inside its dark, capacious interior and made it your own.

Lymphoma. What a funny word! It sounds like a musical instrument, something that emits warm round tones when struck with a soft mallet. Anyway, Dr. Netsulis showed you how to administer the morphine, left several vials in a waxy white paper bag. He has changed so little through the years: the white lab coat, his snow-white hair, long beard, thick glasses, absentminded cheer. He said to me, *Safe journeys and many white days! And six weeks left to live if you're lucky.*

You asked me yesterday if cancer hurts, really hurts. Yes and yes. You say you don't remember the time we rushed you to the clinic in Madona. You say you don't remember telling the doctor that hornets had built a nest with knitting needles inside your ears, that our voices rattled like matches in a matchbox. What you felt in your ears I feel in my lungs, a sharp rattling. Every breath is a short, hard swipe of matches on the striking surface's rough swath. Thank God for morphine.

More like a liquid weight than anything else, I'd say. It pulls me under and I happily let it drag me to the depths. The weight is like that of the radiologist's bib. Remember how during that visit the technician sat you on a stack of thick dictionaries and draped the lead apron over your small body?

The color of doom, that apron. And so heavy! It took all of your strength to keep your five-year-old body still so that he could take the pictures. More about that visit I could tell you: the immediate circuslike sensation your ears provoked among the technicians, the many questions the doctor asked as she trailed her finger along the tawny fur of your earlobes, but it's that weight I'm thinking of. Morphine feels like a soft metal melting in my stomach, pulsing through my chest, hips, thighs, pushing all feeling toward my hands and feet, which are, incidentally, burning hot. I know I told you earlier not to fuss over me, not to bring the pans of ice water for my feet, but I think now I'll take you up on that offer.

You've come to sit beside me. A sheen of perspiration stands on your brow and above your lip. The fading light makes your ears look larger. You've lit the candle. Some people will think it a waste that at eighteen years of age you've devoted yourself to tuning pianos, studying speculative physics, and publishing poetry in the temperance newspaper. But I'll tell you this: I couldn't be prouder of you.

From the open blisters on your hands, I can see that the ground is giving you some troubles. You are digging near Uncle Maris's grave.

It is a particularly unyielding patch of the cemetery, the ground buck-ling, his stone lashed with many black marks and tipped to one side. The earth pushes back what it doesn't want. The fact is, something of your namesake has always lingered with us and I don't mean in the sentimental way that people hoard memories and imagine that a mem-ory is the man. I mean the man was with us. Palpably, tangibly, and long after he passed. We were marked, branded.

I understand now that you've known this all along. From the time you were four, your ears were as large as soup bowls. You could barely lift your head for the weight of them, for all the chatter and noise they collected. As you grew older, you kept notes. The ground spoke to you and you couldn't help but hear the soil's slow heave of stones. You heard the triumph of each slender blade of grass spearing up through the mud and the restless dreams of the dead. Buttons and zippers. Needles and thread, things that fasten and bind. At night, that's what the dead dream of, you wrote. They are unhinging bone from joint, word from thought. Oh, that the needles of the trees would pierce them, would dart and pin body to soul. The unraveling, you wrote, is their greatest source of confusion. What are we without our bodies? This, you wrote, is the question that grinds at the dead like steel wool on a rusted washboard, like gravel splintering the planed pine boards of a coffin.

You wrote that when people die they leave an empty sack they fill with words, murmurs, questions, gossip, complaints. Some empty sacks are bigger than others. Uncle Maris, you wrote, wanted a new pair of leather shoes—nice Italian ones with ornamental fobs—be-cause the walk to heaven was longer than he had figured. He's been gone fifteen years. And still he has so much to say. He is our haunting, present in absence. Hearing what we couldn't, you've known this all along. Maybe this is why you asked me this morning whether I'd like to be buried closer to him or my grandmother Velta.

I said, *Bury me wherever the ground is softest.* I think your hands were hurting; you kept your fingers curled slightly, like a man who handles a shovel all day long surely will. I said, *Sit here a minute because there are things you know and things you don't.*

Mistakes. I have made more than my fair share. When you were a child and claimed you could hear printed words vibrating on pages, or that in the buzz of the telephone wires you heard a week's worth of gossip, I didn't believe you. When you told me that the problem with living things is that they don't last and the problem with dead things is that they do, I questioned your sources. "Uncle told me," you said, and I put the aviator's earmuffs on you and sent you to your room without supper. When you first showed me your notes, I didn't believe a boy of your tender age could have possibly written them. I couldn't fathom the overwhelming noise of the living and the dead, how their multitude of stories in myriad permutations assailed you.

Other failures: shrouding events and people in silence and calling it love. I might have kept quiet, I might have died quiet. But this is the strange thing about illness. Or maybe this is the strange thing about the medication for the illness. I have lost all sense of proportion and value. Every thought, every scrap of any memory, seems as important, worthy even, as any other. All of it begs to be told. I would like to have written everything out for you, but in the same way wool is cleaned and carded before being spun into skeins, the act of writing demands a cleaning up of the facts and becomes an exercise in selection, editing. An artifice. It's better if I simply tell you everything I can think of and let you do the sorting later, cull the extra fibers, sort the mistakes. You've always been able to hear a word and the many spaces around it, and discern what is vital and true. When I said this, your face softened and you smiled such a tender, sad smile. "Oh, Mama," you said, pressing your forehead gently, gently against mine. And then you sat on the blue wooden chair. And you listened.

Your grandfather was a cautious man in possession of a serious nature forged by sorrow and quiet fury. He had buried many people whom he loved, and those graves were written on his forehead, forearms, wrists, and hands. All he had to do was stand in front of a mirror and he could see from the lines around his eyes how long they'd been gone and where in the cemetery all the bodies were buried. In the winter of 1992, Father took your uncle Rudy, who was then sixteen, and me, fourteen, to the cemetery. At that time the cemetery sat much closer to the river than it does now. Magnificent oaks, some of them more than six hundred years old, towered over the many plots closest to the lane while the alders flushed red at their tips near the graves closest to the river. Rudy and I knew the cemetery better than we knew ourselves; we had spent many long hours wandering among the stones, pulling weeds, gathering leaves, or washing Father's shovels and scythes. On this day, Father handed us each a shovel. *Dig,* he said. *Go on, dig.* So we dug.

While we worked, Father talked about things we'd never heard of, things he'd not been allowed to discuss. The president of the Soviet Union, Mikhail Gorbachev, lifted the ban on silence in 1988, but it wasn't until a few more years had passed that many Latvians, Father included, took the ban lifting seriously. This is how we learned from Father that Oskars, his father, had been a camp grave digger. He and Solveiga, a grandmother I never knew, and Father, then a little boy, and some sixty thousand others were deported to gulag work camps in Siberia. Vorkutlag, a mining camp. That's where Oskars, Solveiga, and little Eriks ended up, in the Pechora River Basin somewhere above the Arctic Circle.

How it happened was like this. In 1947, a sweep was made in eastern Latvia. Any excuse, however flimsy, was used to arrest people. One man, for example, made the mistake of wearing an "anti-Soviet smile" and was sent to Magadan, a place few survived. It just so happened that a small contingent of Soviet soldiers searched Oskars's barn and found a Bible. And that was enough. They started a small fire in the brush and would have burned it if not for a certain captain, a Tatar from the Urals.

The captain noted the gilt-edged pages, the mark of a holy book.

"Where did you get this?" he asked, his eyes scanning over the words on the onion-thin pages. And your grandfather explained: "My mother gave it to me."

With his free hand, the captain reached under the collar of his uniform and withdrew a small medal icon. Michael slaying the dragon, I believe, or maybe Saint George. I suppose this captain could have gotten into quite some trouble had his superiors known about that icon. But I have since learned that it wasn't uncommon for Soviet soldiers—generals, even—to wear them, discreetly, of course. The captain kissed the medal right there in front of Oskars. "My mother gave me this," he said, slipping the icon beneath his shirt. The captain nodded to Oskars's shovel, nodded to a patch of mud beyond the barn. Then he bent over his boot and took a very long time to retie the laces. This is how Oskars was allowed to bury that Bible before he was taken away. But this captain still had to send Oskars, Solveiga, and little Eriks to the work camp; he apologized that he couldn't spare them that injustice. A quota had to be filled, and it was the way of the Soviet regime to relocate people as a means of breaking their spirits. The captain made no mention of the Bible in his report and even allowed Solveiga an extra five minutes to gather a few blankets and kitchen utensils for their long journey. I offer this story to remind you that in every period of time, in every place, you can find incredible cruelty but also unexpected kindness.

Your grandfather Eriks felt there is a sacred connection between life and death. A single breath separates the two, and you cannot understand life without experiencing death. Given the task of digging graves for the prisoners, Oskars saw plenty of death at the Vorkuta mines. In those days it was customary to be buried in the nude. They called it "going into the ground Soviet-style." Prisoners did not have the luxury of proper burials with a nice coffin and nice words said at their interment. Sometimes the guards made a point of dragging bodies facedown through the ice or mud. It broke Oskars's heart. Working under the cover of darkness, he dressed the bodies in worn-out work clothing and mumbled passages from Psalms over them even though it was forbidden and could have added time to his sentence. In a twelve-hour workday, Oskars maintained a steady harmony between hand and mouth. As he dug, he recited Psalm 1 through Psalm 150. And then he'd start over again. When he'd tire of the psalms, he'd sing a *daina*.

> *Why, O sun, did you tarry,*
> *Why did you not rise earlier?*
> *I was delayed behind the hills,*
> *Warming little orphans.*
> *I warmed their feet, I dried their tears.*

This was the *daina* he and Eriks sang when they buried Solveiga. She died in that camp giving birth to our uncle Maris. At any rate, after Oskars had served his "tenner," a standard Soviet sentence, the camp administrators released Oskars, Eriks, and Maris. They sent them on their way with thirty rubles and a wolf card, a small paper glued to their travel papers that marked them as former prisoners.

Having a wolf card meant few jobs and no privileges, no rights. Many of Oskars's friends and neighbors, fearing the taint of associating with a former camp prisoner and a practicing Baptist to boot, would not acknowledge him. There was some suspicion at the time that Baptists, also called Shtuntists, were in actual fact German spies. Of course, that wasn't true, but the Baptist faith was viewed by Orthodox Russians and Lutheran Latvians as a dangerous import. And so Oskars became the town grave digger and coffin maker — the only jobs he could get. Working beside him were Eriks and Maris.

Eventually, Oskars's heart seized; he loved butter and, Father said, digging graves had broken his spirit. The brothers built a coffin, measuring boards and joining them without any nails. They dug a hole. All these things your grandfather Eriks told us that winter in 1992. It was our inheritance, he said, to know the truth and be set free by it. But lest we get big ideas and forget our place, he gave us each an ash-handled shovel. From that day forward, if we weren't in school, we were in the cemetery. Even at that time, Rudy could dig quickly and well.

I could not say the same for myself. Assailed by strange longings I could neither name nor describe, I made a poor grunt, jabbing at the hard clay with my shovel in jerky, awkward movements. Not like Father. The shovel was a natural extension of his arm and his digging was a smooth unbroken cycle, like a song that had become a prayer.

And he certainly needed to dig. You won't find this anywhere in the newspapers, but in the months following the Soviet Union's collapse, a series of strange and tragic deaths seized town and country. First, a poet from Lubana awoke from a dream in which she was a wolf, bit her husband's neck, and killed him in the bed they shared. Not long after that, a saxophonist in a klezmer band went crazy and killed his fellow band members — all seven of them — and then beat himself to death with the saxophone. It was tax season. A few weeks later, after swimming in the nude in the newly thawed Aiviekste River, a civil engineer built himself a flying machine and died after falling from a great height. His grieving widow later succumbed to a mysterious urge to throw herself in front of the Daugavpils–Minsk train.

As the local grave digger, your grandfather Eriks was the first to hear about it all through a black phone in our kitchen. In the Soviet days, when someone needed burying, we'd get a knock on the door, but after the fall, orders came from the cemetery's new director and owner, Mr. Zetsche. Though none of us had ever laid eyes on the man, his reputation of largesse preceded him. A German-born businessman, he'd married a Latvian woman of enormous wealth: her family owned a sugar refinery and choice property near Lake Lubans. At his own expense, Mr. Zetsche had installed the phone. You may laugh at this, but we felt smart and privileged to have it: everyone else in town had to go to the post office and place an order to make or receive a call. Through the winters of 1992 and 1993, this phone sounded with increasing regularity. One day brought us news of an overwrought copy editor who had a bad case of frayed nerves and a rope long enough to hang herself. Your grandfather roused your uncle Rudy and me early one morning — all hands to the shovels.

Even then, I sensed that as lowly as our work was it mattered that we did it well. Our work connected us to the living and the dead, to things beneath the earth and above it. When I watched your grandfather working — sanding the boards; measuring once, twice, thrice to make sure the joints married snugly; drilling holes in the coffin for those who asked for it — I often thought he was a holy man performing a holy office. On the day of the copy editor's funeral, we watched a cluster of women dressed from head to toe in black and a procession of men in black hats walk toward the Jewish section of the cemetery. The coffin, a pine box with a domed lid and handles all around, must have been heavy because every ten paces or so the pallbearers stopped and set it on the road to rest for a few seconds.

In bigger towns, Jews had their own cemeteries, but our town was just small enough that we all had to be buried together. Well, near one another. The Jewish graves were separated from everyone else's by a low stone wall. The wall, Father explained, was there to keep the Jews settled. Jews were like Gypsies, always on the move, always prepared to wander, and when they disappeared, it was their way to leave no trace of themselves behind, not even their dead. But in his thirty years of caring for the cemetery, Father said, with a hint of pride, not a single stone, pebble, or blade of grass had been disturbed.

Once at the burial site, four men lowered the box with ropes. Your grandfather had offered to help, but his being Baptist was a mark against his assistance. And so we hovered discreetly should someone need us; for what reason we couldn't imagine. That evening, after everyone had left, Father raked the sandy pathways between the graves so that the spirit of the copy editor couldn't follow the footprints back home to the living.

. . .

The thing you must remember is that most people, including me, speak out of ignorance. We open our mouths and a universe of all we don't know rushes out in a collision of sound and folly. At fifteen years of age, I knew very little about Latvian Jews. Rudy knew even less. Rarely did Jews earn a mention in the history books we read at gymnasium, which made them seem all the more exotic and fascinating to me. In Daugavpils we'd learned of a Jewish man who'd been denied an entry visa to Israel and flung himself out of a fifth-story window. "Jews must be really sad — killing themselves like this," I surmised one night, as Rudy and I crawled into our beds.

"They don't have a land of their own. That's why they are so sad," Rudy said, smoothing the wispy fuzz above his lip and under his chin. Two years ahead of me at school, with only a half year left before graduating, Rudy had acquired all kinds of opinions and pseudo facts. For example, it was his opinion that Jews in the larger cities like Daugavpils were not well liked because they had more money than everybody else, though the Jews in our little town were as bad off as the rest of us. According to Rudy, Jews were the reason why unemployment in Latvia was on the rise. And the émigré Jews from Russia were the worst kind because they didn't even bother to speak Latvian, which didn't seem so bad to me, but many people, including Father, maintained that the sound of Russian fell hard on the ears. Your grandmother felt the same way. *I don't love Russian,* she said, and the way she stretched the vowel in that word *love* expressed the measure of her dislike.

At that time in my life, I listed toward the melancholy and dramatic. While I washed dishes, I sucked my cheeks in so as to affect the gaunt look of a poet gripped by an esoteric thought. Or, if I was scrubbing potatoes, I might fix my eyes on the lane outside the window and adopt a meditative gaze. I can tell you about it now and we can laugh together at my silly posturing, a product of adolescent fancy and boredom, but at the time, it seemed very important to me to strike just the right pose.

At the time, my only friend, Jutta Ilmyen, felt the same way as I did about tragedy, drama, and romance. She talked a lot about suicide and the futility of life — all while contemplating the sky and sighing. She lived in the house opposite ours and looked, according to town gossip, suspiciously German, though in actual fact she was a Jew whose family had come from Belarus somewhere. The house where her family lived had sat empty for seven months, the owners having gone to Australia just like that. In month number eight, the Ilmyens arrived with their many suitcases, an elegant horsehair divan, and a droopy eared donkey named Babel.

Mrs. Ilmyen spoke passable Latvian and always said *lab dien,* good morning, to us when she passed us on the lane. She claimed that her family had been granted automatic Latvian citizenship on account of their having been in Latvia several decades before the occupations and annexations. About Mr. Ilmyen we knew very little: he translated important legal documents in an office somewhere in Daugavpils. It was a job that kept him quite busy as many Latvians from Australia, Canada, and the U.S. had arrived in droves to reclaim ancestral properties that had been illegally seized during the Soviet regime. Your grandmother wasn't sure about Mr. Ilmyen's status as a Latvian or his political leanings. But she admired Mrs. Ilmyen's smart fashion sense, and because of this, I was allowed to visit Jutta. In their home, everything seemed exotic and better: the lace of their curtains hanging in their windows had yellowed more elegantly than the muslin hanging in our windows. And though I knew it was true that the rain pelted our houses equally, it seemed to me that the rain fell from their eaves more musically than it did from ours. And whereas we had only a few books in our home, they had dozens, and in those rare moments of sideways afternoon light, the gilt spines of the books glowed and exhaled a smell of old leather. In a small cabinet where Mr. Ilmyen's chess medals were mounted on black velour, they kept a special silver candelabra. And this was the great thing about the Ilmyens — they were all smart. At least half the chess medals inside Mr. Ilmyen's case belonged to Mrs. Ilmyen and a few even belonged to Jutta.

And the Ilmyens were kind. Once, when I fell against their fence, I cut my hand. Mrs. Ilmyen, who worked part-time at the clinic, rushed outside with gauze and a bandage. She had my hand cleaned and wrapped before I had a chance to have a proper cry. Likewise, after those rare moments of depression when Father got so drunk he couldn't stand, it was Mr. Ilmyen who rolled him up in flour sacks and carted him all the way from the river to our house. "Mr. Ilmyen is a very fine person," Father would say on these nights, as he wrapped his arms around his sides and swayed like a dizzy pendulum. "Even if he does speak Russian." But in the morning, when his head hurt him terribly, the ache was not associated with the drink but with the way Mr. Ilmyen had dumped him onto our kitchen floor. He would foster a low-grade dislike of Mr. Ilmyen, which Rudy told me had far more to do with the fact that the minute the Soviets packed up Mr. Ilmyen had laid claim to one of the better fishing spots on the river and Father had not quite adjusted himself to that harsh reality.

I thought that being Jewish was some sort of vocation and that with the right paperwork and attention to detail anybody could become one. Jewishness was like a job or a calling — the most important one, because Jews were God's chosen people. I knew this because I read the Old Testament and everywhere in those books it seemed God looked out for the Hebrews, hurling thunderbolts and even afflicting the heathens with hemorrhoids. I wanted that kind of attention from a God who parted waters so that his chosen could walk on dry ground. If I had to wander through a desert as the Hebrews of old did, I wanted what they had: unmistakable guidance in the form of pillars of clouds by day and fire by night. But I knew being Jewish wasn't going to be all fun and games. Jews were special — so special they had to suffer for it. And the more they suffered, the more special they became. How exhausting! How dramatic!

I demanded that Jutta teach me how to be a Jew, and she did try. To start, one rainy afternoon she pulled from her father's bookcase a Hebrew prayer book. Within four seconds, I realized my folly. Not only did the letters swim all over the page like birds trapped in strange cages, but Jutta insisted that I read the letters backward from right to left. If that wasn't confusing enough, each letter, according to Jutta, carried special symbolic meaning, and certain arrangements of the letters were more symbolic than others, and some people, she said, spent their lives looking for the right arrangements. "What are they trying to arrange?" I asked, and Jutta blinked as if I had just asked the unthinkable. "The true name of God," she breathed reverentially.

Mother unwittingly reinforced my admiration of the Ilmyens and my desire to be more like them. Each night after Rudy and I climbed into bed, instead of saying prayers or kissing us as other mothers did, she bent over us and breathed: "Rudy, Inara: be geniuses." Mother said this each night because each morning she had to get up at five thirty to ride the bus to Daugavpils where she cleaned houses for a few elderly men who had more money and more things than we did; she assumed they obtained these items through their intelligence. The smartest people in our town were the Ilmyens, and so I decided that my clearest path toward brilliance, and thus Mother's affection and approval, would be to study Jutta and learn how to think like a genius. If I became more Jewish in my heart, if I could suffer somehow for my pains, and thus become slightly more special to God, that would be an added plus. To this end, on the nights before big exams, I studied with Jutta. We conjugated all the regular and irregular German verbs or recited Mr. Gepkars's history lessons. *The stones, children!* Then our talk turned to hopelessly tragic things such as the possibility of romance in a small town for a girl like me — a girl with bad skin, big hips, and eyes set a little too close together. "Oh, don't worry so much, Inara," Jutta would say. "Just put a little lipstick on and always remember: boys like boobs. When you walk, lead with your chest." And then we'd practice walking up and down their narrow wooden hallway, our chests thrust out. We wore Jutta's dress shoes, which weren't exactly high heels, but they weren't flats, either. All the while Mrs. Ilmyen made comments in Russian from the kitchen: "Imagine you are swans gliding on water. Glide, girls, glide."

This I loved: practical bits of advice from a bona fide genius. Jutta was the sister I had always wanted, a confidant who understood me, accepted me, and offered minimal corrections when I said or did something stupid, which I suspected was far more often than I even imagined.

While you were scrubbing markers at the far edge of the cemetery, Mrs. Zetsche—Mildi—came to see me. She had to cross the yard and let herself into the shed, and I could tell this bothered her. She is one for formalities and protocols. I believe this had to do with her involvement with equestrian society. Why did she come? We are not family, and we belong to a different social milieu. Before you were born, I cleaned for her, and because of this, I think she felt obligated to pay her respects. She is a fragile soul and, I do believe, a tormented one as well. She is seeking absolution. "Have I done the right thing?" she asked. Such a lifetime of hurt and woe in those words. The truth is, the Zetsches are at the center of the knot that is our town and our family.

You well know a knot is a snarl, a tangle. You cannot pull one end without troubling the other. But I said to her, *Yes, it is enough.*

I have always felt a little sorry for Mrs. Z. Your grandparents' feelings toward the Zetsches were more complicated. They were of good pedigree, Mother said, well-papered. Also Mrs. Z. had married a German. This distinction automatically elevated her status with Mother and Father as they have always held in high esteem all things German. Your grandfather longed for, and though it is a sin, even coveted, German-made autos. Your grandmother yearned for a Bavarian clock. She wanted those long chains bobbed with pinecones, the dark wooden birdhouse from which bright yellow chirping flew out on the hour. Germans, your grandparents believed, possessed sound, practical minds, and therefore, your grandparents felt they could understand them better than they could Russians. Germans had helped a great many displaced Latvians after the war and that was no small thing. So, when Mrs. A. at the post office told us that the Zetsches were making inquiries about properties for sale, Mother visibly brightened.

The Zetsches arrived in a BMW for their first visit, a Mercedes for their second, an Audi for their third. They made quite an impression with these fine cars polished to a glassine shine that cut through 1993's winter of torrential rains. As they skirted the larger potholes, in the glossy side panels we spied our faces reflecting a mixture of awe and envy. Where were they going? To view the many properties put up for sale. Latvians were leaving the smaller towns in droves to find their fortunes in Riga or even Sweden or Ireland. Velta and Ferdinands's old manor home was located upriver. Would the Zetsches build too close to our ancestral property? What kind of neighbors might they be? All we knew of Mr. Zetsche was the sound of his tinny voice through the black telephone. And as much as Mother admired German things, I think she was a little afraid of the Zetsches. That is until we saw them get out of their car outside the post office.

Short. Impossibly short. We'd never seen such short people. Everything about them was in perfect proportion but presented in the miniature. I believe Mrs. Zetsche wore a child's shoe size, and Mr. Zetsche could not have topped 120 centimeters, and this in custom-made leather loafers with tall heels. They sped from one property to another, and from the town gossip, it became clear that the earlier rumors were true: they were buying up property left and right, and had plans to occupy a manor within the month. That property has something to do with why Mildi came to see me. She has a sheaf of papers that I'd like you to have. They are important. Perhaps you'll consider burying them, which is what our family has always done with anything truly valuable or precious. "Have I done the right thing?" she asked. What I heard was *Is it enough?* I looked at her sad eyes and said, "Yes. It is enough."

You never knew the manor as I did. I never knew it as my own mother did. I could not know it as Velta had. Every town, village, and hamlet has at least one of these ancient stone-and-thatch houses from the old days, sitting lonely, boarded up, closed off. Hidden by oaks and spooling bracken, they possess the irresistible allure of ruin and decay, spur myth and speculation. Such was the way with ours. North of the river, surrounded on all sides by a dense wood of alder, pine, and birch, it seemed like an animal denning deep among reeds and twigs and river mud, reluctant to come out into the light.

"Don't go into those woods," Mother often warned us. "Strange howls and whispers stretch across the water," she'd say, her eyes wide and her voice low. "The Ghost Girl rises up from the river. And that means somebody will soon drown. Water always wants to take a life." When I heard this, shivers rippled up and down my spine. But it only made your uncle Rudy more determined to explore where he shouldn't.

It was your uncle Rudy's conviction that the old manor was built of wood and held together by stubbornness, communal memory, and a little plaster. Not a single brick had been used in its construction, but the plaster had been coated so many times with rust-colored paint that, despite years of bitter winds and driving rain, it still bristled a bright iron-oxide color. On those covert missions, I was not the twelve- or thirteen-year-old Inara with bad skin and stringy hair that wasn't quite blond and wasn't quite brown. I was one of the legendary White Tights, a Baltic female counteroperative, a femme fatale forest partisan engaging the Soviets in necessary resistance.

Skulking beside me, your uncle Rudy always carried his slingshot and, strapped to his back, a bazooka-size beet launcher, one of Uncle Maris's inventions. Whatever we intended, whatever we thought we'd discover, we were always disappointed: covered in thirty years' worth of grime, the first-floor windows afforded a limited view of empty rooms and what looked to be only a few sticks of furniture and a spinning wheel draped in sheets. An oven stretched from floor to ceiling, the brown glazed tiles darkened by time and disuse. I imagined oil lamps lit at twilight, a fire casting a warm glow, shadows flickering on the walls, the reedy moan of an oboe spilling through open doorways to the dark ponds. Paintings of women making hay, an attic full of steamer trunks and rattling ghosts. Beautifully irrelevant things.

Crows lived in all three chimneys and the roof drooped on one side. The third-floor windows were small half ovals, sleepy eyes watching the woods and river. But that didn't diminish the grandeur of the porch with its two stately granite columns or the wide circular drive or what must have been at one time a magnificent water garden. Behind the manor, concentric circles of dark pond water boasted lilies and reeds. In the centermost pond, like an elegant arrow from the middle of a slimy bull's-eye, rose a faux-marble statue of Venus minus a head and left arm, a choir of belching frogs hopping at her ankles.

Mother didn't want us near the manor. It was dirty, she said. And not just because of the dusty floors or grimy windows. Young couples used it from time to time for their trysts; Mother was sure of it because she'd find candles in tin cans and other evidence of common, filthy actions.

"What's a tryst?" I sometimes asked her, mimicking the way her mouth twisted around the word. I asked knowing that my question bothered her as much if not more than the mess the couples left behind. It was those messes, we figured, that drew Mother to the manor. Once, we followed her from a distance, careful not to snap twigs, careful to follow the path through the thicket her body had cleared. We watched as she wrested open a side door. Through the smear of dirty windows, we watched her open drawers, even pull up some wooden flooring. We watched her steam long skins of wallpaper, carefully pulling them away from the many sheets of newspaper used for binder and insulation. We could hardly believe it: Mother, violating the same home she'd so sternly wanted us to avoid. I think that's when we both realized that this must be the old manor that had once belonged to her parents, Velta and Ferdinands. Maybe she was looking for the newspaper articles her father had written. Maybe the very poem that got him sent to the work camp was wedged in the walls of that manor house. Maybe this was why Mother, who believed in abiding by the laws of privacy, felt no compunction about peeling skin after skin of newspaper from the wall, rolling them up, and tucking them under her blouse.

Rudy and I conducted similar investigations. We dug behind the dark ponds; we dug beside the stone walls dripping with ivy and clotted hollyhocks. One day in autumn, when the wind off the river bent the birch trees in sad sighs, we went exploring. Rudy found a box of rifle bullets. I unearthed a tin box. The rusted color of fallen pine needles and large enough to hold a thick ream of papers, or maybe a family album, it had the weighty feel of the sacred or secretive, and therefore it seemed valuable. I broke the hasp, pried off the lid. No books, no photos. Just a bundle of letters bound with butcher's string. Under my coat I carried the bundle, somehow knowing that this might be the secret treasure Mother had been searching for. I took the tin to the cellar and sat with a candle in the darkness. Some of the letters were scratched on thick cardboard-stock paper, others on thin onionskin. Some were in German, others in Latvian. I rifled through a few of these, pausing at a recipe for caraway bread and then at this story in blue ink.

> *I will stitch my dark parable.*
> *I sew a new skin.*
> *With my sharp beak,*

I will order my words by reason of darkness.
I will step inside.
I will sew myself up syllable by syllable.
What if this was my story?

The lonely hedgehog raises his pointed nose to the stars. Cold is his nose, colder still the stars. He would freeze if he stood like that for long, looking for the name of his true love spelled out among those pinpricks of light. He is a bad speller; those are the wrong stars. They don't spell any names he recognizes and he is cold, cold. He shivers and his spines stand on end. He doesn't know that other hedgehogs suffer as well. Loneliness, after all, is a contagious condition. All of them stand in different parts of the forest, their pointy noses aimed at the stars. One little hedgehog sniffles, cries. Another joins in. Soon the forest is all asniffle, and many tears freeze to the points of many noses.

"Well, this is dumb," says one hedgehog, so cold now his words fall to the ground as chips of ice. "Why should we each suffer alone? Why shouldn't we huddle and cling? At least we'll die together."

"Oh! Let's!" cried the other hedgehogs, and in short order, they all found one another and curled up in a big pile of fur and needles. To their amazement, they did not die. In fact, they grew quite warm, huddling and clinging. Some of them even managed to find their true loves whose names they could not see in the stars. And all would have been well for those hedgehogs had they clung and huddled and held stock-still. But as hedgehogs have sharp spines, the slightest tremble, the tiniest shiver provoked endless torments.

Here the letter had been folded into halves then quarters. Velta had written this in a shaky hand.

It is bitter, they cried, to be together, and it is bitter to be alone.

I read another scrap of paper written in a different hand altogether.

> *A girl stands beside her mother's bed, her small hand finds her mother's furrowed brow.*
>
> *"I just need to sleep," the mother was always saying to the girl. "I'm just so tired."*
>
> *"Go on," the mother was saying. "Go on and leave me alone."*
>
> *A stone sat on the mother's chest. She didn't ask for the stone, but someone put it there anyway.*

> *A stone grew in the daughter's stomach. She didn't ask for the stone, but someone put it there anyway. It pushed on her lungs; she couldn't breathe. It pushed on her throat; she couldn't speak. Go on, she wanted to say. Go on and crush me.*

Why had Velta written about hedgehogs, of all things? In whose hand was that second scrap written? I supposed Mother would know. So why didn't I show her the letters? Even now, I don't know how to answer. I imagine I liked the idea of possessing a secret; I am ashamed to admit the measure of joy I felt in withholding from Mother the tin, which I hid under my mattress. I suppose I'm telling you this because it is useful to remember that each of us is a strange, intricate combination of contradictions. This is what makes us a mystery, even to ourselves. This is what makes us capable of surprise.

I wish you could have known your grandmother Biruta in her prime: as unpredictable as the weather and just as strong, few could resist or withstand her energy. She wasn't a tall woman or particularly muscular. Her strength was of the compact, sinewy sort. She could walk twenty kilometers without stopping. She could peel three buckets of potatoes and then start in on a mountain of laundry; if she was tired, you'd never know.

What she loved, she loved with a passion that outstripped proportion or measure. She loved publishing her monthly temperance newspaper, which she pounded out on an old green German Olympia typewriter. She loved presiding over the Ladies Temperance League. She launched both endeavors because your grandfather sometimes liked to go to the river to think. That is to say, he was meeting Mr. Ilmyen or Mr. Arijisnikov for a cup of tea. That is to say, they were getting as drunk as Russian sailors. This your grandfather did three nights in a row, and on the fourth night, your grandmother suffered an epiphany.

Straightaway she began organizing the Ladies Temperance League and elected herself president. It was a lonely post, and in the first month of her presidency, she had managed to convince only two other women to join her society. Mrs. Stanka Ivaska, who had few friends in this world but would join any organization that gave out coffee with sugar, signed up right away. The other woman was Mrs. Ilmyen.

Mother had always held a small secret admiration for Mrs. Ilmyen, who had obtained some higher education and even had the documentation to prove it. Also Mrs. Ilmyen knew how to put on makeup better than anybody else and had two pairs of nice shoes. Now that Mrs. Ilmyen had joined the Temperance League, your grandmother's admiration grew. And when I mentioned one evening as we boiled our cabbage for dinner that the Ilmyens were chess champions, not five minutes later we were on their doorstep knocking.

Mr. Ilmyen answered, blinking in surprise. Mother put her hands on my shoulders. "Inara, as you may well already know, isn't so terribly clever, but could you teach her a thing or two about chess?"

Mr. Ilmyen's eyes swam behind his glasses. "Anything is possible," he said, his gaze now on the clouds. And I knew from the way he said those words that everything Jutta had taught me so far about Jewish suffering had to be true, because it was clear to me that this request of my Mother's had just increased his suffering exponentially.

. . .

We have been sorting through my things, reading Velta's letters.

> *You don't use the same shovel to heel in saplings as you would to dig a grave.*
> *You don't use the same needle to sew a sweater as you would a shroud.*

Odd advice, I agree, but it might make for good reading in your temperance newspaper.

And now this: your Book of Wonder. You opened the thick cloth-bound cover and out of a cloud of dust rose a moth, its wings transparent yellow, fluttering up, up. I took it as a sign that this book of unraveling thread and flaking binder's glue still held life, sudden flight, and subtle possibility. That you can't remember writing in it baffles me. Have you really forgotten so many of your hard-earned discoveries?

Iron in our blood, carbon in our bones, we are built, you wrote, of the same stuff of stars. The moon is slipping off its leash, about four centimeters per year, because, you wrote, even the moon needs to wander. In your careful cursive, you wrote of the dead, their musings, their confusion. Mr. Bumbers, who used to sell apples at bus stands all along the A2, told you that his body was withering, shriveling like the rinds of spoiling fruit. Herta Ozolins, a seamstress who specialized in alterations, said that when she died a fountain of water rushed through her every fiber as if her body were a loose garment and she were in a gigantic whirlpool washing machine, something she'd never owned while living. Mr. Dumonovsky, a kind man who had worked in the bread cooperative during the Soviet times, said he woke up on a stone floor. He heard thunder. His body trembled, as if shaken by an enormous tumbler. Lida Kaulfeds, who in her golden youth had been a principal dancer and had loved cigarettes, described a furnace of terrific heat. Her bones dried up inside her body. Her body turned to paper, then ash. Then she flaked to bits.

A way to quiet the noise, a way to carve order out of the jangling and jostling of so many books and school worksheets full of facts. A way to escape. That's what the book was for. You made it through the first week of the third grade; we had high hopes for the second until Miss Dzelz, the third-grade teacher, sent you home one bright September day with a piece of butcher paper. On that paper you were to draw a stout oak tree with branches blooming ovals for each set of great-grandparents, aunts, uncles, cousins, parents, and siblings. You studied that tree and the empty ovals, and asked, "Whose name should I write in the oval for 'father'—David or Joels? There's not room enough for both," you said, "and I don't want to leave it empty." There it was, your dilemma served up as neat as geometry: one boy, two fathers. One man absent, one present.

In the middle of the tree's green canopy you drew a self-portrait in colored chalks. Your head the size of a plum, your ears as large as tubas into which a spiral of sound, circles upon circles, funneled. And in circles swam eels, dark notes of dark *dainas,* the caviling of owls, your grandmother's latest advice: wear those earmuffs! For the ordinary and acceptable noise, you selected soothing blue and green chalks. But the words of your classmates: *Freak! Monster!* These you drew as jagged electric-white thunderbolts piercing the circles, puncturing your inner ear. And the little raisin eyes you'd drawn for yourself were so sad, so unbearably small and sad that I understood in a blink what must be done.

I consulted with Miss Dzelz, and it was decided that with the exception of special school events you'd stay home. You'd write in that book anything and everything that caught your fancy. We were glad to have you. Everything you needed to know Grandfather, Grandmother, Uncle Rudy, Stanka, Joels, Dr. N., or I could teach you. All of us working in concert, we compiled a curriculum like no other on the planet. We started with ears, of course.

• • •

Crickets keep theirs at the backs of their knees. Whales keep theirs on their broad lips; sound waves travel from lip through a stringlike nerve to the brain. You learned that individual hairs on the body of a spider function as individual ears, each tremble of a hair registering and responding to a whole spectrum of sound.

You recorded how loud a second was, how much it weighed on the stretched parchment of your thin tympanic membrane. The hearing of certain flowers, the hibiscus and clematis in particular, is exceptional as they are all auricle, all ear. The ears are the only part of the human body that never stops growing.

This we knew. For the first few years of your life, we measured and recorded the growth of your ears—Dr. Netsulis in his lab journal, and your grandmother Biruta in her temperance newspaper. *Big,* she wrote one month. *Bigger,* the next. When the fuzz turned to bona fide fur, your grandmother stopped her candid reportage. Her pride in you: unbounded. You were myth made flesh. But common sense had finally caught up with her, as had some none-too-gentle teasing at the Elvi Market and at the swings in the school yard. That teasing provoked a response in her trademark "Kindly Advices" column: *if you can't be polite, then, at the very least, be vague.*

And words! How you loved collecting them.

GNARL growl; snarl
GNAT small winged insect
KNIT to form into knots; to tie together as a cord
KNOT an interlacement of parts; something not easily solved; an intricacy, difficulty
KNURL lump or a knob; a series of small ridges

You found these words in your grandmother's English dictionary, her gift to you on your ninth birthday. You chewed over that word *knot* for weeks. An intertwining or conjunction, you wrote, a knot is a complication. A knot's strength is a result of the snarled strands. If you try to untangle them, the knot loses its integrity. This bit you had underlined with a red pen. The letters g and k in those words intrigued you. Their presence, though unarticulated, is vital; without those silent consonants, the words might mean something else entirely. You wrote that people are like this, too. Some are loud, some silent, all of them necessary to understand the whole.

Loud. Your great-uncle was impossibly loud, or what your grandmother called colorful, flamboyant, lively. In the main, it was his mouth people noticed. He liked to use it. His mouth had gotten him beaten within centimeters of his life, and these beatings had happened in a regular and steady way. He seemed to enjoy the special attention, sometimes asking for more with his lopsided, gap-toothed grin. "What is the matter with you!" Father would ask when Uncle showed up on our doorstep at strange hours, a rag pressed to his mouth or a bandage wound about his head. I think the matter had to do with his left leg, which he lost somewhere in the jagged mountains of Afghanistan. It was the custom of the Soviet regime to dispatch the people least interested in Soviet affairs — particularly Latvians, Estonians, and Lithuanians — to fight the government's ugliest wars. Anyway, Uncle could not forgive the Soviet army for sending him to such a godforsaken place. He couldn't forgive the field surgeon for taking his leg. He couldn't forgive himself for relying on those crutches. Your uncle Rudy and I learned never to ask about his time in the army.

We loved it when Uncle Maris came to visit. All he had to do was smile just wide enough for the gap between his front teeth to show, and Mother could not say no to him. Uncle Maris could put his foot up on the table, smoke indoors, and shave at the kitchen sink if he wanted, because when he smiled, the whole world smiled. This was because he'd gained a certain amount of notoriety as a political protester after he lost his leg in Afghanistan. According to Mother, he had the habit of exhibiting a little too much zeal — even for the protest organizers. But he had a good heart. And, Mother liked to remind us, he was one of the very best vitamin salesmen in all of eastern Latvia. How Uncle Maris became so smart and industrious, she didn't know, except that a hard life, Mother sometimes said, looking at her blaring red hands, had a way of enlightening even the dumbest people. In that winter of 1993, I pondered this quite a lot as I helped your grandfather dig in the cemetery, the way ordinary work provides extraordinary knowledge, and if not that, then a simple, unadorned wisdom.

One night the same winter the Zetsches came to town, we heard a pounding on our front door.

"Maris!" Father and Mother cried, their voices climbing the octaves as they opened the door. Rudy and I stood dumbfounded at the sight of Uncle: crutches wedged under his armpits, and leaning against his shin like a pair of faithful dogs, two small suitcases.

"Don't just stand there like cough drops," Mother yelled at us, and Uncle Maris tipped a shoulder in our direction and beamed.

"Inara! Look at you—a woman already! And Rudy! Such a man!" Uncle was referring to Rudy's mustache, which had taken him a full year to grow. Rudy, his face flushed bright red, grabbed Uncle Maris's suitcases and hurried inside.

That night, dinner was a grand affair. Mother cooked an eel in its own oil along with penny bun mushrooms and leeks. For once we did not eat cabbage. And though Mother had been the president of the Ladies Temperance League for four weeks now, she graciously turned a blind eye when Uncle Maris lined up the shot glasses and broke out a bottle of bison grass vodka. We toasted the eel several times. And with each toast, the eel became more magnificent. At last, when the eel was eaten, Father, ignoring Mother's frowns, brought out his bathtub vodka. Father had been raised a Baptist, and on principle, Baptists in Latvia did not drink. As Father explained to Rudy and me, drinking wasn't a sin, but drunkenness was. When he was depressed or when his brother Maris visited us, Father zealously set out to explore the boundary between those two states.

Father pounded his glass, the signal for a toast, and Uncle Maris raised the bottle. "A story, I'll tell you a story." This we loved, Uncle's verbal arabesques, intricate constructions of lurid detail, supposition, and imagination all delivered with such bombastic gusto that should we doubt the substance of the story we still could be carried along by the power of its delivery.

"Long ago, there was a secret congress of crows. At that time, crows were as big and strong as cows. With three powerful strokes of their shiny black wings, they could fly from one end of the world to the other. They liked to meet in tall forests and tell stories. But they were proud, and for this, God had to punish them. He scattered them throughout the forests of the world and clipped their wings so that they couldn't fly properly and had to hop from tree to tree. To make matters worse, God created man and allowed him to multiply. But man couldn't fly, no, he couldn't even hop from tree to tree, so the crow decided to haunt man wherever he went by laughing at his clumsy ways, mocking him with cries and calls."

I nodded my head. I knew that this was why Mother, who had no time for religion, still hung fish bones in the shape of a cross over our back door. For a crow, she'd explained, hates God in its heart, and the cross or a rifle is the only thing that puts fear into them.

Uncle Maris drained his shot glass and leaned forward. "But Latvian crows are the meanest. They are not allowed to caw in Latvian—only in Russian—and this makes them screech all the more in rage."

"A good story," Father pronounced.

"A true story," Uncle Maris corrected, producing a wad of paper from his pocket. "Language is life, you know."

"What's that?" Mother sniffed.

"This, my dear woman, is a letter of support—a petition calling for a referendum for a new and improved draft of the language law. The minister of education and everyone in the parliament need to hear how thoroughly we Latvians love our language, how completely we want to preserve and protect it. After all, an unspoken language is a dead language." Here Uncle Maris looked at Father. "We will be like dead people." And now Uncle Maris turned his gaze to Mother. "Just think of Inara and Rudy."

"Tell me." Uncle turned to Rudy and me. "What do you know of history? Recite!" Rudy looked at me and I looked at him. I cleared my throat and launched into Mr. Gepkars's spiel that started with stones and stopped with the Swedes. "The stones, children. The stones," I cried in the most Pushkinesque and melodramatic Russian I could. "They are so ancient, so sturdy. They record a vertical history of Latvia, and this is why any discussion of Latvia begins with our stones. Let us not forget the stability provided by the Baltic Shield, that Precambrian—"

"No." Uncle wiggled a finger in his ear. "That's nice, but it's not history." Uncle nodded at Rudy. "Your turn."

Rudy stood up slowly, slowly. Mr. Gepkars had a hump on his back. He'd plod to the blackboard so slowly that if he'd been paid by the hour he would have been a millionaire. And this Rudy imitated, circling the kitchen table as he delivered a weary recitation of how deep, how wide, the changes in our country were as a result of Sovietization, the glorious achievements of that age. From time to time, Mr. Gepkars's canting tipped from bored indifference to befuddlement, as if in the retelling of this old rhetoric something like actual meaning threatened to rise to the surface. This, too, Rudy managed to convey, all the while bearing that imaginary stone upon his back. It was a flawless impersonation.

I giggled.

Mother turned her sharp eye on me. "You should see Inara's marks in Latvian language class. This last round she nearly failed. And we speak Latvian!"

"But it's not her fault when Latvian is the language of instruction only 50 percent of the time in these eastern classrooms. Why are we still catering to the Russians? This is Latvia!" Uncle Maris pounded his crutch on the floor. "If people wish to speak Russian, fine—but they should do it in Russia." Uncle Maris picked up the letter and waved it overhead. "And if a new referendum hurries them on their way, so much the better."

Father pinched the bridge of his nose.

"Times are changing," Uncle Maris continued. "And people either have to change with them or move on."

Mother bit her lip, thinking. I suppose she was remembering her days as a girl at school. She told me how the teacher strode up and down the narrow aisles, asking questions, tapping students on the shoulder for the answers. When the tap came on Mother's shoulder, she was so nervous that she answered in Latvian. The teacher took a strap to her forearms—that's how children in those days were encouraged to remember Russian at the exclusion of all other languages. When we asked her about the scars, she laughed them off, commenting on how they have blended in nicely with so many others and claiming she doesn't harbor a grudge. But I know you understand how a person can carry a thing like that inside, how an injustice large or small swells in time.

So what Uncle was proposing now seemed natural and right: it was time our language replace that foreign one that had been crowded down our throats. And I could tell by the shine in Rudy's eyes that he was memorizing Maris's every word and gesture. I could see that he believed, as Uncle did, that ethnic and political intricacies could be tied as neatly as a pair of shoelaces, and in this way, the problems of our lives could be tidily solved.

Uncle Maris stayed on with us for a week, and then a week became two weeks. He slept on the couch, with his suitcases containing his many bottles of vitamins stacked beside him. Each morning, he got up just as Mother left for work. He dressed in the dark, carefully pinning to his lapel a red plastic carnation that was a call, he said, for unity and a reminder of how much blood had already been spilled for the cause. Then with his suitcases full of smart-looking vitamin bottles clutched against the crutch grip, he walked to the bus stand. He didn't return until late at night, long after Father had locked up the cemetery. It was his strategy, he explained to Rudy, to sell to the towns farthest away then work his way back toward our town, as if he were pulling the drawstring of a net tight. He was good at it, too, often selling an entire suitcase of vitamins in a single day. And he was tireless. In the evening he stayed up late with Rudy and Father discussing politics, the future of Latvia, or plans for a new invention.

Whatever one might say of your namesake, he could never be accused of being idle. Uncle Maris liked to improve and modify inventions already patented and trademarked. He claimed to have made a defibrillator, but his attempts to reconstruct it went disastrously awry and for three whole minutes Uncle left us to visit the angels. He came back inspired to do more, he said. Some of his inventions were smashing successes.

Uncle did a brisk business with his sloth-prevention bracelets. The device fit comfortably snug around ankles or wrists and delivered small "completely safe" electric shocks if a body remained inert for long periods of time. Middle-aged women with unemployed grown children snapped them up even after it became known that some of the completely safe shocks weren't as safe as Uncle had claimed.

Uncle also developed an energy elixir he called Vitality, the ingredients of which were so secret that even he couldn't quite remember what they were. Anyway, I think the real reason Uncle came to visit us was because he needed money. Inventing amazing things requires amazing materials, he explained to your grandfather one evening. Your grandfather could never say no to Maris. The money Uncle used to buy springs and leather and a cobbler's last. He was fashioning elevated shoes. He'd been commissioned, he said, by that funny little German man.

"Who?" Father asked.

"What?" Mother asked.

"Is there an echo?" Uncle looked at the ceiling.

32 *✐* GINA OCHSNER

Chastised, Mother and Father fell silent.

"That man," Uncle continued. "The one who's buying up a bunch of property. He's short and he wants tall shoes."

You have always loved chess. When you were three, your stepfather fashioned chessmen out of white oak. He planed a board, squared and stained it. You would play for hours. I think you understood that chess is a game of strategy, of ordered movement, logical thought. A quiet game, it soothed you. So much so, you often didn't need to wear your aviator's earmuffs. What does the game mean? you once asked your grandfather. Oh, it's about love, he said, without lifting his gaze from Oskars's Bible. The king from one side wants to marry the queen from the other, but first he must negotiate with the other king. No, no, your grandmother said. It's about power and politics. The one kingdom wants to seize everything belonging to the other kingdom. Those squares are parcels of land. That's why both sides fight until there are no chessmen left.

It was that same winter of '93 when both Uncle Maris and the Zetsches came to town that I was trying to learn the game. To me, that board looked like a quilt of white patches of farmland knuckling up through dark patches of water. A secret treasure might be buried beneath any one of the white squares, and certain death lurked in the black ones. I would not move a knight onto a black square and I usually castled my king, hedging him in as soon as I could. You can imagine what a horrible player I was. But my lack of skill worked to my personal advantage. In less than a week, the regional open chess tournament was to be held in the hall and I could spend more time with Jutta.

Everyone was talking about it—even people who didn't care for chess—for nothing quite this important had taken place at the hall in a long time. Every afternoon Jutta showed me opening moves: the gambits, the King's and Queen's Indian, the Nimzo-Indian, and explained to me again and again the importance of controlling the two key middle squares. Then we practiced closing moves—Greco's Mate, the Smothered Mate, Blackburne's Mate, Anastasia's Mate—until Jutta was satisfied I could hold my own with the other beginners and maybe even a few of the intermediate players. Each afternoon we did this while Mrs. Ilmyen studied Latvian grammar texts on account of the language law. Mrs. Ilmyen already had her nursing credential. She worked both at a clinic in Balvi and the one here in town, but she said she needed to prove her fluency in Latvian if she wanted to get a promotion. If any of this was bothering Jutta, she did not show it—that's how good at suffering she was, concentrating all her attention on those black-and-white chess pieces. Each piece, she said, was like a letter of the Hebrew alphabet, each combination of moves and pieces spelled different phrases, the words to different outcomes. But the more I looked at the board, the fuzzier it became, squares and pieces swimming before my eyes. One day, just a week before the big tournament when I thought I'd never have a genius moment in my life and that this was my particular suffering, I discovered I'd trapped Jutta quite suddenly in a Smothered Mate. She was so kind as to allow me to believe I had orchestrated this all by myself. "Well, well." Mr. Ilmyen beamed behind his glasses when he saw the board, and later he patted me on the shoulder as I squeezed past him through their front door.

One night Uncle sat with your grandfather on the divan, a half-empty bottle wedged in the cushion between them. They were watching a low-budget Russian shock-news program. Filmed from the passenger's seat of a careening news-station car, the show captured the day's most cataclysmic or grisly events, most of which were car accidents involving hapless pedestrians knocked clean out of their shoes.

When the potatoes were done, I laid out the table as Mother called the men to dinner.

"You're not getting drunk, are you?" She grinned ferociously at Uncle Maris, but her slate-gray eyes were as hard as flint.

"Oh, Biruta. Calm down." Uncle laughed. "Drunks are people,

too, you know. Young men get drunk because they don't know who they are; old men get drunk because they do." In each hand Uncle held a bottle of vitamins. As he spoke, he shook the bottles, underscoring each word with a percussive rattle.

"I beat Jutta Ilmyen today in chess," I whispered to Mother, my clumsy attempt to steer the conversation to safer topics.

"Oh, Inara!" Mother said, her eyes shiny.

Uncle Maris tapped his fork on his plate. "So tell me — who are these Ilmyens?"

"Nobody," Rudy said.

"Neighbors," I said.

"But not Latvian?"

"Well . . . ," Father hedged.

"So why do you go over there so much?" Uncle Maris asked me.

I rolled my eyes heavenward and sighed. "They're God's chosen people, which is to say they are special, which is to say they are expert in the art of suffering. They are also very smart."

"Well, if they're so special and smart, why do Mr. Ilmyen's elbows show through his sleeves?" Rudy piped up.

Uncle Maris smiled widely. "Well, scratch a Russian," he said. It was an old saying, so old I couldn't remember how the rest of it went, but the gist was that lurking beneath the thin varnish of any ethnic Russian or Russian speaker could be things far worse than mere Russianness. What things those were I did not know. No person could possibly be Latvian enough for Uncle.

"They're not Russian," I said at last. "They are Jews who speak Russian."

"Terrific. Jewish communists — my favorite kind of people," Uncle Maris said. "Inflicting their troubles and woe on everyone else. And the way they go on about it — as if they were the only ones who suffered." Uncle Maris looked at his empty trouser leg.

"Oh, they're all right," Mother said. Later, as we washed the dishes, she made a lot of noise with them, washing and rewashing, as if those plates and cups were unruly children who could be subdued only by vigorous dunkings and scrubbings.

It was early April. Light leaked from the sky a bit longer each day, bringing the birds back to us one by one. I could detect the hard elemental smell of mud thawing. The soil was breathing again, and in early mornings when the vapor hung over the fields, Rudy and I collected worms for midnight eel-fishing expeditions. On the Aiviekste, April is a good month for fishing as the sky never quits weeping, and the eels seem to prefer things that way. We wanted to pickle or smoke as many of them as possible. Uncle Maris loved them, and we hoped that with enough eels on hand, he might regain his old sense of humor that had been evaporating day by day since he arrived.

Mother was on edge, too: she frowned at Maris more and sniffed in his direction, measuring from his body odors how much he'd drunk that day. We figured that either the number of signatures on his petition wasn't to his liking or his vitamin sales were low because one day Maris announced that he'd combed the countryside long enough and that it was time to sell his wares in our town. On a Monday, Uncle Maris took Rudy with him—for moral support, he said. They rode the bus to the outlying homes beyond the school, calling at the Latvian houses, which—he told Rudy and Rudy told me—were easy to spot because Latvians build their homes as if they were planning to stay, while Ukrainians, Jews, and Gypsies cobbled their homes together with whatever they could find because they were too cheap to bother with appearances. Uncle Maris wasn't holding out much hope for big sales in our town full of foreigners ("So tight, they squeak when they fart!"), but for some reason he felt obligated to try anyway, carefully pinning that red plastic carnation to his lapel and checking and double-checking his yellowed petition of signatures. With Rudy in tow, Uncle Maris stumped along the back roads only to find himself turned away from every household—and this before even having a chance to brandish his well-polished arguments about the citizenship laws. By Friday, the day before the big tournament, he'd worked his way to the far end of our road and decided to pay a visit to the Ilmyens.

"At least remove that carnation," Father advised. "It has lost a bit of color and has acquired a strange odor."

Uncle Maris simply smiled. He folded the yellow petition and slid it carefully into his breast pocket then crutched himself double-time across the lane.

We all gathered in our customary places at the open door and watched. As it was Friday evening, the window shades of the Ilmyen home were drawn. Even so, Mr. Ilmyen had the door open before Uncle Maris made it to their front step.

"Good evening, sir." Uncle Maris bowed with a flourish. "I'm Inara's uncle, Maris Kalnins."

"I know who you are," Mr. Ilmyen replied, in flawless Latvian. He pushed his glasses higher onto his nose.

"Then perhaps you'd be interested in the betterment of your body. Vitamins are essential, you know, to good health."

"We don't buy or sell on the Sabbath," Mr. Ilmyen said, politely but firmly.

"Well, then, perhaps you'd be interested in promoting the betterment of Latvian culture."

Uncle Maris withdrew and unfolded the yellow petition. "Latvian language — and indeed the Latvian way of life — must be kept sacred by those who claim to be Latvian. In short, my dear fellow, you should sign this petition to attest to your loyalty to the Latvian nation. You are a citizen?"

"I am a potential citizen," Mr. Ilmyen replied.

"But you speak Russian primarily?"

"Among other things," Mr. Ilmyen said, adjusting his glasses.

Uncle Maris drew himself to his full height. "But language, my good fellow, is identity. You might find it interesting to know that in a recent survey 100 percent of respondents polled agreed with me."

Mr. Ilmyen squinted at Uncle. "How many respondents exactly?"
"Four."

Now Mr. Ilmyen's gaze lifted over the top of Uncle's head and settled on where we stood, shrinking in our doorway. "Good night, sir," Mr. Ilmyen said quietly, shutting the door.

Uncle Maris whirled on his crutches. We all jumped from the threshold and became inordinately busy scrubbing dishes or pretending to study. Later that night, no amount of industry or imagination could block the sounds of Uncle Maris swearing at the TV. And his talk was so raw, so open, it was like gazing upon someone in their nakedness. And though I couldn't make out everything he said, the sentiment behind those words, what I recognized as hatred, was like dark water drawn from a deep cold well.

The night of the big match a lashing rain battered the town. Rain was all about us, routing deep grooves into the roof. We were all jumpy but for different reasons. Mother fussed and fumed in the kitchen preparing a tray of *pirags* and pickled mushrooms—her very best sooty caps—for the big chess tournament. She was in a hurry to set out the crates that doubled as small chess tables and move the piano to the middle of the platform, which was necessary to maintain the fragile equilibrium between two fractious groups of Baptists. They had, at one point in time, been a unified band of worshippers, but an argument arose over the correct placement of Velta's piano: the left side of the platform or the right? No amount of reasoning, exhortation, or recitation of scripture from leaders representing either side could breach the schism. Now each group so thoroughly believed the other to be in heresy, they refused to speak to one another. This behavior was not so odd. A lot of people in our town were not on speaking terms. The Arijisnikov and Aliyev families, Uzbeks, would not acknowledge the Lee or Lim families, Koreans, who, like the Uzbeks, had come from Tashkent. Or maybe it was Bukhara. The Egers family, all nineteen of them, maintained a robust hatred for Gypsies on account of a horse that had been stolen from a distant relative sometime in the 1800s. This kind of hatred had a special name: *principa pec,* on principle, and it meant that if you felt you had been offended or aggrieved you had a right to your grudge for as long as you liked.

After his standoff with Mr. Ilmyen, Uncle Maris hadn't moved from the couch where he drank steadily and watched the TV with Father. Father, visibly nostalgic for spectacular and frequent deaths, kept looking at the phone. "Nobody's died in weeks," he lamented. "I'm a wreck." But as soon as Mother let herself out the back door, Father grabbed a bucket and flashlight, and went into the yard. Rudy followed him, wasting no time in churning up Mother's cabbage rows for worms. At the hall, Mother stationed herself in the foyer behind a long table of pastries and the contribution dish for the Ladies Temperance League. Nearly everyone in town had turned out for the tournament: our teachers from school, all the neighbors, and the fathers and mothers of all the student chess players. In spite of Jutta's fine coaching, I was still in the beginner group. And so I threaded through the crush to the front of the hall where the other beginners—six- and seven-year-olds mostly—fidgeted behind the cloth-covered crates with the chessboards.

I didn't last long. One of the Russian girls in the class ahead of me got me flustered with an Alekhine's Defense and finished me off quickly. The winners then paired with the intermediates, and thirty minutes later, the victors of that round—one of whom was Jutta—battled it out for a turn with the local master: Mr. Ilmyen. By the time Jutta beat her opponent—Mr. Gipsis, the fourth-grade teacher—everyone had finished eating and were settled in the chairs, packed like herrings in a barrel.

Mr. Ilmyen shuffled up the steps and took his seat behind the table. Jutta followed Mr. Ilmyen and took the opposite seat. Mr. Ilmyen nodded to Mrs. Ilmyen standing in the back, and the overhead projector hummed and threw the image of a gigantic chessboard against the back wall. With each move Mr. Ilmyen and Jutta made, Mrs. Ilmyen moved disks over the glass so we could watch on the wall.

"Ooh!" the crowd murmured when Jutta moved her Queen's knight deep into her father's rank of pawns.

"Aaah!" came the sage reply when Mr. Ilmyen moved his King's pawn forward. For twenty minutes this went on. And just when it looked like Jutta would pin her father in an Anastasia's Mate, Mr. Ilmyen blocked with a rook. They were at a momentary impasse: any move either one of them might make would result in the sacrifice of an essential piece. The audience held its collective breath in appreciation of this most delicate position.

And then from the foyer came Mother's voice, high and shrill: "For god's sake, go home, you drunken moron!" In burst Uncle Maris, his face beet-root red, his breath ragged, and the plastic carnation heaving up and down as if it had a heart of its own. In his hand he held the yellow petition, which he raised above his head.

"You don't belong here, you know," Uncle Maris shouted at Mr. Ilmyen. A collective gasp rose from the crowd; it's one thing to think such things, quite another to shout it in public in front of God and everybody.

"My dear fellow." Mr. Ilmyen picked up a pawn and held it suspended in air. "This is our home. Where else should we go?"

"Who the hell cares? You are the expert in suffering. Why don't you just go and die. That's what you Jews do best!" Uncle Maris raised his crutch as if it were a javelin, and then he hurled it. The crutch flew through the air and landed — impossibly — with a resounding *twang* in the strings of the open piano. For three horrifying seconds, the room was absolutely silent as we sat frozen in stunned mortification, contemplating the disaster: the piano, the crutch, those words, Uncle Maris, and Mr. Ilmyen.

At last Mr. Ilmyen stood, brushed the front of his trousers. "And now, ladies and gentlemen, I bid you goodnight," he said in Latvian. It was so sad and sweet — something people said only in the movies, and then only when they were going away for a very long time. Mr. Ilmyen put his hand on Jutta's shoulder, and they crossed the stage to where Mrs. Ilmyen held open the small side door. The spell broken, Uncle Maris, minus one crutch, stumped to the foyer and out the front door.

Everyone spluttered and brayed all at once: "He must be crazy!"

"Even so, he has a good point."

"Such an arm!"

"Horrible aim!"

I slipped out the back, determined to find Mr. Ilmyen or Jutta. But only Uncle Maris was there.

"Help me a minute," Uncle Maris said, leaning his weight into me.

More clouds had rolled in from the east and the sky cracked in two. As we started walking, light shot out in arcs and rain pounded the road.

"You probably think I'm a terrible man for saying those things," Uncle Maris said.

I shook my head, but I wasn't really sure. My eyes were filled with water, and now the rain fell with such force that my skirt stuck to my legs and the road dissolved beneath our feet into narrow violent streams of muddied water. With each step, my shoes filled with mud and I just wanted to get home. But Uncle Maris's crutch sank deeper into the mud of the road and it seemed like we would never make it.

"You're ashamed of me. You wish I never came here," he continued.

"No," I lied, bearing up under his weight. I could see our house in the distance and I tried to pick up the pace.

"You want to know how I lost my leg?"

"Not really," I said.

"I threw myself over a mine," Uncle Maris continued, undeterred. "I saved the man standing beside me, a Russian, incidentally. Now tell me I'm a terrible man."

"You're not terrible," I said, in a voice that I did not recognize as belonging to me.

Uncle Maris leaned close. "I always liked you. Rudy, he's okay, but you're the smart one. Anyone can see you understand the way things are." Uncle Maris lurched, and for a horrifying second, I thought he would kiss me. And then he righted himself with the crutch, doubled over, and retched a colossal amount of vomit onto my shoes. "I beg your pardon most sincerely," he said, wiping his mouth with his sleeve.

I shrugged out of his grip and left him at the edge of our yard, where he retched behind Mother's rosebush. The light was on in the kitchen, and as I came in through the back door, Father and Rudy were at the sink. They'd caught a long dark silver eel, a fully mature adult who'd been reckless, who'd made the mistake of biting our lowly lobworms soaked in pilchard oil. Rudy held the eel on its back. Then with a small kitchen knife, he cut out its angry eyes.

"Where did you catch that?" I asked, astonished at its size.

Rudy grinned. "Where do you think?"

I realized they had fished from Mr. Ilmyen's spot while he had been at the hall playing chess. Mother came through the back door then, and in the open frame of sky and darkness, I saw Uncle Maris, still in the yard. His mouth was moving and the sounds kept issuing forth, a burbling colorless stream of rage.

"He goes. Tomorrow," Mother said. Father tried hard to hide his embarrassment by scrutinizing the eyeless eel. Then Mother turned, looked at my feet, and sniffed mightily. "Get your other shoes and coat on. We're going to the Ilmyens'."

When we reached their house, Mother stood on the step and wrung her hands. We could hear dogs howling in the hills, barking through the dark with their low, dull voices. Finally, she knocked on the door and a few seconds later Mr. Ilmyen appeared. Mother touched the white temperance pin on her coat. "Mr. Ilmyen, you must forgive my brother-in-law. He's an idiot, and besides, he drinks too much. And when he drinks, he talks, and when he talks, unfortunately he says stupid things."

Mr. Ilmyen stared at us and then his gaze lifted to a point above our head. And then Mrs. Ilmyen's voice floated out from somewhere deep in the kitchen: "Go away. Please." So simple a request, so complete. And in her voice I heard the weariness of generations of suffering and abuse at the hands of friends and neighbors. We turned and trudged back to our kitchen, the whole way my heart sitting heavy in my chest, the blood in it tired and unmoving. I would not pretend that I understood the vast and irreparable damage that had occurred in the course of one short evening. But I had lost Jutta, my only real friend. That much I understood. I thought at last I was feeling some of that suffering Jutta had tried so hard to teach me about. And then I realized what an idiot I was — to lay claim to any fraction of suffering when our family had so publicly reminded them of theirs.

Later, Mother sat on the edge of my bed, the springs creaking under her weight. I did not want to be a genius and did not want her wishing me to be one. Though it was dark inside the room, a break in the clouds revealed a slip of moonlight that transformed the window into a box of silver. I could see then that Mother was looking at her hands. "Don't cry, Inara. Nothing lasts forever," she said. "Not love, not hate. Not joy or pain." Mother leaned close, her breath on my hair. She laid her chapped hand on my forehead. And then she kissed me on the cheek. It was the first time she had kissed me in years.

By the time we woke the next morning, liquid light healed over in the west to a dark welt that meant more rain. Uncle Maris had gone. No one seemed surprised: vanishing is what he did best. Also, he'd taken Mother's typewriter. According to the typed note he left next to the sink, he felt like a fox caught unawares by winter and forced to eat his own turds. He would return only when we had all come to our senses, and maybe not even then. In a postscript addressed to me, he'd written: If you can't behave disgracefully, then what's the point of living? Another note, this one left for your grandmother: I'm feeling a nudge for patriotism. Riga calls. Don't worry about the typewriter. It's all for the greater good.

When your grandmother found that second note, she sat at the table, buried her head in her arms, and wept. She would have continued to do so had the oven timer not sung out. "Oh, shit. The Baptists!" Mother grabbed her coat and I followed her out the back door and down the road. As we approached the Ilmyen home, Mother kept charging ahead, but I let my feet slow a little. The shades were still drawn. Light behind the windows turned the shades to paper lanterns. Dark shapes moved behind the lighted scrim. I thought that if I stood still and stared hard enough I could watch the quiet goings-on inside the Ilmyen household as if I were watching a movie. But the longer I watched, the more my eyes burned and I realized that their world was a book written in another language and therefore closed to me.

We had forty minutes before the left-side Baptists were due. Inside the hall, the previous evening's disaster remained untouched: there were chairs overturned on their backs, chessmen scattered over the floor, and plates of half-eaten pastry and plastic cups of stale coffee studded the windowsills. Uncle Maris's crutch was still wedged in the strings of Grandmother Velta's piano. Mother dragged a trash bin from the foyer, and I climbed onto the platform. I leaned my shoulder into the piano's wood and pushed with all my might. And that was my mistake: the piano sailed over the lip of the platform. The resounding crash sent the crows screeching and the dogs barking in the lane. Then complete and absolute silence. Hands on her hips, Mother surveyed the destruction: the collapsed wood, the hammers sheared from the pinblock, strings snapped, the solid soundboard thicker and heavier than any tombstone half sunk in the wooden floor. At last she turned to me, her eyes shiny with unshed tears. "I've never cared for stringed instruments if you want to know the truth."

Without another word, we left the hall and headed home. As our feet churned the mud, I thought of Uncle Maris and how he'd split in my mind into two separate people, the Uncle Maris of my childhood whom I would always love, and the Uncle Maris whom I never wanted to see again. He had changed these last months, and I realized there was no stopping that or helping him. We each of us had to keep taking our steps where they would lead. It was a scientific principle: momentum, and it meant to me that some things — like love, like hate — once in motion couldn't be stopped. Even the piano had not been exempt. But that was the way of life, Father liked to say as we stood on our threshold watching the sad funerary processions. Forward life rolled and only death slowed it down. And even that, Father said, was only a temporary hitch. Even now the rain was falling as steadily as ever and the roads were rising and bleeding to the river as they always did this time of year.

And what of that mangled piano? By bits and pieces: keyboard, pinblock, hammers, and strings, Father gathered it into a wheelbarrow and stored it in his toolshed. The cast-iron plate, the largest and by far the heaviest part of the piano, we carried: Mother and Rudy on one end, Father and I on the other. We picked it up, walked a few paces, set it down, picked it up, walked a few paces, set it down. Though none of us said it, I know we were all thinking how very much like a Jewish procession we looked, how very likely our neighbors were standing behind windows and watching us as we had watched so many others.

We laid the iron plate and soundboard to rest inside Father's toolshed, which was where he stored anything that was broken. Set on end and leaning against the far wall of the shed, the iron plate with the strings, which somehow had not broken ("What a miracle!" Mother intoned again and again), looked like a loom. Every sound, every utterance, set the strings buzzing.

Though Mother claimed she did not care for stringed instruments, she made a phenomenal number of visits to the shed. Father would follow her, assuring her that with the right glue and patience he would have Grandmother Velta's piano trilling tunes that would make angels weep.

CHAPTER TWO

Y OU'VE BROUGHT THE PAIN MEDICATION. You've brought
more ice. And newspapers. Your grandmother would have
turned cartwheels to hear this latest: Madame President
Vaira Vika-Freibergs opened a recent book-fair address with a *daina*.

> *I was born singing,*
> *I have lived singing,*
> *and when I die,*
> *I will fly to heaven singing.*

Because the president had been raised in Canada and because your
uncle Rudy had just had a fight with your grandmother, Rudy, on
principle, didn't vote for Mrs. Vika-Freibergs. But just about every
other voter in the country did. I think her holding a PhD in ethnogra-
phy and having so many *dainas* committed to memory went a long way
with a lot of people.

I thank you also for reading to me from the Gospel of Luke. I've
always liked it for the miracle accounts: Jesus feeding the five thousand, the healing of the demoniac who made his home in graveyards.
What did that man eat while he lived among tombstones? Let's not
dwell overlong on that.

You told me once that Jesus was your favorite superhero. You

46

asked me once, too, if I thought Jesus had big ears. I said yes because He hears our every prayer, but honestly, there is no exact record of what his ears looked like. He definitely liked ears—that much I know. Twenty times, by my count, Jesus said let those who have ears to hear. You remember, of course, his arrest in the Garden of Gethsemane. A crowd had gathered. One of Jesus's followers, and I believe it was Peter because he was such a hothead—though your grandfather assures me that the scriptures do not support this—withdrew his sword and hacked off an ear belonging to a young servant of the high priest. Jesus wasted no time attaching the severed ear to the side of the boy's head. A miracle, and on his way to his own crucifixion. I've often wondered how this action changed that boy's life; if the restoration of a small flap of cartilage on the side of his head did something to his heart.

I thank you, too, for reading from your Book of Wonder.

There's no covering that protects the body of any living thing that excels the scales of a fish, you wrote. Both armor and oil jacket, the plated scales are tough enough to resist bruising, resist the radiation of heat, and keep the fish's skin dry. Having no seams to the body, no seams to the scales, a fish can withstand any amount of water pressure without breach or penetration. This is why a fish can swim at depths no human, no submersible, can reach. Even more amazing, you wrote, is that dark stripe that runs along a fish's side from gill to tail, the lateral line, which registers low-frequency vibrations. A tactile and aural organ, this line senses movement, and like radar, it indicates to the fish how near or far away other objects are and whether those objects are in motion or stationary. Sound, you concluded, was a form of touch.

We had guessed as much from your many visits to the clinic. One doctor in Balvi showed us X-rays. We saw those large hammers and anvils inside your enormous ears.

"He's living in a sound chamber; everything is amplified," the doctor explained. "And as sound is a form of touch, certain vowels in words, certain tones, will cause a faster vibration and pain him more than other sounds." The doctor sent us home with those blaze-orange industrial-strength ear protectors that you conveniently left on the bus.

If the wind blew from the east, you could hear the bells peal-ing in St. Petersburg. You claimed that the monks at Saint Alexander Nevsky Lavra ushered morning in with songs that started bright but stanza by stanza bent to unbearable sadness. That's when the monks jumped, you said, as jumping was the only way to outstrip sorrow. You wrote this all down, how you could hear the gradations of sound on the chromatic scale, half tones, quarter tones that only the monks have mastered. You've assured me that you don't recall having placed your ear to the mud at the river's edge to hear the water's quiet susur-ration, but you recorded with what patience water reshapes shoal and shore. How patient? One particle of sand, one bit of stone at a time.

You have suffered on account of your ears. I am sorry your date walked out on you. That's a city girl for you. I will say that your choice of on-line dating services—Desperate.com—doesn't inspire confidence. At any rate, you did not ask for your ears and I fear they have been a burden, your affliction.

It may be slim consolation, but I assure you we all suffer in some way or another. When I was young, I was afflicted by a ferocious need to prove, if only to myself, that I was a clever girl. I don't know what Rudy's particular affliction was. I think it may have been an over-whelming desire to know love in the physical sense: he had not been popular with the girls at school and this even with a Fu Manchu mus-tache. What was your grandfather's particular affliction? His younger brother, Maris. Agony—your grandfather slept it, wept it, ate it, and drank it on account of Uncle. This is a kind of love: to be tormented on behalf of another, to grieve for one whom he thinks may be lost. I don't know if this is a healthy love, but it is a love all the same.

We could say the problem was one of personalities. They were ut-terly different, your grandfather Eriks and uncle Maris. Your grandfather was a man of the earth, a man who felt keenly, especially as he stood knee-deep in an open grave, gravity and the weight of time pushing on the bones. "The world is all stone," he'd sometimes say, when he'd come home after a long day of digging. I suppose this is why over the years he had become a quiet man. What does one say in the presence of so much weight? And I suppose this is why Uncle Maris was so noisy. Uncle filled your grandfather's quiet with sound. One man's steady drive into the earth the other countered with erratic, brilliant flight. Mother was less generous in her assessment of Uncle. She said he was like the hedgehog, a difficult animal to love as it is a proud creature, slow to listen and quick to make a point. Even if Uncle had not made the scene at the hall, Mother's dissenting vote was almost automatic in nature, as Mother and Father rarely agreed on anything.

Maybe you recall the time you asked them where you would go when you died. "Into the ground," Mother said. "Heaven," Father said. Father believed that the invisible things — truth, time, love, regret, memory — manifested themselves visibly if one knew how to look, really look. Invisible faith takes palpable imagination, but it is apprehended in the smallest of actions. A man stopping to help another to lift a load — that was love. Knees hitting the floor in a prayer of thanksgiving or desperation — that was faith. Faith, Mother believed, was a neurological aberration that occurred in the temporal lobe of the brain. And to acknowledge or name an emotion such as love was to commit the crime of trivialization and sentimentality. Wind, the cruel intelligence of crows. The river. That's what she believed in. The impossibility of fully removing the bright and sure stains of beet juice from linen. She preferred the tangible world of things seen: light, water, salt, stalks of rye, what could be grasped between her hands and understood by the body.

Seeing as how I have little time left, Stanka came by again while you were working. She is in fits and torments. Her roadside business, Fortunes While You Wait, is being taxed. Her solution: send a curse through the post in the form of a long strip of flypaper covered in coarse black pepper. It will ensure at least three weeks of colossally bad luck and robust rounds of sneezing for the recipient. She drank all the milk, by the way. I am glad the two of you have always been such good friends. You once asked me when you were small why her skin was so dark—was it because she smokes Bulgarian cigarettes? You might have been six or seven at the time. "No," I said. "She's dark because she's a Gypsy." This explained her fondness for milk, which she drank, Stanka once told me, so that at least her insides would be white. Even so, she was a cursed woman because she had "gone behind the hedge" and married a *gadjo,* a non-Gypsy, which is the most disgraceful thing a Gypsy woman can do. This is why the day after she married Mr. Pauls Ivaska, Stanka's family, who all lived in Sabile, held a funeral for her and burned all of her belongings and all their photos containing her image. That wouldn't have been so bad, but then a month later Mr. Ivaska went to Riga to play his French horn and forgot to return. Out of sheer loneliness, Stanka then lit the lamp for Uncle Maris.

I thought Stanka had a sporting chance, as she understood men who wandered, but your grandmother held slimmer odds. About Stanka she'd heard Uncle mutter: "Is she just dirty or permanently tanned?" The sad fact was that Uncle Maris had over his years cultivated a deep suspicion of anything or anybody who'd come from the east, which he said was the source of all our trouble. But we've all seen how a very small amount of water can wear down stone. Stanka predicted a streak of winning lottery numbers and Uncle couldn't resist her charms. Stanka also has thick calves and this is something in a woman Uncle admired. They paid their fee and married at the courthouse and I suppose they were happy, though sometimes it was hard to tell. Uncle sustained two concussions in the first year of marriage. Assault and battery, Uncle called it. Tough love, Stanka called it.

Anyway, Stanka combed my hair, what is left of it, gently, gently.

The comb is sturdy, made of white oak. You needn't return it. She left it so you would put it in my coffin. When we buried your namesake, she put a mirror in his right hand and a packet of cigarettes in his left one. A mirror is a window into the next world, and the dead hold it up like a compass to better steer by. The cigarettes? There's nothing worse than the jitters, she said. Even the dead get them. And she told me about Gypsy heaven. The clouds are made of light bread and the houses are made of cheese. No one ever goes hungry, no one cries. The little orange foxes, the chanterelles that smell so much like apricots, fruit endlessly. No one wears white in heaven because white is the color of mourning. The songs are like wheels well soldered, well fit. They turn smoothly and without effort, and this is how it is that in Gypsy heaven the singing never ends.

Why am I telling you in such detail about what might seem like irrelevant conversations that happened before you were born? The short answer: it's a way to keep our loved ones alive, if only in our embroidered fictions. And why am I narrating the stories of people you knew well and even about events you witnessed? A story is a garment made of many threads, sewn by many needles. Our story is a cloak thicker and more knotted than we suppose. *Like a tapestry,* I said the other day. You said, *No, it's more like lace.* We hold lace up and marvel at the beauty of the light shining through it. But that beauty is only possible because of the knots anchoring the empty space. *Our story is like that,* you said, made as much of silence and emptiness as it is of the knots, those anchors of known fact, people. Who are the knots holding us in place? I could say that it was the Zetsches who ordered shape out of our emptiness. Or I could say it was Uncle.

For three years after that fateful chess tournament, we didn't hear much from him. A tattered and road-weary postcard from Tajikistan. (*The watermelons! Wow!*) A cable from Murmansk. (*Cold, cold.*) Once in a blue moon Uncle Maris called and the black phone swelled with his elaborate, overwrought, and altogether pitiful explanations for his behavior that we could only consider as obligatory fictions. For all his charm and brains, Mother explained to me once, our uncle Maris was the kind of man who could never perceive his own bodily stink, only the stink of others. And so she hung up on him whenever he called.

During that time, both Rudy and I graduated from gymnasium by the skin of our teeth. Mother's deepest fears were confirmed: she had not raised geniuses. That next autumn, several of my classmates, Jutta among them, rode the bus each morning to university. There she would pursue a brilliant life, I was sure, just as I was sure that my life was headed for all things dull and dreary. Had the Soviet Union not fallen, it is possible that Rudy and I would have gone to university. Higher education in those times was free, or nearly free. But after the fall, people like us who earned low marks did not go to university. People like us learned trades or worked in factories—if we were lucky. But as we were not lucky, we made ourselves as useful as possible in the cemetery. And then one evening the black phone on the wall bellowed: *eeeeeee-oooooooh!*

It was Uncle. On principle, Mother hung up on him. He promptly rang back and this time Father answered. He'd called to tell us that Rudy would go to university in Daugavpils. Maris had made all the arrangements. "It's the least I can do." His voice boomed through the black receiver. The next morning Rudy rode the bus to Daugavpils and that left me with Mother and Father. Mother applied herself to her newspaper. The frenzied activity in the real estate market she likened to piranhas let loose in a tank of meat. This newly liberated Latvia meant that Latvians, if they could produce the correct paperwork, could reclaim family properties that had been seized during the occupations. Curiously, a spate of fires ravaged the filing cabinets of many regional courthouses. In the absence of essential records, extremely well-forged titles and deeds sprouted up like mushrooms after a fine August rain. I suppose this was why Mr. Ilmyen, who clerked in a legal office in Daugavpils, always looked so tired in the evening. It was all very suspicious and all meticulously reported in Mother's temperance newspaper.

Father thought Mother's interest in the property deeds and sales transactions unhealthy. "At least we still own the manor—and we can prove it," she'd mutter, her fingers stiff and aching, her eyes bleary. And I think Father felt obligated to offer a mild corrective. "Nobody really owns the land," he'd say, a gentle acknowledgment that our family had not been able to come up with the back taxes for the manor; it both did and did not belong to us. We are caretakers, he'd remind us, stewards, and all that we see God has temporarily placed into our hands. There was no mistaking the emphasis he placed on that word *temporarily*. "If we steward well, that is to say, if we trod gently over this land, then there will be no sign of us afterward. Except, of course, a gravestone or something like that," he hastened to add.

At this time, stewardship was heavy on our minds. Even Mother, a thrifty woman who knew how to stretch a single chicken through an entire month, remarked more than once that winter had sharp teeth. A sack of our potatoes had gone bad in our cellar, and what luck we'd had with the mushrooming had run out. Though Mother took an extra cleaning job in Rezekne, spending even longer hours on her hands and knees, and Father dug fresh holes like a madman to accommodate another rash of suicides, we still felt the pinch. Though a series of new hypermarkets opened in Riga and we'd heard rumors of sudden wealth in big cities, such news felt like distant sparking fire: we might see the light but we did not feel its heat. I understood that it was my job to catch as many perch, pike, and trout as I could and preserve them any way I knew how.

I was eighteen. Not an expert angler but not the worst, either. I fished in midafternoon as the light thinned and cold crimped the horizon. By four, four thirty at the latest, full darkness and frost fell. Under this cover of cold, I shamelessly trolled the spots I knew belonged to Mr. A., Stanka, Mr. Lee, and Mr. Lim. I measured the hours by the number of bites on the line, and by my count, I did pretty well, often hooking pike, a greedy fish easily fooled by the flimsiest of bait.

Toward the end of March and into April, the light in the afternoons returned, weak and pale. Rain and more rain. Torrential rains, falling in biblical proportions, and the river rose steadily, covering the rocky shoals, reshaping glides, and flooding the marshy banks. Perfect fishing conditions to land an eel. But try as I might, I couldn't hook a single one. I decided to become more eel-like: sluggish and dull by day, quick and clever by night. I holed up in my room, Velta's letters spread around me. I felt only a little guilty about my theft. My attention to and my love for these letters exonerated me. After all, we forgive, even applaud, archaeologists for their discovery of fragile artifacts, provided those discoveries find their way home. And as this was a family affair, I told myself I was doing no real harm.

Water is life. In mud, a drier form of water, lives every dark dream, good and bad. The Black Snake lives in this mud. And so does Ghost Girl. She swims close to the riverbank. Mud flows through her veins. With her eyes flashing as blue as flaming sulfur, she looks for children as only children can see her. And being a child, she longs to play. She calls to children to come and swim with her, to come and see her watery world, to slide among the eels and the slippery rocks. She knows every child by name, and when she calls your name, she does so with a voice as strong and persuasive as a dream.

If Mother noticed my furtive habits, she did not let on. More pressing concerns held her attention. In April, Widow Sosnovskis ran out of her antidepressants, went to the little Elvi Market, bought out the entire stock of hair dye, all three bottles, and colored her hair lavender. Three of Mr. Arijisnikov's goats went barking mad. The Zetsches had purchased more riverside property. Her fingers plunging over the stiff typewriter keys, Mother turned these strange stories into clacking syncopation, a matter of public record the rest of us could read.

In addition, the low swollen skies had driven the men to drink and attendance at Mother's Temperance League to swell. Mother couldn't help feeling that all of her efforts were paying off at last: the women in town were finally taking the matter of drinking, and to some extent her newspaper, seriously. But her sense of satisfaction was short-lived as that spring Father more regularly climbed the cork. I should remind you that, for the most part, your grandfather Eriks maintained a sober outlook. But sometimes the rain got on his nerves, particularly when it threatened the cemetery. That spring huge swaths of topsoil — some mere meters from the most famous horse in Latvia — washed into the river. This horse, decorated twice for acts of valor during the Great War, in which it had served under Janis Kalnins (no relation to us), was something of a town mascot. It had been embalmed and for several years had been kept on display in a special mausoleum. At some point, the preservative fluids failed and Father built a supersize coffin. He then dug a supersize grave with a nice view of the river, as befits a war hero. But given the rising water table, he was now doubting his wisdom.

Adding to his worries was the driving rain that scoured the gold paint from the stones belonging to two of the best chess players in town: Mr. Spassky — very distantly related to the great Russian chess master — and Mr. Sosnovskis. Before they died, both men requested that Father include a complete record of their wins and losses on their stones, and Father happily complied, painting 273-1-17 on Spassky's stone and 273-1-17 on Sosnovskis's stone. This would have been of no account if not for the fact that Spassky and Sosnovskis hated each other so completely that their hatred infected their widows, who seemed, on principle, determined to carry on the sentiments of their husbands. Made of knitting needles and thistles, the widows Spassky and Sosnovskis spent most of their time lancing and barbing each other. They only stopped every now and then to needle Father, accusing him of laziness or fecklessness. With the patience of a saint, Father bore their withering scowls and assured them that he was doing his best to give their husbands' gravestones the care befitting chess geniuses. I knew that he was: in those rare breaks between showers, he sunk to his knees in front of those stones and blasted hot air from a battery-operated hair dryer—the last of Uncle's inventions.

In those days, if I wasn't fishing, then I was I tucked in the shed poring over Velta's letters. To my surprise, she wrote, obsessively so, of old myths. Wolves. Water. Girls turned into crows. Of their own volition, these girls flew home to their mothers, their black feathers as shiny as an oil slick and their beaks pointy. With their beaks as sharp as awls, they punctured the sky and let the darkness and wind tumble in. *Why, girl,* their mothers would ask, *why would you do this?* And down to the girl they cackled and said, *We've been to see the Devil and the darkness is his cloak and the wind is his meat. We will never be cold or hungry again. We will want for nothing.*

Sometimes I found a fragment of a letter from my grandfather Ferdinands.

We work fourteen hours in the cold. Frozen soot hovers in the air like a shroud. Mining crushes a man in body and spirit. Three men crossed the white line, the warning mark. They crossed the low stone wall, and the sirens wailed. They crossed the red line, and the guards let the dogs loose. The men flung themselves into the barbed wire. "Go on!" they shouted. "Shoot us. We're begging you."

The ravens try to peck our eyes out. We paint eyes on our caps and wear them backward on our head to scare them off. We would eat the ravens, but they are scrawny and nothing but bone and bile. Gaddis got his hand caught in a machine. It sheared off two fingers and a thumb. We put a leather strap around his hand. We looked for his fingers, but the dogs had run off with them.

As I sat with my knees pulled to my chest, my whole body shivering, I knew that I was feeling a fraction of the cold he had felt. When I fished, I told myself that I suffered the way he had, working in the cold and the dark. I told myself that this was my inheritance. Then I'd look and see that I had all my fingers. I was wearing three sweaters, had a hunk of bread in my pocket. I was nothing like Ferdinands or Velta.

Of all the days our family loves and holds sacred, you know that Mid-summer — Jani Day — is chief. Jani Day is a magical time when the trees come to life and dance. All the old stories come true as long as we stand by our bonfires and tell them. It's the time when boys jump over flaming buckets of tar and girls make wreaths of oak leaves. No digging. No burials, no laying outs. Jani Day is the one day reserved for life, joy. Song. Songs for plowing and planting, threshing and spin-ning, baking, sewing, courting, warring, marrying, and burying. We sing them all. Of course, your grandmother Biruta and grandfather's favorite *dainas* were the Ligo songs.

Traditionally, one only sings them on Jani Day, but as you know, we've never stood on formality. We sing them the entire months of May and June and other months, too. This is how we resist the weight that would crush us. The *dainas* are lift, loft, blood in the veins. They are our life. "Do you know," your grandfather once said, in a sermon at the hall, "that the muscle responsible for a bird's vocal chords is lodged next to its keel bone? That is, the architectural structure re-sponsible for balance in flight is intricately linked to the bird's abil-ity to sing. That is, without song, a bird cannot fly true." This is the magic of Jani Day; it fastened wings between our shoulder blades. It also inspired an incredible urge to fish.

And so it was on account of Jani Day that I made my way to the river one evening, carrying empty flour sacks to sit on and a jar full of lobworms soaked in crankcase oil. As twilight wobbled purple and gray, I went looking for the dark pocket the eels love best. The stars swam overhead. The moon rolled about like a cork in water. Being naturally wary, eels don't venture forth on a night like this, but the water was dark and roiling, mixed with mud churning from the riverbed, just the way eels prefer when they go on their nightly hunting sprees. I set my pole signal, a tiny bell no bigger than my thumbnail. If the line went tight, the bell would trill merrily. The flour sacks I spread over a patch of grass and lay back onto my elbows for what I knew could be a long wait. Mysterious creatures, eels. Where they come from few people can say. Rudy and I read in school that Athenaeus believed they were bred by mud. Or perhaps by the sun's heat. Some people believe that eels are born out of the ruination of the earth or from dew. Others believe that eels breed other eels out of the corruption of their old age. In your Book of Wonder you wrote that even the great angler Izaak Walton couldn't say with certainty how eels breed because no one has ever seen it happen. Only two things Walton can say for sure: first, eels simply disappear somewhere in the Sargasso Sea to die where human eyes have never seen. Second, the meat of eels is like no other. Tasting of the salt of warm seas and distant grasses, the meat melts on the palate, and to eat it is to glide on skies.

In the dropping dark I could just discern Mr. Ilmyen dumping the last of his bait into a choice snag, a prize fishing spot for eels. He was done fishing. He lifted his arm and I waved back. I liked Mr. Ilmyen and was relieved that he would still wave to me despite what Uncle Maris had done and said. It had been three years since the crutch-hurling incident, but I knew that, on principle, Father and Mr. Ilmyen had still not gone fishing together and that they had not and probably would not take a beer together.

But as you know, Jani Day, that midsummer celebration of the longest light of the year, recalibrates the world. It was the time young men jumped over buckets of flaming tar or lured young women to the forest for stolen kisses. We celebrated light, heat, song, healing. On Jani Day even the eels pulled on new skins and, forgetting their hard-earned wisdom, swam a little closer to the surface. When Mr. Ilmyen disappeared behind a copse of drooping alder, I pounced upon that prize fishing spot, which was now maximally baited and utterly irresistible to any eel. No sooner had I set my pole than the line went tight and the bell sang.

I stuffed the sack with wet grass and hauled in the line. Pulling taut the line was the largest eel I'd ever seen. Its thick body looked as big and long as a dachshund as it thrashed in the shallow water, its yellow eyes full of hundreds of years of wisdom. I pulled him in slowly. Then I bent and scooped him to my chest. Some eels can be gentle; if you speak tenderly to them, they might curl up in your arms and go to sleep. I'd seen Mother lay eels flat on a wet towel and stroke their long bellies and sing to them until they drifted into soft dreams of wet grass and water. This eel was not of that temperament. Before he had a chance to curl and whip me in the face or bite my hand, familiar tactics each, I pitched the eel to the ground and held it on its back. It made a few token snaps at my hands, shuddered, and then went still. It was not dead; this is what eels do when held on their backs: they go to sleep. With some effort, I hoisted it to my chest, cradled the eel in my arms as if it were a well-fed child, and noted the dark blue spots dotting its silver body. I'd never seen such markings on an eel before. That's when I knew this was the magical eel whose meat brings wisdom and chancy luck, depending on who catches and eats it. I felt a little sorry for having so unceremoniously yanked it from its soft world of water. But only a little sorry. I eased it into the sack, tied off the opening, and rewound my line on a plastic bottle, burying the butt of the pole in the gritty riverside soil. If I had caught one magical creature, perhaps I might catch two.

I watched the line slicing the water and gliding a bit toward the snag. And then I waited. Few people realize how wily and discerning eels are and what a glacial patience it takes to catch them. I didn't mind; I loved this river. I told myself that it spoke to me in a language only I could understand. I told myself that because I understood the river, it understood me. Just then the second pole bell sang out. I jerked on the line hard to set the hook. A larger fish, I thought, because it bucked and fought, nearly yanking the pole from my hands. I stepped on a rock to get better leverage and that was my mistake. My feet slid from under me and I fell into the river. I splashed and flailed, trying to gain my footing, but my boots were filling up fast and the water pulled me down. Even worse, Rudy's pole spiraled away from me, carried off by the fish that was hooked but free. I made one last desperate reach for the pole and I felt myself going under.

"Here!" a man's voice called. "Grab this!" The end of a pole nudged my elbow. I grasped it tightly. I kicked and chuffed, keeping my eyes fixed on the pair of hands hauling me in. At the shallows one hand gripped my elbow while the other hooked my ribs, and I then I was on the bank, coughing up river water and taking stock of my rescuer. Not Mr. Lee. Not Mr. Arijisnikov, but a stranger, taller than Rudy and almost as broad in the shoulder. He had gotten wet past the waist, all on my account. But with the way he calmly stamped his feet and wrung the water from his sleeves, he acted as if he were at home on the river and hauling out girls from it was the most natural thing in the world for him to do.

He turned to me and grimaced. "You know what they say about a river," he said, taking off his coat and draping it around my shoulders.

"No, what?" I studied his eyes trying to decide if they were bluish gray or perhaps grayish blue.

"Never believe, never trust, never ask."

It was a very Russian expression, but whoever he was, he didn't look Russian. For one thing, he had incredible ears. That is, they were enormous and jutted from the side of his head, a little like the gills of a fish. A beautiful sight, these ears, and I could not stop staring.

"I've never seen you on the river before," I managed at last.

"No, you wouldn't. I'm out from Riga, visiting for the weekend."

"Well," I fumbled. "I'm Inara."

"I'm David." He tipped his finger to his forelock, a very gallant gesture, then he set off through the grass.

"Your coat!" I shouted.

David stopped, looked carefully at me. "I'm sure we'll see each other again—just keep it for now." With a quick wave of his hand, he disappeared behind the scrim of trees. I stood there shivering beneath David's coat and tallying the evening's swift reversals. I'd lost the fish I'd hooked. I'd lost Rudy's pole. I'd gotten soaked to the bone. But if I hadn't fallen into the river in the first place, I would not have met David. And none of these things, good or bad, would have happened if I'd not first landed the magic eel.

The eel!

I scrambled through the brush back to the sack where my lucky eel, his belly tight from eating all my bait, lay snoring—lulled to sleep by the falling rain. It was an effort, but I dragged the sack through the cemetery, through our yard, then up the back steps into our kitchen, where Mother bustled from the sink to the oven, muttering to herself. This oven was serious business for Mother, who had installed it herself and knew, understood, and adored every bolt and coil.

I stowed the sack under the table. Mother took one look at the puddle of water pooling at my feet. "Get changed," she said. "We've got to go clean the hall from top to bottom." Mother hooked her chin toward the Ilmyens' house. "Jutta's getting married tomorrow. And what with all their relatives coming in from Lithuania and even one from America, there's no other building big enough to hold them all."

Jutta. Getting married. Impossible. Given the robust nature of small town gossip, how was it that I hadn't heard of it?

I sleep quite a bit. I can't help myself; it is a short walk in shallow water. As thin as a cobweb, as sweet as clover. You wrote that death begins as a fragmented dream. You heard this from Mr. Zetlars, whose grave you dug five weeks ago. The fragments of the dream stretch, one image and kaleidoscope scenario after another binding together in the recumbent fluidity only a dream affords. When the dream runs unbroken, then you are dead. Maybe this is why you keep waking me up.

You have the little key to the hall, and I have no doubt you'll take good care of it. It was your grandmother's intention that you look after that building. As you know, it sits on the only elevated patch of land in the village, and this affords the little wood building a view of the school huddled at the end of the lane, the peaked red and orange roofs of some houses, and a glimpse of the river. This hall was sacred to Mother. Before the war and occupations, Mother's parents had donated the wood and paid for the brick and mortar that went into the hall's construction. Grandmother Velta donated her small grand piano, and it had been, Mother said, their hope that the hall would always be bursting with song and dance. This is why Velta's and Ferdinands's photographs hang in gilt frames on the back wall near the coat rack. Mother carried a special rag in her purse, and each time she came to the hall, she stood before their pictures and polished the glass. As she peered into the somber eyes of her parents, I imagined she was willing them to speak, to tell her what to do. From beneath his large brow, Ferdinands stared out of that picture frame with a gaze that pierced you to the marrow. What need for ordinary speech has a man with such furious vision? He'd been a poet. He printed and distributed a newspaper that included translations of Finnish poetry and a few political jokes. That was enough to get him deported to Siberia, Tomsk, where he repaired rail lines in temperatures so cold that metal shattered.

Though Velta's photo was in black-and-white, I imagined that her thick braid wound around her head was the color of wheat or honey, her eyes smoldering amber. Wide jaw, thin frowning lips, we could have been twins. About Velta, Mother had only two things to say: silence consumed the woman, as if she'd swallowed an ocean of quiet. She'd also been a ferocious letter writer. Whenever Mother said this, I'd feel a wasp's sting at my fingertips; I'd still not given Mother the letters.

We are commanded to honor our parents. Caring for the hall was Mother's way of preserving the spirit of hers. And being one of the few buildings that had withstood the ravages of the war—no small thing—the hall represented pluck and courage. This didn't prevent the Soviets from commandeering it to billet soldiers and show on the little TV *Swan Lake,* which aired any time a Soviet premier died or war reenactments in which the Germans, the bad guys, were always played by Latvians. In the '80s, Mother said, so many big shots died that they had *Swan Lake* up to their eyeballs. Then came the blessed day they learned that the Soviet Union had, in fact, dissolved. Mother put on her best hat, the one with a mess of black netting front and center and two perky black feathers rising jauntily from it. I called it the crow's nest. The implacable shoehorn, your uncle Rudy called it. When she put it on, she meant business. She marched to the hall, knocked on the door, and shouted: "I demand, by right of my Latvian citizenship and heritage, that you restore this building to me." The only occupant at the time was an old army clerk. Having read, sorted, and filed thirty-some years' worth of bureaucratic sludge, he knew precisely which way the winds blew. The door creaked open, and with a trembling liver-spotted hand, the clerk relinquished the key to the hall. Behind him stood a tidy retinue of packed suitcases and boxes. A force of nature, yes, but Mother was also generous. For many years she called herself an atheist—she saw no use or reason for religion and she hated the way politicians invoked religious sentiment, predictably during election years—but she recognized that in our small community such a fine building should be put to use. So she saw to it that the key hung from a little hook. On Wednesdays the Orthodox Russians sang vespers and on Friday evenings the two Uzbek families gathered for prayers. Early Sunday morning the Baptists who favored Velta's piano on the left side of the platform met. As soon as their service concluded, the Baptists who favored the piano on the right side of the platform convened. A rambunctious group of Pentecostals met on Sunday afternoons. They preferred the piano front and center. And so it was Mother's job to move that minigrand three times each Sunday, which I think went a long way toward reaffirming her atheist sentiments.

She loved the hall for its electricity, running water, toilets, and, most of all, the double oven. This explained why she did her level best to make sure that, just as at our home, she was the only one who cooked with it. Sometimes I thought Mother cared more for that oven than she did for me. It never failed or disappointed her, continually cooking with even, reliable heat so that her *piragi* browned gently at the seams and her cakes rose and her carp cooked to perfection, bubbling in their own fat and tasting of warmer, wiser waters.

You know how your grandmother can scrub a thing to within a fraction of its life. But this oven, for all the reasons I've mentioned, she did not clean. Each subsequent meal carried the traces of every grand dish that had come before it. I suspected that while some people kept journals of their days on paper, this oven was Mother's diary, an olfactory witness to every wedding, wake, chess tournament, and society meeting that she had attended, and no sooner did Mother turn the dial than a flood of smells jogged her memory to better days.

So, on that day when we went to clean for Jutta's wedding, Mother unlocked the back door and stood for a moment on the threshold with a stillness that bordered on reverence. She was looking at the picture of her father, your great-grandfather Ferdinands, whose eyes held the look of a man who has seen every kindness, every cruelty. Between his gaze and hers, I felt I was seeing past and present moving toward a slow collision. Mother ran the cloth over Ferdinands's image then Velta's. She touched her finger to her lips and touched her finger to Grandmother Velta's lips. This was Mother's private ritual, one I knew not to ask about. I had divined, on account of the small stone next to hers in the cemetery, that Velta had lost a little one during the early years of the occupations. But the circumstances of the child's death I did not know. That was another topic we were not to ask about.

Mother turned to me, clapped her hands briskly. "Let's get busy," she said, seizing a stiff-brush broom. Quietly, the words barely discernible, she sang the *daina* she always sang when she was tired but still had work to do.

I rose early in the morning.
Dear God rose earlier, yet
Why, God, did you get up?
What did you need so early?

I grabbed a mop and bucket. I'd cleaned this hall with Mother so many times, I knew exactly what she wanted done and how to do it. While Mother swept the carpet on the raised platform, I stacked chairs and mopped the main sitting area. And the song continued.

What would you do, dear girl, if I didn't rise early?
I open all the doors for you; I give all advice.

Mother set to work in the kitchen; I scrubbed commodes and tiles. And then I turned my attention to one of the walls, my ritual. When I was a girl, the hall was considered Soviet property, and as so often was the case in public buildings, an oversize portrait of Stalin frowning behind his oversize mustache had been hung on the wall. The day after the Soviets pulled out and your grandmother collected the key from that elderly clerk, she snatched that picture off the wall and flung it out the hall's back door, as if it were a piece of moldy cardboard. It landed face down in the mud. It stayed there for weeks: nobody wanted to be known as the person who had rescued Stalin. Still, the tyrant had left his indelible mark: having hung on the wall for so long, the picture had shielded that sixty-four square centimeters of wall from the ordinary dirt and grime that discolored everything else. That portrait had been, Mother said, a larger taint keeping at bay smaller taints. But it looked strange: this bright white square surrounded by a sea of duller white. The only real solution, Mother decided, was to hang a picture of the Bear Slayer, Lacplesis. You have always loved this picture. As he grapples with his foe, every muscle of the Bear Slayer ripples. His large hands rip at the bear's jaws. His fur-trimmed ears sit high atop his head, looking not at all strange.

The only trouble with this newer picture is that it is smaller than the old one. A verge of white wall framed the smaller picture, a reminder that Bear Slayer had not always been with us.

We'd been working for some time when I noticed that Mother's singing had stopped. I pulled off the rubber gloves and found her, head thrust inside the open oven, her hands running along the inside panels. Mother withdrew her head, sat on her heels, and examined her hand. "Good Lord!" Her face blanched. "Someone's scoured the panels of the top oven! They're as spotless as the day I installed it!" Mother's shoulders sagged, and I knew that she was taking a quick inventory of her lost culinary calendar. "Well, we'll just have to come back early tomorrow," Mother said at last, wiping her hands on her skirt.

"Why?"

"To mind the oven, of course!" Mother charged out the kitchen door into the rain. I trudged behind her, listening to the sound of the greasy mud wrestling with our boots and not talking as we passed the Ilmyens' house, where each windowpane threw squares of light into their yard. Even though Mother and Mrs. Ilmyen still held Temperance League meetings together, I could not imagine that Mrs. Ilmyen would want us anywhere near the hall on the day of such a big event. And this made me unbearably sad; Jutta and I had once been like sisters, allied against the madness of a small town. We'd hidden frogs in the boots of the boys who teased us; I taught her all the dirty Latvian words and jokes Uncle had told Rudy and Rudy had taught me; we glued chessmen to the board belonging to a boy who was a cheat in math and not even a good one. And there was a time when I believed that I could be like her, able to navigate out of this town into a larger, better life. Jutta had tried to help, showing me how to balance chemistry equations, teaching me how to think two and three moves ahead on a chessboard. But where she could perceive endless possibilities within the fixed frame, I could see only how small the squares were, how short the time on the playing clock was. When we all sat for the entrance exams, I knew before the results were posted on the school doors that Jutta would go and I would stay. Her departure signaled a subtle shift; we had become two different kinds of people.

Once home, Mother went to the kitchen where she found Father touched by drink: a row of beer bottles stood in salute on the wooden table. For a Baptist, Father knew an awful lot about beer. But he was Latvian, and inhabiting and articulating seemingly irreconcilable paradoxes came as naturally to him as breathing or praying or, in this case, drinking. That is, Father was both a Bible and bottle Baptist. And he took both jobs seriously, though when he drank, he did not wear the white gloves that he wore when he read his Bible. At this particular moment, he was aspiring to grand notions. He wanted romance, but not with just a bottle. But Mother had all the excitement she could handle in one day and personally escorted him to the toolshed where she instructed him to sleep it off.

This, I told myself, was the reason why she had failed to notice — again — my magical eel quietly slumbering in her washtub under the table. As thick as a fifteen-kilogram sack of potatoes and twice as long, marinated or smoked, pickled or baked, he would feed twenty people, maybe more. And then I knew why the river had sent this eel to me in the first place: so that I could give it to Jutta and her family. They would eat the meat and have all of the blessing, all of the wisdom. And if by chance there was a bit left over for us, then all the better. I split the eel down the middle and took out the innards and placed the gutted fish in a stockpot. I poured vinegar into the pot, some of Mother's special-occasion wine, and crushed coriander and fennel seed. Then I sat at the table in the dark where I cradled my head in my arms and fell almost at once into an unshakable sleep of utter exhaustion.

And I dreamed. I heard Father singing in the yard: *Then the water had overwhelmed us; the stream had gone over our soul. Then the proud waters had gone over our soul.* And then another voice, both sweet and strange, strangely familiar — the Ghost Girl. You have always loved this story. The way your uncle Rudy tells it, the Ghost Girl emerges from still water, revealing herself one bit at a time: a slim torso, her breasts, her round shoulders, then her dark wings, as sharp as scythes. Half bird, half woman, her beak is as sharp as an awl. She comes for you in your dreams, and you'll know she's visited if you wake in the night and find puddles of water on the floor by your bed.

In the dream she didn't come to me; I went to the river, where she swam in the dark water. She was not surprised to see me. Dark hair, pale face, dark eyes, she seemed a darker version of me.

"Inara." She waved me toward the roiling water. "Ask me a question; I'll answer!" I took one step in then another. I could see that she was not me at all but something else entirely. River weeds for hair, skin the color of mud. Her eyes, gaping black holes. She lunged and bit my shoulder. I woke to the sound of dogs barking and a shrill rooster clearing his throat.

What did that dream mean? you ask me. I have no idea. Maybe the dream was a tiny confirmation that there's something to your grandmother's ghost story. Maybe it was the first time I felt fear. I woke with a start, my elbow knocking against the pot with the eel. A quick look inside, a poke with the fork tines. It wept vinegar, just as it should, so I washed the meat, dredged it through flour. The rest of the ingredients for the sauce — shelled walnuts, hard-boiled eggs, raisins, honey, parsley, and mint — I'd take with me and assemble at the hall. I had just turned on the oven, thinking I'd precook the eel, when Mother came into the kitchen, her hair pinned up in preparation for a full day of cooking. She pointed her nose toward the oven and squinted at the murky glass door.

"You're not cleaning that oven, are you?"

"No," I said. I knew she'd not fully recovered from her previous night's shock. "I'm cooking something for Jutta."

"Oh," Mother sighed. "Well, whatever it is, cover it and bring it with you. We've got to get to the hall before someone makes a mess of that kitchen."

The recipe? I've never written it down. I've never needed to. I can tell you that you must watch over the walnut sauce with care. Too much heat too soon will ruin it beyond remedy. The raisins, by the way, need to sit in sweet white wine overnight.

Thick fog swelled from the river and held to the lane. We set off into the fog, Mother's nose twitching. The distinct smell of chicken rolled through the mist. As we approached the lighted hall, we could see the silhouettes of women working in the kitchen. Mother held the door open for me and we stood on the threshold surveying the scene: Mrs. Ilmyen and the twin aunts whom Jutta had once told me about — Reka and Lida — furiously chopping almonds, dicing boiled chicken, and slicing mountains of leeks. Clearly, Mother had severely underestimated the energy of Mrs. Ilmyen and her sisters.

Mother coughed, and after a long moment, Mrs. Ilmyen looked up. She smiled. "Oh, Mrs. Kalnins! I can't tell you how much we appreciate your thorough cleaning."

Mother grimaced, her gaze taking in the stockpot simmering on the ring. "I thought we'd help out where we could — with the soups, maybe."

"Well." Mrs. Ilmyen straightened a pin in her hair. "That's generous of you, but you've done so much already."

"Nonsense! What are good neighbors for? I won't get in the way," Mother added, as if reading Mrs. Ilmyen's thoughts. "I'll just watch over the oven; it can be tricky."

Mrs. Ilmyen glanced at her sisters, who were still chopping but much more quietly now. Then she reset the pin in her hair. With that single gesture, she acknowledged that in all the years she lived across the road from Mother she'd weathered much worse. She'd get through this, too.

"All right, then," Mrs. Ilmyen said.

Mother wiped her hands on the sides of her skirt and affixed a smile of blistering benevolence on her face. I knew that her stubborn insistence regarding the soup wasn't merely out of spite. Mother sincerely believed that soup making was sacred work because the bad spirits of the air didn't like it when they smelled onions and beets weeping together in the bowl. They seized you by the bones and tried to make you too tired to finish, which was why Mother sometimes needed to sit on a stool and why sometimes she started a soup and I had to finish it. Had Mother and Mrs. Ilmyen been closer friends, Mother certainly would have reminded Mrs. Ilmyen of these things. Instead, Mother stationed herself on a stool in front of the oven and set the temperature dial.

I kept my back to them and my nose lowered over my sauce, walnuts and raisins swelling with spiced wine, and waited for the oven to heat. And I listened carefully for the little morsels women drop while working in kitchens: how many people were coming (sixty, at least); who the big eaters were (the groom's father, who ate half a salmon at a wedding two towns away); where Semyon, the groom, and Jutta would live (in a small room Mr. Ilmyen planned to attach to their kitchen); how Mrs. Ilmyen was handling the stress (good — only one gray hair this morning and so far not a single tear shed from the bride). Through all this talk, the hands of Mrs. Ilmyen's sisters never stopped moving. Reka and Lida were a veritable whirlwind of chopping and rolling and flouring, mixing, blanching and boiling. I marveled at their quick and steady industry: latke upon latke appearing on the trays in endless ranks and files, ropes of braided challah dough quietly rising under a towel. After three hours, the sisters decided to temporarily relinquish the kitchen to Mother and install themselves in the bathroom: Jutta needed help with hair and makeup. I caught a glimpse of Jutta. She had a towel wrapped around her head. Her dark eyes flashed. Catching sight of me, she lifted her hand, wiggled her fingers. With that one gesture, my world was made right.

Before she left the kitchen, Mrs. Ilmyen fixed a stern gaze on Mother. "Promise me, Biruta Kalnins, you will not tamper with our food."

Mother adjusted the heating dial then crossed her arms over her chest. "I will only open and close the oven door — and only then to make sure nothing burns."

I could read utter doubt in Mrs. Ilmyen's eyes, but the lift of her jaw indicated the resigned optimism of a woman choosing to believe. "Okay," Mrs. Ilmyen said, clutching her purse under her arm. "Okay." And she retreated for the bathroom.

For the next hour Mother and I worked in silence, Mother assembling her famous *piragi,* small pasties she filled with meat — smoked ham and bacon and onions. It was completely unkosher, colossally unkosher, but years of cooking alongside Mother taught me to ask no questions, offer no correctives. I passed my sauce through a sieve into the belly of the eel. Then I wrapped the fish with a towel, one of Mother's very best, and slid the entire bundle into the top oven.

"Wait." Mother opened the door of the upper oven and smelled the heat. "What with half this oven not what it used to be, I can't quite judge. My nose is off." Mother thrust her head farther into the oven. It was important, Mother had taught me, to never rush an oven heating. And you should never bake anything without first dancing the requisite twenty drops of oil on the bottom plate of the oven. How the oil beaded, she'd told me, and how it danced told you how hot it was and which dish to bake first and for how long.

"I just don't know," Mother said, withdrawing her head from the oven. From her apron Mother pulled out Uncle's old stethoscope and inserted the ear pieces into her ears. Then she reached for her backup jar of pork lard and dropped a thick white crescent from the spoon onto the racks. Another cataclysmically unkosher move. We watched the lard drip to the bottom panel. Mother held the scope near the panel and listened to the lard sizzling. It was better to use olive oil, but Mother had always maintained that anything could be substituted for something else if the situation was dire enough.

When Mother, satisfied at last, returned the stethoscope to her apron, I slid my eel, now fish in a cloak, into the upper oven. And

Mrs. Ilmyen's somber warning? We meant well—didn't that count for something? Mother turned her attention to the two oversize bowls of dough for Reka's latkes and Lida's challah. She thrust her fingers into the dough, noted how quickly the dough flaked apart. She spooned a little lard from her jar into Reka's dough and folded it in with muscular jabs of the spoon. So much pork lard, so much unkosherness. It was too much, even for me.

"Mother," I gasped. "What are you doing?"

"This is a small repair, not an alteration," Mother said.

"You know, some women are a strange mixture of pride and humility. Wanting help but uncertain if they should ask for it," Mother said. "A wedding—now this is a big event, so big it overwhelms. If there's a small thing I can do to help, then I want to do it." Mother smiled. "It'll be my gift to her."

Fortunately, it was at this time that the musicians converged at the back door: a cellist, two violinists, and an oboist, a man with a white yarmulke stapled to a red toupee. He annoyed Mother greatly by repeatedly addressing her as the mother-of-the-beautiful-bride and asking if the ensemble could be paid in advance for their services.

At last, the groom and his family arrived. And with them the rabbi, a tiny man in a black suit shiny at the elbows who was supported on both sides by the groomsmen. The rabbi did not walk so much as he shuffled, the weight of his beard pulling his chin to his chest. The entourage tottered to the platform where they all took their places beneath the chuppah, a shawl tied to four poles Mr. Ilmyen had erected on the platform. This canopy, bowed in the middle like a long-winded prayer, didn't look like much to me. But back in the days when I thought I could become a Jew, Jutta explained to me that the canopy was God sheltering and protecting the bride and groom. No doubt they'd need it, I thought, so near to the river where rain and stork crap fell from the sky in a far-too-predictable manner.

And then in a billow of white came Jutta, her dark cherrywood hair bound up with beads. Her cheeks flushed (with a little help from

Mrs. I.'s flat of rouge) and her eyes as bright as May marigolds, Jutta glided past me, her gaze fixed on Semyon. She joined Semyon under the chuppah and bent over a low table where they signed a piece of paper. Then the rabbi read a bit from a musty-looking book. Melodious and odd words in a language I did not know, but they had the effect of quiet enchantment. I was standing tiptoe on the threshold of something sacred: love.

After the reading, Semyon peered intently into Jutta's face before lowering her veil. Happiness, I knew. He was divining in the face of his bride where his happiness lay. But even from my spot, on the threshold between the kitchen and the hall, I could see the love between them, apparent and apparently ample, and I felt that bite of ancient envy. I wanted that kind of love. Not the flimsy kind I'd read about in books, but the sturdy sort of love that would not disappoint with every change in the weather. I wanted that boy who didn't notice my hips or my hands but looked steadily into my eyes and liked what he saw.

A groomsman placed a glass on the platform, and Semyon smashed it under his right heel, a reminder of the fragility of human joy in this lifetime. Everyone clapped and shouted, "Mazel tov." Mother rushed for her whisk broom and dustpan, but not before clicking her tongue, calculating the cost of such an elegant piece of glassware utterly destroyed.

Mr. Ilmyen climbed onto a chair, a glass of wine raised in his hand. "As you know, we named Jutta after the famous chess prodigy Jutta Hempel who gave simultaneous chess tournaments on TV when she was only six years old. Just like that, Jutta, our Jutta, has always known the right move in life. And why should it be any different in love?" Mr. Ilmyen nodded at Semyon's parents. "So a toast to the parents of the groom for having the imagination and foresight to orchestrate their first meeting. At a chess tournament, no less!"

"A brilliant move!" Semyon's father called out. And then he climbed onto the other chair and put an arm around Mr. Ilmyen. "You can't have the sweet without the salt. Every fisherman knows this. Sweet water rushes headlong to the sea where it runs to salt. Both kinds of water are good; both waters nourish life. But let us not forget the inherent risks of living. Let us not forget that joy and sorrow are shadows cast by the same tree, and this tree we also call life."

"To life!" Mr. Ilmyen cried, and the shout went up: "To life!"

Outside, Mrs. Lim, Mrs. Lee, and Stanka pressed their noses to the sweating panes. I went to the kitchen and let them in.

"I'm sorry —" Jutta's uncle Keres materialized behind me. "This is a private party."

"What's private around here?" Stanka elbowed past him. "We're friends of the bride."

Mrs. Lee said, "I taught her how to tie her right shoe."

"And I taught her the left," said Mrs. Lim.

I followed them over the threshold into the hall that had been transformed now by laughter and music and movement. Jutta and Semyon each clutched separate ends of a hankie for dear life while they were carried aloft in their chairs and twirled about. Jutta had never looked happier, and where I had just moments before felt envy, a knot between my shoulders, I now felt a simple undivided happiness for her. The music was nothing like the staunch Baptist hymns, and before I knew it, I was tapping my feet. How could I not? This music flew and skipped as if the musicians had never heard of the sturdy 4/4 signature or the open chords of the major keys. Tipping from joy to sorrow in a half measure, the music was like each one of us there in the room: intricate and sometimes discordant motifs brought together to make a song that every now and then clarified into a single melody. Where was I in this song? A half step away, near joy but not in joy. I felt myself tearing up.

Stanka nudged me with her elbow. "Don't be sad. Her life isn't gonna be all fun and games, chess or otherwise."

I smiled. Stanka always knew when I needed cheering up.

"A girl like that! All books and big vocabulary. I'll bet she doesn't even know how to take out her own eyes." It was the Romani expression for orgasm. Clearly, Stanka didn't think Jutta, as smart as she was, would know how to satisfy in the bedroom, let alone experience the ecstatic state for herself.

"Psst! Inara!" Mother called from the kitchen. "Stop lounging around like a cough drop." She pointed to her trays of *piragi* cooling on the sideboard. "Carry these out."

"What about all Reka's latkes?"

"Oh—she's busy dancing. Let's put our food out first." This I did, but I couldn't help but notice that only Stanka and Mrs. Lee touched Mother's meat pies. Not a single guest even approached the table.

During a break between numbers, Mrs. Ilmyen took Mother aside by the elbow. "About your hors d'oeuvres, Mrs. Kalnins; we cannot eat them."

"What?" Mother blinked. "What's wrong with them?"

"It's not part of our tradition."

"What tradition?"

"Traditionally, Jews do not eat pork. Your *piragi* are loaded with pork and are, therefore, forbidden to us." Mrs. Ilmyen spoke with the same overly patient tones she used when I'd visit Jutta and ask impossible questions.

"Can't the rabbi just bless it?" Mother asked. She was not a stupid woman, and I believe she genuinely did not mean to offend the Ilmyens. She simply couldn't see how something so elemental to Latvian cuisine could be at fault, and she hated to see this measure of our generosity go to waste.

"No," Mrs. Ilmyen said. The weight in her voice pulled her words to a place beyond any suggestion of emotion—to the physical state of pure exhaustion: Solomina Ilmyen was not angry; Mother had simply worn her out.

Crestfallen, Mother returned to the kitchen where a great clanging of pots and lids commenced. The musicians started another song, but not before Jutta caught my eye and raised her hankie. Jutta knew me and she knew my mother. No one had to tell Jutta what was going on, but she was so happy she didn't care. Instead, she wound her way through the moving bodies until she stood before me.

"Inara." Jutta clasped my hand in hers. "It's time for the gladdening of the bride." Stanka coughed and rolled her eyes.

"I don't dance," I said.

"Nonsense. Everybody dances at a wedding. It's easy—just follow the person next to you."

I looked at Jutta, so happy now and determined to share her happiness with me. And I wanted to feel it, too—real happiness. I had a few doses of sorrow, and for one hour I wanted to trade them for joy. Which is why I allowed myself to be pulled into the current of bodies, turning in a ring first clockwise then counterclockwise. And I was surprised to feel how light my feet could move.

And that's when I saw, above the weaving ring of women, a pair of ears, ears of such grand proportion that they were irrefutably the same set that belonged to David. The circles of bodies rotated, and when he and I were opposite each other, he clutched my hands and pulled me out of the circle. David had blue eyes to the bottom of a river and back. So blue, it was as if they'd taken a clear summer sky and wrung the color out of it.

"Why, it's the girl from the river—I almost didn't recognize you in those dry clothes!" David stepped back and examined my appearance.

I couldn't help noticing that his gaze seemed stuck at my hips.

"What are you looking at?"

"You have, er, elbows of enormous construction."

My cheeks burned.

"I was thinking the same thing about your ears. They're really quite marvelous."

This time it was David's turn to blush. "Each year I think I'll grow into them, but every year they seem to get bigger."

I looked at my hips. "I know the feeling."

David laughed. And that's when I knew I was looking at the boy I would marry. David pulled me closer and maneuvered us away from the too-enthusiastic oboist.

"So, Inara, do you have a last name?"

"It's Kalnins."

David stopped midstep then caught up. "Kalnins? As in the Kalnins who narrowly escaped indictment for trademark fraud?"

"Yes, the same."

"As in the Kalnins who salted the birch trees belonging to that Alpine yodeler until all the trees died?"

I nodded. "Yes."

"And claimed to have invented the cadmium loop as well as the world's first environmentally friendly antigravity jump boots?"

"Okay. So okay—you've heard of my uncle."

"It's just that your uncle is legendary. His *We Are So Smart* science programs are still aired—usually around three in the morning."

My face burned. I recalled that moment when Uncle hurled his crutch at Jutta's father and the horrible things Uncle said.

"Hey—I'm only teasing." David touched my chin with his index finger. "Let's just dance."

"I think you should know that I sleep with your coat under my pillow. I suppose I should give it back to you."

"How about at the river—for old times' sake?"

To tell someone of the opposite sex that you want to meet at the river is to say you want to kiss that person. But as David was from a big city, he might not know this, and I was only too happy to educate him on the matter. Later. "Okay," I said. "What time?"

Before he could answer, a scream pierced the air. The orchestra fell silent. I pointed my nose toward the kitchen, toward the source of the noise and the unmistakable smell of smoke.

Mrs. Ilmyen and her sisters raced to the kitchen, where I found

Mother standing stock-still in front of the open oven doors. Dark clouds of smoke billowed and purled up the walls and across the ceiling. Apparently, we'd used too much lard, so much so that it had dripped from the back of the top oven into the bottom. Fire blazed from both ovens, top and bottom. Now it was every cook for herself.

Stanka lobbed a tureen of coffee grounds at the fire. And still the flames raged. Though I could see it killed her to do it, Reka hurled an open sack of flour into the ovens. Mrs. Ilmyen scrambled to cover the trays of latkes, lest the flour contaminate them, but there was no help for it. The flour hit the flames in a big white cloud that traveled from inside the ovens and dusted every surface in the kitchen — animate and inanimate.

"My challah!" Lida shrieked, even as the flour settled in her hair and on her skin. And still the top oven flamed.

"My eel!" I cried. I wrapped a dish towel around my hand and pulled at the rack and the baking pan. I could not have held that pan more than three seconds, but it burned through that dish towel all the same. The smell of burning flesh revived Mother: she hurried me to the sink and thrust my blaring red hand under the faucet. I could not look at my hand. Instead, I looked at Mother, covered head to toe in white flour. I smelled coffee grounds in her hair and I knew she was, like me, ashamed.

Mrs. Ilmyen sat on a stool and buried her face in her hands. "Everything is ruined!" she sobbed. Through the open doorway I could see the guests whispering nervously. Mr. Ilmyen climbed atop a chair to better assess the catastrophe.

Mrs. Ilmyen took a big breath and held it. "Mrs. Kalnins . . . Biruta" — she attempted a smile — "if you'd kept the oven clean like any decent cook, none of this would ever have happened." Mrs. Ilmyen swept her arm toward the oven, her flour-dusted sisters, the chalk-white challah, my burned hand.

Mother drew herself to her full height. "Please, do not besmirch these ovens. They are absolutely faultless in the matter." Mother sniffed mightily. The flour had gotten into her nose. She sneezed. This, too, on Lida's challah.

At this, Mr. Ilmyen, still perched on the chair, raised his glass: "To life!" he shouted. "To life!" everyone in the hall cried. It was only a small pause in the celebration—the Ilmyens and Semyon's family would dance and forget that any of the rest of us had ever been there. I stood on tiptoe. David moved away from me in the mix of bodies. I knew I would not get another chance to talk to him about the river, and even if I had, he would not want to meet me there. Not now.

On the way home we didn't speak a word. Music poured out of the hall, now a box of sound and light shrinking behind us. In my arm the pan cooled to a leaden weight and I was never so glad to see our laundry still flapping on the line, our dingy back steps. Mother paused at the rosebush to compose herself, but I forged ahead.

Inside the kitchen I snapped on the light. Father sat at the table, white gloves on his hands, his Bible open before him. He'd been reading in the dark, which is how he read when his head hurt. With a loud *thunk,* I set the pan onto the table.

"What's that?" Father peered charred remains.

"I call it fish in a cloak. But you can call it dinner," I said. I pulled my hand back but not before Father saw the angry welt still rising in the middle of my palm.

"You're hurt."

I shrugged. "Not badly," I said, but I kept my hand under the table where nobody had to see it.

Father poked at the smoldering lump with a knife. "Carp?"

"Eel."

"I love eel," he said, sawing at the charred mess until the meat yielded. Mother came in at last—still covered in flour and as white as a ghost. She sat across from Father, who studied her and chewed for a long moment. At last he cleared his throat. "I like what you've done with your hair. You look very dignified."

Mother made a savage pass at her eyes with her sleeve. She managed a wobbly smile. "That's why I married you—you don't talk much, but when you do, you always say just the right thing."

Father considered this carefully. Then he sliced another chunk of meat from the pan and put it on a plate for Mother and me. Together, the three of us, we ate that entire eel, every burned bit. And then we went to bed so that in the morning when we woke we would be wiser.

CHAPTER THREE

JUTTA CAME BY THIS MORNING. We watched the starlings being seized by a collective flinch that launched them upward in a blink, as if of one body. How do they know to do this? Is it a shift in the wind, the sound of grass bending differently? A snap of a twig or the sudden awareness of being observed? They swirled, twisted, folded in upon themselves, danced. What is this movement called? I wanted to consult your Book of Wonder, as I was almost certain you would have the answer in there. Jutta scolded me for trying to move too quickly and for not wearing warmer socks. She said, "You just sit there and let me help you." Then she told me a story. This is the gift, the blessing of coming to one's end and having the luxury of knowing it. People shower me with stories.

Her story came from her father. As a boy in Minsk, he'd been schooled, as so many Jewish boys were, at a heder. The rabbi kept in his study a wide mirror, as tall as the man himself and framed in dark cherrywood and mounted on a wooden stand. In those days every boy had a chore in the school; some cleaned the floors, some the wooden stairs leading up to the rooftop where they held evening prayers. Others cleaned the tables and chalkboards. This boy's job was to run a dry rag over the spines of all the books in the rabbi's study. The rabbi enjoyed smoking a pipe every now and again in the study, and as we both know, smoke will settle. One day the boy noticed that the mirror was covered in dust. The rabbi was a great and devout teacher, the kind of man who would have wiped the sweat off of God's brow if there had been a cloth large enough. And because it bothered this little boy that a man so holy should have such a dirty mirror, he ran that cloth over the mirror's surface. As he did, the boy contemplated his own reflection in the smudged glass. Maybe he was remembering the rabbi's teachings from earlier that morning: a divine spark resides in each of us. We are made in the Maker's image. And the boy, forgetting the dangers of a mirror and perhaps thinking that if he gazed into the glass long enough he'd catch a glimpse of that image, leaned in.

The silver hummed, softened. The mirror turned liquid, the wet metal folding and pooling in on itself. The lull and lure of both his changing reflection and the changing mirror pulled at him. As a swimmer parts the water with his hands, he opened a passage in the glass and aluminum, and climbed through the mirror and vanished. How could anyone know this? Because one of his shoes had been caught in the mirror as the liquid silver closed behind him. A warning against the dangers of vanity? The tacit endorsement of escapism? "No," Jutta said. It was a reminder that a flimsy, whisper-thin membrane separates us from this world and others.

We stand at all times on the threshold of mystery. I tell it to you now to remind you the reason for stories in the first place. It is a way to pluck the loose stitching of a garment so capacious one cannot tell where the top is, where the bottom is. In this way our words take full sail and lift us to another time and place.

Because he dug so many graves, people often asked your grandfather if there was a good way to die. He'd say in the bosom of our Lord. And because he was a man of the earth and a man of the book, they asked him to hold his hands over them and pray. Not so much a prayer of healing because when people sent for your grandfather they knew they were beyond healing. More often, they wanted to make amends, to recount their wrongs, as if Father were an ordained priest and could offer absolution. This is how we learned about Mr. Sosnovskis's many trysts. We learned, too, that Mr. Spassky had once cheated his way to a chess win.

Though these deathbed confessions made your grandfather uncomfortable, he did not dissuade the dying from telling their stories. Their urgent need to confess, he believed, was both natural and necessary and a need, he said, we carry to the grave and beyond. "Just as the body decomposes, the soul likewise must uncompose," Father explained to anyone who wanted to hear and sometimes even to those who didn't. The soul's work, he believed, was to both tell and untell the wrongs of the body. He called it taking a moral inventory, an accounting that included an exhaustive examination of one's attitudes, will, imagination. Jealousy, selfishness, misplaced ambition, the brilliant and false illusions of oneself so carefully groomed over a lifetime, every failure of large and small compassion—all these had to be acknowledged, exposed. That is why, Father said, some people flop about so much in the first weeks after they die. "Dismantling the tyranny of self—it's quite exhausting work," Father explained. "And noisy."

From your notes I detect it was this noise that in your teenage years pulled you to the cemetery. You wrote that Lida Kaulfeds, the brilliant dancer, had in her home life-size bronze sculptures of herself in various poses. In both her youth and elder days she had many lovers. Of each she demanded bouquets of carnations, roses if they could get them, and obsessive, slavish homage. You wrote that with some remorse and bewilderment she confessed she could not remember any of her admirers' names.

Mr. Ozolins had fathered a child with one of his employees. He would not recognize the child, had insisted he wasn't the father. His failure to love what he'd been given gnawed at his bones, turned his teeth to chalk.

Mr. Bumbers admitted that he'd made all his money, which wasn't much but enough to put his daughter through school, by selling distressed fruit at top price. Spray paint and fructose injections figured prominently in his small frauds. The worst thing, he said, was that he believed the lies he told himself: his small deceptions were no more egregious than those of his competitors. And yet he could not deny his deep sense of shame or the need to confess.

The dead are not alone in their deep need to rectify accounts. But my reasons for telling you our family stories are not so much for confessional purposes as they are for corrective ones. You know how I love your uncle Rudy to the marrow of my bones, but he is an inveterate talebearer. What more clever means of misdirection than a story, these beautifully extravagant lies? He would have you believing that great-uncle Maris's around-the-world-in-eighty-minutes experiment involving a bathtub, tanks of hydrogen, and a town full of stolen bedsheets was a smashing success. Let me be clear: it was not. Your namesake only managed to clear the tops of the birches before all the women, recognizing their pilfered laundry floating away from them, lobbed stones and brought Uncle literally to his knees. Ditto for Uncle's hope-of-our-nation Olympic campaign. Alpine yodeling is not and has never been an Olympic event.

I do not wish to be contentious, but I do believe it's wrong to knowingly tell a lie. I should have told my version of the family stories to you sooner and more often. I should have remembered that we find ourselves and locate the meaning of our lives in the stories we tell. We are setting a string of buoys, lights in a deep water of darkness. It's an attempt to find a way closer to the raw and aching truth of ourselves and it takes a lifetime of telling to travel there. Agony to articulate, agony to hear. But what sweet relief to be released through our words.

I believe you know this agony and release well. The yearning to find the words for the inexplicable, the inchoate — that has been your torment. Your Book of Wonder, this playground of ideas capriciously arranged, that was your release. They have been a great comfort to me, these notes. That you've taken to writing in it again, that you allow me to read your thoughts, pleases me beyond measure. You've written that time is a series of looped threads. Of this I am living proof; I am here in the present, but many of the ruminations of my internal landscape are tied to the events of the past as if there were two of me, the one talking to you as you sit in the blue chair and the other a twenty-one-year-old girl pulled by longings that elude my attempt to clothe them in words. What ties these two girls together? You.

You've asked what kind of a person I was that summer I met your father. Awkward comes to mind. I was not and would never be a beautiful woman, and I was just vain enough to know it and care. I had not heard from David, wondered if I ever would. Not knowing brewed a restlessness in me I had never before felt. No, not butterflies. Having butterflies suggests beauty, a gracefulness to my agitation. All I had was a desperate sense that I was inadequate. If I possessed some skill, some talent, some secret knowledge, I told myself, I could make up for my many shortcomings.

I turned my eye to Velta's rusted tin. At the bottom, wrapped in lace, I found a coil of her hair, a deep chestnut brown that turned copper when I held it to the light of the window. I liked touching the rough paper of her letters, I liked this act of possession. In Velta's letters I left the known world of precarious fact for the elastic, forgiving terrain of a vividly imagined, vividly confused internal landscape. With each reading, a little more of that unknown woman came to life. She did not come willingly, this woman who wrote in fragments, in *dainas* and, in some cases, recipes. About herself, her thoughts, her feelings—not a word. More often she relayed old wives' tales, kindly advice, observations regarding the world outside her window. I had to fabricate Velta from the flimsiest scraps: at night the trees, shameless gossips, tell tales. The moon is a brazen voyeur. The coarse thread from two fishing nets yields one sweater, and even then, it's not a great sweater. Eels caught in wintertime should be dipped in icy water and hung from the rafters. On New Year's Eve one must eat every last yellow pea on one's plate. Failure to do so results in grief, a year of tears for each uneaten pea. Something she called number ninety-two appeared in several letters:

> *Tell me, dear girl; Tell me, dear girl,*
> *What is heavier than a stone?*
> *I would not be a maid*
> *If I could not tell you*
> *What is heavier than a stone.*
> *At my side a youth is sitting*
> *Who is heavier than a stone.*

I suppose this was a courting *daina,* but I couldn't help but think of old Mr. Gepkars, who adored every bit of Latvian sandstone, clay, and limestone: *The rocks, children, the sturdy ancient rocks. They tell our story if only we will get on our knees to read it!*

Other bits Velta had written on backs of recipe cards.

> *Bleach, bluing, and lye. In a dress made of paper and ink she wandered in the rain, bleeding a river of words between her legs. What words are there for this song? She will have to borrow a new body, a new voice to make a new song. She will sing through the water.*

I shuddered as I read this letter. I could not help thinking of the Ghost Girl, could not help making associations where maybe I should let well enough alone.

Mrs. Zetsche — Mildi — came to see me again. She sat in the chair you are sitting in now, her feet dangling. Sometimes I forget how small she is. And old. Horizontal lines score her small troubled forehead. She looked out the window and told me about a distant relative of hers who'd been a general in the Austro-Hungarian army. He'd kept ostriches on some ancestral estate, had broken them with bit and bridle, and on St. Demetrius's and St. George's days he held ostrich races for the children in town. She gave me a recipe for apples in nightgowns for your next issue of the paper. She told me a story: "In the beginning the animals received their fur or hair according to the place each slept their first night. The hedgehog chose the mountaintop, and as the sun rose in the morning, he marveled at its brilliant rays. This is how he acquired his radiant coat of spines." I agree with you, it's a strange story to tell a woman who has lost most of her hair. Perhaps she realized it, too, as she launched straightaway into another, her gaze on the burzuika stove. She told me about her grandmother, Emilija, a woman who talked and talked. She talked about the raid on their village, how the bombs fell and flattened it, turned it to rubble. The rubble was crushed to pieces. Those pieces ground to grains of sand. The name of their town erased from every map. Punishment for having revolted against the landlords installed some hundred odd years ago. Burned flat, the town was. People shot while attempting to flee. Weren't they the lucky ones for having escaped? "Shut up," Mildi's grandfather said to her grandmother. But Grandmother Emilija couldn't shut up. She had to tell what she'd seen. She'd tell it to her schoolteacher; she'd tell it to the cashier in the market. Mildi's grandfather punched Emilija in the mouth. "Shut up about politics or you'll get us all killed," he said. "Shut up before you bring a curse on our family." Emilija's teeth fell out soon after that. So she wrote her words down in white chalk on blue slips of paper. Letters to the spirits, she told Mildi, then still a little girl. If no one living would listen, then she'd tell the dead. Her face had a sunken look to it, like a shriveled apple. I have made mistakes, Emilija said, while rattling a glass that held her teeth.

"You may wonder," Mildi said, leaning toward me, her amber eyes glittering like sequins, "why I'm saying these things."

Behind her words I heard the rattle of teeth in a jar. "No," I said. I didn't wonder one tiny little bit.

Incidentally, Mildi brought gifts. That long silver platter. Not silver plate. Silver through and through. She is haunted by guilt. How to repay your grandfather for the torment they caused him. It's another mystery, an unanswerable question. I assured her again and again that Eriks was not the kind of man to hold grudges. "Why?" she asked, blinking in wonder. I told her what I've told you all along, love keeps no records of wrongs. Love steps into the river, wades in to the knees, thighs, and hips, lets the river carry everything where it will.

She had her help bring that oval mirror set inside a leather ox harness. It's enormous, that mirror. A visual picture of vanity ringed by brutish servility. It would be best to cover it with a sheet.

When you were six, I led you to the cemetery where your grandfather was working. He wanted to show you the patience it took to dig a grave, and he wanted to show you how to prepare your heart for the future. He told you that someday he would go away. He was getting older, and he explained to you that he'd have to leave you because where he was going he had to go alone. It was the first of many riddles. "Nobody stays in the same place forever; nothing stays the same," your grandfather said. "Rocks do," you said. But you furrowed your brow and added, "But water can move rocks."

"Yes," your grandfather said. "Water can move anything if there's enough of it."

"And time," you said to him, "rearranges people and things, too. But time is heavier than water."

Grandfather stopped digging then because I suppose he realized he was in the presence of a poet and philosopher. I'm telling you this because you say you can't recall much of your childhood. I find it odd that you could hear so much and so well but remember so little. Odd and a little sad. I suppose, being saturated by so much sound, your brain simply had no space left. But you were such an interesting child. You deserve to know that.

· · ·

While you were out, Dr. Netsulis brought more medication. He clambered into the shed, catching his shin on the piano's sharp edge. The grandfather I never had, he dispenses small bits of wisdom. "Stop scratching!" he said. I'd been raking my jagged fingernails along my shins. This is the problem with our bodies. They flake and peel. Bright bruises, an astonishing bloom of color dots my arms, legs. A map of my undoing — how can I resist reading it?

Jutta stopped in to change the linens. We watched the light climb the wall. We listened to the clock's steady ticking. She brought some thread and a needle. She is sewing my shroud. Before a child is born, she told me, it possesses all knowledge. All wisdom. But at the very moment a child enters the world, an angel of the Lord touches it on the forehead and all knowledge and wisdom vanishes. We spend our whole lives dimly aware that we once grasped the deepest mysteries of the universe and that we are wholly unable to remember any of it. But at the moment of our death, that same angel touches our foreheads once again and we remember. The veil is lifted and we pass through to the other side of understanding.

Jutta lifted the fabric to measure it. Stretched long and thin, it shivered over my body. Breath rising, breath falling. *It will breathe for me,* I thought. And in that last moment, wisdom will pull me by the wrists through the veil.

Why this harping about wisdom? I suppose I'm taking stock of what I have lacked and what I hope to gain. Perhaps my trouble was that I did not fundamentally know myself and what I did know I didn't like. I had a fabulous imagination, but a completely ordinary intellect and a downright disappointing body. But I was a good mushroom hunter. At nineteen years of age I could find almost every kind. I knew that if you found the red-freckled saffron milk cap it meant you'd fall in love soon. The sulfur-yellow chicken of the woods, which loved to crawl up the bark of the yew, meant good luck. But the jack-o'-lantern, whose orange gills glowed in the dark, meant death if you ate it. It was the same way for the toad-brown panther cap. Its looks weren't nearly as exciting as the lantern's, but it was just as deadly. By far the most elusive fungus was the cornflower bolete. A homely looking mushroom with its straw-yellow pores, it holds healing properties in its chambered flesh. If you cut it with a knife, it turned a cerulean blue.

I loved hunting the mushrooms, fair or foul. I cherished every gill, wart, and wrinkle, inhaled with affection the fusty reek of damp and mossy places beneath the alder, pine, and birch. It was the dank smell of the earth turning leaves and needles to rich soil, a beautiful rotting boletic smell that meant mushrooms. But I did not always hunt well. My mind was on David, replaying the image of his climbing up the black steps of the old bus. We had not managed that first kiss by the river. This was the best we could do: I stood on the gravel at the side of the road and David, sensing my gaze fastened to his back, turned and lifted his hand in a wave. I imagined Velta on a similar road watching Ferdinands, a prisoner, loaded onto an old Soviet truck juddering on its chassis. Did they wave? Did she say, as she did in her many letters, I kiss you with a thousand kisses? Did she stand and watch, as I did, the bus retreat into the distance, a veil of dust rising up in waves behind it?

In those days I found myself scouring my memory for every detail of his face, the angle of his cheekbones, wide jaw, those enormous ears, his blue-silver eyes. I kept his coat under my bed, and every now and then I'd pull it out and sniff the collar and cuffs. I looked to the woods for a sign. If I found a milk cap or a chanterelle, then I'd see David again. If I found the dog mushrooms, those gray fungi that are no bigger than a little finger and utterly worthless in a culinary sense, then I divined bad luck was on the way. Imagine my delight when one day I managed to fill my trug with the prized cornflower bolete. But as I laid the mushrooms on a sheet over the kitchen table and gently pinched the stalks, they bled crimson from the gills. When Father saw the mushrooms, and then saw my hands, he went white and had to sit down.

"Mushrooms like these mean someone in the family will die soon," Father said.

"Oh, that's an old superstition," Mother said, dragging the kettle over the ring. No sooner were the words out of her mouth than the black phone bellowed deep and low.

Father jumped from the chair. "Yes." Father said, holding the phone to his ear. "I understand completely." Father slid the phone gently into the cradle.

"What is it?" Mother asked.

"It's the hospital in Daugavpils. They want us to come for Maris. He is too ill for treatment."

I realize that most of what I've mentioned about your namesake isn't terribly flattering. Perhaps I needn't have mentioned the twenty-kilometer-long underground rubber tubing that stretched from a vodka still in Estonia to his yard or the slightly toxic peppermint bark he made and donated to a children's home or the lasting gastric impression it made. I will say that Mother had a hard time forgiving Uncle for taking her beloved Olympia typewriter. But Uncle Maris's footing the bill for Rudy's education went a long way toward fostering something like forbearance. And when family is in some kind of trouble, you overlook past grievances. This is why, after that phone call, your grandfather wasted no time in collecting Uncle from Daugavpils and installing him in the shed.

Though it seemed unkind to closet Uncle amid shovels and rakes, it was the best place for him: he could be as offensive as he liked and there was little chance any of the neighbors would hear or smell him. Mother lit the old Soviet-style burzuika stove and propped two pillows behind Uncle's head.

Uncle smiled and it was then I saw that he'd lost some teeth. "A gift. For you, Biruta." Uncle nodded to one of his suitcases.

Mother opened it and found her green Olympia typewriter nestled in some papers. "The keys for the letters K and O and S are missing," Mother observed.

Uncle thumped his chest with a fist, and said, "Inconsequential." And then a fit of coughing seized him.

Mother and Father backed out of the shed. I stayed in the shed.

"What's wrong with you?" I asked Uncle, pulling a blanket up to his chest. My voice set the piano strings buzzing. He had always been larger than life: bombastic and unflappable. Now his face was ashen. Except for a few defiant gray wisps, his head was bald, his body stove in. He was as mortal and small and defeated as the rest of us.

"Inconsequential," he said, and snapped his fingers. I brought him his other valise, which yawned open on its rusty hinges. Inside were the last of his vitamins and something new: rows and rows of cigarettes, some short and squat and packed with loose tobacco and some long and elegant but a little hollow looking.

Uncle retrieved one of the shorter cigarettes and lit it.

"Those long ones, they're nicotine free. For all those health freaks who really think this life is worth prolonging."

"Are they any good?" I asked. Stanka had taught me to smoke her Bulgarian cigarettes, and I just couldn't imagine cigarettes that didn't taste like a newly paved road.

"Doesn't matter. Do they appeal to a hidden need in the consumer? That is the better question." Uncle Maris exhaled a halo of smoke. Then he snapped his valise closed, and with a quick wave of his fingers, he dismissed me from his shed.

Death is a slow advance on the joints. It's a cough that won't go away. It's a stone that can't be swallowed. It's the weight that draws us into the ground, folding our chests to our knees. Having grown up in the Vorkuta mining camp, your grandfather Eriks knew death so well he could smell it a month away. He heard it in the tight chafing sound of his brother's voice, the rattling in his lungs, and that is how your grandfather knew, and I did, too, how very ill, as good as gone, Maris really was.

All that evening we fluttered to and from the toolshed. With blankets. With broth. With birch-bark tea and pain medications. With newspapers and lozenges. Each time I opened the shed door, I reminded myself to lower my gaze. The loss of all his dark hair and this harrowing cough were strange enough. But Uncle had changed in other ways, too. He'd been in the shed a full three hours and hadn't once spluttered about the Jews or the smelly Russians or the Ukrainians with his trademark vitriol. I thought perhaps in the time he'd been away from us that he had learned to love people more or hate them a little less. But when I brought him his last dose of pain medication for the evening and asked him about this, Uncle corrected me. "No, I still hate everyone. I just don't have the same energy to let them all know about it the way I used to."

But Uncle was working hard to fix that problem. In the two years he'd been away, he had invented a new vitality drink, certain to restore him to his right self. "Watch this," Uncle Maris said, and he downed an entire can of the stuff right then. This inspired a coughing fit complete with red-flecked spume. Uncle collapsed onto the tall bank of pillows. Five minutes later he drifted into a troubled sleep in which he muttered nasty things about Baptists, field surgeons, and Russian cuisine.

I took heart from Uncle's dyspeptic ranting. I thought it meant Uncle's elixir was working. But Mother took one look at Uncle's pallid face and frowned. "We'd better tell Stanka about this," Mother said. "She may want to get one last whack with a frying pan in before Uncle leaves us all for good."

Not three minutes later Stanka burst through our kitchen door.

"Where is he?"

"The shed."

Stanka turned on her heels and stomped back the way she came, her sandals slapping the porch steps. As I followed her through the yard, I studied the brown skin of her feet, the white rind of her cracked heels, and her substantial ankles, for it was on account of those ankles and the thick calves they supported that Uncle Maris had first fallen in love with her.

At the shed Stanka flung open the wooden door and stood there a moment, her arms crossed over her chest, her eyes adjusting to the dim light cast by the stove.

She took in the jaundiced tone of Uncle Maris's skin, his bald head. "What's the matter with you?" Stanka demanded.

Uncle Maris lit one of his fat cigarettes. "A crippling case of post-Soviet syndrome." The piano strings hummed in agreement.

I leaned toward Stanka. "He's got cancer of the lungs."

"Well, if you've got lung cancer, then you don't need these any-more!" Stanka plucked Uncle's cigarette from his lips and ground it under her sandals. Then she gathered all of Uncle's cigarettes — even the healthy ones — and tucked them into the waistband of her skirt. With a quick turn, she was out of the shed.

"Oh, it's bitter!" Uncle moaned, and the piano strings moaned with him. It was his way, I knew, of letting us know how much he still loved Stanka and how badly he wanted those cigarettes.

I followed Stanka out into the yard, where she ploughed a path through the laundry. And then behind the scrim of flapping linens, I spied Rudy, and beside him the most beautiful and delicate girl I'd ever seen.

"Rudy!" I cried.

Mother turned. She saw the girl with Rudy and dropped her laundry basket.

"This is m-my friend, L-Ligita. She's studying dance at the university," Rudy stammered, as we approached. Mother squinted at Rudy while I gazed openly at Ligita, unable to fathom how Rudy managed to bring home such a beautiful girl—and an artistic one. The closest Rudy ever came to art was the time he filled in for a sick band member at a school production. And even then the director allowed him to stir the triangle only intermittently.

"Well." Mother wiped one chapped hand against the other. Rudy glanced at the shed. "How bad is Uncle?"

Mother looked at me, then at Ligita, who was sizing up our wooden privy. "Let's all have some tea. We'll get acquainted."

Rudy ushered Ligita into the kitchen, where Mother was boiling water. I stole covert glances at Ligita. She was utterly perfect, every part of her body in proportion to the other, every movement graceful. The bones of her face were like fine china, her cheekbones high and wide, her chin sharp, her dark eyes shrewd and intelligent—she could not be real, I thought, as I poured tea into Mother's best cups and noted the rise of Ligita's eyebrows, which were plucked to mathematical precision. And yet there she was, slurping our tea through cubes of sugar. Sitting next to Rudy. Who blinked and stammered, flabbergasted by his incredible fortune.

At last Father thumped up the back steps and opened the screen door. He stood at the threshold and pulled off his boots.

"This is Rudy's new friend," Mother said to Father. "Ligita . . ."

"Samoylich," she said, and I caught sight of her teeth, jagged and stained. "Samoylich—that sounds"—Mother screwed up her eyes—"Russian, or perhaps—"

"Ukrainian," Ligita said.

"Of course!" Mother beamed.

"Ukrainians are very brilliant people." Father gently set his boots on the top step and gave each of the tongues a solid tug to help the boots breathe. "They invented bison-grass vodka. Yes, in general, Ukrainians are very fine."

"She's got a three-day holiday before her ballet auditions," Rudy said.

While Rudy spoke, Ligita's gaze roamed the kitchen, looking for some cultural point of commonality. Finding none, she sighed. Even her sighs held the air of a thoroughbred.

Mother laid out supper and put a bowl of salt in the middle of the table. "For Uncle," she said, pinching a few granules and tossing it over her shoulder. Rudy and I did the same while Ligita observed the fallen salt on the floor.

Father kept his hands folded in his lap. "I will say a prayer for Maris," he said.

I knew Mother would rather pray to the concrete moon that changes boys into bears and returns them to their old strength than pray to God, whom she said was very unpredictable. But she respected Father. So when he started praying, Mother lowered her head for a split second. Then she went back to ladling the cabbage.

Dinner was a quiet affair. Ligita refused every dish Mother offered, as she was in training. She also wouldn't use our dry toilet, preferring instead to relieve herself in Mother's finely scrubbed porcelains at the hall.

"Well, she is, after all, very refined," Mother said to me, as we observed Ligita skirting puddles on her return from the hall. "The smell of our shit probably offends her."

That night, after Rudy delivered broth to Uncle that Uncle returned ("Too salty! Too thin!"), Mother, crestfallen that another meal had been refused, put a clean sheet on the couch for Ligita. It was Rudy's hope that he'd sleep on the floor beside Ligita, but Mother wouldn't hear of it. "You'll catch your death from a draft!" she exclaimed. Like most women in the east, she had a dread fear of wind and currents, and it was something we did not joke about in her presence. And so, as we had all the nights of our childhood, Rudy and I slept side by side in our separate beds and watched the moon through the window casting its pale sorrowful eye on the houses along the lane and listened to Mr. Ilmyen's donkey, Babel, protesting Uncle Maris's proximity.

In the morning we woke to the bellow of the phone: *eeeeeee-oooooo*. It was Mr. Zetsche. In a few days he would inspect the cemetery; afterward he'd hold a town meeting in the hall. The news sent Mother and Father into a frenzy. It was autumn, Mikeli, the time when the aspens shake off their gold leaves to make a carpet for the ghosts. Your grandmother Biruta believed in ghosts. If the hall kitchen and basins weren't scrubbed to perfection, she believed her mother and father would scrape their fingernails against our windows at night. She also wanted to make a good impression on Mr. Zetsche. For his part, Father worked even harder to scrub the moss of the more remote stones and touch up the gold paint on the Orthodox crosses of the Russian stones. Rudy and I sat in the living room and watched spellbound as Ligita executed a series of stretching exercises, necessary, she said, in order to keep her limber. And limber she was: first, she raised one leg behind her, lifting it so high that it almost touched her ear. Then she lowered that leg and the other one went up. She was like a human protractor: Ligita's slim torso held stock-still over one leg, while the other leg swiveled about with unimaginable flexibility. "Wh-wh-wh-what a figure!" Rudy breathed, enchanted by the amount of daylight he could see between her legs. But the more he watched her, the more agitated he became. By noon, his stuttering rendered him completely unintelligible. "For god's sake," Mother, back from the hall, said. "Go out and do something!" Ligita froze mid-pirouette, but Mother simply waved her on. "Not you, dear." And so Rudy turned to his slingshot, his second love, and went foraging through the woods.

I spent the day attending to Uncle Maris. His ire inflamed by the injustice of sickness in general and by his suffering our fierce attentions in particular, everything now provoked him: the light from the lightbulb was too bright, my tread on the floor too heavy, Babel's braying from across the lane too loud. And then there was the trouble with Stanka.

"Oh, it's bitter!" Uncle Maris cried. Yes, he still loved Stanka terribly despite all that he had done to suggest otherwise. This was the one endearing trait about Uncle: he could be an ass, short and abrupt and spiteful beyond reason, but he was capable of love. What he loved, he loved to distraction. He did, in fact, love women in a constant way, forgiving them their minor faults and moments of pettiness. He loved women in general because they were nothing like the men he knew. And because Uncle Maris believed it was better to die in the embrace of a woman than to die alone, he was prepared now to do or say anything to reconcile with Stanka.

Uncle Maris rolled onto his side and gripped my wrist. "You have to help me. You have to be my legs and my lungs." Uncle reached under the cot and withdrew his beloved fishing pole. "I'd ask Rudy to help, but your mother tells me he's so tongue-tied in love, he's practically useless." Uncle paused to string his rod with some line. "But you, Inara — you don't have anybody yet."

Uncle was right: with my bad skin and wide hips, I did not turn heads.

"What do you want me to do?" I asked.

Uncle opened his auxiliary valise. In it was a sheaf of papers that looked to be quite old, yellowed with time. With them was a bundle of letters. They looked uncannily similar to the ones I had hidden under my bed: the same jumbled assortment of all kinds of papers, all of it bound up with a leather strap.

"Where did you get those?" I touched the letters. A lopsided grin stretched from one side of Uncle's face to the other. "Ask no questions, tell no lies." He patted the bundle tenderly and pushed it toward me. "Go on," he said. "Take them. They make good reading. But before you read them, I want you to mail this envelope at the post office. It's important."

The envelope was the kind used for legal documents, and judging by the weight of it, there were quite a few papers in there. A will, I figured.

"Thirdly, set a bait trail for Stanka."

"Bait?"

Uncle sighed in exasperation. "And I used to think you were the smart one." Uncle opened his second valise and withdrew a confectioner's wax-paper bag. Inside were black Dutch buttons, the kind that are so salty they make grown men weep. At the bottom of the bag, the confectioner's prize: a button double the size of all the rest, as big as a horse chestnut. Uncle took this oversize button and pushed his hook through it. Then he handed me the white bag.

"It's a full moon on the rise tonight and Stanka will be hunting the sooty milk cap. You set out a trail of buttons from her door to mine. And make sure I get my last dose of meds early; I want to be at the height of my charm when she gets here."

As the sooty milk cap looks remarkably like a Dutch button, Uncle's plan was a sound one. And the fact that Uncle was scheming again gave me hope that his vitality drinks were really working. Bit by bit, he was coming back to us. Just then Uncle set down the rod, turned his shoulder sharply, and started coughing. It was a terrible sound, as if everything he'd ever known and wanted was working its way loose from the bottom of his lungs.

I wrung my hands. "Do you want me to pray for you?"

"Pray?" Uncle spat into Mother's metal basin. "As in pray to God the Father, Jesus His son?"

I nodded.

"God the Father—He's an entrepreneur, a negotiator. I can deal with him. But Christ"—a blue blood vessel rose to the surface of Uncle's forehead—"He's a tyrant. Crawling up on that cross to die, knowing full well he'd come back from the dead. All this just to inflict himself on everyone." The piano strings buzzed and Uncle's nostrils flared with his old familiar rage. "Well, two can play that game. I'm going to kick this thing in the teeth! Watch me now!" He was like a wild animal, cagey and unpredictable. Uncle Maris drove his crutch into the sod and pitched to the floor.

"Oh," Uncle moaned. "It's bitter."

I helped him back onto the cot. I opened a vitality drink for Uncle, but he only grimaced.

Uncle withdrew a small pouch from his hip pocket and shook out a small mound of tobacco. "What I want is rolling paper."

We did not have rolling paper. I knew what I had to do. I ran to my room and retrieved my Bible. It had soft calfskin covers and gold edged the onionskin pages. Father had written: *sword and shield, my strong buckler is you, Lord, oh Lord.*

Father had given it to me on the same day Gorbachev had allowed Bibles back into Latvia. I was only ten at the time, too young, he said, to go with him to Daugavpils to see the heavy-cargo Ural transports roll into the middle of the old town square. There was some concern that this was a trick, that the transports would be stuffed stem to stern with soldiers and a riot would ensue. Father went anyway. The cargo trucks arrived. No soldiers. Just boxes and boxes of Bibles. Within four minutes the boxes were emptied. He told me this, tears streaming down his face, as he gave me that white calfskin-bound book. I loved this book. I loved my uncle. And right now he needed it more than I did. And so I returned to the shed, my Bible trembling in my hand as if it sensed its fate.

I handed the Bible to Uncle.

"Well, it's not rolling paper, but it'll do."

Such sacrilege, it pained me. I bit my lip. "Just promise you'll read each page before you light it up." I left Uncle. I took the large envelope to Mrs. A. at the post office. And then I set the trail of licorice. I did not know if nicotine withdrawal or pain relievers had driven Uncle into a temporary heresy or if I was at last seeing Uncle stripped down to his truest form: a man who really did not hate people so much as he hated the God who made people, the God of resurrection who promised life in those New Testament books and had left him on this cot in this shed to cough himself to death.

• • •

Back inside the living room, Rudy had his hands full. Ligita had stretched and danced solo all day long and now she needed a mule, she told Rudy. "Imagine that I am a bird of paradise and you are the strong stalk of support," she said, turning on her toes, unfurling her body.

"Now lift!" she commanded.

Rudy grabbed her by the waist and flung her over his shoulder in a fireman's carry. He twirled in a wide ungainly circle.

Father smiled at the fireplace; Mother bit her lip.

"Clumsy!" Ligita shrieked. "Put me down!" Which Rudy did as gently as possible, but with Ligita flailing about, it wasn't as smooth a landing as she might have hoped for.

Fuming, Ligita raked at her hair until she had restored her bun and composure. She turned to Rudy.

"You will never be a good dance partner." Ligita spoke each word carefully as if each one carried a mysterious weight that needed time to sink in. "You're not even a good mule."

"It's true—I don't lift well," Rudy said, his gaze on his feet. "Can you do anything well?" Ligita asked.

Because Father had taught him to be a gentleman, Rudy only ducked his head. But as he slid his slingshot into his pants pocket and passed by me for the kitchen door, I detected something desperate in the hunch of his shoulders.

You asked once what kind of a person Rudy was when he was younger and what kind of person I was. I said he was the kind of person who would walk a thousand kilometers to rescue someone who needed saving. He would defend the defenseless and love the loveless.

He'd do this without apology. His only flaw, in my opinion, was that he'd do these things indiscriminately, wasting the best of himself on people unworthy of it.

I did not love others as deeply or openly as your uncle Rudy. I suppose it is a shortcoming on my part because I know very well, and you do, too, that the Bible entreats us to love our neighbors as ourselves.

But I had a hard time answering the question, Who is my neighbor? The Ilmyens, of course, and I did love them. Stanka I loved. But this girl, this woman, whose every word seemed intended to harm, I could not love. And I felt shame and guilt stirring inside of me. If Rudy saw fit to love her, why couldn't I?

By dinnertime, Mother stood over the stove, cursing a pot of uncooperative sorrel soup. Ligita sighed with the distracted air of one who was profoundly bored. Of one who was wishing a comet would drop on our roof if only for the novelty of a spectacle. And then, just as Mother set out the sorrel, Rudy returned. In his hands a rabbit swung by its heels. Spots of blood dotted its snout and gummed the whiskers.

Ligita gasped. But Rudy, undeterred, presented his gift to Ligita, it being his conviction that women long to be showered with the fruits of nature, dead or alive.

"That's very nice, son," Mother said, with a wink in Ligita's direction.

"Please tell me that there's something else people do here for fun." Ligita sighed. I saw the liquid shift in Rudy's eyes as he hung the rabbit over the salting board.

Then I looked at Ligita. In her I saw every beautiful girl who breaks every good boy's heart. And I got an idea.

"We go mushrooming," I said.

"Really!" A cardiac glow bloomed over Ligita's pale face. Outside, the harvest moon loomed large and bright. In the air I could smell the ground cooling, the snap of seasons changing. A perfect night for mushrooming. As we passed the shed and wandered toward the river, I stepped over the licorice trail for Stanka. And I talked. I explained to Ligita what I knew of the invisible properties of mushrooms, namely the kinds you should feed the cows if you want them to come into season, which ones to fry with onions, which kept well in a freezer. I told her what your grandfather and grandmother had taught me. In short,

I was testing her to see if she'd listen. Was she worthy of such knowledge?

As I talked, Ligita raced toward a stand of birch. "Ha!" she cried, triumphant. She'd spotted some fringed parasol, which were nice to look at but bad for the bowels.

"No. Not those." I cautioned. And when she spotted the oyster mushroom, its dark tongues bracketing the bark of a tree, I said the same thing: *no*. Ditto for the liberty cap, which was slightly hallucinogenic. On this went, and as we approached a copse of birches, I could tell Ligita was getting frustrated. And I was glad. I wanted to wear her out. I wanted her to see that, like her, we were artists — talented and smart in our own fashion.

Ligita dashed toward the trees. "Chanterelles!" she cried, filling the trug. This time she wasn't far off. What she'd found was a nice troop of false chanterelles, which were known to cause acute nausea. In the dim light, hers was an easy mistake to make.

"I wouldn't eat those," I said.

"I know what you're all doing to me. Making sport of me at every turn. But I've been to university. I know reverse psychology when I hear it." Ligita shoved the entire mushroom into her mouth and chewed furiously. It occurred to me that not only was she angry, but having skipped so many meals, she was also probably very hungry. And she was right; I did want her to eat that mushroom.

Throwing caution to the wind, Ligita ate another. And another. And then I realized what I was allowing to happen. I took a few steps and dropped to my knees. There under a birch was a fine fruiting of bay bolete — one of Father's favorites, as it carried an air of nobility. Also, their fleshy stalks and caps were good absorbers of stomach acids. "Here." I handed Ligita a bolete. "Try this one instead."

Ligita stopped eating for a moment and contemplated the mushroom in my hand. "I need to use a bathroom," she said.

I looked around the woods and shrugged. "Just squat behind a log."

"It's a very unattractive position, squatting," Ligita said, but her voice had lost its starch and she weaved on her feet. I hooked my arm around Ligita's tiny rib cage and steered her back toward our yard.

"Stanka! My love, is that you?" Uncle Maris called, as we passed the shed. Babel trumpeted and Ligita moaned. She lurched for the back steps, draping herself over the bottommost one.

"I need a bowl," she said, and fished from her sleeve a bit of perforated fabric: a very fine lace handkerchief. As she did, I spied a purple line that ran from the inside of her wrist to midforearm. A scar thick and deep. Perhaps her life wasn't as enchanted as I had assumed.

I dashed into the kitchen and returned with Mother's orange polka-dotted mixing bowl. And not a moment too soon. One look at the bowl's busy pattern and Ligita began retching. When they heard the powerful heaves of a stomach turning itself inside out, Mother, Father, and Rudy rushed to the steps.

"What have you been feeding her?" Mother's eyes were flat with fury.

"Mushrooms." I lifted the trug. The mere mention of the fungi provoked an explosive response from Ligita's stomach that was no match for the finely perforated lace, which acted only as a sieve. She retched like this for a solid twenty minutes, Mother holding her hair out of her face the whole time.

"The audition!" Ligita moaned.

Rudy carried Ligita to the couch while Mother made tea. Rudy sat on his knees and dabbed at Ligita's cheeks and neck with a damp cloth. Every now and then, he'd lean in and brush a quick kiss on her forehead. And because she was so weak, Ligita couldn't bat away his hand or hurl insults. Rudy had never looked happier. And Mother was happy, too. This girl—so petite and fine she could never have been borne of Mother's bones, a girl so unlike me it hurt to look at her—was at last allowing herself to be comforted. I didn't know if I liked Ligita for pleasing Mother in this way or if I hated her a little more for it.

Then from the lane came a colossal ruckus. It sounded like Babel braying, trumpeting as if the end of the world had started in the lane and was moving toward our yard. Then I realized it was only Stanka.

"My eyes! I cannot believe my eyes! Dutch buttons!" Stanka shrieked. And past our windows she went for the toolshed, one button at a time, her jaw pumping hard and fast. I slipped out the back door and followed her. Uncle had left the shed door open just wide enough to afford a glimpse of the confectioner's prize balanced now on the threshold. Stanka crouched to get a better look. Uncle snored with exaggeration. Just as Stanka reached for the button, the line jerked. The button flew. And following the button, Stanka careened into Uncle. He held her hard even as Stanka worked that enormous button off the hook into her mouth.

"Forgive me, Stanka. For everything. I'm begging you," Uncle implored. Her mouth full, Stanka couldn't argue, couldn't refuse. "You really are dying, you bastard," she managed at last.

Uncle coughed. And coughed. Each cough was a gouge, a rip in his lungs. Each cough set the piano strings rumbling, an orchestra of discordance, as if the piano were dying, too. I took a blanket from the corner and draped it over the soundboard and strings. Then I went for Mother and Father. When we returned, Uncle was still coughing. Nothing we did could make him stop, could end that terrible wet sound of a man drowning inside of himself.

Uncle looked at Father. "Please—cremate me the Gypsy way."

"What?" Father could not hide his mortification.

My open Bible lay next to Uncle's cot. He'd smoked Matthew, he'd smoked Mark, he'd smoked Luke, and he was now well into John. And as these were the books in which Jesus did all his talking, I wondered if our Lord's words had finally driven Uncle to complete madness.

"But you're not a Gypsy," Mother said.

"And we Roma in Latvia don't burn our dead, dear," Stanka reminded.

"Doesn't matter. I never asked for much. And what a man asks for on his deathbed he should get."

Father hung his head. Cremation, in his opinion, was only one step shy of burning in hell. "If you must insist on this bodily blasphemy, at least put your heart right in the sight of God," Father pleaded.

"What's God ever done for me?" Uncle asked, and Father pulled his cap onto his head and went back to the house. Such a question was so stark, so blunt, that even as I followed Mother out of the shed I could not help despairing for Uncle, who would travel through the door in the dark — all alone, without even God.

The morning light thickened outside our windows. Rain began to fall. Ligita, as pale as bleached paper, appeared in the kitchen, her small bag packed in readiness for the seven-fifteen bus that would make a brief stop at the end of the lane.

"Here." Rudy put a hand at her elbow and held Ligita's coat for her. "At least let me walk you to the bus stand." Ligita took the coat from his hands, opened the kitchen door. "I will walk myself," she said, descending the steps with great dignity.

Rudy stood at the threshold and watched her go. Mother and I watched, too, observing Ligita as she stopped in at the hall to make a final deposit in the shiny porcelains. "I suppose she was too refined for us anyway," Mother whispered, her gaze fastened to the tattered floor mat flapping on the line. Beside it hung Ligita's lace handkerchief. We'd never get all those stains out.

In the course of that day, we emptied Uncle's basin fifteen, maybe twenty times.

He was peeing and peeing, draining himself dry, peeing his strength and will into that basin. Where could all this water come from? I asked Father, who merely shook his head slowly from side to side. Uncle was weak; he could barely lift his head.

"There she is." Uncle nodded at a dark corner of the shed. "Dripping wet and all dark wing."

"Who?"

"The girl from the river." His words were failing him and it took all his strength to simply breathe. By late afternoon, he couldn't even cough, and to see him like this — so quiet, so agreeable — was utterly terrifying. Father sat on a folding chair at the foot of the cot, and Stanka sat on a chair at the head, where she held Uncle's hand in hers. He lay on the cot, his gaze fixed on a point above Stanka's head. That's how he died, his hand in Stanka's. Mother pulled a sheet over him and for the next hour we sat at the kitchen table. We did not speak Uncle's name. Mother knelt in front of the open oven, her head thrust inside so we wouldn't see her tears. Father held his cap in his hands. His shoulders shook as he wept quietly. And across from Father was Rudy, his hands shielding his face. Uncle Maris had once been his hero and now he was gone. Also gone was Ligita.

Stanka scrutinized Rudy for several minutes. "Your heart is broken. But I know the remedy for that," she said, rising from her chair and approaching Rudy. Rudy's eyebrows lifted. We both knew there was no herbal tincture or mushroom in the world that would mend a wounded heart not done with its weeping. And it sounded so strange to hear Stanka say this when her own eyes were dark and wet with tears.

"Stand up," she said. Rudy rose from his seat.

Stanka stepped out of her sandals, stood on her tiptoes, and put a hand on Rudy's shoulder. The other hand she placed gently in his open hand. "Now close your eyes and dance." Rudy shuffled his feet first one way then the other, Stanka steering him with small squeezes on his shoulder. Then Father and Mother sang a song for Uncle.

> *What if our song is silenced?*
> *What of it?*
> *Go on singing!*

Mother kept her eyes on Stanka's feet, those stout ankles that knew sadness but had known happier times, too. And before long, the

melody brightened and Stanka's feet moved quickly and lightly. Whatever her heart felt, whatever sorrow she held in her eyes, her feet were
finding their way toward joy. And through it all, Rudy, his eyes still
closed, kept up.

"You are a wonderful dancer," Stanka whispered. "Now open your
eyes and don't forget."

Without another word, Stanka stamped out the back door and
down the steps. The hour of grieving had passed and now Uncle
needed us. We followed Stanka into the yard, Rudy dragging our plastic washtub behind him into the shed. Rudy and I held Uncle up by the
armpits while Stanka and Mother washed his body. First, they poured
water over his head and neck then his right arm and everything on the
right side down to his foot. Then they did the left side.

Three buckets of water were used—no more, no less. After
Stanka dried Uncle with a towel, Mother and I dressed Uncle in Father's best suit.

All that day Rudy and Father planed boards from a felled acacia Father
had been drying under a tarp. At nightfall, they'd joined the boards
and carried Uncle from the shed to the coffin. Stanka lined his body
with the remaining cans of vitality drink and all the cigarettes. She
put a mirror in his hand. Mother tucked his crutch beside his good leg.
What was left of my Bible I stuffed into the breast pocket of the suit.
For some time we stood in the rain contemplating Uncle in his coffin. We all knew what Uncle wanted: to go out in flames, refined and
annealed by fire into his elemental parts, his iron will and that metal
crutch. And we did our best. Rudy and I piled wood, the driest we
had. We lit match after match, but one by one the rain doused them.
The rain had fallen so hard and so long that every stick and every bit of
wood was bloated and warped with water. Whatever Uncle's wishes,
however badly we wanted to carry them out, we simply couldn't.

Rudy, Mother, Stanka, and I all stared at Father. Father stared at
the pyre. It was the first time Father didn't know what to do.

"Now what?" Rudy asked.

"Tomorrow we bury him — the proper way," Father said.

"But what do we do right now?" I asked.

Stanka wiped her face with the hem of her skirt. Then she stepped out of her sandals, and standing on tiptoe, she placed her hands on Rudy's shoulder. "Sing that song," Stanka said to us. "Sing it louder this time."

And we did.

CHAPTER FOUR

MY THOUGHTS FLY LIKE A SHUTTLE through a loom; I am grateful for your patience with me. While you went to make tea, I slipped into a sleep where memory and dream mingled so thoroughly I could not tell one from the other. I heard a voice call my name. I went to the river. I saw the spiked umbrel crowns of the tall cow parsley. I wanted to collect all that lace, make a bridal veil from it. I pulled one off, then another, and another. A man shouted, *For the love of God, stop!* It was Mr. Gepkars, sitting behind his wooden desk at gymnasium. His shoulders shook with sobs, and I knew it was because someone had whispered, "Siberia." *Siberia.* *Siberia.* The smell of burning sugar filled the room, and I was riding on the old blue bus to Rezekne to clean house for a new family. As the bus hurtled over the road, the seats shuddered and groaned. My teeth rattled. Rattling of cups and saucers, the waxy paper bag, and then I saw you, your gray-blue eyes filled with questions, and I remembered that there is much I never told you. I start a thing, stop. I forget what is and isn't important.

You explained to me the movement of electrons, and this seemed as important as anything else I've ever heard. I am in awe that life is built of something so small. My talking to you can only happen because of their buzz and dance, their frenetic exchange of energy that I think must look something like bees wild with the possibility of flight. Behind every bit of creation is a push for movement, change. And what's true for the living things holds true for the dead as well. Your grandfather believed that for the first few days in the ground the dead lay still, snug in their dark warrens, quietly adjusting to their new reality. They must learn to see in the dark, navigate by sound. What flimsy fabric the body unreeves, tendon and muscle, joint and bone. It was your grandfather's conviction that this separation of the body from the soul resembled that of a tooth rotting, rotten, falling from the gum. Only after the tooth has fallen can the raw oozing socket begin to heal. Only after the body sloughs away do the needs and demands of the soul make themselves felt.

Simple, but not easy. That's what Mr. Bumbers told you. He floated in a cauldron of boiling water, like an overstuffed piroshki bouncing about. Long sheets of skin floated beside him in the water, clung to the sides of the pot. The superfluous, the unnecessary, it takes great heat to loosen them, you wrote in your book. But there's no going back, no way to undo the wrongs except to admit them one by one.

You told me the other day about Mrs. Ozolins. Shame burned in the place where her heart used to be. Regret pinched like a vise on her neck. The only remedy: to identify the source, as a laundress noting the stains on a garment, to say here, here, and here. That's when she felt the flood of water. The beauty of this washing was that she could actually feel the taints and stains lift from the fabric of her soul. Mr. Dumonovsky said that he rattled about like seeds in a dark pod. But it was this agitation that he so dearly needed, so desperately craved. Each rattling, as wheat from chaff, shook loose his sin. He was threshed; as olive oil is refined, he was beaten to light.

Your grandfather would have taken such satisfaction from your notes. It was his conviction that the soul's hard work, though uncomfortable, was utterly necessary. Without it, he believed, the soul remained root-bound, held fast in the mire of its own making. Groaning under the burden of stagnation. Which wouldn't be so bad if not for the fact that all of creation yearns for change. It was a theory shored up by many hours of reading Oskars's Bible in general and specifically by a passage in Saint Paul's second letter to the Corinthians.

For we know that if our earthly house of this tabernacle were dissolved, we have a building of God, an house not made with hands . . . For in this we groan, earnestly desiring to be clothed upon with our house which is from heaven. For we that are in this tabernacle do groan, being burdened.

That our bodies should both desire and undergo a transformation does not surprise me. I think of caterpillars bundled in their cocoons erupting into flight. I think of Izaak Walton's account of the eel. No other creature, he reports, embarks on such a long journey nor does any animal experience such a remarkable physical transformation as the eel. He writes in *The Compleat Angler* that when eels are newly born, somewhere in the Atlantic Ocean, they are no bigger than a child's fingernail. As flat as ribbon, as thin as paper, and as transparent as glass, these little eels bob and ride the currents. As they do, their bodies lengthen; they grow teeth. Impulse or maybe genetic memory directs some of the glass eels, now elvers, to head south and west to America and some to head east for the North Atlantic. As the eels continue their journey, small permanent teeth push out their larger juvenile teeth. Their jaws change shape and their bodies, previously flat, plump up like enormous cucumbers.

Under your grandfather's tutelage, you copied this passage of Walton's several times: in blockish print, in looping cursive. How can a creature breathe in saltwater then live in fresh? How is it, you asked in the margins of your notes, that the eel could begin its life suited for one kind of environment and become a creature built for quite another kind?

The eel's design, that's the real magic. A fish has a single long nerve running along its back that registers change in light, pressure, movement. But every centimeter, every cell of the eel detects sound and pressure. You wrote in your book: it is as if an eel is all ear.

What happened at the meeting? I never finished telling the story. The day before the meeting, a soughing wind bent the birch trees in half, unlatched screen doors. We heard a thumping at the back door. I imagined it was Uncle, whacking the gates of heaven, or maybe hell, with his crutch. "If that's Stanka, tell her we're out of milk," Mother called from the living room where she was beating the cushions of the divan with the business end of a golf club Father had found in the cemetery.

I rushed to the back door and opened it cautiously. Widow Spassky stood on the back step.

"So sorry to disturb," she said, sounding not at all sorry.

"Come in, Mrs. Spassky," Father said from the kitchen, pulling out a chair for her.

Mrs. Spassky crossed the threshold but did not take the chair. "There's a meeting tomorrow evening. At the hall. To discuss the cemetery." She enunciated each word carefully, wrapping pauses around each word, as if she knew the damage each might do and wanted to see its effect upon Father.

"Yes," Mother said, pretending to make tea. "Mr. Zetsche already rang us up."

"Well, I'm sure you know your own business." Mrs. Spassky withdrew a heavy yellow card with thick black print on one side. She set it on the table and shuffled toward the door, a malevolent gleam in her eye.

Father sat in the chair, his hands trembling. There was a time, in the Soviet days, when humiliation and shame were used as tools of instruction and correction. For example, Mother knew a trolley driver, a good woman, who'd fallen out of favor with her superiors. One day she received a summons to the public library where all of her fellow colleagues, coworkers, childhood friends, family, and neighbors had gathered. As if at a funeral, they one by one trudged to a microphone and said something about Galya. Only they didn't say nice things.

They related how she'd been slow to learn how to properly tie her own shoes, how she'd received poor marks in secondary school, how silly she looked in her threadbare clothes, and so on and so forth until Galya was reduced to pulling her hair out in clumps. That is how people were given the boot in those days. It was a public spectacle and free entertainment for the masses. And it started with the arrival of an announcement on thick card stock.

"Well." Father pushed back from his chair. "I feel a little sick," he said, exiting for the latrine. The afternoon of the meeting, your grandmother and I went early to the hall. Father stayed behind, taking his time shaving over the sink. If he was to be publicly humiliated, at least he would be clean shaven. As we aligned chairs in rows, the foyer of the hall slowly filled with our neighbors: Mr. and Mrs. Lee and Mr. and Mrs. Lim whispered in Korean, and every now and then one of them would send a sympathetic glance in our direction. The Arijisnikovs came with tureens of tea, Stanka set out her boxes of sugar, and Mr. Bishofs, the German teacher, plugged in an overhead slide projector. Then the people we saw only at funerals arrived: the Liepins, the Jacobsons, humpbacked Mr. Ignats, the Gipsis family — all seventeen of them — and, of course, the widows Sosnovskis and Spassky. Father arrived and I knew he was a nervous wreck: tissue clung to the many spots up and down his neck where he'd nicked himself with the razor. At last, Mother arranged the chairs to her satisfaction and everyone took up their positions: to the left of the podium the widows sat together as a united front while Mr. Ilmyen and Father sat to the right of the podium. It was a reconciliation of sorts, the two men sitting so close. In spite of a lifetime of small and large misunderstandings, Mr. Ilmyen and Father were true friends. Likewise, Mother and Mrs. Ilmyen sat together in the second row, whispering, their foreheads almost touching.

Outside the hall, a far-off mechanical whine grew louder as it approached. The dogs barked and Babel brayed. Everyone in the hall fell silent, listening to the sound of Mr. Zetsche's approach. Finally, the hall door sang on its hinges. All bodies swiveled in their chairs. Brisk footfalls echoed as Mr. Zetsche, dripping with swagger, strode to the platform. Not an easy feat when you are a mere 120 centimeters tall. In fact, he seemed impossibly smaller than before. He also had a purple birthmark that ran the length of his neck and was the exact shape of Italy, the boot of which looked as if it were kicking his Adam's apple.

"Ladies and gentlemen." Mr. Zetsche stood and nodded to the widows, to Mr. Ilmyen, and to Father, who was gritting his teeth, bracing for the worst. "As you all may or may not know, I am quite a successful businessman in possession of a great many, er, things. And one of my holdings is a piece of riverside property here in town that is positively choice for development. So you see"—Mr. Zetsche aimed a smile at Father—"I intend to create jobs."

Mr. Zetsche nodded to Mr. Bishofs, who flipped the switch on the overhead projector. The small fan hummed to life and then we saw for ourselves every detail of Mr. Zetsche's plan thrown onto the wall.

"Imagine a Latvian Riviera complete with a promenade and a band pavilion. And, of course, lodgings for the many tourists such an attraction would bring. The first step is to reshape the banks of the river whereby we'd build a retaining wall of the stoutest quality." Mr. Zetsche's high-pitched voice assumed the round museum quality of an artist admiring his own work.

"This is very interesting, but what does it have to do with the cemetery?" Widow Spassky asked.

Mr. Zetsche smiled. "Geological surveys indicate that the best place for development is the cemetery. So, of course, this means our first step is to move it."

A collective gasp rose from the audience. Mr. Ilmyen wagged his head slowly from side to side. Father and Mother looked as if between them they'd swallowed a bucket of ashes. For a long moment, the only sound in the room was the hum of the projector and Stanka snapping sunflower seeds, eating as if a famine were knocking at our back door.

At last, a Gipsis said, loud enough for everyone to hear, "I think his plough has jumped the furrow." Yes, Mr. Zetsche was quite mad. But he was well dressed and he drove a nice car and that meant something to some people.

Mother stood slowly and gripped the back of Stanka's chair for support. It took some effort, but at last she manufactured a smile. "So, my husband here will dig new holes and move all the bodies, just like that? It all sounds conveniently foreign." Her voice was pure acid.

Mr. Zetsche grimaced. Even he knew that this was a reference to the way that the Soviets had moved people left to right and up to down during the occupation, changing and rearranging people and borders so that even God couldn't find some of us. No one had ever found Mr. Zingers or his Baptist wife, and we'd heard that atrocious things had been done to the Orthodox priests who'd been railed into the Soviet interior. The only evidence some of us had been here at all were our graveyards, which is why Father cared so thoroughly after each plot and stone, and also why the spiteful campaigning of the widows Sosnovskis and Spassky hurt him so.

"My dear woman," Mr. Zetsche began. "It is not as if I have no feelings. But there are other outside considerations to, er, consider. In the end, we'll all be better off because, while this town is undeniably beautiful, it is also quite depressed." Mr. Zetsche glanced at Widow Sosnovskis. "That is to say, economically speaking."

Mr. Arijisnikov jumped to his feet and appealed to the audience. "Do not be wooed by the cold heart of commerce."

"Hear, hear!" cried Mrs. Arijisnikov.

Stanka rose slowly to her feet. She narrowed her eyes at Mr. Zetsche. "A curse falls on anyone who disturbs the dead." Stanka's voice shook with the weight of terrible prognostication, and among the rows of Christians, Jews, and Muslims, heads nodded in agreement.

"Old superstition," Mr. Zetsche replied. "We can still venerate the dead. We'll just venerate them, er, elsewhere. Because, with so many changes in our county, it's time to consider the living now." Mr. Zetsche's gaze fell on Rudy. "This is a new Latvia—we must think of the future and what we can provide for our children and their children."

And when he said this, he touched on a painful and raw economic reality of life in a small town. From the bobbing of heads and the slow wagging of others, I could discern a clean division between the old and the young, the murmurs of assent and dissent separating into a canticle sung by two choirs.

The next morning we found Father in the cemetery. He held a hoe loosely in his hand. On his face he wore the look of utter bewilderment, as if he were waiting for someone to tell him what to do. At last Mother turned to Father. "Don't you know that there's some people and some things you just can't stop?" she said.

"I know it," Father said. Then he turned away to walk among the wet stones and, I suppose, remember each of the people he had helped to bury, remember them in the cemetery where they always had wanted to be.

But within three minutes Father was back in the yard, "Inara! Biruta!" he called, waving us toward the cemetery. Mother and I ran toward the gate. Uncle Maris's stone had tipped and a portion was broken off.

"It's an omen," Father said. I kept my gaze trained at the tree line, hoping for a hint of kindness from the skies. We listened to the roaring of the wind through the trees, and then I saw movement—a shudder of white.

"Look!" I pointed. "A stork."

Mother and Father followed the bird with their eyes. Mother put her calm hand over Father's shaky one. "A stork," Mother said, "that's an omen, too." She squeezed Father's hand. "You see the stork building that nest above our cemetery. It doesn't know that in a week or maybe a month this"—her gaze swept the cemetery—"will all be gone. It builds anyway because that is all it knows to do. Because life is for the living."

I've been thinking about all I've told you. I've said quite a bit about your great-uncle Maris, your grandfather Eriks, your grandmother Biruta. I told you about Mr. Zetsche's plans. I'm a little shocked at how little I've said about your father, David. Maybe after all these years, I still don't know how to make sense of him or where he fits in our lives. I consider this a shortcoming on my part. After all, I've had plenty of time to consider this. His powers of hearing weren't exceptional as far as I can remember. And, no, I don't know if his parents had large ears. I'm sorry I don't have a photograph of him. All I have are his letters. I started writing to him after Jutta's wedding. At some point into the third draft of the first letter I realized I did not have his address. Fortunately, in a small town like ours, it's not too hard to find out where someone lives. Mrs. Arijisnikov had a photographic memory, which she helped along by scouring the contents of the trash bins each night, looking for discarded envelopes and cancelled postage stamps. This was how she not only knew the precise address of each person in our town but also the addresses of the people they corresponded with. In exchange for small gifts, she almost always shared what she knew. It took only one marinated pike and few minutes for her to locate David's address.

"Ah! The university," she said. "He must be so smart."

I nodded, reaching for the scrap of paper with his address written on it. Mrs. A. curled her hand around the scrap, put her other hand on top of mine. "So"—she looked at me over the tops of her glasses—"how does your uncle know Mr. Zetsche?"

"What?"

"That big envelope. The one with extra postage. It went to Mr. Zetsche's home in Madona."

I shrugged. What business did I have with Uncle's dealings? Maybe he had designed another pair of tall shoes. I had bigger things to think about. Namely, was your father thinking at all of me? This is how infatuation works. All other details of reality are irrelevant, nonexistent even. Stars might supernova, but I wouldn't have noticed. I was on a mission.

The next ten months, as one season bled into the next, if I wasn't cleaning or helping Mother with the newspaper, I wrote letters as if possessed. Mother thought I was taking a class by correspondence, an assumption I did not try to correct.

I know that I have seemed careworn, even stern at times. But remember, I was girl once. And I was in love. Being in love ushered a heightened sense of perception and perspective. The green of the moss gloving each fallen birch and oak along the river acquired a hue of such vividness and texture that it seemed to glow with an interior light, its color being sufficient unto itself. And while it is true that when girls fall in love their vision intensifies, it also narrows in scope. Did I care about Mother's newspaper? Not a whit. The secret life of root vegetables bored me utterly. I wanted to know about the woman who penned the odd letters hidden in my room. I plied your grandmother Biruta for details. I wanted to know how Velta and Ferdinands met (at a dance, incidentally). I wanted to know about Velta's piano. Ferdinands's newspaper. Anything. Why, you may wonder. Why the obsession over a woman I had never met? I believe each one of us has a mystery we are compelled to solve; this mystery is our peculiar haunting. We are given few clues and often don't recognize them as such until many years later. My particular haunting had to do with Velta. My clues were many: the manor house, the beloved and much-battered piano, the framed picture at the back of the hall, Mother's silence. Velta's many letters.

A ripple of fingers over the white teeth of piano keys. A child's sharp cry of delight, the heavy jingling of coins, whistles from birds in the hedges. What if our world was built of these sounds? In a world of touchable, tangible objects, a world of solidity and weight, these sounds etch a permanent record. Yea, on the tablet of my heart. Sing me that song, the one you sang in Siberia. Sing me your dark melody.

She wrote of locusts that razed the rye field then came back four weeks later to do it again. I puzzled over her words, imagining that if I could wring some understanding from them I would know Velta, I would then know Mother. Maybe I was like that boy who climbed into the rabbi's enchanted mirror. Perhaps, like that boy peering at his own reflection, I thought that if I attended to the visible details of Velta's life I might cross the threshold of the ordinary here and now, and step into the mysteries of the past. I would see how one woman can inhabit another in the small gestures that flit from hand to shoulder or expressions that pull at the eyes and mouth. I would see how easily one woman becomes another.

I can tell you how afraid we were to take off our shoes and socks, to walk in the fields blanketed in lime. To churn white chalk under our feet. For fun, for sport, they said. Why don't you dance while you're at it? We did. They said, "Sing." We sang. We churned the soil with our feet, the skin of our heels sliding off. Is this a kind of love, to give oneself to the ground?

I confess. I read these letters and I wanted to be Velta. I wanted the clouds of white air filling my lungs, burning me from inside out. I wanted to be the one who had made sacrifices and could later write about it so poetically. I told you I had a habit of posturing. The sad truth was that not much was happening in town. Other than facts Mother gleaned from post-office gossip (former Game Warden Lukin was in stable condition after his wife hit him about the head and face with her prosthetic leg, one of the tie-dyed T-shirts given to the Lithuanian basketball team at the Barcelona games in 1992 was currently on eBay for more than five hundred dollars, Jutta now looked like she'd swallowed a cabbage), I didn't have much else to write to David. So I used Velta's letters as fodder for my own. I wrote: *A ripple of fingers over the piano's white teeth, a child's sharp cry of delight. Is this a kind of love?* Posturing and petty theft. Guilty on both counts.

To my extreme delight and relief, David replied to my letters. He apologized profusely for not writing to me first. In his missives he joked about the hygienic shortcomings of his roommates, the difficulty of his many exams, a recurring problem with headaches, and how much he wished my eel hadn't caught fire in the hall kitchen during Jutta's wedding reception, preventing our meeting at the river that fateful night. He was so kind as to assure me — repeatedly — that even though eel was not kosher, had the ovens and their contents not gone up in flames, most certainly he would have eaten it with terrific relish because my hands had prepared it.

Heartened by this endorsement, I borrowed Father's Bible, put on a pair of white gloves, and copied verses from the Song of Solomon, that surprisingly steamy book of the Old Testament.

> *By night on my bed I sought him whom my soul loveth:*
> *I sought him, but I found him not. I will rise now, and go about the city in the streets, and in the broad ways I will seek him whom my soul loveth.*

As I copied passages from Solomon's book, I became the Shulamite girl, separated temporarily by time and distance from the one her soul loved. And with each passage I copied, David became more and more like the lover of the Shulamite girl. Each new letter I wrote was another small test, a fleece by which I could gauge David's true heart by his responses. If he retreated to banalities of weather or, worse, hockey, I would have my answer: he was merely being courteous to a girl with big hips and bad skin. But if he replied in kind, then I would know he liked me. After I posted a letter, my moods careened as I imagined the worst until the day I received his reply.

> *Thy teeth are like a flock of sheep that are even shorn, which came up from the washing; whereof every one bear twins, and none is barren among them.*

> *P.S. You're right about Jutta—she's due to have a baby in a week—a boy according to the ultrasound. If all goes well, I'll be there for the celebration.*

We women up and down the lane had figured that Jutta was expecting: she'd been sighted in a bus carrying squares of soft fabrics—the kind used for making baby things. We'd also observed her circling their yard, clearly trying to hasten things along. Mrs. A. had been taking bets on the due date. Reading the news written in David's hand is what made her baby real to me. That was the week I dredged a new path to the post office. With each trip, I slowed my pace, straining to hear the sharp and fitful cries of a newborn.

What else could I do? My entire body was possessed with a restlessness that nothing—not even hunting the spring morels—could quiet. I thought perhaps I had contracted an illness. But one morning when I was on my way back from the post office, Stanka stopped me and examined my face carefully. Then she laughed. "A donkey should piss in my eye! You're in love—I can't believe I didn't see this sooner!"

"No, I'm not," I said. For some reason I could not name, I did not want to tell Stanka about David. Not yet.

Stanka clasped my hand in hers and squeezed her eyes closed. "Yes, you are. And all these trips to the post office mean he lives out of town." Stanka squinted. "Yes, I can see quite clearly, you are in love with a man of greatness."

I sighed. "It's just his ears. They are quite enormous if you have to know."

Stanka uncurled my fingers and peered at my open palm. "Soon you will be together. You will marry — in the hall, of course — and you will have many, many children." Stanka smiled and patted my hand.

The next day Jutta didn't appear in the yard. I knew it could mean only one thing.

It was on an evening of lashing rain that we heard pounding on the back door. I ran to the door, hoping it was Stanka with news of the baby.

"Finally," Rudy said, shrugging out of his coat. With him was Ligita. Apparently, they'd kissed and made up. Rudy bustled past me for the kitchen table where he pulled out our best chair. He waved Ligita to the chair, where, without a glance at me, she sat and pulled her purse — cheap imitation leather — into her lap.

Sensing another female presence in the house, Mother rushed into the kitchen. Behind her came Father.

"Rudy!" Father cried. "Such a surprise!"

"Usually you just call us on the phone when you want something," Mother observed.

Rudy blushed and looked at Ligita. Rudy had washed out at university, but he had managed to get into one of the best technical schools where he was now only weeks away from earning a surveyor's license. Rudy cleared his throat. "You remember Ligita."

Certainly we did.

Ligita seemed glued to the chair. She looked as if she'd poured herself into her clothes or perhaps the clothes had been spray painted onto her body. Yes, her jeans and sweater were just that tight, and looking at her filled to overflowing, her cup running over, looking as if abundant life had overwhelmed her, I knew she was pregnant.

"We're marrying right away," Rudy said.

"Why?" Father was incredulous.

Ligita folded and unfolded her hands in her lap, and stared at Mother's dishes in the cupboards.

Rudy blushed again. "For all the usual reasons." Rudy patted Ligita's stomach and then it was her turn to change color.

"We're in love, quite obviously," Rudy said.

"Quite obviously!" Mother beamed. "Love. Marriage. Another wedding. We'll hold it at the hall, of course."

"Of course," Ligita said. Her dark eyes shone like obsidian. In less than a minute she had Mother figured out entirely.

"Well, I, too, am in love." Father passed his hand over his heart.

"Really?" Ligita ventured.

Mother tucked a strand of her dark hair behind her ear and snorted. "Don't encourage him — please."

Though it was Mother's habit to pour water over Father's words so they wouldn't have a chance to firm up, Father merely winked at her. "Oh, yes, and they are beauties, each and every one possessing speed and balance and perfect symmetry." For years Father had maintained a theoretical love affair with German-made automobiles. Whenever that slick magazine arrived at the end of each month, Father immediately retired to the latrine, where he gazed with sustained admiration at the many shiny pictures, the only luxury that Father allowed himself.

Father sighed, a sound of vast longing that conveyed decades of wistful desire.

"Someday I will have one of these lovely ladies for my own."

"What would you do with such a car?" Mother asked.

Father looked at Mother as if she'd grown a third eye. "Why, drive it, of course."

Mother and Father wasted no time in setting up Rudy and Ligita in the living room. I repaired to the shed, where I felt I could pursue my literary endeavors without interruption. But that very first night, Rudy and Ligita rattled the wooden door and let themselves in without knocking.

"I didn't want to mention it, not in front of Mother and Father; they're upset enough as it is. But there was a fellow on the bus asking after you."

"He had absolutely enormous ears," Ligita piped up, and it seemed to me she was smirking a bit.

"Anyway, this fellow wanted me to give you this." Rudy handed me an envelope. I waited for them to leave then tore open the letter.

For, lo, the winter is past; the rain is over and gone. The flowers ap-pear on the earth; the time of the singing of birds is come, and the voice of the turtle is heard in our land.

P.S. Dusk is the best time to hunt for the magic fern that blooms. And the river is the best place—no?

I glanced at my reflection in the window. Not cute. I whisked a tube of lipstick over my lips, pinched my cheeks for color, and pulled on David's fishing coat. As luck would have it, Mother was busy show-ing Ligita the inside of her oven. I hurried through the cemetery. The rain had quit, and the earliest of the spring birds flitted and darted from the understory of the trees. The last light, fallen now behind the lowest layer of clouds, cast a horizontal beam that illuminated every drop of water studding silver and gold the buds of every twig of every branch of every tree. Suddenly, I was that Shulamite girl in a garden of diamonds.

"Inara—over here!" David emerged from the brush. His gaze swept the open collar of his fishing coat and the neckline of my dress underneath it. "You look wonderful."

Behind his words, I heard Solomon's script scrolling like a ticker tape. Dramatic, sure. And crazy. For me to fall in love not really knowing what love is but sure that I was consumed by it and that this must be a good thing. But it was easy to do as the clouds had folded down for dusk and twilight blurred sharp edges, forgiving any blemish. It was easy to allow myself to feel, to be carried away by feelings larger than any I had ever encountered before. David linked his arm in mine and we walked by the water. Eventually, our steps led us through the cribbed aspen to the manor house. It was the only tangible evidence that our family had once owned something fine, and I wanted him to see the crumbling stone statue of Venus rising from the dark pond and how the loss of her left arm and head only added to her noble bearing. I wanted him to hear the strains of waltzes spilling through open doorways. I wanted him to imagine, as I did, that we might someday live here together.

We walked over the flagstone, which at one time, judging from the grout of weeds between each stone, had been pieced and fitted to such precision that a woman in rustling silk could walk without soiling her dress or feet. The mullioned windows of leaded glass and the intricate loops and curls of the decorative wood latticework wrapping the entire upper story of the structure suggested an elegance belonging to a forgotten era. And now, at sunset, when the last stabs of light lanced through the birch and oak, those windows turned to mirrors, casting light all about, honey thick and viscous. I wanted to drink that light, bathe in it.

We approached the back of the house where the side door hung crookedly on its hinges. We did not light a lamp. We did not need to: by this time the clouds had thinned and the moon, round and full, threw rectangles of silver light over the stone floor. I unrolled his coat and spread it over the floor.

When you were quite young, you asked about your father, the circumstances of your birth. You asked where he was. You asked me why I did not love him enough to marry him, and that was the question that convinced me, matters of tact and dignity aside, that I should tell you everything. You are my son, blood of my blood. You are David's son, blood of his blood. And so I will tell you he had eyes as blue as a cloudless sky in August. In certain light they looked purple, in other light, silver. No one before had noticed me in the way a girl wants to be noticed. I loved him in the frenetic, anxious, giddy, soul-consuming way a girl does when she falls in love for the first time. I stumbled headlong and clumsily through a tumultuous array of emotion. Time moved in two speeds at once: dizzyingly fast as darkness fell around us, and at the same time as slowly as an old camera, the kind with a shutter snapping one frame after another: a look, a breath, a gesture.

I know you understand. You've written that we inhabit mysteries we don't have words to express. To read your explanation of the latticed nature of the universe makes perfect sense to me. I have witnessed the way needle ice grows slowly, knitting itself into sheets so solid they can support the weight of an army of elephants. I have rooted for mushrooms, have seen the thin white tendrils of the mycelium, that network of roots that binds one fruit of a mushroom to another that might fruit ten kilometers away. I know that the strength of lace rests in the knots that anchor the empty holes. That we are built of more space than solid substance seems in perfect accord with the larger architecture of our visible and invisible world. All fundamental forces of nature, all particles, you wrote, can be thought of as vibrations of tiny strings. A network of thread corseting the heavens, binding the deep. Strings finer than the finest hair, so fine no needle can work it. This intricate warp and weft of thread, this quiet industry, weaves itself on a vast loom that never stops growing.

And so there we were, sitting beside each other. I had waited ten months to see David, but nervousness seized me and I could hardly breathe, let alone speak. And whatever ailed me seemed to afflict David, only it turned him strangely chatty. He told a joke about three retired Estonian race-car drivers. Jokes about the famed unflappable calm of Estonians is a sure icebreaker in almost any social setting. When David launched into an anecdote about a rabbi, a priest, and a mullah, I put a finger on his lips. "You didn't come all this way to tell jokes."

"No." David squeezed my hand.

I looked at David, at his gray-blue eyes, and I saw the eyes of the famous lover, one who is beautiful in his coming and going, one who found beauty in an unlikely candidate, the dark Shulamite girl, misunderstood, shunned. So when I looked at my beloved, I could say, as the Shulamite girl did, that his head was as fine as gold, his locks as bushy and black as a raven. His eyes were the eyes of doves by the rivers of waters, washed in the milk and fitly set. His cheeks were like a bed of spices, as sweet as flowers. When I looked at David bending toward me, he was more than David the person, he was David of those passionate letters. David cradled my head under his arm and his lips were lilies dropping sweet petals. *Let him kiss me with the kisses of his mouth: for thy love is better than wine.*

When I looked in his eyes, they replied in that same language, a language beyond words.

Then I kissed him. And with that kiss, I was transported, divided. There were two of me. One kissing David and the other one hovering close by, watching. It was as if my life were a movie and I were both actress and audience. When he pushed my dress above my hips, I kissed him. And when he pulled my dress over my head, I kissed him because there was nothing dirty or shameful in any of it. I loved him and he loved me, and in this moment, we were finding the unsaid part neither of us knew how to say. As surface slid against surface, our soft geometries, we made a soundless language between us that only we two could speak, a language beyond words. And I suppose, as the audience part of me watched myself, that I was putting some distance between the act of love and the feelings of love. Because the truth was, the act wasn't living up to my romantic imaginings. In fact, there was a moment of actual pain. Sharp pressure, wetness down below, wetness above. A tear rolled down the side of my face.

"Are you okay?" David studied my face, the part of me beneath him on the coat. "Did I hurt you?" And I smiled, both versions of me did, because not for the world would I tell him that he had. After all, what's a little blood between people who love each other? We pulled on our clothes; it was cold after all. I rolled up the coat, a spot of blood on it now, and both versions of me were glad for the incumbent darkness.

Afterward, we walked back to the river.

David pulled at a tuft of tall grass and worked it between his fingers. "What happened between us just now is the most sacred thing that can happen between a man and a woman."

"Oh, I know it," I said. It was so sacred and special that I don't think I'd ever heard Mother talk about it outside our house, or inside of it, either.

"So, in way we're married now, you and I." David knotted some grass into a loop, slipped it as a ring around my finger. "This is a solemn seal between us."

I rubbed at the grass ring with my thumb. It was beautiful because David had made it, but it wouldn't last a day in the kitchen.

David squeezed my hand. "I have to go back to Riga tomorrow and I won't return for at least two weeks."

"Why?"

"I have to take some tests."

"Oh — more exams."

"No." David reached for my other hand. "Different kinds of tests. For those headaches. I probably just need new glasses or something. I'll be back before you know it."

"When?"

David smiled, tapped the faces of both his watches. "Two weeks to the day. I promise. I'll be here." David planted a kiss on my forehead, one on each cheek, and another on my lips. "'Many waters cannot quench love; neither can the floods drown it.'"

I smiled. "That's chapter eight, verse seven."

"Don't forget it."

Through the cemetery I scurried. I had cleared the toolshed when the latrine door flung open.

"Inara!" Father bellowed. "Where have you been?"

"At the river." I clutched David's coat tightly to my chest.

Father shined his flashlight on my high heels. "Quite obviously you weren't fishing."

"No. I was reading."

Father shined the light into my eyes. "Reading?"

I squinted into the light. "The Song of Solomon."

"Oh—the Bible—that I'm glad to hear. But if you are going to study God's Holy Word, promise me that next time you will cover your elbows. Please don't ever let me see you dressing like a Russian again." The light panned my face and neck. "And wipe that mess off your face. It's trashy." Father pulled shut the toolshed door.

My eyes stung. Never had your grandfather spoken to me like this. And then I felt ashamed. His eyes had measured me and found me wanting, and now I could not get to my room and wipe the makeup off my face fast enough.

The week after I met your father at the river, we were nervous wrecks, each of us for our different reasons. Ligita listened to a German radio station in the dark and commented on her frayed nerves, which was why she couldn't help in the kitchen or hang laundry. But she was tireless in her arguments with Rudy, possessing the stamina of a champion interlocutor who knew how to grind out an infinitesimal advantage and convert it to palpable gain. That is, she talked and talked and talked, her tongue the grindstone by which she wore Rudy down into numb submission.

With a flashlight wired to his cap, Father spent long hours drawing maps of the old cemetery and the new cemetery. Mother worked longer hours, stockpiling for that grandchild she hadn't planned on. And the weariness of a lifetime of hard work was beginning to show on her. Late at night when we washed dishes, she'd startle at the sight of her own reflection in the window as if, in the small signs of aging, she'd become a stranger to herself. Mother was not a vain woman, but she'd been proud of her hair, which all through the days of her youth had been as dark and shiny as wet stone. Over the last couple of years, she had acquired some silver hair on the crown of her head, and it seemed to me that these hairs were a growing record of the major stress-producing events in her life: the fall of the Soviet Union, the first democratic election, the hyperinflation that took nearly everyone's savings, Uncle Maris's boisterous decline and eventual death, and now this: the news of a grandchild, which announced itself as a bright silver streak at her temple. But I couldn't work for anything. All I could think about was David. Was he thinking about me? How were his tests coming along? Was he leveled by those headaches and, dear Lord, I wondered, could I be the cause of those headaches? After I broke the third plate in one night, Mother tossed her rag into the sink. "What in the world is the matter with you?" She touched my forehead.

I bit my lip. "I'm in love," I said.

Though the light in the kitchen was dim, Mother shielded her eyes with her hand and squinted at me fiercely. "You have too much common sense to fall in love. Love is for girls who can't manage anything else." Mother folded her arms across her chest.

I studied the tops of my hands. Her comment was a compliment and an insult at the same time: I hadn't had the brains for university, but at least I wasn't so foolish as to hitch my hopes on any passing boy. I twisted the grass ring between my finger.

Mother frowned. "Just how well do you know this boy anyway?"

"Well enough to know we're in love."

"And just who are his parents?"

"You saw them yourself—at Jutta's wedding. They are very fine people," I said.

"Oh." Mother's face went tight. "Relatives of the Ilmyens'?"

"Yes."

Mother threw open the window and thrust her head over the sill. "For God's sake," she called over her shoulder. "Don't tell your father about this; he has enough worries already."

"Tell me what?" Father called from the shed.

"Inara's in love — with a Jew," Mother shouted.

Father sprinted across the yard. He stood on the porch for a moment, catching his breath. Then he opened the back door and sat at the kitchen table. Though I could hear his heart thumping erratically in his chest, his voice was steady and calm. "We like Jews. The Ilmyens, as you know, are, for the most part, magnificent people. So then you also know that we absolutely believe in being neighborly to Jews in general."

"But that doesn't mean you have to go around marrying them!" Mother said, reaching for a scrub brush.

"Why not?" I asked.

Mother fell to her knees and scrubbed the floor with the vigor of a woman possessed. "Because," she said at last, "they aren't real Latvians. Not Latvian Latvian. They are more of a European variety of Latvian, which is to say they have acquired that weedy continental look of people on the move. They also possess a harrowingly Hebraic sigh that discourages frank and open relationships."

I looked at Father. He lowered his gaze to the scored tabletop. There was no use arguing or attempting to adjust this opinion of Mother's. She was not a mean-spirited woman, but she had always appreciated the certainties of classification; it was her way of keeping tabs on what seemed to her an increasingly unruly and disheveled world. "Besides," Mother continued, resting a moment on her heels. "People who don't believe the same way can't be happy together. Trust me."

Father winced. But Mother continued. "We aren't trying to ruin things. Really. We're only trying to help." Mother glanced at the living room, where Rudy and Ligita's voices rode the rise and run of a swelling argument. "Anyway, don't think for a minute you're marrying anytime soon," Mother whispered. "You'll not upstage Rudy and have him jumping in puddles."

I fingered David's grass ring. Time. Everything yields in time, I told myself. The time it takes for water to wear down stone. Eventually, even the sharp edges of Mother's unassailable logic would blunt to nubs. Mother was right—I could wait. And while I waited, she would see how unhappy I was, and then some unknowable part of her heart would soften.

CHAPTER FIVE

DUSK FELL ONE GRAIN AT A TIME. I heard Mother singing out in the yard, a work song we all knew by heart:

> Trouble, my big trouble,
> I put it under a rock
> and kept on singing.

I know she's been gone for some time. But I heard her voice as clear and pure as cold water, and I hoisted myself up out of bed fully expecting to see her washing her coal-black hair in that old metal tub we keep next to the shed. I saw instead pigeons, light gray smears fluttering at the eaves of the Ilmyens' house. High above the red tin roof, the geese, those dark knots, pulled a peasant's twilight in their wake. Enchanted by the lull of this quiet spectacle, I floated adrift in a dream, extravagant, strange, and dark. Mother rose up from the river. *Inara, come and drink this water that is so cool and sweet,* she said. *I'm not thirsty,* I said. *Come to the river where you can wash and I will baptize you,* she said. *You don't believe in such things, Mother.* I said. Her arm stretched long over the tall cow parsley, stretched long over the grass. Her strong arm hooked around my body and drew me to the water, pulled me under, held me down. No amount of thrashing from my arms and legs could free me. I struggled. I called out.

I woke with a shout, my legs tangled in the blankets, my sheets drenched in sweat. I lay there bathed in quiet, bathed in gray light, my baptism. A puddle of river water beside my bed. You said, "Rest now, rest now." But I heard "Go on and dig." And I thought, *Go on and bury me.*

I'm not crazy; at least I don't think I am. But I will admit there have been times when I'm not sure which girl I am: the one in love with the man by the river or the one lying in bed talking to the man in the blue chair. Which story will this girl remember? In the days after I met David, my moods swung wildly between elation and despair. I thought often of the Ghost Girl. They say she crawls on her knees and knuckles through the river grass. She can assume many shapes. As you sleep, she broods over you with her dark wings. You know she's been near if you wake with a sudden thirst and find water in the foot of your shoes. I knew of a farmer who found dark feathers as long as a scythe beside his pillow. He drowned his beloved dog to make her go away. I clung to those stories, to Velta's letters, for their lurid strangeness, for their vivid detail, for a world made known by small solid things: forks and dance shoes, clover and eels. Only the act of reading and writing letters tethered me to a sense of time and place. I recounted for David how hundreds of storks—black and white—returned to their nests the day after he left or built new ones high in the riverside oaks and lindens and in the crotches of telephone poles.

Father returned to work at the cemetery. Mr. Zetsche assembled a crew from Jekobpils to move the contents of the cemetery, and now he needed Father to write the names of the dead on a blueprint of the new cemetery to make sure everyone arrived in their proper place. "It's very simple," Mr. Zetsche assured Father one night over the black telephone. "The two land parcels are mirror images of each other. The only difference is that the old cemetery falls to one side of the lane and faces the river and the new cemetery rests on the other side of the lane and faces, er, other things."

Whereas the old cemetery featured stately black alders and ash that yielded gradually to a birch at the river's edge, anemic birches that year after year neither flourished nor withered marked the four corners of the property that was to be the new cemetery. A lone oak anchored the center. This parcel of land sat on higher ground than the old cemetery, a fact Mr. Zetsche was quick to point out. "You'll thank me later," he said again and again.

Everyone else realized in no time how unalike the two parcels were. Those who determined that their family plots occupied the choicest spots—the ones nearer the lonely oak and the memorial for Old General, the most famous horse in Latvia—privately rejoiced. Those who guessed that their plots would be too near the plot designated for our uncle Maris uprooted Father's string lines or switched markers. In short order, chaos reigned, and every morning Father tramped through the new cemetery and pulled out Mr. Zetsche's map, looking at it this way and that. Then he'd shake his head and reset the string lines, knowing that by nightfall they'd all be moved again.

Adding to Father's worries was the fact that three of Mr. Zetsche's crew, Jews from Daugavpils, quit and notified the Jewish Burial Society of Mr. Zetsche's indelicate plans. Mr. Zetsche had no choice but to promote Father to project supervisor, foreman, and community liaison. Though this meant that Father would do the digging as usual, now he also had to endure the evening visits from the widows Spassky and Sosnovskis, who were now best friends. They brought rum cookies and birch juice, and begged Father to place their husbands in plots befitting their position of honor in the chess world. They provided Father with a new plan for the cemetery, which looked uncannily similar to that of a chessboard. Naturally, their husbands were to occupy the king positions.

I wrote about all this to David; my frenetic writing was my way of shortening the days between our agreed-upon meeting, a way to dampen my worry that David had not replied to my letters. When the appointed time for our meeting came, I pulled on Rudy's fishing boots, and despite Father's strong sentiments regarding cosmetics, I applied to my face a generous coating. Then I went to the river. For the first three hours at the river, I fished. I caught a woman's umbrella, which offered no help whatsoever when the clouds lowered and rain fell sideways and pounded the river like a thousand tiny fists. I stood on the soggy bank watching the water rise over the tops of Rudy's boots. I stepped forward, felt the water at my shins, then my knees. I told myself I would wait for David for as long as it took. The rain quit and the light folded quietly bolt by bolt until the sky bled rose, bled lavender, then a deep blue. A horrible thought seized me: a good-looking and smart man like he was might have found someone else. I could not help myself. I sobbed big body-wracking sobs so powerful and grand that I was surprised by my own sorrow.

> *I rose up to open to my beloved; and my hands dropped with myrrh, and my fingers with sweet smelling myrrh, upon the handles of the lock. I opened to my beloved, but my beloved had withdrawn himself and was gone . . . I called him, but he gave me no answer.*

I stepped forward. Water pulled at my hips. I had that sensation of being utterly split. Of there being two of me present at the same time: one in the water, bawling as if there were no tomorrow, the other one wondering, *How much farther can I wade and still haul myself to shore? How strong am I really?* I thought about my childish desire for water, weightlessness. I took another step and my breath came in sharp pulls. The cold forced a shift in my vision, and I saw myself from outside my own body. I saw how I looked as viewed through a camera placed at a distance then through the lens close up. I was a fat Ophelia, as sloppy as an unspun sonnet; my hair — a tangle of wet ropes — clung to my neck and face.

I imagined David observing from the trees, somber and sad that he'd driven me to this. And then I took another step. I was in up to my chest. The water was so much colder and harder to push against than I had realized. I could neither fight the current nor find my footing; the boots had filled with water and each step pulled me farther out into the middle of the river. If I opened my mouth to call for help, the water would rush in. And who, on a night like this one, would hear me? And for the first time in my life, I doubted this river. For the first time in my life, I was afraid of this water.

"Inara!" An orange float bobbed past; I grabbed for it. The line pulled me and I kicked for the shallows, where I imagined I'd see David. I sank to my knees and panted like a carp.

I looked up. Not David, but Mr. Ilmyen, his sides heaving. He wiped at his face with a handkerchief. I crawled onto the soggy bank, and he pulled off my boots, dumped the water from them. "You know this river as well as anyone." Mr. Ilmyen tossed one boot at my feet then the other. "You are a good girl and a good swimmer. But you are not a fish. What were you thinking?"

I shrugged. "I don't know."

Mr. Ilmyen tipped his head, considering the possibilities. "Oh, Inaraleh, you have always been like another daughter to me." Mr. Ilmyen wrapped his coat around me and I buried my face in his shirt. I cried, quietly at first, and then, because Mr. Ilmyen was so kind as to let me continue, even patting my back, I wailed and bawled until I had cried myself into quiet exhaustion and stained his shirt with my inky tears.

You know your grandmother was a wise woman. She could look at people and see who they were at their core. A single squint and she'd divine your very essence. Though I often thought that she was too busy banishing every offending particle of dirt to see me, this was a failure of my imagination. The fact was her vision was never as sharp as it was that night I came back from the river. I found her kneeling in front of the oven, the earpieces of Uncle Maris's stethoscope in her ears and the scope held to the back panel. She caught my reflection in the oven's back panel. She maneuvered her head and shoulders slowly out of the oven and sat on her heels. "Every time you come back from the river, you are sopping wet and wearing somebody else's coat. What were you doing out there?"

I bit my lip. "Fishing," I said.

Now Mother looked me over carefully. "What did you catch?"

I looked at my hands. The grass ring David had made for me was gone, lost in the river no doubt.

"Nothing."

Mother frowned. "Let me make you some tea." She wiped her hands against her thighs and dragged the kettle over to the stove. "With honey."

I sank into a chair. Mother wet a tea towel under the faucet. "And let me clean your face. Maybe I should have said this more often." Now Mother cupped my chin in her chapped hands. "Maybe you don't know. You are so beautiful — in every way. You don't need this paint." Mother scrubbed at my face with the towel. "Besides, in my day only trashy girls wore makeup." As she withdrew her hands, one of her fingernails raked my cheek.

That night, as I studied my reflection in the darkened window-pane, I detected a tiny smear of blood on my face. I left it there. I lulled myself to sleep, and as I did, old words from an old song wove themselves into the loose fabric of night, a crow's calling in the distance.

> *Strange news flies up and down,*
> *Strange news is a-gathering.*
> *My true love has left town.*
> *My true love they are a-burying.*

The crow flew darkness into my sleep, where I dreamed my loves and I dreamed my fears. The Ghost Girl of the river called my name: *Inara! Inara!* I walked the river, took that old forbidden path to the manor. My feet sank to the ankles in a bog. The bones in my heels disintegrated, and with every step I took, my feet sank deeper into the mud until I went under, swallowed whole by the dark mire. I held my breath and I grew scales — beautiful periwinkle-blue scales, but no one could see them in the dark. *Inara!* David called to me. *Come find me!* I realized that I had never lost David — all this time David had been waiting patiently for me deep beneath the mud. But I could not swim to him: my arms had not yet changed to fins and I had not yet learned to breathe through my skin.

I found Stanka two kilometers downriver. Though she advertised her dream interpretation services in Mother's temperance newspaper, we all knew her claims were dubious. Still, I reminded myself that even a broken weather vane tilts in the right direction once in a while. She was hunkered over the riverside underbrush. In autumn she liked to look here for choice sooty milk caps, a mushroom good for marinating with onions. In spring she came to read the mud for signs of her family, as this was once a place they used to pass through on their way to the towns where they liked to buy and sell horses. But every spring it was the same story: the only tracks were those made by Mr. Ilmyen or me in our separate bids to catch fish.

"I just had a strange dream," I said. "I was wondering if you could interpret it for me."

Stanka merely grunted.

"David appeared in the dream," I pressed on. "He was supposed to meet me yesterday and didn't. What do you suppose it means?"

Stanka straightened. "It means you should wake up." Then she scurried off.

I turned upriver. As I passed the school, the windows of Mr. Bishofs's classroom had been thrown open and the voices of his second- and third-year students conjugating German verbs at the top of their lungs rolled over the back of the fog. Mr. Bishofs believed in fresh air, though Miss Druviete, who taught in the room opposite, had a terrible dread of drafts. The two teachers spent most of their short lunch breaks opening and closing windows. They would probably get married.

The Ilmyens also believed in the power of fresh air. As I climbed their front step, Little Semyon's wails ripped the air into shreds, though Mrs. Ilmyen was doing her level best to sing her new grandson quiet with a lullaby I knew well: *aija zuzu, laca berni* and then another, something simpler and ancient and much sadder: *bai, bai, bai.* When I knocked, Mr. Ilmyen answered the door.

"I'm looking for David. He wasn't here yesterday and he promised he would be."

Mr. Ilmyen pulled the door closed behind him. "I know, Inara, I know."

"Why hasn't he come?" Dread, thick and full, spread across the floor of my stomach, rose in my throat.

Mr. Ilmyen gathered me into his arms. "He wanted to, Inara. He very much wanted to."

"But where is he now? Tell me."

"I am so very sorry; I thought someone had already told you," Mr. Ilmyen said. Then he raised his gaze to the clouds. And that's how I knew David was never coming back. Those headaches had not been about poor vision. He'd been ill all along and now he was dead.

Mother met me on our back porch. "I'm sorry about your friend," she said.

"You knew?"

Mother withdrew two letters from her apron—both letters in my handwriting, both returned to sender unopened. "I had guessed," Mother said. "Mrs. A. delivered a black letter to the Ilmyens. I put two and two together. Also, Mrs. A. had steamed open the letter."

For the next three days I did nothing but wander up and down the lane in a daze. "You'll find somebody else," Ligita offered, by way of consolation. From time to time Father patted my head. Mother, too, only her hand held a scrub brush. *For me, work,* she was saying. It was the only way she knew how to purge herself of tragedy. Stanka brought me black licorice wheels. On the fifth day, after I'd exhausted her supply, Stanka sat with me at our kitchen table. The dishes were drying in the racks by the sink. I put my sorrow to good work and scrubbed the floor, but still I could not stop crying.

"Inara," Stanka sighed. "You can't fart wider than your ass."

I wiped at my eyes. "What?"

"There are limits. To everything." Stanka slid her feet into her sandals and left the kitchen, a trail of sunflower hulls dropping in her wake.

I walked through the woods. I thought this is what Velta would have done. She would have turned her sorrows under her feet, trod them like a stone, and kept on walking. So I walked through the scrub alder and birch to her manor house. I wasn't happy and I knew I wouldn't be for a long time. But I thought the sight of a familiar place, a place I had shared with David, would somehow bring comfort. I skirted the dark ponds, thinking I'd peer into a dark window and see the other me, a girl in a white dress with rush lights in her hand and man who loved her sitting in darkness. Instead, I saw a long flat piece of thin wood. On it seven crows had been nailed spread-eagle. They'd been left to rot. Feather, beak, and bone. That's all that was left of them. A message, a warning to other crows, as death is the only thing a crow respects. But who would want to send this message here?

"Hey!"

I whirled on my feet. A man in overalls shook his fist at me. In his other hand he held a bucket with a trowel and brush. "This is Zetsche property. You're trespassing."

That evening I tasted the salt on my skin as I tumbled into a fitful night of watery dreaming. Bloated with sorrow, my body was a buoyant sea, rising and ebbing. Three times in the night I had to go outside and use the toilet. In the morning the air smelled metallic and wet, like rusty keys or old wire fencing. The Arijisnikov dog, a herder with long teeth that was best avoided, took a sudden interest in the smell of my skin at the back of my knees. No matter what I drank — tea, coffee, juice — my mouth tasted bitter, like a new filling in a bad tooth. And I couldn't eat.

Always, I'd had a healthy appetite, but now the smell of Mother's cooking lard and the sound of her pans rattling on the stove top turned my stomach. Four mornings in a row I did not sit with Rudy and Ligita at the table for breakfast. On the fifth morning Mother followed me outside to the toilet where I threw up, as faithful as the hands of the clock are to the hours.

"You're pregnant," Mother said.

I wiped my mouth with the back of my hand. "Yes."

"Stupid!" Mother slapped me across the face. "Stupid girl!" Mother stormed back to the house.

I want you to understand that I have always considered you the greatest gift ever given to me. You are living proof of the love that transcends the limits of a single human body, of time and space. They say that because God is omnipresent God loves us in the past, in our present, and in our future. I believe this not because I know so much about God, but because the moment I realized I was pregnant, I loved you. I loved the idea of you, the fact of your existence. I knew I would love you in the present and I loved imagining your future. Maternal affection pounded inside my heart, pushing on the seams and bursting forth like rushing water during a sudden spring melt. Such a surprise to me to learn that while I thought I had been so large hearted in my love for your father it was nothing compared to what I felt for you.

You should know your grandmother Biruta loved the same way: beyond measure and without limitation. You must also understand that her not speaking to me for the next thirteen days (on principle, I knew) was because she had been raised in a traditional household. Hers was the traditional response. It would have been different if I had been a man, if I'd been Rudy. A boy who gets a girl pregnant is fulfilling a natural function, and as long as he marries, the whole world nods and winks. A girl who gets pregnant is a tramp, a source of shame to everyone who knows her. And whereas I had felt little shame before, and it surprised me that I could waltz around such a large emotion unscathed, I did feel the sure and hard knowledge that I'd disappointed Mother in ways she'd never imagined I could.

One morning Mother followed me into the latrine again. This time she held my hair while I threw up. Then she wiped my face with a handkerchief. I knew that by these gestures she'd forgiven me.

"Does Father know?" I asked.

Mother tucked her handkerchief into her dress pocket. "Not yet."

"I have to tell him," I said.

Mother laid her rough hand on the back of my neck. Though her hands were not smooth—never smooth—they were cold and the pressure of her hands immediately calmed the nausea. "I'll tell him," Mother said at last. "Later."

I followed Mother inside the house and washed my face at the sink. Through the window I watched Father digging in the new cemetery. Even from my place behind the window I saw how hard it was for him to dig, how heavy the rain-soaked earth had become. And I could see, too, that Father was not as strong as he used to be.

Rudy returned from school a week later. He moved Ligita and her small wardrobe into our living room. From a hook on the wall, she hung her ballet shoes, drooping with disappointment. As she snapped open the wardrobe doors, we heard her anger. She flung a suitcase on the floor. In its thud we heard her fear and disappointment. About living arrangements. About money. About life ambitions. From room to corridor to kitchen, a small thunder followed behind her.

Ligita fought with me, too. Quietly. As we both began our days with touchy stomachs, each morning it was a race for the privacy of the outdoor toilet where Ligita had a small plastic bucket stashed for her own use. "What's the matter with you?" Ligita demanded after I'd been inside the privy for a good fifteen minutes with my own small bucket.

I pulled a big breath through my nose. "Bad food, I think," I said on the exhale.

"It's your mother's cooking." Ligita brushed past me for her pail and emptied her stomach. But after a few mornings of this, I knew from the way Ligita narrowed her eyes when she looked at me that she'd guessed I was pregnant and had gotten that way simply to upstage her. Since then, on principle, she wasn't talking to me, relying on Rudy instead to deliver messages, requests, and instructions. Especially at mealtime.

"Please pass the plate of greens to your sister," Ligita said one evening. "Folic acid is very important to the healthy brain development of the unborn." She delivered a significant look at my stomach.

"Greens are good for everybody!" Mother said, with tepid cheer. Judging from the bewildered look on Father's and Rudy's faces, they didn't know about my pregnancy.

I excused myself from the table and went to my room. Though there was a chill in the air, I opened my window and lay on my bed.

"Burying them six inches closer just to make room for more plots," a woman's voice lamented. "Never in my life!"

"This new cemetery is screwed up like Russia, but with German precision," a man's voice replied.

Later, as dusk brewed, the talk turned uglier. Every town, I knew, had its secrets: stories, fables, and lies sewn together with silence, that most formidable stitching. This history lurks, literally, beneath the surface of any town, as we were all learning. Now that Father was disinterring the graves, it was as if that stitching had been broken and he were dredging up from those plots every stain and taint associated with each family, the things we knew or suspected but dared not voice: that someone in the Gepkars family had bribed certain members of a Soviet unit dispatched to our area with Bavarian cuckoo clocks (this was why no one in their family had been deported to Siberia); that it was because Game Warden Lukin's wife regularly offered herself to a Soviet official in Riga that Lukin was given such a choice job; that certain people had provided certain information about certain other people and now those people had disappeared. Yes, Father had his work cut out for him, and though death was his business, I knew that the overlap of the living in the territory of the dead caused him the most heartache.

Father rapped softly on my bedroom door. "I'm awake," I said.

Father sat on the edge of my bed and stared at his hands. At last he turned his gaze on me.

"You're angry," I said.

Father rubbed his hands over his face. "I'm too tired to be angry. But I'm disappointed. I won't pretend that I'm not."

"Rudy and Ligita are having a baby."

"This is different."

"Why?"

"Because you are my daughter. Not somebody else's daughter. My daughter. And there is no man to marry you." Father ran his hands through his hair.

I couldn't help myself then. I cried. My nose ran. I honked into Father's handkerchief.

Father patted my back. "Don't cry, Inara. God has big hands."

I blinked. "What is that supposed to mean?"

"His hands are big enough to carry even this." Father nodded at my stomach, but his voice was sad and I knew this heartache I had caused, was causing, would be one more thing he had to carry.

"Well." Father stood slowly and pulled the window closed. "I hope it's a girl. I hope she will be like you were: a happy child." Then Father did something he hadn't done in years: he pulled the cover up to my chin and kissed me on the forehead.

I tumbled into a thick, hard sleep that left no room for dreams. When I woke in the morning, spring had shaken hands with winter. Across the lane shoots of fern and crocus pushed through the mud and with them a quiet shock of blues: Anna-on-the-ice and a clutch of Siberian iris. Father called this color crucial blue because he said it meant the ground had turned from its sleep and was ready for life. I sat on the edge of the bed, my stomach calm but my heart astonished by the change a single day brings.

That week Father worked with the backhoe by night and heeled in the stones by day. By the end of the week, most of the holes had been dug and place markers set, and Father was ready to move actual remains. Very sensibly, he removed the bodies in the graves closest to the lane and worked his way back toward the river. And by the start of the next week, he'd moved most of the Christian bodies, our uncle Maris included.

Meanwhile, a Mr. Serotsin from the Daugavpils Jewish Burial Society wrote a heated letter to Mr. Zetsche. This was intercepted by Mrs. Arijisnikov, who had the good sense to steam open the letter, call Father, and notify him of its contents before sending it along to Mr. Zetsche. Did Mr. Zetsche not understand that moving a body once it had been interred was the highest offense? Had he no regard for ritual or tradition? Mr. Serotsin asked.

A few hours later the black phone bellowed. This time it was Mr. Zetsche. He had received and read the letter from Mr. Serotsin.

"Tell the Jewish Burial Society that they have my sympathies, of course." Mr. Zetsche's brittle voice rattled Mother's dishes. "They wish to revere their dead, which is fine. But they want to do it on the site of my future Riviera, which is not fine. Tell them to do what they need to do, but you've got to move the rest of those bodies. Soon. Subgrade is going in in a few days, and after that, the concrete will arrive."

"But, sir," Father objected. "I am just one man working here; I have no crew left."

"Oh, not to worry. Moving, er, things from one place to another is something Jews are especially good at. Just make sure they have plenty of rope. They'll know what to do," Mr. Zetsche assured Father. "But don't let them operate the backhoe," Mr. Zetsche added. "It's new."

. . .

And what of our manor house? I listened, shameful I know, at doors and windows. Mother and Father spoke in hushed words, but even so, I could hear their anger, frustration. Only once did Mother raise her voice and only once did she ever use that black phone on her own behalf; and in both instances it was to call Mr. Zetsche. She demanded to know how he had obtained the title and deed to the property. She had signed no paperwork and would have never in her right mind sold off her parents' home. "It's simple," Mr. Zetsche said. "I've paid the back taxes. Also, I have a power of attorney on which your signature appears and just beneath it your husband's. This is a perfectly legal and binding sale."

"Those are our names, but not our signatures," Mother objected.

"If you want to take this to court, I understand completely," Mr. Zetsche droned. "But, really, my hands are tied. I've done nothing wrong."

I could not escape the logical conclusion that all this was Uncle Maris's doing. All that business with the yellow envelope, his insistence that I not ask questions. Uncle Maris had forged your grandparents' signatures and sold the ancestral manor from under their noses. The money he'd received had funded, no doubt, any number of his exploits and possibly put your uncle Rudy through those first few years of school.

Mother slid the receiver into the holster.

"Is it gone?" Father asked.

Mother's gaze never lifted from the wooden table. "Yes." In that one word I heard years of hope dashed.

True to Mr. Zetsche's word, the Jewish Burial Society came to town on the early bus. They walked the length of the lane toward the cemetery with such solemnity, it was as if they could feel beneath their canvas shoes how badly worn the earth's overcoat was. The arrival of ten men carrying shovels provoked instant curiosity in the same way a crowd attracts a crowd. Soon everyone who didn't have jobs,

that is, nearly all the men and a handful of women, Ligita and I included, gathered outside the cemetery, not even bothering to conceal
our open interest. Father introduced himself to the oldest of their
number, Mr. Serotsin. Then Father followed them into the cemetery
as the men walked among the plots, touching the stones. One of the
men chanted a prayer in front of each of the Jewish markers, and after
this prayer, each of the men balanced a small pebble on the marker,
which seemed odd to me considering the fact that the stones would
be moved soon. After ten sets of hands touched every Jewish marker
and everybody resting beneath had been remembered in a prayer, the
men sang a song. Maybe it, too, was a prayer, but it was so sad that the
magpies and corncrakes went silent.

"Let me help dig. It's the least I can do," Father said.

"No." Mr. Serotsin shook his head. "We will do it — our way."
With a nod from Mr. Serotsin, the men split into two groups, each of
them carrying shovels and ropes to the farthest Jewish graves, where
they began to dig. When the first group cleared a deep trench around
a pine box, the second group worked the ropes through the large
pulleys and snatch box that had been erected over the plot. Without heavy machinery, this was the only way to pull a casket from the
ground onto the thick linen drop cloths. Then they began the slow
pull over the grass.

All this Ligita and I watched from behind the gate. It reminded
me of the times when Rudy and I were younger, watching the slow
procession of the Jewish pallbearers carrying their heavy load. The
men would take a few steps, stop, and carefully lower the coffin to let
it rest for a moment. Then they'd pick it up and carry it a few paces
more. And it was much the same way now: the men pulled the cloth
sled several meters over the grass. Then they'd stop for a moment, as
if to let the soul, tired now and perhaps disoriented, catch up with
the box.

The next afternoon, a Friday, the men of the burial society — all
ten of them — stood at the bus stop, the place in the road where the

shoulder widened a bit. The last body had been reburied. Sabbath was only a few hours away; they were anxious for the bus to take them home. Overhead, a damp tent of clouds sagged onto the tops of distant pines, making the hour seem later than it really was. Father, with his cap in his hand, waited with the men. At last the bus rounded the corner. It grumbled toward the shoulder, jerked to a stop. The old door folded open with a hiss and one by one the men filed up the steps, the youngest first until only Mr. Serotsin stood with Father.

Father touched Mr. Serotsin's sleeve. "You must believe me, we're not bad people. Not really." In his voice I heard that ancient question: *Is it enough?*

Mr. Serotsin looked at Father then turned his gaze to that dark sky lowering. "Every blade of grass is breathed upon and so blessed by the divine creator." Mr. Serotsin reached for the door grip and hoisted himself onto the lowest step. "And you've kept the grass in the old cemetery remarkably well-groomed." With that, Mr. Serotsin climbed the last steps and slowly found his seat near the front of the bus. The doors snapped shut and the bus rumbled down the lane, leaving as quickly as it had come.

CHAPTER SIX

YESTERDAY, WHILE WE WERE WALKING among the stones, liquid weight gathered in my joints. You said that our bodies are two-thirds water. I think in my case the ratio is something like three-quarters. I wonder if this is how the eels feel, both buoyed up and pressed upon by water. It's as if my body is being bent, stretched, reworked to become better suited for my next home built of a different air.

You've written about the secret lives of river rocks. Their yearnings for movement. Their dreams of an ocean of dry water. Their desire to sublime in fire, of being spun as light as ash so as to fly on the hot breath of a quaking mountain. Of liquefaction. Transformation. I think of your uncle Maris's spectacular attempts at flight, both figurative and literal. The push for a different air, for weightless buoyancy. I understand the urge. All of creation, after all, trembles and groans in anticipation of change. Some of creation groans more loudly than others. You have my sympathy.

You told me about a dream Uncle had the other day. He sat astride a camel thirty hands high and as black as ink. They crossed the dark sands of the Karakum. Uncle rode four days without a drink of water. He rode so long that the camel's fatty humps, having lost all their water, slid to its ribs and belly, where they bounced flaccidly. Even so, the camel strode across the sands without pause. Uncle was undoing the days of his life, one day per each massive stroke of the camel's legs. He had done many wrongs, Uncle. This was going to be a long ride, he realized, as his tongue swelled inside his mouth.

"It's a hurting thirst," he told you. "It can't be quenched with ordinary water."

I find it odd that Uncle has grown so vocal of late. You theorize that he is talking his way, ever so slowly, toward something like the truth. I love this generosity in you and I hope you never lose that.

And I agree with you entirely: all of this life is preparation for the journey to come. This is not to say every creature is so keen for movement. I think of your grandfather's work in the cemetery that summer I was pregnant. After all the bodies, Christian, Muslim, and Jewish had been relocated, it was time to move Old General. Father trenched around the oversize grave with Mr. Zetsche's backhoe and discovered that the wooden crate containing the equine hero had rotted through and through. All that remained: wet amber-colored wood chips that crumbled to a chalklike paste at the slightest touch. The good news: Old General looked as fine as the day he'd first been laid to rest. That is, he was just okay. Father and Rudy managed to fit Old General in a harness and sling that they attached to Mr. Zetsche's state-of-the-art winch. Five times Father put the motor in gear. Five times the sling jiggled and snapped tight, five times the winch stalled and the motor groaned. Father then looped a rope through the sling. He and Rudy and Mr. A., who enjoyed a spectacle for its own sake, all pulled and strained. Nothing. Old General didn't budge a bit.

Every attempt Father made with the winch to dislodge Old General produced an equal and opposite force. That is, Old General wouldn't budge.

"That's it." Father dropped his lead on the rope. "I'm whacked." The men went their separate ways. Rudy and Father trudged up the back steps, defeated. I drew my shades and lay on my bed. Headaches popped and fizzed like soda water. I felt as if someone had strapped a helmet of pushpins around my head. And this pain clarified my vision;

everything I saw fell into two sharp categories—colors that hurt and those that didn't. Deep green and blue soothed. Anything lighter than pigeon gray brought a low thrumming pain. Red, orange, and fuchsia—the shades of Ligita's nail varnish—were excruciating stabs of brightness and saturation. Only in the dim light of dusk, in that time of seeing but not seeing, did I find relief. In darkness the world turned to stone. The blue-silver light of the moon fell heavy inside our rooms, heavy on our bodies. Heavy on our eyelids. You swam, a fish no bigger than a grain of rice, navigating your world of water. I couldn't swim. I'd swallowed the moon. I was like Mrs. Lee's chickens that eat tiny pebbles along the lane. Without constant friction inside their gizzards, they cannot digest anything of the outer world. What they need and what they want they must crush inside themselves. This is how the world becomes knowable: in tiny broken pieces.

And then one day the stone lifted. The glaring blocks of light at the window didn't blind me. That morning I let Mrs. Arijisnikov at the post office know that I needed a job. I knew she would put the word in her husband's ear. Mr. Arijisnikov had a mobile knife-sharpening service and always knew who'd just been fired and why. Sure enough, before true nightfall, Father went down to the river with Mr. A. to fish and "take a cup of tea." That is, they were down at the water's edge sharing a bottle, a necessary procedure before, during, and after any transaction, business or otherwise.

That very afternoon Mother burst into my room. "Hurry," she said, helping me into my scrub clothes. "Mr. A. got you in with the Zetsches."

"Who?"

"Mr. Zetsche!" Mother exclaimed.

"Where?"

Mother bit her lip. "At their new manor house." Our old manor house. She was not fully resigned to the loss of the manor, I knew this. But she'd bite her lip till it bled before she said a word about it to me. "They need a cleaner who knows what a scrub brush is made for."

Mother bent and tied my shoes. She didn't have to do this for me, but her doing that so I wouldn't have to produced in me a sudden rush of emotion. I kissed Mother's cheek.

"Don't get carried away now," Mother said, handing me her best bucket and even her gloves.

The Zetsches seemed both ordinary and incredibly mysterious. Was it that they'd cleared a grove of birch to make way for their circular drive with the walnut-size chunks of rock and agate? Or was it the new miniature iron stallions lining their drive? Five horses, each no taller than a meter, anchored the verge of green lining the drive. Each horse had been cast in a different pose: one ran, one grazed, another looked as if he were nuzzling an invisible open hand while another reared on its hind legs with its forelegs scissoring the air. *Extraordinary,* I thought, trying to calculate the cost of such ornamentation. But as I made my way to the rear of the house, the place where every worker knows to go, I could not help noticing the sheer volume of bird droppings smearing the head of each horse. This struck me as exceptionally ordinary.

I rang the bell and kept my gaze on the intricate hinges, metal tongues that curled to flames. Ancient and anciently familiar, I'd seen this door many times when Rudy and I crept around the property. But in those instances, the door was a portal to our own past, a fragile invitation. Now I felt like a voyeur, an interloper eavesdropping on a conversation that had at one time included me.

A small shadow moved behind the glass pane. The door opened. Mrs. Zetsche stood there, no higher than my shoulders. She surveyed my shoes, my legs, my hand gripping the bucket and brushes. As she did, a veil of stale air, heavy with cigar smoke, hit me solidly as a slap. I blinked.

Mrs. Zetsche grimaced. "My Mr. Zetsche loves to smoke. It's not good for him, of course, but every man needs his vices." She laughed, a high-pitched twittering that settled on my shoulder. She ushered me through the rooms: the billiard room, the kitchen, the pantry, the wine cellar, the downstairs lavatory, the dining room, Mr. Zetsche's downstairs and upstairs smoking rooms, the upstairs lavatory, and her pride and joy: the indoor/outdoor conservatory where she kept Meyer lemon trees and even some pots of weedy looking bamboo. They'd renovated the interior so completely that, had I not trespassed so regularly as a girl, I would not have recognized it.

"My Mr. Zetsche had only the best glass installed for the conservatory. He knows how I love my lemons." More twittering.

I could hear how terribly Mrs. Zetsche loved Mr. Zetsche, and this spoke volumes about the kind of man he was behind closed doors. And he did give Father the slightest of raises last year when so many people died in the same month and Father had to dig like a man possessed. But as the day wore on, I realized that the Zetsches were, at least in the domestic matters of housekeeping, more ordinary than mysterious. Even though Mr. Zetsche's trousers were cut smaller than those of most men's, his clothes and bedding needed the same amount of soap and bleach as ours did. And Mr. Zetsche's bathrooms looked and smelled like any other bathroom. The only difference was where most people only had one toilet to dirty, Mr. and Mrs. Zetsche had two.

And then there were those miniature iron stallions. As I cleaned the windows, I watched the birds — pigeons and crows in the main, but even a stork from time to time — swoop low over the drive. They let loose with green spatter, spotting the drive and back steps but more often than not smearing the proud horses.

Mrs. Zetsche followed my gaze. "Every day, Inara, you must clean and polish the horses before Mr. Zetsche comes home. This"—Mrs. Zetsche held a forefinger in the air—"is why we had to let the last girl go; my Mr. Zetsche once rode a racehorse to the winner's circle and now there is nothing Mr. Zetsche dislikes more than to see an unkempt horse."

I nodded solemnly. Mrs. Zetsche handed me a soft-wire curry brush and a yellow polishing chamois.

All that week I washed sheets, sanitized bathroom sinks and commodes. I aired the gauzy sheers and heavy brocade draperies that hung floor to ceiling at the windows. I even polished Mr. Zetsche's hunting medals: a row of discs the size of gold coins that he was awarded for superior marksmanship. On the first floor, envy assailed me at every turn. Oyster spears, nutcrackers, and even the ice bucket scooped out of lunar silver caught in the act of hardening. I wanted these sleek implements that exuded elegance. I wanted the sheers and the heavy brocade at the windows, the long rectangles of oil paintings on the walls. I wanted the fine leather-bound books, the sets of encyclopedias. I wanted Mr. Z.'s gardenias forced into blooms of cobalt and calamine. I wanted the vermillion and orange Kilim floor runners that softened my every footfall.

But on the second floor, a strange unease crept over me. Despite Mr. Z.'s exhaustive renovations, from time to time I came across an old drawer pull, a door handle, or something as intangible as light streaming through a sheer that reminded me that Velta had lived here. And then there was that mirror. It was set within a cracked leather ox harness anchored to the wall. *Who puts a mirror in a harness?* I wondered, as I approached the glass, a bundle of laundry in my hands. A hush, a close stillness, descended as if I were in the presence of something hallowed. I put the laundry on a plush-backed chair. The mirror warped, wrinkled, bulged as if water had gathered behind it. Rivulets of silver upon silver ran down the glass. From behind that water a woman stared at me. *Not Velta,* I told myself. That is not Velta, her hair plaited round her head, her somber eyes gazing at me. Not her white hand, her white hand with the long white fingers beckoning me toward the glass. She is not reaching out to me from the other side; it is not her voice calling my name.

One day I came home to find Father at the kitchen table, his head resting in his hands and the trumpet of the phone out of the cradle.

I knew from the slump in Father's shoulders that it was Mr. Zetsche on the line.

"But, sir," Father said, "Old General served in one major war and lived through two occupations. Such a grand animal deserves some dignity."

"Listen." And we all did. For a small man, he had a big voice and it carried through the line and filled the room. "I have known many stubborn horses in my day. You have to take a firm hand with them — it's the only thing they respect."

Father held the trumpet of the phone away from his ear and stared at it.

After a long moment, we heard something like a whinny. "Just fill the dirt back in around the body a little. Maybe place a spray of carnations nearby. But first things first. I've set a stake to mark where I will stand and say a few words. Before everyone arrives, I want you to turn over a few shovelfuls of soil."

"Why?" Father could not contain his bewilderment.

"I'll be wearing my tall shoes," Mr. Zetsche said. "I don't want to fight with the shovel."

The rain fell all night and through the next morning, but by the time of the groundbreaking ceremony, the clouds stretched and lifted. The sky was still gray, but a lighter, brighter gray. Pearl gray Stanka called it, sniffing at the sky with suspicion. As we approached the emptied cemetery, now the future site of the Riviera, I had my eyes and thoughts trained on the soil. This ground had been broken many times, of course — during the wars, during the occupations — but history seemed of no consequence to Mr. Zetsche, a man with his eyes cast toward the future.

On principle, half the town did not participate in the festivities. In those days, Mother still cleaned for Dr. Netsulis, who became famous for once engineering a cow with five stomachs instead of four. Now he spent most of his time making messes in his home laboratory. On principle, he did not attend community events. The Ilm-yens stayed shut up inside their house, tighter than green walnuts. Even Babel wasn't at the fence. As chief caretaker, Father had to at least make an appearance beneath the dark alders. But the rest of us couldn't resist. We had nothing better to do. Girls wearing foil costumes greeted us all, handing out cigars to the men and sleek silver-wrapped Laima chocolates to the women. Mr. Zetsche, in his tall shoes, smiled benevolently. He gripped a gold-plated shovel in one hand and a microphone in the other. He held the shovel over a patch of freshly turned earth as if it were a talisman, a compass, a bit of enchantment. And then he talked. And talked. Father gazed wistfully at the gold-plated shovel, but I found myself unable to look anywhere else but at Mr. Zetsche's neck, in particular his Italy-shaped birthmark that burned as brightly as red wine on his face. At one point, when he spoke again of the prosperity we'd all enjoy with the advent of the Zetsche Riviera, the toe portion of the birthmark knocked against his Adam's apple.

"Motivation is when dreams roll up their sleeves and get to work!" Mr. Zetsche pronounced, raising the shovel high and giving it a shake. That was the cue and the band struck a triumphant tune. Mr. Zetsche turned his back to the river, thrust the head of the shovel into the dirt Father had prepared for him, and tossed aside a shovelful of dirt. And another shovelful. And then another.

"Well, he has a strong work ethic," Mr. Gipsis observed.

"But no sense of pacing," said old Mr. Vehovskis, who in his youth was forced by the Cheka to dig a mass grave. "Look at him go!"

Inspired by his own words, Mr. Zetsche seemed determined to single-handedly carve out of the ground his beautiful dream Riviera; he just wouldn't stop shoveling. And shoveling. Busy digging and dreaming, Mr. Zetsche had not noticed how soft the ground was in places, how during his speech the water was carrying away his property chunk by chunk. Had Mr. Zetsche been aware of these things, perhaps he would have taken a break, perhaps he would not have kept digging so close to Old General. And with such vigor.

We all saw it coming: a bad idea growing like an abscess, worse by the second. But we were collectively powerless, not a single one of us able to caution, to warn, to shout what we knew we should: "Stop! No more! Not another shovelful!"

Finally, Mr. Zetsche leaned on the shovel and wiped his brow. At this precise moment, Old General, freed at last from the mud, swam away. From where we stood that's how it looked: Old General's head and neck bobbing in the water, the front half of his body remarkably buoyant.

Father shook his head slowly from side to side. Mr. Arijisnikov whistled long and low. "No, no!" Mrs. Zetsche waved her arms as if instructing Old General to turn back to shore. The band struck up another tune, something that sounded like a military dirge.

A smile slowly spread over Mr. Zetsche's face, the kind one wears when one has discovered he's just stepped in soft poop. He clapped his hands and the band stopped, all but the trumpeter whose final note wilted obscenely in the air.

"Well, well." Mr. Zetsche brushed imaginary dirt from his hands. "Let's dance!"

Hearing her cue, Mrs. Gepkars, dripping in magenta faux ostrich feathers, emerged from behind the band. She'd been hired to teach us a new dance, and in honor of this event, she'd dyed her hair an oily purple, the shade and luster of mussel shells. She had also wound her hair into tight curls, all held in place with a multitude of metal pins. As she glided over the makeshift dance floor, large squares of plywood set on the mud, the wan afternoon light made it seem as if she had pinned tiny purple sausages to her scalp. Even this might have passed without notice if not for the fact that Mrs. Gepkars, a woman of ample body, had upholstered herself in an evening gown two sizes too small. Squeezed by the whale-bone armor of her unforgiving corset, her bosom resembled two cantaloupes buttressed to the point of bursting. In vain Mrs. Gepkars crooked her finger and tried to convince one after another of the young men, and the older ones, too, to be her partner. "For educational purposes," she said, again and again. Calculating the risks involved, the likelihood of bodily injury, they politely declined down to the man.

The Merry Afflictions kept on with the tune and then started another. And still, except for Mrs. Gepkars, and Miss Dzelz, who had graciously assumed the male role of dance partner — for educational purposes — no one danced.

Then, in small mincing movements, Mr. and Mrs. Zetsche took the floor. A baffled hush fell upon us as we watched them. It wasn't that they were such great dancers; we simply had nowhere else to place our focus. And that, I suppose, was a part of the trouble; with nowhere else to look, we looked even more intently at the Zetsches, who danced as if this life were a waltz meant for them alone, this entire town their dance floor.

From two of Rudy's friends standing nearby came low grumblings. From behind us, the tensile murmurs of unrestrained resentment. "Hard to believe," Mrs. Inkis whispered, "that Mrs. Zetsche's had been a farming family, Latvian and poor." Another female voice: "And who is he, to come back so long after the troubles? Who is he to tell us how to live?" The unguarded envy in those voices — unmistakable. The Merry Afflictions doubled their efforts, tried to make the tune livelier. Still, we could not stop staring at the Zetsches.

Could the Zetsches discern our growing resentments? Did they regret the ignoble loss of Old General? It's hard to say. But by the next morning, they had already left in their Mercedes. As they believed in taking continental vacations, they'd be gone a good six weeks, touring the Swedish islands, competing in shooting matches, Mrs. Zetsche explained in a note she'd left for me.

You'll be our chief housesitter. Therefore, with the exception of polishing the horses in the drive or taking meals with your family, we expect that you'll spend most of your time inside the house. Please launder your own sheets. Also, limit your use of the downstairs bathroom. No more than two flushes per day. We are conserving.

So it's true; for a time I lived in the Zetsche manor. And it's true; I have always been curious, perhaps to a fault. I wanted to know who those people were whose likenesses graced the walls in enormous portraits: our family or theirs? To whom did some of these items belong and what else might be hidden in the walls, up the chimneys?

Without Mrs. Zetsche buzzing about the house, time moved like slow viscous water, one drop at a time. One spoon. A fork. A pass of the mop. I thought about David. I tried not to feel sorry for myself, told myself that because he was already gone I could never lose him.

I had time to think about what kind of a person I wanted to be for my baby. I did not want to be the kind of mother who smothered her child and called it love. I wanted to believe that the kind of love I had for you could be limitless and that the more I loved, the more I would learn of love and be able to keep loving. But I wondered, as I rubbed that silver and caught slices of myself in the shiny metal, could this kind of love even exist? Was it possible for two people, a man and a woman, say, or a woman and her child, to love with this more perfect love? I looked at my stomach. Yes, I decided. It had to be possible.

I sang to you in my belly as I cleaned. I cleaned the upstairs, avoiding the mirror in the corridor. I worked clockwise through the rooms, the way Mother had taught me. She'd also taught me to work top to bottom, dusting and polishing first, laundering second, disinfecting basins and showers third, and scrubbing and waxing floors last. This was good for the body, she believed, as it was natural to start the day upright and then, as gravity took its toll, finish on one's hands and knees.

One day, I made a minor discovery in the cellar: wedged between planking, pages and pages of musical scores. Imagine: a house built of song! Song springing out of every gap in the wall, floor, joists. Dark melodies rose and fell, penned in what I recognized as Velta's hand, her script leaning hard to the left.

It was wrong to do this; the house was no longer ours, nothing in it ours. But I rolled up those pages of scores, took them home. How Mother would have liked to see them, I knew. But I kept them to myself. It was a way to hurt her a little. I didn't like that I had this meanness in me, but I did and I hadn't quite forgiven her for that slap, for her words. Each letter of each word was a dark note, another bird flying, skipping, stuttering across the measures, those lines that look like telephone wires. By this time, I had learned to read music well enough to decipher that certain musical notes corresponded to certain letters of the alphabet. I made a chart. The first letter of the alphabet, *a*, corresponded to the middle a note above middle c. The letter *b* corresponded with the b note, and so on. The letter *j* corresponded with the high a note, *k* with the b note and so on until every letter of the alphabet had its partner on the musical scores. I congratulated myself; not every girl is so clever. But my triumph was short-lived when I read what I had decoded.

We had wallpaper. So we boiled it and made a broth of glue and fiber. Our thoughts stuck together. We ate flecks of paint. Colors bloomed brightly in our dreams.

We had pots. So we put our tears in them. We scooped up our sorrow, ladled it out, filled our children's stomachs with our salt. To the hungry, every bitter thing is sweet.

Those words were dark blots of ink against snow, darkness flung against light. What did I know of hunger? A chicken and an onion stretched over a week. Sure. But a gnawing in the gut that drove people to eat binding glue and the tongues of shoes? Never. And sorrow?

I had only waded up to my hips in it. I was not the sojourner Velta was. Maybe this is why I couldn't understand what I read. Perhaps certain experiences can only be articulated and known through hyperbole, euphemism. Maybe this was yet another code, a more difficult language of metaphor and emotion that I might never learn to crack.

"The black snake," she wrote, "burrows in the dark bed of the river." Her first pregnancy she described as an ocean. She swallowed the tides and rocks bumped along the floor of her stomach. The goat at the neighbor's farm had eaten rotten potatoes and had died. The post office had been repainted. A neighbor's laundry line that used to hold all sizes of shirts and socks now hung limp. She seemed compelled to catalogue the world outside her back door, the world down the lane, what could be seen through her leaded bull's-eye windowpanes: a man, a dog, a transport truck. Conjuring her world one small word at a time as if to say *This exists, this, and this.* To keep her words a private matter between husband and wife, she'd written these observations of the ordinary in musical code. But the significance that these quotidian observations held for the two of them eluded me. That was the second code she employed. Cloaking importance in the mundane. Wrapping a layer of ambiguity around the words so that no amount of scrutiny revealed a clear message.

Old Widow Druviete had crossed the veil. We opened all the windows and doors so that her soul could come and go as it wanted. We placed her body in the washing chair, her feet in a tub of water. We washed her with three long cloths. Afterward, we buried her. We burned her clothes; we burned the washcloths. We pounded a nail into the floor where the chair had been and bathed it in brandy.

I suppose she was re-creating a world for her husband, a quiet world he'd recognize, a world of old traditions and customs she did not want him to forget. And stories.

A man who'd been turned by a witch into a wolf ran out onto the road. We could tell because of his eyes. He wept at his fate. He could not remember the blessing that would turn him back into a man. So we gave him a bit of bread, because it is the Christian thing to do. He ate all the bread. He bit our hands; he lunged for our necks. He howled and said ungodly things. But we kept feeding him and feeding him until his stomach burst.

In handwriting belonging to neither Velta nor Ferdinands was something like a *daina*.

> *One girl sings in the river.*
> *One girl sings from the stone.*
> *Both sing the same song.*
> *Could they be daughters of the same mother?*

When the swifts dove from the lower limbs of the birch and burst from the eaves, signaling evening's approach, I put away the cleaning things, tucked that music inside my coat, and headed homeward. The house was dark except for a sliver of light from the back room. I heard Mother speaking. "This happens sometimes. A little bleeding is normal." I pushed open the door and saw Mother leaning over Ligita and dabbing at her brow with a wet cloth. Ligita lay on the bed, her face chalk white and her hair stuck to the sides of her face. A small dark blot of red stained her bedsheets. When Mother saw me, she drew Ligita close. I pulled the sheets off the bed, set pots of water to boil in the kitchen.

Sometime in the night, Ligita shrieked. A solid wall of sound that pushed every other noise out of the house. The house went utterly still, as if it were holding its breath. "Inara!" Mother shouted. "Come quickly!"

I grabbed some clean towels and rolled Ligita toward the wall.

More blood and this time something else: a baby smaller than two pats of butter. Mother touched the baby once with the tip of her finger then wrapped it in a towel. I put the bundle under my shirt, holding Ligita's baby to my chest where my heart pounded. I thought maybe my heart would be warm enough and strong enough to beat for this baby, too. Rudy and Father met me on the back steps. I gave the bundle to Rudy and we made the short trek to the cemetery.

Sometimes I forgot how intuitive Father was, how much he understood without saying a word. Already he had dug a hole, small and deep, not far from where our uncle Maris lay. Already he had found a small wooden box, the same shape and size as a cake box. Rudy held the lid and I placed the small bundle inside.

"Shall we sing for this little one?" Father asked.

Rudy's gaze was glued to the box. "No," he said, and turned for home.

After your auntie's little one passed, darkness set up residence inside your uncle Rudy. He did not speak often, and when he did, it was to complain or make a sarcastic comment. He brought home a TV and watched it for hours on end. Sometimes he'd go out at night and not return for days. Your auntie would have drowned in her own tears if not for your grandmother. While I worked at the Zetsches', your grandmother looked after Ligita. By look after I mean to say she put her to work. It was the best way to manage grief: putting up vegetables, laundering sheets and towels, digging a new root cellar. This is how Ligita learned the *dainas* her own mother hadn't taught her: your grandmother at her elbow reciting the words, keeping time with her fist as she beat dough for bread.

For the next five weeks I kept on at the Zetsches', scrubbing the heads of the small stallions until they gleamed. One day Father came by to visit me. Mr. Zetsche's spare car, another Mercedes—this one soot gray—was parked on the drive. I could read in Father's eyes how badly he wanted to drive this auxiliary Mercedes with the faux-leather bonnet, clean now from the grille to the side vents to the spoiler, the interior fumigated with an ozone box and each tiny slat of the air vents in the dash swabbed with cotton-tipped swabs, every surface loved by a golden chamois. But Father had his dignity. Father touched the chrome molding tentatively. He thought for a moment then opened the driver's-side door. "I just want to sit inside. For a minute. Or two." He slid into the leather seat, inhaled deeply. He ran a fingertip along the dash and then recoiled as if he'd received a shock. The gold key dangled from the ignition. Powerless against such temptation, Father turned the key. The ignition fired, the engine hummed—a smooth liquid sound of a well-oiled machine.

Father turned a knob at the end of the shifter and the windshield wipers swished up and down. Up and down. Then he turned on the radio and a Wagnerian opera commenced. It was a sledgehammer of sound disguised as orchestral music. Father twisted the knob gently and found Sibelius on another station.

"Sit with me," Father said. I opened the passenger's door and slid in beside Father. We inhaled the rich leather scent of good breeding. We watched the precise synchronization of the windshield wipers. Father's hand trembled at the shifter then fell to his lap. He shook his head. "I can't—it wouldn't be right." He opened the door and climbed out, leaving the keys in the ignition, the engine running.

I sat in the car alone and listened to the plaintive strains of violins and the swishing of the wipers. I studied Father's stooped form. I thought about him, about Mother. I thought about the things each one of us had wished we had done in our short lives. And then I thought of our many compromises. We settle too quickly, our gazes falling lower and lower, until we forget our small dreams and then, worse, we forget how to dream at all.

It shouldn't be this way, I decided, as I slid over the shifter into the driver's seat. I ran my hands over the cherrywood steering wheel; I would do what Father told himself he couldn't. It was the least I could do. I switched the radio back to the furious Valkyries. Transmission in gear, I pressed the pedal.

The car shot down the drive into the first miniature stallion. *Clank,* then a loud *lug, lug,* a shrieking whine as cast-iron hind legs tore at the undercarriage. Then *clunk-clunk* as the back tires rolled free of the fallen beast. *Clank, lug, lug, scree, clunk-clunk* as I plowed rank-and-file over every horse. Finally, the drive shaft of the Mercedes high centered on the raised front legs of the last stallion.

Father opened the driver's-side door. "Inara!" he gasped, pulling me from the seat. We stood and surveyed the carnage. Steam hissed from beneath the crumpled hood. Father rocked on his feet. He doubled over. He roared with laughter.

"Oh, Inara." Father clutched his sides. "If only your uncle Maris could have seen this!" Father rested his hands on his knees and waited for his breath to return.

I handed Father the keys. And then I went to Mrs. Zetsche's linen closet and found her oldest sheets, one for each of Mr. Zetsche's black stallions.

"I'll be fired," I said.

"Oh." Father rubbed his chin. "Most certainly."

"I should look for another job."

Father put a hand on each of my shoulders.

"Time for that later. I'll help you lock up. Then you can come home. We miss you at the dinner table."

A few days later, the Zetsches returned from their continental vacation. The battered Mercedes we had pushed into their garage. The fallen horses lay shrouded in Mrs. Zetsche's sheets. When popping gravel announced the Zetsches' arrival, your grandfather and I stood on the drive like soldiers awaiting inspection. Slowly they passed the draped figures until they reached the garage. Mr. Zetsche climbed out of the car and stood for a moment studying the battered and broken Mercedes. Then he walked to the drive where he stood before each toppled sculpture, lifting the sheet quickly then letting it fall. All this time, Mrs. Zetsche, in shock, sat trembling in the car, murmuring, "Oh dear, oh dear."

"About the horses," Father began.

"Yes — vandals, pranksters — I presume."

"No."

"Who then?"

Father contemplated Mr. Zetsche's shoes. "It was an accident. We thought —"

"We? Who is we?"

"Inara and I."

"Thought what?"

"Thought it wouldn't be such a bad thing to drive such a wonderful car. Just for a bit, you see."

Mr. Zetsche waved his hand at the crumpled vehicle. "It was a repossessed vehicle. It wasn't worth a pop. But the horses, you see, are a little more, er, problematic."

"We will pay for all repairs," Father said. "How much do you think we'll owe?"

A smile devoid of any warmth surfaced on Mr. Z.'s mouth; the Italy-shaped birthmark deepened to a brilliant maroon. "Hundreds upon hundreds upon hundreds — as many needles on a hundred pine trees." An indigestible sum. With that, Mr. Zetsche spun on his small heels and marched back inside his mansion.

CHAPTER SEVEN

I USED TO MEASURE TIME by how long it would take to wash, dry, and stack dishes. Hang laundry. There was never enough time for all the work to be done. That there is so much of it now stretching the ends of days while simultaneously Dr. N. tells me I've only a few weeks left is a strange conundrum. If your grandfather was here, I would ask him about this fluid time I'm living in and if it is how I am being prepared for the next life. Is this how, I'd like to ask, God sets eternity in our hearts and each thump from that wet engine pushes us just that much closer to the threshold?

At any rate, I've decided not to count the hours between doses. Instead, I will measure the change in light around me. Between the cracks of the jamb and door, roof and wall, light leaks in, a grainy dust swirling in viscous air, a galaxy of swimming stars. You are quite right: light is both wave and particle, I can see this now. This light pulses in my veins like electricity, febrile and alive. Insistent. I lie here and listen to you and Little Semyon working in the kitchen on the temperance newspaper. The clacking of the metal strikers sooting the paper becomes one and the same thing with the wild rye rubbing its rough stalks against the shed. The rattle of words is music to me, percussion to my rambling thought. This is how perception shifts and the ordinary becomes something hallowed and sacred.

· · ·

I managed to get up and about without you today. I went to the cemetery. I wanted to watch you work. I passed Mother's stone, Father's, Uncle Maris's. My stomach wanted to head north, my bowels south, so I sat on the wall to let myself recalibrate. It was a trick of the morphine, making me believe that I had my former strength. I made it to that wall and there I stayed.

> In the pine woods
> My rye has been sown.
> In the pine woods
> Are my hollowed oak trees.
> The rye blooms, the bees hum.
> I am beside myself with joy

This is the *daina* I wanted to sing. Instead, spent and winded, I sat on the wall and waited. Patience is the other half of courage, Joels used to say. Or, in my case, it is the accidental product of my foolishness. I had it in mind that we would sit, you and I, on this wall and listen to dusk spool up from the ground. We'd listen to dark wicker down in gnat and needle. Instead, it was Little Semyon who came along and—thankfully—saw me here. He carried me to our house as easily as if I were a child.

"Don't ever do that again!" Jutta scolded. I laughed. Long and loud. Where did this laughter come from? It may be the effects of the painkillers, but I'd like to think that at last I am laying hold of joy, which is not the same thing as happiness—a capricious feeling as flimsy as thought itself.

Anyway, while in the cemetery, I touched up Uncle's stone. What's left of it. I thought maybe if I sat quietly enough I would hear his voice as you do. I sang: *Soul awaken, soul arise, soul push that stone away.* That his long and relatively quiet dormancy should be broken—and so noisily, so urgently—in these last few weeks has been a puzzle to me. My theory is that he's been chattering away all along, but it is only now that he's saying anything of importance.

Hell, he said, was to be abandoned to yourself, left utterly alone with your own self-awareness and memories. "Not quite what I had expected," Uncle said. "This singularity of self. It's one thing to maintain this position while alive and amid others. Quite another thing to do so when dead, and"—here, you say, he paused significantly—"all by oneself."

Why, you have wondered, did I name you after such a cantankerous man? David, Joels, Eriks, Oskars, these are all good, strong, and worthy names belonging to good, strong, and worthy men. And you know how a name binds together the bearers as a loop, a link from past to present. I suppose it was an act of faith, my belief in the redemptive power of language, my belief that the boy might redeem the man. It isn't correct Baptist doctrine, this idea that the action of the living can influence the soul of the dead. But the belief that names carry inherent power is.

I imagine you're right. This must have been about the time when I stopped reading Velta's letters. I should have given the letters, those I read and those yet to be decoded, to Mother. I should have done a lot of things. Instead, I hid them and told myself I was justified in doing so. We had plenty of other concerns, and those letters seemed a small thing at the time compared to my larger wrongdoing, what Mr. Zetsche termed *assault, battery, and willful violation of possessions most precious*. It took all of Father's savings to pay for the damage to Mr. Zetsche's car. Some good news: after a thorough examination, Mr. Zetsche determined that his miniature cast-iron stallions came through the fray with minimal damage. All they needed was to be reinserted into the ground. And so Mr. Z. had Father dig deep holes ("You're good at that!" Mr. Zetsche joked over the phone). Then Rudy and Father reseated the horses on their pedestals and anchored them into the wet concrete. Mr. Zetsche was so impressed that he hired Rudy on the Riviera project as a surveyor's assistant. It would be Rudy's job to shoot lines and distances with a theodolite. When the trucks came with the crushed rock and cement mix, he could then tell them how much was needed and where.

Though she was not happy, probably would never be happy, Ligita took some consolation in his wages. The job paid well enough for her to buy blouses so sheer that we could read Mother's newspaper through them. Rudy gave to Mother and Father the money left over from Ligita's shopping. And how they needed it. Mother's hands had turned so red and raw that when she tried to scrub the floor or wash a dish blood wept through her skin. She could no longer keep house for her clients in the city. I don't think she minded — she wanted to spend more time with her paper. Quite a lot had been happening politically and economically. Parties were merging, new scandals were being revealed and there was lots of talk about the EU. If Latvia joined, as other countries had, Mother speculated that emigration would go through the roof, as all the good jobs were elsewhere. That was bad. On the other hand, instead of ten drunks lying about in a ditch, we'd have only two. That was good. Then there was the matter of carrots. Would the quality of imported vegetables decline or improve? As writer, editor in chief, and publisher, Mother was having a hard time keeping up. And so, as she had done for so many years, I made her rounds cleaning the hall, the school, and for the elusive genius Dr. Netsulis.

He was by far Mother's favorite client. He never patronized her, never pretended to be interested in her personal life, her temperance newspaper, or our family. Nor did he seem, she said, to expect her to display undue admiration for his many smart inventions such as the automatic venetian-blind cleaners and candlewick trimmers, both of which commanded brisk business in Sweden. It was a working relationship and Mother preferred it that way.

"But to be frank, he wore me out, that one," Mother confided to me the night before I was to make my first visit. It seemed that furniture, on principle, didn't like him. In the days when Mother cleaned for him, she often witnessed his stumbling into chairs, tables, wardrobes, setting off a crash of dishes, an explosion of glass test tubes. The genius walk, Mother called it. Her advice: get out of the way or follow with a mop and bucket at the ready. It was also Mother's conviction that the smarter her employers, the sloppier their bathrooms and kitchens. "They can't help it," Mother said. "Pondering all those intricate thoughts, they are utterly distracted."

From the looks of Dr. Netsulis's manor house, a three-story stone structure set in a boggy hollow, his intricate thoughts were of a phenomenal sort. I determined right off that I would need to devote two days a week — maybe three — just to set the kitchen and mudroom in order. While I cleaned, I made rhymes of the names of ingredients. I inserted lines from *dainas,* sang songs, moved around little pieces of sound, rubbing them into Dr. Netsulis's transparent glassware. I told myself that you could hear me. As small as you were, you were listening.

On week three, as I cleaned the first-floor hallway, Dr. Netsulis burst from his lab and stumbled into my oversize mop bucket. One foot tangled in the wringer and one foot on solid ground, he stood and puzzled over my appearance. And I puzzled over his. In those days he was as thin as a rake's handle. He looked like a big wind might carry him off, which is probably why he had such heavy looking glasses — standard genius impedimenta designed to anchor his brains in place. A speckled film of dandruff, a constellation of stars, coated the lenses. And then there was the matter of his snow-white beard, as long as a goat's and thick. Somewhere behind it was a mouth. And then the mouth appeared, a small dark circle.

"You're not Biruta Kalnins," he said at last.

"No. I'm Inara, her daughter."

"Oh. I didn't know she had a daughter." He took in my work clothes, my hands, my work shoes — canvas sneakers with cracked sides. A look of kindly abstraction settled over his features. He withdrew his foot from the bucket and motioned me toward his lab. The door to the lab stood ajar; the smell of cherry-flavored cigar smoke filled the hall. A quick glance beyond his shoulder revealed two long tables, shoals of test tubes and glass microscope slides, all of them dirty.

Dr. Netsulis followed my gaze. "Ordinarily — you can even ask your mother about this — I keep a clean house." A slight twinge of shame crept into his voice. "But I'm in the thick of a new top-secret project called Joyous Bovines."

"Bovines," I repeated dully.

"Terrific animals, cows," Dr. Netsulis said. "But you needn't worry yourself about them. My assistant, Joels, feeds and milks them. But if you wouldn't mind mucking out the stalls every now and again . . ." he said, bowing slightly and vanishing into his cherry-smoke-filled lab.

Dr. Netsulis was a quiet man and simple in his habits. Breakfast was always curd cheese over porridge, a meal, he said, that kept his brain from falling to distraction. He needed to keep his wits about him; he had five different dairy farms to study. It was his hypothesis that the atmosphere and general conviviality of a barn and pasture directly influenced the flavor and quality of the milk a cow produces. To this end, he made copious notes regarding the color of paint inside the barns, the type of music piping from the radio, and the quality of jokes the milkers told in the presence of the cows. And, of course, he collected a colossal number of milk samples in test tubes, all of which needed cleaning.

Spring arrived on the ground and above it simultaneously. The bark of the birches peeled and trembled with every breeze. The shedding bark looked like tissue paper upon which long and short dashes, dots and lines, had been branded. These slender gashes on the tissuelike bark were like Velta's letters, silent music composed of scars. The catkins dripped gold. The ferns steadily unfurled their green standards as if to say that there was no stopping life. The storks returned in droves to their enormous nests atop the telephone poles. Violent windstorms shook the boughs of trees, upended old birches, and lifted roofs from barns. But those nests, amazing feats of architecture built of twig and mud, held fast. As light stretched the ends of the days, the construction crews worked longer hours at the Riveria. First grading and leveling. Compacting. Then slab after slab of concrete. Footings, of course, to receive hardware that would anchor walls, the studs, and the supports. Then the framing. A strange numb exultation seized the town. We were watching our economic salvation emerge one wooden joist and beam at a time. But it was slim consolation. Once the framing went up, Mr. Z. gave Rudy the boot.

When women experience a sudden loss, your grandmother said, they blame themselves. When men suffer loss, they blame the entire world. Judging by the dull flinty look in Rudy's eyes, the set of his jaw, I understood that his grief had clarified to anger and resentment toward Mr. Zetsche. The same suppressed rage that I had seen on Uncle Maris's face now settled over Rudy's.

Mother turned her attentions, predictably, to the hall. A sanctuary, a strong tower in the time of tempest, the hall gave her the quietude she could not find at home. Noise was all we had from Rudy and Ligita, who argued steadily. Ligita's voice droned like a bagpipe, blaring with constant sound and volume. The key points of her complaints had to do with their living arrangements—she wanted to live in subsidized housing, something other young couples were doing. But Rudy's abrupt dismissal ruined their chances for applying.

To escape the nighttime noise, Father retreated to the dry toilet, magazines about sleek German automobiles tucked under his arm. I believe it was at this time that Father had some kind of crisis of faith. He no longer drank and he spent more time reading the Bible. In the morning, I'd hear him working long passages forward and backward. This was something his father and his grandfather had done in Vorkuta, but also when they returned home. Knowing the Bible by heart was part of being Baptist. Verse by verse he worked himself toward a personal revelation. Now that he was going to be a grandfather he had to consider what kind of example he would set. And so, out the bottles went to the woodpile, where he tucked them as tenderly as nostalgia.

At this time, my ability to separate one part of me from the other part of me grew. An imaginary zipper ran from crown of head to sole of foot. I could, as I walked down the lane, unzip myself, step outside of my body corseted in flesh. The spirit part of me hovered at the elbow, documenting the toilets I cleaned, the linens I washed. The spirit part of me imagined she was Velta, she was Mother, she was every woman, any woman. She imagined she had tilled lime into dark soil. She imagined she was one of those women along the A2 holding hands in the Baltic Chain. The A2 is a long highway running from the capital of Estonia to the capital of Lithuania. Along some lonely stretches, there weren't enough people to stand shoulder to shoulder. So they strung sashes between them. They made an unbroken chain of fabric and song. While I cleaned, I sang. The body part of me and the spirit part of me agreed that my voice was the sash binding you to me. After work, I sat at the piano in our little shed and tapped the keys, struck hammers on those strings, put pencil to paper to coax forth Velta's dark parables. Water will not always love us, my dear. The rocks groan beneath our feet, keeping time in low sighs. And I congratulated myself for every note, felt certain I was a little less ordinary for this effort.

These elevated feelings soon evaporated. As I returned home from cleaning the school or from Dr. Netsulis's, I'd make my way to the river, to a lonely stretch that was not part of Mr. Zetsche's Riveria development. Our river was changing. Construction debris littered the grassy shallows. The wailing of buzz saws and the steady pounding of hammers assaulted our quiet. How altered the lay of the land was near the water. Gone that choice fishing snag, gone the eel. One evening I walked near the new construction. Another alder had been felled. I ran my hand over the stump. Rough and inexpertly cut, it snagged on my chapped skin. It was bad luck to chop down a tree. But if the crew was worried, they didn't show it. At the present moment, two men were contemplating a series of vandalized joists decorated with loud graffiti: KRAUT GET OUT!

There was a time, you wrote in your Book of Wonder, when the faithful walked by sound, not by sight. Having no open vision, people relied upon prophets who could hear the word of the Lord, as a man hears a friend whispering into his ear. Such a man was Samuel. Nowhere in the old accounts do we have a physical description of those ears. No measurements. But his hearing was fierce. This, you contended, was because no razor passed over his head. Like Samson, the strongman of old whose long hair was the source of his power, Samuel's hair was his strength, the reason for his incredible ability. Reading this in your book, I have made two conclusions. First, you have drawn connections between yourself, Samuel, and our national icon, the Bear Slayer. Your grandmother would be delighted. Second, I understand that you have not quite forgiven me for delousing and shaving the fur on your ears. I am sorry. The fur looked a little natty and it seemed a good idea at the time.

This morning Stanka turned the ox-harness mirror to the wall. As you may or may not recall, she has strong opinions about mirrors. No problem to bury the dead with small ones, she said, but is it bad luck to have one near the dying? Colossal! Fooled by the pale world returned in the glass, souls fly into the mirror and are trapped. Being stuck, unable to free themselves but fully conscious of the world of the living, they *tap, tap, tap* on the glass with their long fingernails.

You tell me that at the root of the word *mirror* is miracle or wonder. I have always believed in miracles. I credit your grandfather for this unshakable belief that the inexplicable, unbidden, and wholly wondrous can and does occur. And I believe in blessings. You cannot be wondrously healed if you haven't first been terribly wounded. Doesn't the pelican in the wild places pluck her breast and nourish her young upon a freshet of blood? you asked in your book. You drew a picture of a bird brooding over her nest. Doleful eyes of the Madonna, motherly torment in the long neck folded toward her clutch. It is she, not her brood, whose heart has been pierced. It is, after all, a mother's way to bleed for her children. We can't help ourselves. We spend our youth wondering what we were made for, holding ourselves in, storing up every good thing. And then, in that moment we apprehend life outside of ourselves — perhaps in a child, say — we willingly bare our breasts so that our hearts can walk outside of it. Where does this heart walk? Inside that child. This is a story about where love comes from and that is a story that has no beginning and no end. It's a story that has a thousand versions, all of them true.

In those days I cleaned for Dr. N., he was something of a celebrity abroad. In September he went to a scientific conference in Geneva. He chattered on and on about a subatomic particle called Higgs. I thought it was cute that scientists named itty-bitty things that no one could see. Maybe someone would name a subatomic particle after Dr. N. Then he'd get a fat grant and we'd all eat butter on our bread and drink pricey cognac. Meanwhile, I cleaned and mucked. Dr. Netsulis's new assistant, Joels, sometimes had to leave the barn to run tests in the lab. I always knew he was inside the house because Joels was very careful to leave his muddy boots — the largest I'd ever seen — in the mudroom. I liked to put my boots next to his and imagine that while we worked our boots carried on lengthy discussions. Like I did, Joels preferred to work unobserved, and so I timed my visits to the stalls to coincide with his visits to the lab. I didn't want him to think I was some kind of stalker. If he appreciated my keeping my distance, I knew he'd never say so. Joels was from Estonia and therefore uncommonly quiet. He had hair the color of rust and in certain slants of light his beard looked like a finely bristled brush of copper. But every now and then, as I left the barn for the mudroom or he left the lab for the barn, we'd catch sight of each other. And then he'd smile — just a quick flash — and then it was gone. Such a smile from an Estonian meant only one thing. He liked me. A little anyway.

When Dr. Netsulis returned from Stockholm, Joels and I, each of us forgetting our reserve, rushed to help him with his suitcases. Dr. N. took one look at me. His caterpillar eyebrows jumped.

"My God, Inara, you've gotten fat!"

I bit my lip, looked at Dr. N.'s bags. I could not bear to look at Joels.

"I'm pregnant."

"Oh. Of course. That explains it, then. I can see that now, it's as obvious as an axiom."

Joels reached for the bags, his gaze glued to his shoes.

The next day, Dr. N. ushered me into his lab. "How would you like to work for me — full-time?" He scratched his beard. "Yes. Mornings you come and do housework. Afternoons you can clean in the lab."

"I'm not good at science," I said.

Dr. Netsulis nodded at my bucket of bleach. "You handle chemicals every day. That's science. But, please, wear gloves — always. And from now on, let Joels do the mucking." As I had at the Zetsches' manor, I cleaned the top floor and worked my way down. In the afternoons I washed glassware in the lab and mopped the floor. From my lowly position, I had an excellent view of Joels's oversize feet. I admired the care with which he lifted beakers and stirred solutions, each movement calibrated so that he never expended more energy than necessary. And he was mindful of where he put his huge feet, never treading over the places I had just mopped.

One afternoon I watched as Joels made his observations and wrote down notes, ever so slowly working his way to where I stood at the oversize metal sink. Joels stole a glance at my hands.

"I imagine you are a busy person with many, er, friends and passionate interests," he said.

"I'm not busy and I have absolutely no friends or passionate interests," I said. Better to tell the truth, no matter how pathetic. Joels smiled. His gaze had now traveled to my knees. "As it so happens, I know a good jazz café. We could"—now his gaze had reached my stomach—"have tea or something."

We met at a café where I drank tea and Joels downed a beer in good Estonian fashion. He did not approve of drinking in theory, he said between gulps. But in practice he drank. "To thank God that I am not a drunk," he said. And this made perfect sense to me. For a time, after Uncle died, Father had battled with the bottle. This is how his grief worked its way from the heart through the body. It did not necessarily make a man a drunk.

"Why did you ask me out?"

Joels glanced briefly at my face. "You have very nice patellas and clearly you are a hard worker." It was, I knew, almost a profession of love. "Anyway, why did you accept?"

"You have enormous feet and you are a very hard worker," I said.

I am glad that you kept your self-portrait. Moses had his stutter. Paul had his thorn in his side. You have your ears. A curse, a blessing. You have been teased, persecuted. Burdened with more than one person should ever have to hear. And the family tree. That was a burden, too.

You did your best to complete it in spite of my failures, my omissions. Digressions. During many chats, I've set forth certain facts and observations about your grandfather, your grandmother, your uncle

Rudy, even your great-uncle Maris. You must have noticed how little I've said about David, and now I'm telling you about your stepfather, Joels. A sloppy genealogy. Where to start and with whom? I've given you the key to the hall. And now these strange objects around which every story seems to revolve: the shovel, the letters, the mirror. There are, of course, people and things that ought to be here and aren't. Your father, David, for one. You asked when you were younger what he looked like and I said, *Look in the mirror.* This you did for a solid hour or more. *What did you see?* I wondered. Your eyes, not gray but silver and luminous, are just like your grandmother Biruta's. Your square jaw—that I gave you. But your ears! You stood and pondered your reflection. You ran your index finger over the rims of each auricle so carefully, with such awe. The wonderstruck expression on your face reminded me of an infant in that moment it discovers its own hands. But I keep losing the thread of the story. You wanted to know how Joels and I became a couple. I think you are really asking why we became a couple.

He was solid and sturdy. He would not vanish. He would not leave me. You asked me what love looks like, and I can tell you that love is choosing to stay when one has every reason to leave. This is not an indictment against your birth father. God knows, he had no choice in the matter. But you wanted to know what I saw in Joels and it was this: a steady man as solid as stone.

Joels tapped his fingers on the tabletop. "Jazz," he said, "is like life. The sorrow is in the frontbeat and joy breaks out on the backbeat. You have to have both halves to make a whole beat."

I nodded as if I understood.

"Look—here they come."

A tall spindly man with legs that looked as if they might snap at any moment dragged a bass across the stage. He looked oddly familiar, yet I could not quite place him. Joels leaned across the table. "That's Buber."

Then a young man wearing an enormous trench coat stationed

himself in front of Buber. He had no hair, not a single strand on his head. For several moments he ran his hands over his shiny head, as if it were a genie's magic lamp. Then from the inner recesses of his coat he withdrew a shiny trombone. He held it beside his face and executed gymnastic movements with his lips.

"That's Vanags. He's stretching his lips," Joels explained.

Two old men shuffled across the floor. Their bodies bent like hinges at the waist and they had linked arms. It was not clear who was helping whom. But somehow they both arrived at their destinations, one man behind the drum set and the other man at the piano, where he performed scales in such rapid succession, I wondered if he'd hidden inside his shabby coat an extra set of young and limber hands.

"Ludviks is on the drums and Mengels is on piano."

"Twins?"

"Father and son."

"I know I've seen them before." I turned to Joels, squinted fiercely. "I've seen you with them. At the groundbreaking ceremony."

Now Joels's gaze reached my nose. "I wondered if you would remember."

A series of warm-up riffs, clashing with Mengels's zippy high-hat glissandos on the piano, pulled Joels's gaze to a long black box beside the piano.

"That's your band. You should be with them," I said.

Joels smiled gratefully then leaped onto the stage. Ludviks counted out a measure and then the Merry Afflictions launched into a number. I could not pry my gaze from Joels, who was becoming before my very eyes an entirely different man. As he forced air through his gold saxophone, coaxing a long and sad melody, he was no longer the same man who carefully recorded the demeanor of cows or the quality of their milk. And it was equally clear to me that the rest of us were undergoing a transformation as well. Whatever we carried inside of us—the dark thoughts, the grim despair—Joels had given it voice with the wails and moans of his sax. We did not have to carry these things any longer if we didn't want to. We could let the music wash it away, at least temporarily.

Perhaps this is why, when Joels slid into a wrong note, he raised his hand and brought the number to a full stop. Then he made the rounds, first to Buber on bass, "I beg your pardon"; to Mengels on the piano, "I beg your pardon"; to Vanags on trombone, "I beg your pardon"; and finally to Ludviks, who looked so frail now that he could barely hold the sticks, "I'm terribly sorry — do forgive me." The melody thus corrected, they picked up right where they had left off.

I tried keeping time with my foot. That's when I felt movement, a quick flutter. The evidence of life — there, inside of me. I had done the biological actions necessary to make life but had done nothing to deserve it. That God in his heavens might be far more generous than I had imagined overwhelmed me, moving me to tears. Then I felt it again — another small twitch behind my navel. That twitch was you. Mother's words came to mind: every good thing starts in water. You asked me how I could so quickly, so easily, fall in love with Joels and I think I loved him because you danced when he made music.

"You were wonderful," I said to Joels afterward, as he walked me to the bus stand. "I made some mistakes," he said.

In the distance a rim of purple trees exhaled sweet darkness. Birds and bats scissored dark patterns into night's dropping hem. Joels hummed jazz tunes until the old bus arrived. When the doors creaked open, Joels and I shook hands. All in all, a very successful first date.

That night I fell asleep thinking of your father. Thinking of you my only link to him. I wondered if my dating Joels was a betrayal, and if so, was it a forgivable offense? I slid into sleep, dreaming of the woods near our house. In the manner of a dream, illogical smudges of sound and image, I found myself gathering penny bun mushrooms in a basket made of hedgehog quills. As I reached into the basket to examine my haul, instead of mushrooms, I withdrew a baby, no bigger than a beating heart. I touched its navel, a tight pink throbbing knot. "How dare you!" the baby cried in a tiny baby voice. Its amber eyes were furious. And afraid. Of me. If I unknotted the navel, I would undo his fragile body and he would disappear. The very memory of him would vanish. And then the baby bit my hand. From far away came the sounds of a woman. Not me, I told myself, not me crying, smothering my cries. Not me smothering my angry baby. Again, a womanly cry. Ligita, crying for the one she'd lost.

Our first date ended with a handshake. Our second date ended with a proposal of marriage. It was late August, twilight, and we went to the river to stand on the little footbridge, the only good thing that had come of Mr. Zetsche's enterprises. The railing was strong and could bear the weight of many fishermen and their poles. From this small height we could see the moving water below us. Above us, the storks sat in their enormous nests wedged in the telephone poles and oaks. They clacked their beaks and made strafing calls, what they did just before they flew to their winter grounds.

"Not a musical sound," Joels remarked.

"Not pleasant, no," I agreed.

With massive ungainly flapping, they were off in droves, darkening the sky. A beautiful sight, birds and the sky becoming one dark thing together.

From my pocket I withdrew a few buns. I'd put extra anise seed and butter into the dough because the fish liked it better that way. From a black pocket of still water carp broke the flat skin of water with their kisses. Other fish, trout and perch, nosed to the surface. Dark gray, calamine blue, olive with spots of yellow, a riot of color swam beneath us. As they fought over the mayflies, the blue of one fish so near the green and yellows of another, the water turned gold before our very eyes. A shifting darkness above, a shifting gold below.

We stood there together, not speaking, not needing to. The water went flat and stars swam on the surface.

Joels put his elbows on the railing and leaned over the water. "You know what makes the light of the stars so sharp, so raw?"

"What?"

"They're lonely."

I looked at the stars on the water. "In the old story," I said, "the lonely hedgehog in the forest must huddle with others of his kind in order to stay warm. In huddling, they harm one another. But if they don't do this, they most certainly will die of cold. The huddle is worth the hurt."

Joels studied me for a moment. "Inara," he said, "you are absolutely normal. I hope you don't think this is too forward. But it seems to me that I could use a wife and you could use a husband. And"—here his gaze settled on mine—"I like you well enough to marry you."

There was something completely adorable in the way he worked himself toward genuine affection, and because Joels was Joels, as honest as the day, I knew whatever he said, it was exactly that—genuine. "That sounds reasonable to me," I said at last. "If we marry, I will walk with you the whole way." These were the very words Mother told me that Grandmother Velta had said to Grandfather Ferdinands when he asked her to marry him.

Our nuptials became a matter for your grandmother's "Kindly Advices" column: *Received a sudden proposal of marriage? Say yes before he changes his mind.* This suggestion received a record-breaking number of responses, all outlining the number of swift courtships and subsequent marriages that had ended disastrously. Of course, this necessitated a lively barrage from "Biruta Responds!" Your grandmother was the happiest I'd ever seen her.

Women, take a firm hand with your husbands. They are like large children. Feed them then tell them what to do. Failure to do so will allow them too much free time and we all know what a danger that is!

And then, as she so often did in her columns, she gave helpful tips on how to read an oven, how to marinate an eel, how to remove pills from a sweater. For the segment on home remedies, she relied on Stanka.

Got gout? Soak a cabbage leaf in vodka for two days. Then drape the leaf over the gouty parts. No, really. Do it.

Words knock like the stones of plums against my teeth. They tap against the shed. I don't know if it's Mother tapping at the typewriter or if it's you and Little Semyon working in the kitchen. Is this how words travel from one place to the next, from one body to another? They won't mean the same things those words: *stone, river, salt, thirst.* But they make the same sounds. I should have remembered this. *Siberia,* someone said, and Mr. Gepkars threw his hands up like he'd been shot. *Go on,* he said. *Go on and laugh. Go on outside and play in the dirt. Go on,* he said, *go on.* But his voice sounded like a shovel turning dirt.

That was my dream, as thin as an eyelash. And *tap, tap, tap* I heard the typewriter. *Go on,* it said. *Go on, bury me.* I woke up on fire, flames in my feet, soil in my mouth. I felt afraid. I said, *Read to me, read anything, anything at all. Go on. Go on.* You read from Velta's letters.

Meanwhile, the sun cut itself on the jagged horizon. Night was a knock on the door. The crows tapped their beaks, winged their dark witchery over the land. Meanwhile, the woman took a hammer to a stone. She broke the stone into chunks and the chunks into smaller bits. She poured water over those bits and stirred it into a slurry. They have taken our men and our boys to quarries and mines. They will break our boys to bits. She stirred the slurry, tipped the bowl, and drank it dry.

There you are in Joels's blue chair watching me now. I'm no longer afraid. *Are you very tired?* you ask me often. *Sleep and I'll watch over you,*

you say. *Dream,* you say, and I think that's what I've been doing all this time. It is harder for me to parse night from day, then from now. It's like trying to separate water from water with a comb; there are no teeth fine enough. I sometimes wonder if it's even you sitting in the chair. Maybe I'm dreaming you. But then I'll see a stack of letters, musical scores, the photos, and I'll remember. I was telling a story. No story should be left unfinished.

My long walks down the lane to Dr. N.'s, the dig and pitch of the muck shovel in the barn, rocked you to sleep. I loved the grainy air in the barn, damp, chalky with the smell of hay and warmth. I loved the smell of Dr. N.'s tobacco, vanilla, cherry, apricot. He carried entire orchards in that pipe. As I cleaned the lab, light warmed the windows. And I found myself often looking through them, awaiting the arrival, or the return, rather, of Dr. N. and Joels. It was their habit to ride the little red scooter to nearby farms at four and five in the morning. Around nine, they'd return, their two large bodies balanced carefully on that scooter that strained beneath their combined weight. The rest of the day they ran tests of the milk samples and looked after the cows in the barn, the control group, Dr. N. called them. These cows were fed a steady diet of genetically engineered grass. Now that we were an item, Joels and I were under strict orders not to smooch in front of the cows or say anything remotely amorous or humorous. "It's all about the ambiance," Joels explained, in a reverential hush.

I tried to wear the latex gloves while washing. But my hands had swollen, my fingers turned to thick sausages. So, as Mother always had, I cleaned without gloves. By autumn, I had washed so many of Dr. N.'s test tubes in bleach water that my fingers always felt slippery. One day I showed Mother my hands, blaring red at the palms, white at the tips. "Oh, they do that at first," she said. "Eventually, you'll lose feeling altogether at the ends."

Closer inspection revealed that I'd lost my fingerprints. I was like those birch trees, shedding skins and forgetting with each passing season who I was. I could understand now — just a little — why Mrs. Lee corrected anyone if they referred to her as Chinese instead of Korean and why Mrs. Arijisnikov was quick to work the topic of Almaty, her hometown, into any conversation. Why Uncle Maris had been so bombastic about his service record. These were verbal fingerprints pressed into conversations that became a second, better skin. But who was I becoming? I could not read my skin as it was shedding daily, and daily I was being rewritten.

At this time, Ligita and I made our wedding plans. My engagement forced theirs as it's the height of bad manners for the younger to go ahead of the older. Jumping in puddles, they call this. Complicating matters further, Mother and Father could not afford two church weddings or even two dresses. This reality brought on waves of tears from Ligita. I believe she wanted to float in gauze down the aisle of a grand cathedral. I, too, had privately nursed such fantasies. Mother wasted no time in setting us straight.

"In my day girls rode the bus to the city and registered with the civil clerk. We dressed as smartly as we could and had our picture taken. All in all, it was very nice. I think you two girls could do the same. Afterward, we could have a reception at the hall — if we do it on a Saturday."

Sensibly, we both agreed. The date set, Mother and Father felt it high time they meet the groom. The next evening Joels arrived with a bouquet of marigolds for Mother.

"Inara says you are Estonian?" Mother ventured, as she set out the tea things.

"Yes." Joels's gaze remained on the tabletop.

Mother sighed. "A very clean country."

"And how do you feel about cemeteries?"

"I adore them," Joels said.

"And are you a drinking man, then?" Mother scrutinized Joels's face for signs of liver strain.

Joels coughed. "Only to fortify my intestines and give the bowels something to think about."

A thorough silence descended. Once bowels are mentioned, it's hard knowing in which direction to steer.

"Inara is pregnant, you know," Mother said at last.

"Oh, yes." Joels found my hand under the table and gave it a squeeze. "She is great with child and I am ready to support a family."

"Well, this has been a very good talk," Father said.

"I always did like Estonians." Mother turned to Joels. "I've known several who could be quite sensible and generous — when the occasion called for it."

In three weeks time, as we had planned, Ligita and Rudy married first, and on their heels Joels and I registered with the clerk. Each of us paid the registry fee and acted as witnesses for the other. "So happy," the fuzzy-haired clerk murmured. "I'm sure you'll all be so happy." A tepid smile said she doubted it. We rode the bus back to town.

Anxious to make their appearance at the hall, Rudy and Ligita went on ahead while Joels and I walked toward Mr. Zetsche's new footbridge. This was something newlyweds did — walk by water. Some newlyweds wrote their sins on stones and threw them into the water. Others scratched their names on padlocks and hung them from the rails of bridges. Joels and I stood shoulder to shoulder and watched the pass of clouds on the skin of the river. After a while, Joels withdrew a padlock from his pocket and snapped the lock around Mr. Zetsche's new railing. He had had our initials engraved on the lock. "Here." Joels pressed the key into my hand. "You do the honors."

I held the key in my hand. "I will walk with you all the way," I said.

This is what Velta had said to Ferdinands once she finally decided to marry him. And then I threw the key as far as I could downriver.

By the time we reached the hall, the wedding celebration was in full swing.

"Here they are, the lovebirds!" Mr. Arijisnikov called out, and the men made good-natured jokes in poor taste until Mrs. Arijisnikov flung open the door and herded us all in.

When they saw us, the Merry Afflictions struck a chord and everyone clapped. "It's time for a toast," Mr. Lim cried, and cups of black balsam made the rounds.

"May happiness brood over them." Mr. Ilmyen raised a glass. "May the tears soon cease to flow," Mr. Gipsis said.

Father and Rudy and Joels lifted their glasses and the band launched into "Many White Days," a song mandatory at Latvian weddings. Joels guided me across the floor through the entire song and halfway through Charlie Parker's "Bird of Paradise," the whole time counting the beats under his breath. As happy as we both were, I knew he would be happier if he was playing his saxophone. I touched his elbow. "Just play," I said. "I need to sit down anyway."

Joels smiled at me gratefully. "You are better than normal," he said, planting a kiss on my forehead.

Oak boughs hung from the beams, and Mother had made swags of birch and pine for the sills. Every table had a candle, which I knew had Mother in a high state of alarm, but for our sake, she'd stretched herself. She stood at a long table, beaming from behind a platter of *rasols,* a potato salad Mother wouldn't dream of serving without herring and pickles, beets and sour cream. She handed a plateful to Mrs. Gipsis. Mother liked Joels; when she said his name, she lifted her chin slightly. And she was happy to see so many people in the hall. The beautiful thing about weddings is that songs flow freely, as does the beer. Everyone attends even if they find the bride or groom utterly loathsome.

Father, too, was happily conversing with Mr. Baltmanis about the theological implications of certain vegetables in the Bible. "Sadly, there is nothing written in the entire Bible about potatoes."

"What a shame," Father concurred. "The hidden part of the slumbering vegetable is the most fascinating. It's the unseen that holds greater value than the seen."

I thought of you turning silently in my womb.

"Inara!" Jutta squeezed my shoulder. "I think marriage agrees with you. You are positively glowing. And your groom up there — what a man!"

I blushed. "Yes, well. He's a—"

"Very hard worker. I know, I know." Jutta patted my hand. "All work and no play, well, you know what they say about that, too." Jutta winked and waltzed back to her family. No wonder she and Big Semyon kept the shades drawn.

"Ahem." Dr. Netsulis stood before me and bowed. "I am an old man with few pleasures." He extended his hand.

I rose and put my hands on Dr. N.'s shoulder while he searched for my waist. We laughed. And then we danced. If anyone, Stanka said, could have read my future and told me that everything that had happened, both good and bad, would have led me to this man who made the music my feet now danced to, I would never have believed it. I would have never guessed that happiness could find me twice in one lifetime when so many people never find it even once.

Dr. Netsulis danced me closer to the back of the hall where Mrs. Gipsis had cornered Ligita.

"And where is your father, dear?" Mrs. Gipsis shouted. Having taught the sixth-grade class for so many years, her hearing was not the best and she refused to wear any helps for it.

For her part, Ligita, being half Ukrainian, was plagued with the western Slavic intonation that prevented most people from understanding her, especially when she mumbled. But Mrs. G. furrowed her brow and persisted: "Speak up, dear. The music is so loud."

"He is in Liepaja!" Ligita's voice climbed to a volume that turned a few heads.

Befuddlement seized every muscle in Mrs. G.'s face. "But why is he there when you are here?"

"He is in PRISON!" Ligita shouted. "He stole a gun and shot a man in the head." The music stopped for only a measure, and then Vanags launched into a lively reel. Mrs. G. patted Ligita's shoulder and brought her a tissue. Poor Ligita. There is nothing like living in a small town to reveal your nakedness again and again. But there were benefits to this kind of life. Yes, now everyone knew where her father was. And we sympathized. Because in every household there was a missing father or uncle. A grandparent sent to Siberia. An alcoholic. A wife beater. Knowing these things, the hard things, we could come together and pretend that those things didn't mark us forever.

I watched Joels. Did he wonder what others were thinking about him, of our marriage, of this baby I carried who was not his? Was he thinking about his family—Aunt Tufla? Or was it Tevya?—the one who had raised him and had chosen not to be here? Was he remembering her stingy love? Feeling it an injustice that she should be saddled with her dead sister's child, she clothed and fed young Joels grudgingly. Every day at five in the afternoon, regardless of the season, she sent him to the mudroom where he had a cot. She forbade him to rise until seven the next morning. You asked him once how he had committed so many musical scores to memory, and he told you he had lots of time on his hands to do so. But he didn't tell you how he did it. While his aunt wrote her scholarly papers for the academic journals, he sat on the edge of his cot and imagined measure after measure of music unspooling over the gray walls of the mudroom. The rufous-sided towhee trilled in soprano. The frogs belched baritone. Crickets were his violin section. The oboelike calls of the owls became his wind section. The wind roared like kettledrums and the rain *tap, tap, tapped* percussion on the windows and roof. In a few years' time, he had composed entire symphonies, score upon score of joy and sorrow. And now all the pain and hurt and harm he carried came out of the sax, his instrument of joy and sorrow.

That was him telling his story. And he was doing it for us, people he did not know. But that was the beauty and power of music. It undressed us all and made us honest in ways that nothing else could.

Around midnight people began making their way home. Dr. Netsulis blew everyone a kiss then climbed onto his scooter and spluttered into the darkness. The Merry Afflictions packed up their instruments with the care one bundles the most fragile of children. Vanags brought around his ubersturdy Pobeda. The instruments they stowed first, the string bass in the front passenger's seat where the safety strap was still in good working order. Ludviks, Mengels, and Buber climbed into the back, folding their legs to their chests. And then they sped off at breakneck speeds for the nearest bar.

Joels and I walked down the lane and through the yard to the shed. Mother had propped open the door to let it air. Father had moved the bed from their bedroom into the shed and dressed the mattress in her comforter and freshly laundered sheets. They had even stockpiled wood and kindling next to the stove, and strung a clothesline from one wall of the shed to the other. A fire sizzled and cracked inside the burzuika, casting an orange glow of shadow and light. Joels scooped me up and carried me over the threshold as if I were as light as breath. He set me on the edge of the bed. And then he spied the wheelbarrow full of the wooden parts of the piano. He surveyed the soundboard, the cast-iron plate, my clumsy attempt to secure the strings. He sank to his knees before the plate and board, as if in supplication. He ran his hands over the wooden pieces in the wheelbarrow and then again over the hammers and keys.

"I can fix this." Glowing reverence for the piano, for a piano needing him, warmed his words. I motioned to my dress, our bed. "Later," I said, rising to my feet. Joels unhooked the clasp of my dress and helped me step out of it. He laid it carefully on the back of the chair. I helped him out of his suit jacket, hung it on Mother's good wooden hanger. The same for his trousers, so the creases would hold crisp, and his dress shirt. His long dress socks. Then we stood before one another, contemplating our feet.

"Well," Joels said.

"Well." I studied the fire in the stove. "There is one bed and it is bedtime."

We looked at the bed. We looked at each other. "Do you have special preferences?" Joels asked.

I coughed. "I-I don't think so—no more than the usual person." Now Joels blushed. "I mean for sleeping. Do you prefer the right side of the bed or the left?"

"Whichever side is closest to the latrine," I said, pulling back Mother's best eiderdown. On the sheets lay a metal rake, a hoe, and a shovel: each pristine and shining. It meant good luck for our marriage, but they were very bad for sleeping on. Joels laughed, set the tools beside the fire, then we climbed into bed, Joels stretching his long large body beside mine. He hummed a few bars from a song. This is how for the first time we lay together, side by side, as man and wife. We listened to the dogs barking up and down the lane. In the comfort of darkness we spoke—quietly, of course. Layer by layer, Joels talked his way through the worries of his heart. Which is how I learned that he had entered an international coffee-flake jingle competition. He'd submitted three jingles. The winners would be announced in a few days, but Joels was in such a bundle over it that his bowels hadn't moved in a week. Dr. Netsulis had given him some stewed figs, but that had only added to the problem.

"Oh, Joels," I said, stroking his arm. "I am so sorry."

He sighed. "The long and short of it is that my capacity for passion is utterly displaced."

"It's all right," I said. "It can wait." I took his hand and placed it on my stomach, which was hard and tight like an early watermelon.

I could feel the muscles at my hips quivering, signaling a contraction taking hold. Practice twitches, Mother called these. My body was teaching itself what to do when the time came.

Joels lifted his hand. "Does it hurt?" he asked.

"No," I said. "But watch this." I rolled to my side and repositioned Joels's hand. Just then you kicked so hard your foot threw Joels's hand into the air.

"Good God!" Joels exclaimed.

I nodded my head solemnly. "I know."

CHAPTER EIGHT

EVERY CREATURE CARRIES WITHIN ITSELF an internal clock, an unerring sense of when it is the precise time to do or not do something. I think this is what Solomon meant when he wrote that for every season there is a time. That stars slowly burn out and their light reaches us many years later or the fact that the seeds of certain trees cannot be released if not for a sudden and terrific heat confirms to me that we live in ordered chaos. I know it's not fashionable to believe in God these days. This flabbergasted your grandfather, who saw in the veins of leaves and the striations of rocks evidence of a creator who loved his creation. He saw eternity strung in the stars and brilliant economy in the way, after a forest fire, the first trees to knuckle up through the scald are the same ones whose bark and sap we use to heal a burn.

No, it wasn't anger; it was more of a sorrow that he felt. I think there were days your grandfather actually grieved for God. *Can you imagine,* he asked me once, *having your handiwork, the culmination of all your creative thought and dreams, dismissed as an accident or, worse, a mistake?*

Sharks expel their stomach once a month in order to clean them. Such tidy creatures! That is something, you wrote in your notebook, you very much wanted to see. The life cycle of a female octopus fasci-

nated you, too. Once she has mated, she finds a secluded den and flat-
tens herself in its dark recesses. She may brood thousands of eggs, and
once they hatch, as small as sequins, they hang suspended in a lace of
her making. All of her energy is devoted to caring for her young; she
will not leave the den — not even to hunt. Once they are able to float
free of the den, her final act before she dies is to exhale and send them
forth on a current of her breath.

You wrote about flecks of light buried in certain rocks. Reading
your Book of Wonder, your words returned me to a time when I had
a heightened sense of awareness and awe for every living thing.

It was as if I had been blind, deaf, and dumb, and now in everything I could perceive order and design, be it found in a creature as
small as the bee, whose drowse and hum I now pair with the fall of
the apples and their hard turn to vinegar, or something as vast as a
field of rye and the wind sighing through it *shhhh-shhh-shhhh.* By mid-
October, the abandoned storks' nests atop the telephone poles had
sprouted thick ferns. It was now Mikeli, the time the ghosts knock on
windows and doors asking for a cup of water. If you give them one,
it means you will die next. If you feel a sudden thirst, you shouldn't
drink lest you drown on that water. Certainly, you should not go to
the river.

Your grandmother recorded all this in her newspaper, and I do believe that her devotion to this kind of folklore was therapeutic. But the
ferocious attack of her fingers on the typewriter keys suggested to me
that she'd not quite forgiven Uncle for selling the manor house. You
can't hate a dead man forever, but she did bear this loss heavily. It was
a good thing the German Olympia was such a sturdy model; few others could have borne her fury.

Meanwhile, your grandmother ran some racy advice supplied
by Mrs. Lim called "Your Cabbage and Furious Fermentation." Apparently, cabbage, when left unsupervised, yielded a robust alcohol;
three squirrels and one hedgehog had died after imbibing. "Keep that
stuff away from my cows," Dr. N. said to me, as I cleaned one day.

And then he added thoughtfully, "But I myself wouldn't mind a sip. Or two."

My feet had grown so heavy I thought they were anchors pulling me into the ground. I couldn't bend over without losing my balance. Dr. N. lowered the seat of his scooter so that I could duck walk it through the hallway. I attached the mop to the backseat and this is how I cleaned his floors without ever getting down on my knees. If I sidled it up to the laboratory sinks, I could wash the beakers and test tubes while sitting. "Like a lady," I told Mother, though I had to strad-dle the seat, which wasn't so ladylike.

At Dr. N.'s manor house, Joels hovered constantly, asking, "Can I bring you anything?" His attentiveness was so sweet that sometimes I said I could use a glass of water when I didn't need one. Joels had al-ready collected the data from the various cows at the nearby farms so now Dr. N. worked in furious solitude. All Joels had to do was feed and muck the cows in the doctor's barn and contemplate more jingles. He'd placed second in that coffee-flake jingle contest, to the great re-lief of his knotted bowels. About this same time, Chem-Do Dry Toi-lets announced that they were sponsoring a jingle-off for their newest line of outdoor mobile toilets: the Tuxedo Toilet. Joels immediately set about finishing repairs to Velta's piano.

This he was doing late one afternoon. Darkness fell in damp folds outside the shed.

I folded laundry inside and watched Joels. There is something beautiful about a large man doing delicate, intricate work. With such care, he secured the pinblock and hammers; with such tenderness, he tapped the keys. I loved his devotion to the small and fragile. Anyway, after some plinking, Joels leaned back on his heels. In the air his hands drew a tall box, as big as a coffin but wider.

"Imagine if you will a completely sanitary, completely dignified, and completely private portable latrine experience. Imagine the Taj Mahal of toilets."

"All right," I said, closing my eyes. "I'm imagining."

"Okay. Now the jingle: If you must go, then go in style. Tuxedo Toilets: a class act."

"That's very good," I said. Sometimes it was necessary to refrain from saying difficult things, like the truth, for the sake of a healthy relationship. We called it "speaking through flowers." Some people call it lying, but I prefer to think of it as compassionate avoidance.

"Or how about this: cushy-tushy—so comfortable you'll never want to leave." Joels, I noticed, had his eye on his sax standing at the ready.

"Also good."

Joels reached for his saxophone, dug in his hip pocket for his mouthpiece, licked his lips, and played a few measures. He sang the jingle. "Don't have a moment, have an experience—classy assy." Joels paused. "Well?"

"It's nice," I said. "It's very nice," I said again. Maybe Joels had heard of creative avoidance as well; he threw himself into cleaning his spit trap as if his very life depended upon it.

Night school. I think it's a fabulous idea; plenty of people your age and some much older have done quite well by it. The suggested reading list has me a little perplexed. Pushkin makes sense to me, but *The Sorrows of Young Werther*? Is it a good idea for a young man who makes his livelihood digging graves to read such a depressing book? You assure me that it is most suitable for a moral education. After all, in Mary Shelley's *Frankenstein,* the monster has it at the top of his reading list.

You've lit the burzuika and I'm glad for crackling heat that dries the jelly in my joints. I do not wish to complain, but you asked me what it felt like to die and I'm telling you. Pinches at the wrist, a buzz in the back of the brain. And the pain is a harmonic series of sensations, each piled on top of the other. On knees and knuckles, the cold creeps in. I feel it tighten over my ribs with each draw of breath. Cold is the devil's carpet, ice his only friend. He rides the bitter winds looking for a place to land. Restlessness is his soup and bread, but all the devil really wants is sleep. This is why, if caught out in the cold, you should never let yourself succumb to the urge to close your eyes. The devil will seize your body, pull your skin over his, and sleep inside your body for a thousand years.

It's a kind of hell, desiring sleep and not having it. You tell me that Uncle complains of insomnia, how it burns holes through his stomach. I don't understand why his experience should be so different from others. Mr. Dumonovsky told you that after he felt himself thrashed and threshed his mistakes, sins if you will, were milled to a fine powder and carried off on a wind. He was never so glad to see a thing go. Afterward, that same wind shouldered through what was left of him, passed through him as breath on paper, as paper on a comb, and made music of him. That this has not happened to Uncle puzzles me. He does not make music. Itches that can't be scratched. A thirst that can't be quenched. A story that won't be finished. Death is a furious irritation, he told you.

"What could be preventing his passage, his transformation?" I mused.

You leveled your gaze on mine. "You are," you said.

As autumn settled in, Mr. Zetsche's Riviera grew a good two meters taller than the tree line. Father didn't like this new construction because of the afternoon and evening shadows the building cast over the new cemetery. Our town seemed beset in a gloom we could not name nor shake. Ligita, unable to pass the hiring screenings for any of the future Riveria jobs, spent her days wandering up and down the lane and through the woods. She wasn't looking for mushrooms—it was too late in the season for boletes, and she'd never regained her appetite for fungi after our ill-fated hunt together. What she was after was harder to find: a stalk of corn with two ears on it. A fruit or vegetable that had grown together. Any such sign that boded well for a woman who wanted to get pregnant. And though she might wear herself out looking, I was glad that hope in second chances had pulled Ligita out of our house. This was not a problem afflicting Rudy. We rarely saw him that autumn. He drank with other men at the *kafenica*. He attended political meetings. He brought home newspapers and flyers bristling with nervous, angry energy. Though Mother made no mention of Rudy's dark demeanor, there were days when I'd see her standing at the kitchen sink, a dish passing from one hand to the other. And over her face, worry settling as a shadow. We were changing in ways she could not control or even imagine. Only our traditions remained the same, or nearly the same.

Every spring we had the Push the Swing ceremony, in summer we had Jani Day, and in winter we held a Christmas pageant in the hall. This meant that every October the Christmas pageant steering committee gathered to determine who would play the various roles. Every year Mother tried to excuse herself from the madness, citing her atheism. But she always ended up going, for fear someone might try to use the oven. This year was no exception. The only difference was that Joels went with me for moral support. Also, Miss Dzelz, on account of being the most recent hire at school, had been elected committee president.

An energetic woman, she seemed perfect for the job. She was a ferocious stick walker, an exuberant style of walking that looked a lot like cross-country skiing minus the skis and the snow. On weekends Joels and I had observed her stabbing the new concrete pavement of Mr. Zetsche's waterside promenade with her poles. Where and how she found such energy I did not know. She was at least twice my age: a spinster who made no secret that she was on the lookout for a husband. Each month she dyed her hair in an unprecedented shade of magenta we only knew to call Dzelz Red.

In years past, the steering committee meetings earned a reputation for boisterousness. This was because the widows Sosnovskis, Rezniks, and Spassky, not wishing to succumb to the sins of sloth or spiritual boredom, insisted each year on participating. This they did with their whole hearts. And everything else, too. They could argue the seventy-two angles of a circle, which is why Mother was so vital to these meetings. She brewed the tea that kept everyone going, usually three tureens but sometimes four.

Miss Dzelz called the meeting to order. Of course, Widow Spassky lodged her protests immediately. Being Orthodox Russian, she wanted to celebrate Christmas a solid thirteen days later than everyone else—just to be difficult. Back and forth the argument swung: Was Jesus an Orthodox Russian Jesus or a Baptist Jesus or a Lutheran Jesus?

Finally Mother arbitrated. "We'll hold the program on January 1. At noon. Exactly halfway between the two dates in question. All in favor say aye."

The room fell silent. It was a near-blasphemous proposition, but it also smacked of good old-fashioned pragmatism.

"Aye" came the response. I could hear only one quiet nay, and this from Mrs. Friemane, a forlorn nihilist who nonetheless lent her talents as resident costume designer year after year.

"Now, then." Miss Dzelz consulted her clipboard. "The cast. Mr. Gipsis's class will be the sheep. Mrs. Gepkars's class will be the multitude of angels. The three oldest boys from Mrs. Inese's class will be the shepherds tending their flocks by night." Miss Dzelz paused and smiled at me. "Mary will be played this year by Inara Kalnins, er, Henriksen. For obvious reasons, she seemed the natural choice." At this, the widows exchanged significant glances. "And then, naturally, the part of Joseph has fallen to Inara's husband, Joels."

Joels shifted in his chair. "Actually, Miss Dzelz, I must respectfully decline. I am uncalibrated in my feelings about Jesus."

"But I've written into the script several potent thinking poses for you."

Joels took a big breath, held it, then let it out slowly and steadily as if he were playing an imaginary solo on his saxophone. "I would consider playing the saxophone—from a distance. I would even consider building the set. But I cannot participate in a Christmas program."

"Why not?" Miss Dzelz asked.

"The truth is, I'm Jewish."

Miss Dzelz frowned. "Is it Jesus the man who's troubling you or Jesus the baby?"

"Jesus the man."

"Oh, that's fine then." Relief flooded her voice. "We're not the least bit concerned about the man and we're certainly not interested in any of his messianic claims. We're focusing only on Jesus the baby. And the sheep. And the cows. By the way—does anyone know where I can find a few cows?" Miss Dzelz looked wildly around the room.

Mother rolled her eyes toward the ceiling.

Joels touched my elbow. "I didn't actually agree, did I?"

"You did, actually. At these meetings, silence is consent."

I patted his knee and Joels excused himself for home. A good thing, too, as no one was finished arguing yet. The solo part had yet to be determined, and this was the point at which good manners strained, friends and neighbors sometimes coming to verbal fisticuffs.

"Little Ksinia should have the solo," Widow Rezniks said.

"She had it last year," Mrs. Lee said.

"And a fine job she did, too," Widow Spassky piped up.

"Let little Aija sing. Ksinia sang last year," Mrs. Lim said.

"And a fine job she did, too," Widow Spassky insisted.

"Everyone should have a chance. This is Latvia," Mrs. Gipsis said.

"Do we want equality or do we want quality?" Widow Rezniks asked.

"Do you hear what you are saying?" Mrs. Lim asked.

Widow Rezniks slammed her palms on the table.

"Every cow licks her own calf," Mother muttered.

"What?" Widow Rezniks swung her head toward Mother.

Mother smiled, slung her purse over her shoulder, and rose from her seat. "I need to pee. I'm going home now. All I ask is that nobody messes up the kitchen." Mother plucked at my sleeve. "Let's go."

We went to the bathroom, where we listened to the women. After all, they still had one more tureen of tea to argue through. Once the topic of politics had been introduced, however obliquely, the floodgates had been let open. Imagine the noise: fifteen women arguing the finer points of immigration law and the theoretical versus practical differences between occupation and annexation. I sat on the toilet and hung my head. Mrs. Lim and Miss Dzelz discussed why a woman would and would not make a better president than a man. And from Widow Rezniks, a bitter lament that Latvia could and never should join the EU as long as ethic Russians like her were being persecuted.

"Persecution!" Mrs. Baltmanis bellowed. "Let me tell *you* about persecution!"

Mother knocked on the divider between the two stalls. "What's the best thing to feed a Latvian?" The answer: another Latvian. I groaned. It was a tired joke in the east.

Mother unbolted her door and stood at the sink. "All this fuss over a *baby*," she muttered. By how she said the word *baby,* I understood the trouble I was causing her and would continue to cause her. Tears welled in my eyes. I coughed and sniffled, did all I could to contain my tears. I made excuses until finally Mother went home without me.

"Inara? You all right in there?" Miss Dzelz knocked lightly on the stall door.

I dried my eyes with my sleeve, unlatched the lock on the stall. "I'll bet the real Mary didn't break down and cry," I said.

Miss Dzelz crossed her arms over her bony chest. "I'll bet she did. I'll bet there was never a girl so afraid and so misunderstood. But she had some strong supporters."

"You don't mean the donkey."

"Think about it." Now Miss Dzelz linked her arm through mine and guided me out of the bathroom through the tiny vestibule and out of the hall. "She had her guy who stuck beside her. And she had God."

"Is that enough?" I asked.

Miss Dzelz stopped walking and peered into my eyes. "I don't know. Is it?"

We rounded the back side of the hall. Down the lane we spied Dr. Netsulis kneeling beside his red scooter. It looked as if he were praying over his scooter, or perhaps to it.

Miss Dzelz squeezed my arm. "Who is that man?" There was no mistaking the admiration in her voice, her readiness to hand her heart over to him as soon as the introductions were made.

"That's Doctor Netsulis. He's a part-time doctor and full-time genius. Joels and I clean his house and barn."

"Barn?"

"He keeps cows. Latvian Browns."

"Cows!" she cried, rushing past me for the good doctor, who jumped to his feet as if he'd been shot in his britches by an arrow.

The day the pageant arrived, I was a jumble of nerves. I couldn't sit still. My hands wouldn't stop shaking. I visited the latrine every ten minutes.

"You are just nervous. Though I can't image why," Ligita said, on our way to the hall. "All you have to do is smile at a swaddled plastic doll." I chalked up her withering encouragement to grief.

Your grandmother stomped ahead of us, her boots punching through the thin crusts of needle ice. We passed the Ilmyens', we passed Stanka's. "Merry Christmas!" Stanka rushed out of her house and joined us. Jesus didn't thrill her much, but she absolutely adored Christmas. Each year she contrived to erect not one but two Christmas trees festooned with mistletoe, wrinkled white snowberries, and bordello-red ribbons.

Like a bucket on a bulldozer, your grandmother lowered her head and forged on. Having already achieved the pinnacle of her holiday spirit, she muttered, *Go to hell.* Now you know where my toilet mouth comes from.

The Merry Afflictions lent their services for moral support. But the instant Ludviks tapped the opening drumbeat, my back seized. A cord inside my stomach, only lower, pulled tight. I bent over Dr. N.'s red scooter, now adorned with faux fur and long drooping donkey ears. "I don't feel well," I whispered to Ligita, as I straddled the machine.

"Just hold it in!" Ligita hissed.

The angelic host, with their glad tidings for the shepherds keeping watch, huddled in the wings. Miss Dzelz gave the signal, and the angels lined up in formation behind the curtain. The little opening between the two partitions had been built to allow the passage of normal children. But these were no longer ordinary children. They were angels and they had sprouted wings of enormous proportion. In actuality, Mrs. Friemane had obtained used Thighmasters from somewhere in the USA. The architecture of these contraptions was such that, once strapped to the backs of the children, the wings were fixed in the open position, and it took tremendous arm strength to fold them in. In no time, they'd bottlenecked themselves in the narrow passage leading onstage.

"Oh, for heaven's sake," Mother sighed, placing her foot on the backside of each little angel and unceremoniously pushing them through.

I squeezed the throttle and rolled slowly down the aisle. In the middle of my grand entrance, the scooter bucked then stalled. I gripped the handlebars and panted. And I groaned.

"No, no!" Miss Dzelz called from the wings. "It's not time for that yet, Inara."

"Too soon!" Ligita hissed.

"I know," I moaned. A warm rush of fluid ran down the insides of my thighs.

Dr. Netsulis rushed to my aid, his stethoscope on the scooter's engine. "Where did all this water come from?" he asked me.

"It's the baby," I panted. "It's coming. Now."

And then what? I suppose Miss Dzelz ushered all the children outside. Mrs. Arijisnikov and Mother bustled around the kitchen putting on pots and looking for clean towels. Ligita hung a sheet for privacy purposes. From Dr. Netsulis's trouser pockets appeared latex gloves.

I folded my body in half as I lay on the straw. Joels rubbed my back.

"I am very uncomfortable with this," Dr. Netsulis confided to Joels. "It's been a while since I've delivered a baby."

And then I felt a dagger ripping me in two.

"Push!" Stanka said.

"But don't push too hard," Mother cautioned. "Breathe," Father advised gently from the kitchen.

"But don't forget to push," Stanka said.

I felt trapped within a Latvian parliamentary session. Everyone was full of advice, most of it contrary. Thank God, nature will do what it must. My internal chorus of self, of my too-many, too-loud, too-self-aware selves merged. Collapsed. To a tightly funneled sensation of pain.

"God!" I screamed.

"Oh, yes," Father said. "Turn to God. He hears. He most definitely does."

"God!" I screamed louder.

"But he isn't deaf," Ligita chimed in.

"Breathe," Joels and Dr. N. whispered in unison.

The pain shot through me from stem to stern. I did not feel strong enough to bear it.

"You can do it. I believe in you absolutely," Joels whispered.

And that is when I looked at Mother and saw her face changing before my eyes.

There was something she could see that I couldn't. "What — what?" I demanded.

"The baby," she said, and she began to cry. "I can see the head."

Dr. N.'s brow furrowed. "Don't push anymore," he said. Stanka and Mother piled towels beneath me. Joels held my hand and counted beats to imaginary measures. Jingles in the making.

Then Mother said, "A boy!"

Stanka held you while Mother cut the cord. Father wiped at his eyes with a handkerchief and even Ligita seemed subdued in a nice way. At last Stanka placed you in my arms and I saw for myself what a beautiful boy you were. You had a shock of black hair and gray eyes, so unlike the eyes of anyone in our family. The whole time you held as still as stone, your eyes trained on mine.

Mother cupped a tiny heel in her hand. "What will you name him?"

"A good name," Stanka said.

"A strong name," Rudy said.

"A family name," Father said.

I looked at you, so tiny, so wrinkled. I did not deserve such a miracle. And yet, I held one in my hands anyway.

"Maris," I said. And nobody said no.

CHAPTER NINE

I DREAMED OF MOTHER AGAIN LAST NIGHT. She hovered over water, wreathed in fog, her hair ink black, her hair like coal. Her mouth moved. She was singing. I said, *Come closer, I can't hear you; come closer.* She took a step into the river and I heard: *Bring a mouse, sweet sleep to a little baby.* Dove gray and soft were her words. She stood in the shallow water on her side of the river; I stood on my side of the river. I sang, *Sweet sleep to a little baby.*

We were two girls singing the same song. *Come closer,* I called to her. *I don't know the rest of this song.* She said, *Throw the rope, a rope knotted at each end and I will pull you over and tell you the rest.* So I knotted the rope and put a spoon in the knot. I cast the rope over the river where it landed at her feet. I hung on to my end, to my knot, because the knot is where one grasps any rope, the knot being what connects the girl to the daughter. And what did she do?

She fell to her knees, unknotted the spoon from the rope. Then, spoonful by spoonful, she drank the river dry. *I'm just so thirsty,* she said, sitting on a rock. *Why won't you die and be still and rest like dead people are supposed to do?* I asked. *Oh, that's so clichéd,* she said, winding her hair into a thick braid, a noose she draped around her neck. *People think that when they die they'll simply shut their eyes and sleep. That's not it at all. It's work and more work.* Her fingers unraveled the ends of her braid. *If I don't work, I'll die.* I walked through the dried riverbed and I sat on the rock next to her. *But you're dead already,* I said. *I know it,* she said, *but what else can I do?* She shrugged, her shoulders rising and falling in helpless wonder at her impossible situation. *My little wolf rumbles, my little wolf hums. My little wolf has a white paw. If this doesn't make it better, it won't make it worse.* She smiled a sad, tired smile. And then she took the spoon and dug in the mud, looking for more water.

I woke up. Her thirst, my thirst; her branding, my branding; her wounds, my wounds. So much misunderstanding between us and yet we are so much alike. Though I am tired, I know I have so much work to do still. The song she sang, incidentally, is a cradle song. We all took turns singing this one to you in those first few months of your life. Joels sang his coffee-flake jingles to you and even your uncle Rudy sang.

> *The bee, the bee,*
> *The dweller of forests,*
> *Hums on the heath,*
> *And stings our fingers*
> *And faces and ears,*
> *And gives us honey.*
> *That is his work.*

> *Oh man, Oh man,*
> *Look at the bee—*
> *You sting enough*
> *In the heart, the heart;*
> *Nevertheless, give sweetness*
> *To your own brother.*
> *That is man's work.*

When Rudy sang, he rubbed his palm over the fuzz on your little head, the fur on your ears, and I thought his singing was evidence of some tenderness left in him. The truth was, I worried about your uncle Rudy. He drifted from Madona to Balvi to Daugavpils looking for work. Mr. Zetsche took pity on him and hired him to work in the Rimi store, a Swedish grocery franchise featuring Swedish-style shopping. What this meant was that we could openly salivate over the gloriously displayed rolls, buns, bins of German candy, and fruit. Fruit! Row upon row of apples of two and sometimes three varieties with root vegetables, cabbage, and lettuces forming tidy edible phalanxes. So, too, the cheese wedges and bright cellophane packages of biscuits and crisps. We could, and did, stand dreamily in the aisles, bright yellow baskets on our hips, and moon over the neatly arranged abundance that we could touch, put in our basket, then take out of the basket and tenderly put back on the shelf. I couldn't help noticing that Rudy often came home with small items: packs of chewing gum, lip balm, cigarettes. I feared that your uncle Rudy was exploring—quite regularly—the elastic boundaries of a free market in this new social context.

When Rudy wasn't at Rimi, he sat on the divan watching cartoon episodes of *Well, Just You Wait!* in which the clever rabbit always outwits the flea-bitten wolf. It was the only time he laughed. Even then, his whole body pulsed with a quiet anger that in time, in an older man, would lead to resignation. But when Rudy held you, his hands were calm and steady. Every mother believes her own child to be remarkable, but you had a palpable effect on anyone who touched you. This was the miracle of a baby, of you. A baby slows the quick and mutes the loud. People even breathe more gently and rhythmically around infants as if they were in the presence of something both holy and fragile. I suppose this is why I kept you as close to me as possible. Wanting neither sound nor air to break the connection between us, I kept you strapped to my back or chest. One morning, with you bound to my back, we took the long way through a thick swale of tall grass to Dr. Netsulis's. That is, I went through our yard, through the old/new cemetery, and walked slowly past the new shops of the Riviera. In addition to the Rimi grocery store and the *kafenica,* the Riviera now boasted a confectioner's shop, and Mr. Vaido, a self-taught magician, operated a small pharmacy. On the sidewalk outside the shop, Mr. Lee sold newspapers: *Diena,* the daily from Riga, and *Kurzemes Vards,* a newspaper Mother didn't like because of the racy ads for gentlemen's clubs. There was a Hasty Pasty pushcart and LazyQuick, a shop that made photocopies and could crank out résumés faster than people could think up false credentials to list. And, in a stroke of entrepreneurial brilliance, Stanka convinced Mr. Zetsche to allow her to sit in a lawn chair and tell fortunes and advise on lotteries and stock markets.

Stanka spied us from a distance and leaped from her lawn chair and hurried toward us.

"A prophecy! Good news and bad!" she cried. "Which do you want first, the good news or the bad?"

You fussed and squirmed. "The bad," I said.

"Trouble with stones." Stanka's voice turned deep and mysterious.

"Like in my kidneys or what?"

"The graveyard. There's terrible unrest there."

"What's the good news?"

"I see your porch steps bathed in butter and oil. And twenty white ponies — sorry — twenty white bunnies."

"Bunnies?"

Stanka's nose twitched. It was the season of dark morels and their pongy, musty scent beckoned. "Do not question my sources!" she cried. And off she went in search of dark treasure.

I think I've told you that I didn't pay too much attention to Stanka's special powers, but even a spent arrow manages to hit its target from time to time. I made short work of Dr. N.'s house then we went to examine the cemetery.

In almost any eastern Latvian graveyard, marker by marker, name by name, you can travel to Russia, Ukraine, Germany, Poland, and even Mongolia. And, of course, the plots say as much about the living as they do the dead. Your grandmother thought these stones were ostentatious means to measure loss. A weird celebration of one's grief. She would cite the competitive manner in which various families erected swags of fir boughs, staked plastic wreaths on stands, and in some cases placed stone benches to allow for longer, more comfortable contemplation. Though it was expensive to do this, a few of the Russian families had even ringed their grave sites with waist-high black metal fencing, the kind with the slim vertical bars punctuated with little metal spikes. They hung candles from the trees, built icon boxes, all in an attempt to make the gravesite look a little more Orthodox, hallowed, separate. I tiptoed around the stone for Rudy's little one. I tiptoed past the stones for Velta and Ferdinands. I showed you your namesake's stone. I could see that the grass around his grave had been disturbed, as if Uncle had been turning in his sleep. There were lash marks, boot blacking or paint, on the side of his stone.

I have tried to tell you things as I saw them then and as I now understand them to be. Every memory invites correction, adjustment, validation against the memories belonging to others. The trouble is, of course, there are few of us left. My telling of these stories I realize now is a flawed one. The act of telling is an act of preserving, but sometimes words wring out unintended meanings from an idea. And who will correct me when I am gone? I've set forth what I can recall in a particular, peculiar order, and I'm not certain what configurations they will impress upon you. I have tied knots into a long rope. I have said, *Here and here. This is important, and this.* The knots are the places on the rope where you will grab hold. The rope will pull, will run through your hands, as you grasp the knots while one after the other they will tear your palms. They will burn you; they will brand you. But a story started must be finished and told as fully and completely as possible. And so I must tell you, though it is not a nice story, about the swing your uncle Rudy built.

. . .

Traditionally, Mr. and Mrs. Vicins hosted the Push the Swing ceremony. You wouldn't remember them: a few years after you were born, he threw himself in front of a milk truck. She became extraordinarily Catholic and refused to eat or drink anything but the Eucharist: a bit of bread and a thimble of wine each morning. She starved to death, poor thing. Anyway, a spring ritual, this swing, a very Latvian expression: the master and mistress swinging to bring good luck for the fields and all who worked them. This year Mr. and Mrs. Zetsche lobbied hard to host the celebration on the rolling green beside the Riviera, the same green that once had been the cemetery. Because so many of us were in some way employed by the Zetsches and because the Zetsches wore us down with their endless petitioning. "This Riviera — it belongs to everyone," Mr. Zetsche implored on one occasion over the black telephone. "It is our commercial heritage. It only makes sense to push the swing at a place where people would be gathering anyway. To shop, that is. Plus, we'll provide the beer." So it was decided.

A few days before the ceremony, I found your grandfather in the cemetery. He sat in his keeper's shed, his elbows resting on his knees, a bucket and rag at his feet.

"Uncle's stone —"

"I know," he said. "His is just one of many."

I reached for the bucket. "Tell me where and I'll clean them."

"Dear girl." *Dear girl.* Such weariness in those words. "You and Little Maris should not be near these chemicals. Go home and help your mother."

We left your grandfather to his work and moved toward the yellow squares of light pouring from our house. Mother had already laid out dinner: a mixture of meat and onions and shredded cabbage and carrots that she called lazy pigeon. It was lazy because Mother hadn't rolled everything up in cabbage leaves. But she'd spiced the beef and she'd cut the cabbage and onions thin and fine.

It didn't feel right to eat without Father. We made small talk.

Rudy relayed a city joke a surveyor from Rezekne told him: "Why do you throw a black cat into a new apartment before entering?"

We waited for the punch line.

"To make sure the floor will not give beneath your feet," Rudy said.

Ligita rolled her eyes. "That is so unfresh." In truth, structures thrown up in haste and their quick collapse had been much discussed in the local news and touted as one more reason why people should not live in large cities.

"Egregious corruption," Joels concluded.

"Nothing changes," Mother said. "It's like this. Crows sit like fists on the limbs of a tree. Someone shoots a gun and they all scatter. But in a few minutes other birds alight on the same limbs. That is corruption in Latvia: same tree, different birds." Mother drained her teacup in a single swallow.

"The mayor in Ventspils wears loud sweaters purchased with taxpayers' money," Ligita offered.

"What I don't care for is the way foreigners come in and throw up a stick or two and grab land." Rudy looked earnestly at his food. "These people are just squatters with a little more money."

"If they buy it fair and square, then it's legal," I said.

"Latvia is for Latvians," Rudy said.

I looked at Mother, expecting her to say something, but she merely looked at her empty plate. Father came in through the kitchen door. Rudy took a large spoonful of meat and chewed vigorously.

Mother jumped from the table and brought Father some tea. She made a big deal out of bringing more tea to the table, first carrying the pot then fussing over the sugar and milk. Joels ate steadily as if this talk were water moving around him and he were a stone, implacable and unhearing.

"About the Push the Swing ceremony," Father addressed Rudy. "It would be nice if we wore our Jani Day shirts, I think. Your cuffs—they are clean?"

"Yes."

"And the swing. It's hung level?"

The muscle along Rudy's jaw tightened. "Yes."

"And the ropes?"

"I checked and rechecked and rerechecked. Everything is fine." Rudy pushed back from the table and strode out the back door.

That night Joels and I slept on the pullout in the living room. Rudy did not come home again. Ligita spent long hours on the back step talking to girlfriends on her cell phone. Held between noise and quiet, sleep and wakefulness, I could not fully enter either world. I studied the wavering wash of light the moon cast through the sheers onto the living-room wall. Everything, I decided, was beautiful when the light is dim enough. In the darkness I heard Mother and Father's cautious whispering.

"What was it at the cemetery?"

"Obscenities, same as before. And a hammer and sickle. Only this time it was with spray paint."

"Whose stone?"

"Mrs. Zetsche's uncle."

"Which side did he fight for?"

"Both, I think."

A long pause. "What did you use?"

"Muriatic acid."

"Will it come out?"

"Well, if not, I can make it look like something else. A star maybe."

Another long pause.

"Mrs. A. tells me that Mr. Zetsche is thinking of getting a dog. You know, the kind with teeth, the kind that bites."

The bed creaked.

Then from Mother a protracted sigh. "Sometimes I think I do not understand a single thing about this world or anyone in it."

We heard the Merry Afflictions before we saw them. From Joels's sax came a few mournful howls and some flatulence from Vanags's trombone. Ludviks stirred his sticks in anxious rasping noises over the drums. It was a perfect day. The promise of free beer had catapulted everyone into high spirits.

From behind the oak, Rudy and Mr. Lee steadied the seat of the swing. With the help of a stepladder, the Zetsches mounted the swing, their feet on the seat and their hands at the ropes. Rudy and Mr. Gipsis gave a cautious push. And then another. And then another. Higher and higher the Zetsches arced through the air; harder and harder Rudy pushed. The Zetsches, as stiff as human metronomes marking out a soundless tune. Mr. Zetsche wore a grin, but an expression of pure terror had seized Mrs. Zetsche's face. The swing had acquired a list, and one end drooped a little lower than the other. Mrs. Z. was turning colors.

A few of the men coughed. "It is enough," Father whispered to Rudy, for clearly Mrs. Zetsche was in trouble. But it is considered very bad luck, or at least bad form, to interfere with the swing once it's in motion. And so we all stood and watched.

"You're doing marvelously!" Miss Dzelz called. That is when Mrs. Zetsche turned her stomach inside out.

But as long as beer is on hand, such occurrences are only minor hiccups in the general festivities. The only remedy is to drink more beer as quickly as possible. Mother and I helped Mrs. Z. from the swing while Mr. Z. signaled for the beer and the Merry Afflictions struck a resplendent tune. The conversation jittered along like an epileptic on a high wire bouncing from talk of the economy, which was by all accounts in the crapper, to the beer, which was just okay, to talk of the EU ("We must join! We must progress with the times and merge with the larger European community!") back to the beer, which was running low, to talk of whether a woman could really be a president (Mother chimed in loudly that women make fine presidents) to talk of the ceramics factory that had shut down to talk of latent Russian aggression (Widow Sosnovskis kept her eyes averted from Widow Spassky, however). Back to the beer, which was definitely not okay because it was now gone. The crowd quickly thinned. To make matters worse, Mrs. Zetsche passed around marzipan that sunk like a chunk of lead in the stomach.

"Not enough almond," Mother said, and turned for home. As did everyone else. The Merry Afflictions packed up their instruments; Vanags brought around his gray Pobeda. Joels remained on the green. We stood side by side, Joels cradling his sax tenderly to his chest, I cradled you. Small yellow pieces of paper littered the green and the wind kicked them toward the river.

Mr. Zetsche stood beneath the oak tree, his hand on one of the ropes of the swing. The seat of the swing listed steeply to one side. He was looking up at the oak at the place where the ropes looped over the branch. One rope was frayed, much more so than the other. In fact, it looked as if the slightest bit of friction and weight would cause it to snap. Mr. Zetsche was talking, but I could not see to whom he was speaking. His gaze was trained on the space between the two banks of the river narrowing fast into darkness.

"I'm not as happy as I look. You know, I have my troubles, too." In Mr. Zetsche's hand was one of those yellow flyers. "I'm a man of principle. I did what I said I would do. I brought jobs to the town. The thing is, I'm not a land-grabber. The thing is, I love this land. My grandfather did, too, before the war. Before all of . . . that."

Now Mr. Zetsche turned and looked at us. He had known we were there all along. "And we paid fair and square for the manor property. So why do things like this happen? Why so many broken windows. I don't mind so much, but it's not fair to my Mildi."

Joels approached the swing. A few saws with his pocket knife and it tumbled down.

Mr. Zetsche handed the yellow paper to me. LATVIA FOR LATVI- ANS, the slogan made popular years ago by a fatherland political party. I felt that old weight, dread, growing inside me. I think about that moment on the green with the broken ropes as the first time I recognized my own naïve complacency, complicity. I realized that whatever our intentions, collective or individual, we would find ways to punish the Zetsches.

In the following weeks, the ground thawed, releasing a steam in the morning that convinced me that soil sleeps, wakes, and breathes just as we do. With each exhalation, the last dreams of winter rolled over the dark ground in white rasps that were sublimed to light. This was how winter left our lane, leaving the gate open for Lent. Father gave the Easter messages at the hall for the two groups of Baptists. As he spoke of the reviving power of water, we looked out the windows of the hall and watched a world of possibility slowly emerging: runnels of rainwater coursed through the lane that guttered alongside the hall. In the fields powerful rills laid bare the soil in dark gashes. It was the season of surprising changes and none of us were exempt. Joels, who had been beating himself up all winter working on new jingles, finally received some good news: a fledgling vodka manufacturer in Kaliningrad purchased three of his product names and tunes. The first name, Eternal Fire, struck me as a little dyspeptic. The bottlers hoped the second, Rear Naked Choke, would entice fans of mixed martial arts — a growing target market, they assured Joels. Lastly, there was Skak, or "at a full gallop" for the Russians who fancied themselves very bold. Factually speaking, it was all the same vodka bottled by the same manufacturer. Although they hadn't yet sent payment, they had sent twenty cases of their product. The timing of this delivery was, in my opinion, divinely inspired. *No! It was serendipity!* Mother insisted later when she recounted the story to Father. She just happened to be in the yard hanging laundry when the man in the delivery van tooted his horn. Not two minutes later, she had the cases safely stowed in the root cellar, the place Mother put things she did not want anyone to know about. She had, after all, her reputation as president of the Ladies Temperance League to think of. But it was clear in the manner of her recitations how very proud she was of Joels.

· · ·

Dr. Netsulis, never one to sit about idly, also had been hard at work all winter boiling different currencies in various solutions: euros, lats, rubles, pounds, and dollars. As it turned out, the Swedish kroner was the most stable currency in nonbuoyant and turbulent environments. This, he maintained, explained the urgent longing so many young people had for the Scandinavian countries. As if to confirm these findings, no sooner had I cleaned all the grimy test tubes (the American dollar has a tenacious ink that clings to glass like no other) than Dr. Netsulis cut my hours. "They were glorious, these last experiments, but now"—he hung his head ruefully and the two ends of his mustache drooped into his white beard—"my funding is kaput. I can afford you only one day a week—to look after the stalls."

I will confess that during those early three years of your life I moved and lived as if I swam in thick, viscous water, my thoughts and perceptions sheathed in a fog. Sleep deprivation does that to a woman. You told me once that sound never vanishes, is never lost. Once created, a sound wave travels infinitely. I believe this to be true. I have witnessed how sound returns, called back by a scent, a wrinkle in the clouds, a thought. Mother used to tell me that our words are like arrows. Once spent, they fly from us and we can't call them back. This is true and not true, given the way a word, just one, hovers at the edge of memory, treads at the threshold of waking and sleeping. Which word? *Work.*

Mrs. Ilmyen put in a word for me at the clinic, and three times a week I cleaned the front office and surgery. In the evenings I cleaned at the school. Mother tended to you.

I wanted to help, but Mother wouldn't hear of it. "You and Joels work; I don't. I might as well make myself useful with the boy."

I understood the ethic to which Mother subscribed: we find ourselves in work; work makes us who we are. This had to be why she set about caring for you during those early years, more thoroughly, in certain ways, than she had for Rudy and me. Though you weighed more than two stones, she carried you in her arms. She shielded you from every draft, real or imagined, by wrapping you in blankets and shawls. And she told you things she'd never told me: rye blossoms for two weeks, ripens for two weeks, and dries for two weeks. Then, and only then, is it time to harvest. After the harvest, the cutters and gatherers always leave a little bread in the sheaves for the fields. "How do you know so much about rye?" I asked her. Great-grandmother Velta's farm, I knew, had been seized and collectivized when Mother was a girl. She could not have possibly grown up in the fields. But Mother simply shrugged and kept singing.

I'd never known Mother to sing so much as when she held you.

> *God grant satiety!*
> *Bear's strength,*
> *Midge's gut,*
> *The ease of hops!*

Be as strong as a bear, every mother's wish. Be satiated with as little as what satisfies the midge, and as you walk the long road, may your step be as light as hops.

I am unraveling one hair at a time. I have a hank of wispy thin hair at the base of my skull, all that has and will ever return. Not silver, not white. It's the same tarnished color Mrs. Zetsche's silver acquired when it needed polishing. Ligita and Jutta came to sit with me. Ligita unearthed an old can of Uncle's vitality drink. Uncle was quite right when he said it tasted like shit. Jutta combed those brittle wisps that break at the slightest touch. At any rate, she asked me how I would describe the difference between mortal and immortal. *Fragile,* I said, and we both laughed. I am not a theologian or a philosopher, my faith is of a diaphanous sort: semirigid, light but strong. I know what I believe; my experience bears witness. I said, that being immortal, we recognize we are mere sojourners here; this is not our true homeland.

Being mortal, we cannot bear to leave. Which makes Uncle's present situation all the more strange. Human fortitude, divine caprice, the injustice of a causality. He burns with indignation all while spouting psalmic phrases amid his habitation of stones. He is bored. Fifteen years dead and as stuck as ever. *If Uncle had been a Jew,* Jutta said, *his stay in hell would have been no longer than twelve months. This is the problem with Christian hell,* she said, *there are no firm boundaries in time and space. And purgatory, too,* Ligita added. *This is why,* Ligita explained, *Catholics can be at all times and in all places utterly miserable.*

Anyway, I've been thinking about those early years when you were just learning to speak. I wish now I'd written down more of what you said. It would fill your Book of Wonder. We suspected that it was on account of your ears that your speech was so delayed. But when you did talk, right around your fifth birthday, you tugged on Father's pant leg, and said, *Night is when God puts his hands around the sun.*

Father spun in circle, amazed. "The boy is a poet!"

The sky, you said, *was nothing more than a thinning lampshade stretched to paper; God was light moving behind it. Darkness was light standing still.*

Transported beyond joy, Father carried you to church every Sunday, believing that you possessed a prophet's clear ear for divine messages. "He could preach someday," Father proclaimed, in a manner that suggested it was certainty. And the pride on Father's face was the kind reserved for a most favored son.

By this time, I couldn't wear you on my back any longer. When I hung laundry, I kept you tethered to me. With that sash. Not a leash, a sash. Let me be clear.

I am grateful that you and your uncle Rudy have always been close. He taught you how to catch eels. He taught you how to smell the edges in the wind and adjust your line accordingly. He loved you as if you were his, and I tell you this lest you think for a moment that my love for him wavered. He was, in those years of your youth, a haunted soul. In the evenings when Rudy should have been working at Rimi, he'd be else-where. At the *kafenica,* I figured, where the manager allowed Rudy and his friends to run tabs while they talked radical politics. They had plenty to discuss—at last count twenty-three political parties had put forth a presidential candidate. One of them was a woman, which pleased your grandmother to no end. But Rudy's absences provoked more complaints from Ligita, who updated us on his lack of motiva-tion at the evening meals. Her biggest complaint: he hadn't achieved success—that most mighty word in Latvia. Her disappointment set-tled over the table like a transparent veil: through these nightly narra-tives of dissatisfaction, we could readily glimpse a virtual widow des-tined for even larger heartbreaks.

What none of us could bring ourselves to discuss was Rudy's drinking, which had a dogged, determined quality about it. He never drank in the house, but in the yard I found bottles of Skak-Eternal-Fire-Rear-Naked-Choke clumsily stashed behind the woodpile. This was an added disappointment to us all; he wasn't even bothering to conceal his drinking in an artful, convincing manner. For a while, I attributed the change in his demeanor to a special form of male grief. If he stayed out all hours of the day and night, if he had sudden bursts of anger, long stretches of silence, if he smelled of mud and vodka, who could blame him. It hadn't been that long since he'd put that cake-boxsize coffin into the ground.

Joels and I talked it over in whispers at night. Could he have fallen in with a bad sort? Who were those men at the *kafenica* he argued pol-itics with? Why did he wear his church shoes to town on some days and creep around in his boots on others? Was he, perhaps, merely fishing?

"He can't possibly be as inert as Ligita claims," I observed late one night. "He gives Mother a five-lat note every Sunday morning. He must be doing something."

"Yes," Joels said. "Of that we can be certain."

· · ·

In time we might have forgotten about Rudy's drinking. But then two things happened: one of Mr. Zetsche's Riviera shops, a pharmacy, caught fire, and Father turned sixty. We heard about the fire first from Stanka who regaled us with detailed accounts of how much square footage had been burned to a crisp and what she had calculated the cost of the damages to be. Rudy, at home that day just long enough to change his clothes and douse himself with cheap cologne, contended that Mr. Vaido had bungled some new magic trick. We had all witnessed Mr. Vaido's illusions at children's birthday parties and we knew he wasn't much of a magician. "How many years did we buy our aspirins from him?" Mother's eyebrows arched. "Too many," Father said. "We are lucky to be alive."

To recoup his losses, Mr. Zetsche cut Father's hours at the cemetery from halves to quarters and raised the rent for all his Riviera shop tenants: Hasty Pasty, LazyQuick, Rimi, the *kafenica*. The shop managers all retaliated in kind by redesignating full-time employees to part-time employees, and part-time employees received the full boot. It became clear to us that between all of our part-time jobs we needed to find more work. But where? Any person older than fifteen and younger than forty who wanted to do more than study the bottom of a bottle moved to Riga or took a job outside of the country if they could. Rudy talked of Sweden, of immigrating, a word Mother would not abide. Father tried to find work in Daugavpils, but he had no specialized training other than what he'd completed at technical school. Ligita made some attempts at finding work, ringing up girlfriends on the black wall phone to see if any of them knew of anyone who was hiring. Of her five friends in Daugavpils, three had already found lonely men in Wales to wed and the other two friends were in open competition for the same jobs. In desperation I made the trek through the brambles to Mrs. Zetsche's, a bucket, rag, and turpentine in my hands. I stood on the back porch and collected myself. What a ridiculous proposition: a girl who'd been fired for mowing over the cherished stallions presenting herself as if nothing had happened. A girl, well aware that her would-be employers had just that week given her brother the boot, begging for a job.

Mrs. Zetsche opened the door, and the scent of cedar and pines wafted out around her.

If I didn't work, I'd die, I told her, aware of how desperation rendered my words overly dramatic.

"The thing is." Mrs. Z. dropped her voice to a confidential volume. "We have a cleaning girl already." Mrs. Z. stepped onto the porch, pulling the oversize manor door closed behind her not quite fast enough. In the crescent of space between the jamb and her shoulder, I spied movement: a dull streak of brick red. Ligita.

I shifted the bucket from one hand to the other.

"But if you're serious about working, we could use help with grounds keeping. And then the cast-iron stallions always need some attention. But times being as they are, I can't offer you much." Mrs. Zetsche held her hand upturned at the wrists as if she were carrying invisible trays of cocktails.

I studied the cleaning bucket in my hand. Did Mother ever settle for our sakes? Yes. Yes, she had. All too often. And she never said a peep about it. "I would work for less, Mrs. Zetsche."

And I needed to. In two days Father would turn sixty. For those two days the house was all sixes and sevens: Mother in a dither rushing from oven to sink to oven, adjusting and correcting her sauces, hanging laundry, overseeing my paltry attempts at twisting bundles of wheat stalks into a wreath. The big night finally arrived and we gathered for a grand celebration: your grandmother, Stanka, Dr. Netsulis, Miss Dzelz, Rudy, Ligita, Joels, you, and I. Mother brought out a special cake called Chernobyl that required not one but two cans of condensed sweetened milk boiled and caramelized, several eggs, and walnuts. Upon seeing the cake, a trembling behemoth of refined sugar, Dr. Netsulis, Rudy, and Joels hopped from their chairs. In the tradition, they lifted Father in his chair, raising him high above the table and back to the floor sixty times, one for each year of life. It was a good thing Father was not a large man and Joels, Rudy, and Dr. Netsulis were. While the men recovered, Ligita and I supplied them with a pale restorative: birch juice for the doctor and Father, and Skak-Eternal-Fire-Rear-Naked-Choke for everyone else.

Mother tapped her fork to her glass. "A toast!"

Just then the phone sounded low and loudly. We all looked at it as if it were a rude and unwelcome guest.

"Pretend we're not home," Mother begged, but Father had already crossed the kitchen and lifted the receiver.

"Yes," he said, after a long moment. "I understand." Father slid the receiver into the cradle and sat down slowly. "That was Mr. Zetsche," he announced. "He thanks me for my years of service, but he has decided that tending the cemetery is too demanding for a man of my age."

Rudy jumped to his feet. "That little bastard! He's cheated us—again!"

"No, son." Father shook his head and motioned Rudy to take his chair.

"A toast," Mother said again, this time more quietly. But Father merely shook his head once more. "When your heart is as full as mine with good things and bad, rich and poor, heaven and earth, what more is there to be said?" Father turned his gaze to his cake. He took a breath, held it, then blew. *Poof.* Out that candle went. He sat down and folded his arms across his chest and it was as if with that single exhalation all of his words evaporated—everything he'd been thinking about or might have wanted to say.

You set your spoon in his bowl and wiggled a finger in an ear canal. "A lake dries out; the crows fall in," you said. It was a riddle Mother had taught you. What it meant was that when the bowl is emptied the wooden spoons clatter to the bottom. It was a puzzling saying that somehow made perfect sense: in his emptiness Father was full. Or maybe it went the other way around.

Inside the house silence reigned supreme. For weeks Father would not talk. He'd been exiled from the only place he'd ever felt he could do bodily good. No one would love those stones as much as he did. No one would remember to rake the footprints on sandy gravel outside the cemetery. No one would know how to remove graffiti and other signs of unrest as well as he did. I knew that this is what he was thinking. Mother and I tried to coax him toward happy memories. I reminded Father of the proper cemetery etiquette, beer and whiskey passed to guests at the wake and salted dried peas and beans at the graveside. The peas symbolized the tears before a burial. The beer was a reminder to seek joy. Mother reminded Father of the great care Oskars exercised as he built coffins: he hollowed out a big broad beam of wood. The lid he made by squaring a plank to fulfill the custom: an eternal coffin, a temporary lid.

Every morning Mother read to Father from her newspaper: a ceramics factory in Latgale closed and another sugar refinery had shut its doors. The unemployment rate soared. As she read, Rudy supplied his own interpretations. About the university graduates exiting the country en masse, "No jobs for real Latvians, here," he said. Rudy referred to the new development outside Rezekne as "shameless land-grabbing by those Krauts and lefse-eating Norwegians." As he spoke, he'd twist the paper napkins into nooses.

Still, Father would not utter a word.

We decided repetition would break his silence, wear him down the same way water bores though stone. We told stories, our words like string winding around itself into a ball: no beginning, no end, just a steady sound of the human voice. We told of Uncle's proposal for an all-Latvian, all-nude female pro soccer team. It was a suggestion that had made him extremely popular in some circles, less so in others. Rudy told about how Uncle once lured geologists from Finland to a nearby forest, claiming it was full of meteorites. They came in droves, those Finns, and when they saw they'd been duped with pieces of worthless kimberlite, Uncle sold them cell phones and offered them free classes in the art of water witching.

Mother reminded Father of the time Uncle parachuted into a dairy farmer's pasture and scared the cows milkless. The farmer presented Maris with a bill for all the milk the cows should have produced, a slip of paper that Uncle stuffed into his mouth and chased with a glass of milk. We wanted to hear Father laugh. And so we talked and talked while you sat listening to every word we said, turning your ears first this way and that, your ears funnels for sound and your eyelids blinking as if you were silently storing away every word we said.

Father sat in his chair and smoked his pipe. While we talked, blue-gray clouds wreathed his body. If our words penetrated that smoke, we did not know, for his eyes remained fixed on the mantel clock that ticked and sang on the hour. He had willed his tongue to dry up in his mouth, and I wondered, even if he had wanted to talk, if would he be able to.

Seeing him this way twisted my stomach in tight, cold coils.

Mr. Zetsche had done this to Father. Had Mrs. Zetsche known this was coming? Could this be why she rehired me, her way of making amends preemptively. I don't know. And I didn't let her act of kindness diminish my hatred for Mr. Zetsche. It was the first time I really and fully hated someone. A few years earlier after the Pushing of the Swing, I had watched Mr. Zetsche by the oak tree. As he surveyed the frayed ropes of his swing, I had felt sorry for him. Now I felt overwhelmed by an animal sadness, for all this time I had secretly believed that I was above hatred. I realized now that I was not. I was as small and ordinary as anybody else.

· · ·

For three weeks I hated Mr. Zetsche. It was during this time that I dismantled the phone. *Dismantle* suggests a gentleness to the action. Actually, I ripped it from the wall. I shattered it with a hammer. I threw the pieces into the root cellar and hoped they would turn to mold. Each morning as I went to work, I could hardly look at Mr. Zetsche's horses, which symbolized to me foolish excess and vanity. Mr. Zetsche had two good and fine cars. Father had none, and the closest he would get to a fine and fast machine was the backhoe and now even that was taken from him.

Only Joels understood. He lived in the world of music; if one instrument fell silent, he noticed its absence. And if another instrument produced sour or false notes, this, too, he noticed immediately. But he was not an alarmist. He set about studying the situation—that is, me—and one night as we lay in bed, he regarded me carefully.

"The depth of a person's hatred is the measure of his or her limitations."

I rolled to my side away from Joels.

"Inara, do not hate that man."

"Why not?" I fumed.

"It disrupts consonance and continuity. It will consume you, and nothing will purge it but a greater consuming fire."

"How do you know this?"

Joels ran his hand through his hair. "Because I've hated before." Then he closed his eyes. He was a believer in the restorative powers of sleep. Sleep, he had explained more than once, makes everything new: the stones in the river, hues and shades of color, our words, and even the letters in the scriptures once a year are renewed in sleep.

Now, as I had then, I laid my ear on his furry chest. A steady rhythm of wet percussive beats throbbed in an even pattern. Sleep, I believed, was the time we each make a quiet music. How beautiful his heart and the music that it made. I think of that as the moment something inside me changed. I felt gratitude for Joels, the fact of his being there. Gratitude that I could feel gratitude and recognize how I felt.

Joels shifted his shoulder, pushing me off. Then he began to snore. Yes, I was grateful and awed that, given his circumstances and mine, he had chosen me. Now he rolled to his side and his breath whistled through his nose. I could feel something solid and elemental shifting in the bed of my heart. I would love this man whose love I could not match or understand, a man whose love for me was better than my love for him. And, even if it killed me, I would take his advice: I would not let loyalty for Father feed my stupid hatred. Father, after all, had not uttered a single word against Mr. Zetsche.

In the morning I followed Ligita in to work. We did not talk as we let ourselves in the back door. Though we'd both been working for the Zetsches since Easter, three months now, she still did not talk to me — not about Rudy or her chores for Mrs. Zetsche. Instead, she held her cell phone to her ear and pretended to talk. I happened to know she let her contract with the phone company lapse, but I also knew how important it was to keep up appearances, especially if that was all you had.

We stamped our feet on the grate and took off our shoes. From down the long ash-wood hallway came the footfalls of very small feet. Then Mrs. Zetsche.

"Inara." Mrs. Zetsche gripped one hand in the other. "Ligita." I had never seen her so distressed. "Please." Mrs. Zetsche gestured toward her chairs grouped around the table she only used when she was expecting fine company.

Ligita and I sat beside each other in plush straight-backed chairs with ball-and-claw feet while Mrs. Zetsche sat opposite us at the end of her very long well-polished table. She bit at her lip, tugged at a lock of hair. She put her hands on the table, spread her fingers, and looked at them for a moment.

"Girls, this is so terribly difficult, because you know how I feel about the both of you."

I looked at Ligita. Beneath her angry maroon bangs, Ligita looked at me. Mrs. Zetsche's feelings for us were of the utilitarian sort: she liked us as long as there were no discernible marks or blemishes anywhere in or around her minimansion.

"I've been counting the silver and silver-plated serving pieces. You know the ones?"

We nodded.

"Well, I'm three short. And I wouldn't have even mentioned it, except last month I was short four pieces. I'm not making an accusation, you understand, merely an observation." Mrs. Zetsche studied me carefully.

"I understand," I said.

"You and Ligita are the only hired help who have keys to the back door."

"We would never steal from you, Mrs. Zetsche," Ligita said at last, her voice pitifully thin, and yet there was a discernible trace of defiance. Ligita would go away from this encounter determined that it was she, not Mrs. Zetsche, who had been wronged by this theft.

Mrs. Zetsche's chin trembled. She plucked at her sleeve and a handkerchief flew to her eyes. She was crying openly. "I know it wasn't you, Inara. Or you, Ligita. But this is so troubling. Because, you see, there's just been so much happening to us of late."

Her tiny hand slid a yellow sheet of paper over the polished table-top. I recognized the flyer—PATRIOTIC LATVIANS FOR AN ALL-LATVIAN LATVIA. "Someone keeps sliding these papers under our door."

I rose to my feet and snatched the yellow paper from off the table. "I'm so sorry, Mrs. Zetsche. It's rubbish—pay it no mind."

"Just some stupid kids trying to make a point," Ligita added.

I made my way home, that old stone pushing my shoulders forward. I looked at that sheet of paper and felt shame. What did I know, really, of her troubles? We did not know where they had lived before they came here or under what circumstances they had left. Nor did I have any real knowledge of just how very hard it was to be a foreigner or, at the very least, a newcomer. I thought about Mrs. Zetsche, who had furiously dabbed at her eyes with a scented tissue. What provocation did I have, really, in disliking her so? She could not help who she was or where she was. She could not help it if she had things when others didn't.

Ligita and I found Rudy beside the woodpile where he was exploring the limits of the potato's not so secret revenge. A bottle of Skak-Eternal-Fire-Rear-Naked-Choke stood wedged in between thick pieces of hardwood set out to season. I showed him the yellow paper.

"Tell me you are not involved," I pleaded.

"Most men are cowards or slaves," Rudy said.

"Which one are you?" I asked.

Mother, who'd been conveniently hanging laundry, appeared from behind a scrim of wet sheets. With one hand, she led you; with the other, she balanced her basket in the crook between her hip and ribs. Rudy didn't see her approaching. Drink had made him effusive, garrulous, loud.

Rudy shrugged. "We are going back to the land. We are taking back what is ours." Mother dropped her basket and Rudy startled. Mother regarded Rudy as if he were something alien and slightly dangerous. Mother took another step toward us and leaned her whole body toward Rudy.

"Never will you talk like this."

Rudy's face underwent a strange transformation. "But he took our ancestral property."

"No," Mother said. "We sold it to him."

It was as if his face were a bowl of still water and she'd troubled the surface with her hands. Whereas his face had been serene, even smug, now his brow lifted, his eyes widened in genuine surprise. Over his face passed a panoply of expressions: alarm, amusement, irritation. At last he settled, a placating smile filtering over his features.

"You were coerced, you were manipulated. If we play our cards right, we can still get the manor house back."

Mother frowned. "Most men grow wiser as they grow older. But, son, I worry for you."

Rudy's voice hardened. "Think about it. When has Latvia really ever belonged to Latvians? We are smart people and capable people. We have ideas and energy and resources. We just need to come together for a common cause."

"And what cause is that?"

"The redistribution of wealth to those who need it most." Rudy grinned. "Imagine a small band of modern-day Robin Hoods." Rudy pulled a five-lat note from his pocket and set it on top of the remaining laundry in her basket.

Mother glanced at the note. "You are not the son I raised."

"I am exactly the son you raised. Aren't you the one who said that all the wrong people benefit from the hard work of Latvians? I'm just settling the score."

Mother's face turned ashen. "Get out of here." Her voice trembled.

For five very long seconds Rudy stood still. And then, as if he'd been touched with an electrical current, he sprang backward and ran down the lane. We did not even hear his boots crunching on the gravel.

CHAPTER TEN

W HAT IF THE WORLD WERE MADE OF STORY? What if a bedrock of words girded the ground beneath our feet? What if the sky were a brattice of sound, hum, and hymn holding us in an invisible embrace? What do I think of this, a poem for the newspaper?

I don't know if your grandmother ever received hate mail. Certainly there were heated exchanges, particularly regarding politics or recipes involving carrots. She was not a fan of them, as you may or may not recall. She usually got the last word in with her "Kindly Advices" column. *If you can't say anything nice, then shut up already!* Did people appreciate her labors with the newspaper? Probably not. Her pearls, as Father would say, had been scattered before swine. But I believe she would have been delighted to see how you are reviving her old column and writing something new: "Mishaps with Camels in Kyrgyzstan!"

And the old pictures. The one you showed me this morning was her favorite, bar none. The legendary Baltic Chain. She wrote an article about what it was like standing along the roadway outside of Riga amid a long line of people holding hands. Where the gap between them yawned too wide, they held a sash. In this way, the chain remained unbroken. Mother wrote of the day she and Mrs. Ilmyen rode the bus to Balvi and another bus to Riga and then finally another to a town just south of Riga. She wrote what it felt like to join hands with people she'd never met: a truck driver from Daugavpils on her one side and an Old Believer in her long skirts and snug snoodlike head scarf on her other side. Mrs. Arijisnikov, standing a few paces down the chain, had likewise linked hands with people she'd never met. All along the A2 more than one million people joined together and sang. This is how Balts lodge a protest, your grandmother explained to me. We don't throw bricks. We don't lob grenades. We come together and we make a chain with our hands and our words and our songs. We say to our oppressors: you cannot pull us apart. We come together and we sing.

You have always loved the story of little Samuel. No other boy in the Bible had ears like he did. Speak, Lord, your servant is listening. He'd been promised to Eli the prophet, to serve the older man and be mentored in the ways of the temple. Didn't Eli have other sons, other protégés? Surely he did. But they were as lazy as fallen chestnuts.

Eli was an old man and he spent a good portion of his time listening to God with his eyes closed. This he was doing when God spoke to little Samuel. *Samuel! Samuel!* And the boy, thinking Eli had called him, runs to the old man's room and says, *Here I am.*

Go back to sleep, Eli says. *I didn't call you.*

This happens again: *Samuel!* And the boy goes to Eli. *Go away,* Eli says. *I didn't call you,* and even in the spare King James text, you can sense the ire in the aged prophet's voice. Maybe he thought the boy was playing tricks on him, depriving an old man of one of his few pleasures in life. The third time Samuel hears his name called and wakes his master, Eli finally understands. If this boy could hear so clearly and well at that young age, then he was beyond the need for mentorship. I have been thinking about how the young outstrip and surpass the old. If the old have mentored well, it's natural and right that this should happen. I'm no prophet, no saint. I have made mistakes. But I am singing the old songs, telling the stories. I am weaving a cloak of knots small and large. I am holding the sash.

You stand in the middle of this song, hearing what I can't. "I have made mistakes," Uncle told you. When the devil whistled, he jumped. And now he feels some guilt. And unease. A foot in search of a shoe. A cup looking for water. So thirsty, Uncle is, he could spit nails. At least that's what he's been telling you. This unrest, you say, is our fault: Father's sorrow, Mother's irritation, my anger, Rudy's adulation, all kept Uncle hemmed in the mud none too comfortably. "I am poured out like water, and all my bones are out of joint. My heart is like wax . . . I may tell all my bones." This, you say, is his enduring lament.

"That's from Psalm 22," I said, my heart leaping. Uncle was reading the Bible — at last. "Yes," you replied. "And it's boring holes through Uncle's hip bones." The ink branded his skin, etched indelible marks upon the tablet of his heart. Yes, I've made mistakes. I realize now that I am his haunting, and all this time I thought he was mine.

In those days after Mr. Zetsche gave him the boot, your grandfather took you at night to walk in the dark among the stones of the cemetery. So much of his life your grandfather had spent in that place, fretting over every stone, marker, and icon. He couldn't fully abandon them to the hands of the new caretaker, a Slovenian, who wisely made himself scarce in town. At dusk you'd go, leaping over the back gate, where I imagined you and your grandfather soundlessly wading through tall grass. I wondered if these long walks among the quiet world of the dead weren't his way of firming the seams between the life he'd made for himself and the one that had been given to him. Red clover, vetch, and the bee, did they carry him back in scent and sound to some early memory, a time before words? I wondered if this was why, even before he abandoned his voice, he didn't talk when he worked in the cemetery. As he cared for the plots containing people, some of whose families had left and likely would never return, was he thinking of his own mother and father still in Siberia, buried in the yellow dirt by his young boy's hands? Was this why he had always cared for the cemetery and everything in it with a tenderness that defied reason (yes, *tenderness* is the only word I can supply when I conjure the image of Father kneeling before those stones, touching up the paint or scrubbing with a small brush at dirt and mud).

Whatever the reason, it was a good thing your grandfather did this. It had rained so much in the prior few months that water stood on the ground. Some of the stones had fallen over. Mr. Z.'s new hire did a fair job of keeping the leaves raked into piles, but it was Father who cleaned the moss off the stones, Father who made repairs in the middle of the night, Father who scrubbed off the graffiti someone had painted on the stone belonging to one of Mrs. Zetsche's distant relatives. This is what love looks like: caring for others even when your care is unwanted.

By this time, you were ten and would have been in the fourth grade. You had not grown into your ears and had accepted the fact that you never would. But neither would you wear those aviator's ear protectors. You said they made the world as blank as bleach, as tasteless as a bus window. You preferred instead to grow your hair long and wear a woolen cap. You almost looked like the other boys. But you have never walked like other people. This is not to say that you aren't coordinated or graceful. But whereas some people — your aunt Ligita, say — walk with their hips propelling the body forward or other people — such as your grandmother sniffing the changes in heat from her oven — walk as if led by the nose, you have always been pulled by your ears. It was as if sound were a living thing pulling you by the right ear this way and then by the left ear that way. You could not ignore these tugs of sound even if you tried.

After some of those late-night walks through the cemetery, you would return home, your hair on one side of your head wet from where you'd placed it against the stones. "I don't think Mrs. Ecis really died of indigestion," you might say. Or "The grass is brown at Mr.

Berzin's grave because he's angry that his daughter doesn't visit often." Though Father was still not talking, he would exchange a significant glance with Mother, as would Joels and I. Later, as you drifted off to sleep, listening, I suppose, to the scratching of the stars etching their distant traceries in the darkness, we'd scribble on slips of paper our diagnosis: his powers of hearing weren't really that keen. These were the lively musings of a ten-year-old's imagination asserting itself, testing its limits via exaggeration. My easy dismissal, I realize, is a failure on my part. Why was I unable to allow in you possibilities that outstrip my own imagination?

How I wished in those days that I could dampen the noise around you. We choose which chords we strike first in any conversation, in our lives, in our loves. And because the words that follow are a natural progression of that first fateful chord, I wanted my words to be gentle. A strange unrest had enveloped our little town, and over the last few years, it had grown more robust. Even Stanka's dog was not immune: every day he nipped at Mr. Arijisnikov's ankles as he went to and from the river. Sometimes Mr. A. complained. When he did, Stanka merely shrugged. "Oh, that's just his way of showing affection. If he had any real rancor, he'd have drawn blood."

We could attribute some of the despair to the two sugar refineries that closed down and the textile manufacturer in Rezekne that shut its doors. There were even rumors that the *kafenica,* the place where some of Rudy's friends sat at tables drinking tea and other things, might whittle back its hours. It was a rumor that kindled even more grumbling and speculation—the shops at the Riviera were failing. I blamed the cold and the unending rain. In the older homes of the elderly pensioners, winter hit hard. Two old women, unable to pay for heat, had frozen to death. Stanka had taken to stuffing Mother's back issues of the Ladies Temperance League newspaper into the spaces between her roof and siding. Others who had lost their electricity now relied on their ancient carbide lamps. But if I'd walk past the *kafen-*

ica, I'd hear blame cast in other directions: at the corruption of certain government officials and agencies, at inadequate leadership, at foreigners who, on account of our joining the European Union, were free to roam in and out of Latvia and, in some cases, even buy land. To hear people talk, foreign investors were either shameless speculators or our financial saviors.

I didn't know what to think. All I knew was that for all our hard work—our clean-as-a-whistle school, the brilliance of Dr. Netsulis, our root cellar full of Skak and temperance newspapers—we were still trying to figure out how to stretch our pickled eel and potatoes through the winter. With the exception of Mr. Ilmyen, who translated important official documents, the income of most people in town had not grown but withered. Mr. Zetsche's market had fewer and fewer items on the shelves, but prices had steadily climbed, and last week he'd sacked another employee, a man with whom Rudy had gone to school. Mother pounded on her typewriter, the hammer striking the ribbon with such force the entire typewriter trembled.

Trouble with taxes? Simply don't pay them. Nobody else does.

Feeling depressed? Join the club! The latest World Health Report ranks Latvia in third place for the highest number of suicides.

Amid all of this noise, some of it loud and strident, some of it cloaked in sighs, as if assigning actual words to our troubles was too much of a strain, I wanted quiet.

The posters of political candidates whose mouths had been scratched out with a key or a coin or, in one instance, had thumbtacks pressed into the place where the eyes had been: that was caricature, petty vandalism, nothing a boy should pay any attention to. I pulled down those posters. The hateful slogans written in chalk on the playground—I dumped tubs of wash water on them. Love, I figured. This was love and therefore what a good mother does: she absorbs all that seems unbalanced, disturbed. As a mother trims tough crusts of old bread, serving up only what she thinks her children can chew, I would whittle the discordance of a swiftly tilting world into smaller sounds, words, and nonwords that would fall to a quiet hum we might ignore.

In one activity you found solace. Chess. Once a week, to combat the general toxicity about town, Mother held a temperance meeting. Stanka and Mrs. Ilmyen, founding members, came faithfully, as did Miss Dzelz and Jutta. Jutta always brought Little Semyon, who wasn't so little anymore, and I brought you. The two of you had fallen into one of those effortless friendships that come quickly for children who sense in one another the spirit of a fellow sufferer. You were both quiet boys, and because of this, neither of you had many friends. The other boys mocked Semyon on account of his bookishness, his unfamiliarity with sports—the things other boys judge one another by. But when you two met on Tuesday evenings, the world around you ceased to exist. The chessboard out, the chessmen arranged rank and file, you'd engage in soundless, intense warfare. Sometimes you and Semyon would call the white chessmen Latvians and the blacks Soviets. Sometimes the whites were Germans and the blacks were Soviets. And then there were times when the whites represented all underdogs everywhere and the blacks were the classmates who had mercilessly teased you.

It was at one of these temperance meetings, which, I will admit, had degenerated into something more like a gossip fest, that Miss Dzelz had something like an epiphany. We were airing our complaints. Mrs. Ilmyen didn't like the looks of the young men gathered at the *kafenica*. Their drinking struck her as dogged and desperate, as if they were making up for lost time. Mother agreed: the consumptions of spirits in our town had escalated while displays of community service had fallen in decline. That is to say, contributions to her newspaper had dwindled. Stanka was in a sour mood because Mrs. Lim had beaten her to a choice morel patch and picked it clean.

From her enormous purple faux-alligator-skin purse, Miss Dzelz retrieved a history book. The history book. The only history book anyone had ever used or seen in use at Elementary School Number Two. Yes, the very same one your uncle and I had chucked out the classroom window all those years ago. We were haunted by this book, it seemed. But no one was more haunted than Miss Dzelz, who actually read its pages. What fits and torments they gave her! She swayed side to side on her chair, a human pendulum of woe. "This book," she said, her voice shaking. "This book contains inaccuracies of such grand proportions that I fear, yes, fear, for our children. Our history and our traditions are the ties that bind, and I fear we are in grave danger of losing our grasp."

Some people believe the maintenance of cultural memory is a moral obligation. But to grasp hold of a memory, collective or otherwise, is to walk through a fire barefoot. Perhaps this is why Stanka winced. "The problem with any talk of the past is that it's all so muddled. Fact stands on one bank of a river and memory stands on the other. History is the mud in between."

Mother passed around cups of dark tea. Her face, normally fixed into an expression of firm determination to conquer whatever task was at hand, now held a look of uncertainty.

"It's worse than that," Mrs. Ilmyen said. "Talking about history is like tapping each of your teeth until you find the one that hurts. Just when you thought you'd subdued the offending member, it reasserts itself in bites and pinches. And we all know how it can bite different people at different times."

Ligita made a face and rolled her eyes. The future concerned her most of all. In particular, she'd heard of the high-heel dash held for girls who loved and lived by their cosmetics. The winner of the sprint would be named this year's Amber Girl and given a truckload of cosmetics and a photo shoot in Russia. Maybe even Bulgaria. It was no secret to any of us that late at night Ligita practiced a tottering trot over the broken sidewalks to improve her ankle strength.

Miss Dzelz would not be swayed. "Of course, you are right. Of course. But as everyone wants to write our history for us, it seems we ought to join in, if only for the sake of steering the conversation closer toward the truth, and if not that, then mere accuracy of fact. For example"—now Miss Dzelz held up the old orange textbook that had been in her lap—"there's simply no Latvia in these history texts, none of our rich culture, our many contributions to sciences, our keen intellect, our music, and our dancing. Our *dainas.* Nothing!" Miss Dzelz was almost shouting.

I understood her frustration. Written in the clumsy self-congratulatory language of Soviet-era rhetoric, the text focused on military achievements and economic development. About Latvia the book had little to say except that Latvia was a leader in the production of televisions and that Riga was an important commercial port. About the near genocide of Latvians and the forced deportations—15,000 in 1941; 60,000 in 1945; and another 33,000 in 1949—the book said nothing. Nor were there any mentions of the Baptists who were shot by the Soviets or any discussion of the many crosses of the Orthodox churches that were pulled down and drowned in the sloughs and marshes. Such events, if they were ever addressed, were mentioned obliquely, speciously referred to as "ethnic engineering" or the "isolation of hostile elements."

Miss Dzelz's voice dropped to a whisper. "There's no mention of 1940."

"What happened in 1940?" Ligita piped up.

Mother's jaw tightened. She was grinding her teeth.

Miss Dzelz ran her finger over an open page and began reading: "In the summer of 1940 Latvia was received by the USSR. The Soviet Union was not a democracy, but it was an example of a good and just society and a reference point for millions of people throughout the world."

"'Received'?" Stanka looked at Miss Zifte, Mrs. Ilmyen, Mother. "Did we ever ask to join?"

It was this question that was like an arrow piercing the mark true. We put it to a vote and agreed unanimously. Our children would weave with words a better and truer version of our own history; we would hold a history fair.

I'm sorry I'm not more help to you with the "Kindly Advices" column. How to stretch a single chicken through a whole winter—that I can tell you. Jokes about Estonians, clean and dirty, I have in abundance. And you are right: removing unwanted body hair with sandpaper or other such abrasives is always a bad idea.

I can tell you something I remember of your younger days. You announced to Joels and me that you wanted to start a mining company. Your grandmother asked, "What will you mine? Silver or gold?" And you looked at her as if you felt sorry for her lack of imagination. "Stars," you said. "I will harvest stars."

And so you did. You dug and dug. One meter, two meters, three meters deep. Was it a week after you started digging or two when you burst into our shed? You had a rock in your hand and you'd broken it with a hammer. Mica or quartz, I didn't know. But the dark rock glittered. "Stars," you said. A galaxy of stars in the heart of that rock. That God could create hidden universes of light and bury them—because He could—astounded you.

Stanka visited again today. This time she brought compounds of gentian, a virulent purple tincture that she claimed would help my acute nausea and "hectic" red cheeks. She surrendered her prize black licorice to help the constipation and procured banana extract in the event of galloping bowels. She concocted an orange-peel poultice for the falling of the womb, which struck me as wholly irrelevant. She also brought a book of homeopathic remedies and anecdotal instructions. I thank you for reading to me from the wrinkled leather book, "There is no class of person whose system, owing to its peculiar structure, is more liable to derangement than a woman's."

I don't know where she found the book, but I imagine it will make for lively conversation in your column.

I told you that the light through the window spins lace on the walls. You were kind enough to pretend that I hadn't already said that once or twice before. Everything in this universe, be it as fine as lace or as fragile as memory is spun of absence and presence, darkness and light. Dark matter. It's all you and Dr. N. have been talking about lately, this mass everywhere present, nowhere seen. Mass that neither emits nor absorbs light. Mass that exerts its own gravitational pull. I imagine galaxies of lace, the visible planets and stars and meteorites spinning tight knots in the darkness.

What lace corsets and binds the depths of the earth to the vault of heaven? You laugh at my questions and I laugh with you. *Go on* I am saying with my laughter. Impossible questions are meant to further the mystery of existence, not solve them. A saint, an important one, I think, said that. I believe it.

For a time you stopped writing in your book. You said it was childish. I said, *No, it's childlike.* The reverence and appreciation—wonder—that you expressed for the act of living and for every living creature held a childlike purity that astonishes me. Evidence of your infinite curiosity, these notes. "Every part of a bumblebee is covered in hair," you wrote. "Every three days a person has a new stomach lining. The hummingbird is the only bird that can fly backward. It can even turn somersaults in air." Your education in those early years was glorious, strange, and quixotic. Whichever way the wind listed, that's what you pursued. "The horn of a rhinoceros," you wrote, "was not made of bone but of dark coarse hair, compacted and condensed." That something soft could become so hard was a mystery you pondered for many days. "Where do you find all these facts?" I once asked, and you smiled the way a child does when he knows more than he will say.

You wrote of the planets etching their elliptical traceries around the sun. You wondered at the sound of light and if the gnawing, grinding noise you dimly detected was the sound of the universe's growing pains. As you grew older, your notes turned more philosophical. Your fascination with sound, gravity, and light all culminated in a series of conjectures helped along, I suppose, by your many talks with Dr. Netsulis. The problem, you've written, is that our universe is expanding faster now than ever before. It has outstripped the relatively weak grasp of gravity. Our world is one tiny buoy among billions of buoys in a vast and ever-widening sea. Our universe resists reduction.

I would love to assure Mrs. Zetsche, who visits me almost every morning, that the slow-moving fire burning inside of me is God. Embers in my lungs, I fan flames with each breath. What water is wet enough to put it out? She cannot answer my question. So we read together your "Kindly Advices."

> It's a sin to tear paper.
> It's a crime to trample bread.
> Salt is more precious than tears, and a spent word can never be recalled.

I told her stories from your childhood. That triumphant discovery of yours: the galaxies caught midwhirl in dark stone. Aren't those bright bits of memory? Reflective surfaces that remind us: we are here, we exist, this is what we know.

She wanted children of her own, and I thought this was a small thing I could do, share the strange and miraculous observations you made as a child. She didn't attend the history fair. She and Mr. Z. were on a horse-riding and shooting holiday somewhere. I remembered that. So I told her of your research methodology and your selection process. How you pulled out that family tree and scowled at all the ovals. You were to choose a departed family member and tell or reenact scenes from his or her life. It is perverse of me, I suppose, but

I had hoped for the history fair you would pick Uncle Maris. I thought that if people had the opportunity to learn how generous, funny, and energetic he had been, they might recalibrate their opinions. He even had a sensitive side. Once I asked him if he remembered Siberia. He was quite sick by this time, his face waxy pale and always a standing sheen of perspiration on his forehead. He lay on the cot in the shed. It was dim, the burzuika casting a dull orange glow. His eyes filled with tears, and he made no attempt to stop them as they streamed from cheek to chin to chest. And then he did the most incredible thing: he answered my question.

"Singing. I remember the beautiful songs, sung quietly, as quiet as slow water in deep, dark night." He looked at me. "If not for the rocks, a river would have no song," he said, and I will never forget that.

I told Mrs. Z. how you sat at your chessboard and moved the white king, the black king, moved the pawns this way and that as if such a decision could be worked out only with the chessmen. You plunked odd tunes in minor keys on the piano in the shed. Then you spent a long evening among the family tombstones laying your ear against each one. Finally, you decided; you'd be Grandfather Ferdinands. You made many visits to the cemetery that spring. Sometimes with your grandfather. More often alone. You said to me that you were researching for the pageant. Also, you were collecting an outrageous number of corks. Another project for Miss Dzelz. I did not argue. We'd all agreed to allow you to pursue your own interests when it came to your education. You told me one afternoon that you didn't think there was a body beneath that smaller stone that rested beside Velta's marker. I said, *Of course there is. A mother always wants to lie beside her children.* You gave me a look that said you knew better, and I felt a chill like a rush of cold air brush past my arm.

I told Mrs. Z. how you pestered Mother day and night about the details of her childhood. If Mother furrowed her brow, then you asked about Velta, questioning Mother with a tenacity I had to admire. Of course, when we were your age, Rudy and I had made our attempts, wondering aloud what happened to the two sets of grandparents we had never known. Who were these absent people whose presence became palpable beneath Mother's loving pass of the polishing rag? Why was Velta's mouth pressed into a flat line? Was she biting her tongue, keeping back a world of mystery or was she merely angry?

"What was she like, really?" you asked Mother one afternoon. The fair was less than a week away. Mother had opened the windows, and an unseasonably warm breeze blew through the rooms. "What color was her hair? Did she dance? What was her favorite song? Was she as good at catching fish as you are?" Judging from the cadence of your queries, hurried and breathless, it must have occurred to Mother that the storehouse of your questions had no end.

She regarded you for a moment then plucked at your sleeve. Together you walked down the corridor to Mother and Father's room. From her open bedroom, I heard your high-pitched murmuring, your voice pure and open in the way children's voices are when they have no idea what they are asking. Mother's voice, uncharacteristically accommodating, rumbled quietly as she answered your every query. *Maybe it has to be this way,* I thought, creeping on tiptoe down the hallway. *Maybe stories skip a generation. She could tell you the hard things she couldn't tell me.* Jealousy pinched at my heels as I walked carefully, holding my weight on my toes.

"This is Velta," Mother said.

I could not see in the room, but I could sense your deep scrutiny of Velta's image behind the glass, her white wedding gown with ribbons, that Jani Day wreath on her head.

"She's wearing a tree on her head."

Mother laughed. It was a liquid sound that filled the room; a sound I'd not heard in months and months. "She's only nineteen in this photo. You can't see her hands, but I wish you could. She had long graceful fingers and she played the piano. Music poured out of her every fiber. She was hardworking, too." Mother tapped the frame with her finger. "She spun wool into long skeins even when it wasn't fashionable to spin anymore."

I didn't need to look through the crack in the door—I knew this photo. Beneath that oak-leaved wreath, Velta's hair is plaited into long ropes and wound around her head. I imagined that her hair, the leaves, and those skeins she wove were one and the same thing, all of it held together, pinned by the dark notes of music.

"It wasn't long after this photo was taken that the trouble started. Soviets first, then the Germans, and then the Soviets again." A scuffling of a wooden object being dragged over wood—Mother was reaching for the other photo. I knew this one, too: a picture of Grandmother Velta taken a year after Ferdinands returned from the camp. She did not even remotely resemble the girl in the first photograph. She had the frizzled hair that told of malnutrition. Her face had turned flat and angular. She was bodily present for the making of that picture, but her spirit had flown away.

"You look like her," you said. I hoped, so hoped, it was the picture of the young Velta you meant.

Your feet padded softly over the floor. I pressed myself flat against the wall, watched you turn for the kitchen, and sighed, relieved that you did not see me hiding.

"You can come in now, Inara," Mother said. She stood at the dresser, peering at Velta's image. "A quiet woman. A quiet woman," Mother said. "Quiet in the shape of a woman. It is a kind of sleeping, that quiet. Like a blanket, the soundlessness. Like snow, that quiet. It could be snowing inside that woman. For years and years, she gathered breath, held it, held it, until it turned cold and white inside her. She lived in a quiet so complete that after a while I suspect she forgot the reason for her silence."

"Because of the baby who died?"

"We all thought that at first. The baby died while Ferdinands was in the camps. And we all know how grief changes a woman. Her only recourse was to write letters, write her way toward a world worth living in. For eight years she waited, wrote letters. Then Stalin died and people like my father were released—rehabilitated."

Mother traced the outline of Velta's face. "She didn't like the dark. Every year, at some point during the winter, she'd refuse to get out of bed, would not eat, drink. And every winter a white truck came for her. Two men wearing white uniforms wrapped her up in yellow blankets, buckled her to the stretcher, and trundled her into the back end of the white truck. The whole time Mother sang songs. Strange wandering songs about walnuts and marigolds. Belted to the board, her eyes on the clouds, she'd lick her lips and say, 'The clouds taste flat today. Not enough salt.' Every winter this happened. And then four maybe five weeks later, the white truck would come around again, and the orderlies would walk her to the front door, or maybe it would be a neighbor who'd gone to fetch her and bring her home on the bus. She'd stand on the threshold, bewildered, her hair cropped to the scalp, her eyes hollow. Each time this happened, I'd think they'd finally cured her. I'd say, *Speak to me, Mama, tell me something, anything.*"

"Something bad happened to her in winter," I suggested.

"Yes," Mother said. "Me. I happened in winter."

You have always shown a keen interest in the legend of the Ghost Girl of the River. You asked quite a lot about her that spring of the history fair. I thought it a macabre obsession, but then we are a family of grave diggers. So I told you that the voice calling across the water is not a woman's, but a girl's. She rises as a mist on dark foggy nights. She cries for help. She calls people by name. She places a pair of sharp scissors beside your head while you sleep. The truth is, a little girl had been drowned in the river. They say that she is seeking revenge or reconciliation. No one knows for sure which because no one who sees her and goes to the water ever returns.

You heard her call your name. I believe that now. I believe in the conductive power of water. It's pull, pure and undeniable. How else can I understand why you went to the water's edge a few nights before the history fair, why you walked in as if it had been waiting for you all your life? I followed you to the cold water. The river, still frozen at that time, lay under a mantle of windswept ice as shiny as silver glass. A mirror. You walked as if firm ground were just a few centimeters beneath the surface. As if you believed the myth of your own life: you were the Bear Slayer and the river was your true home. And then you remembered who you were: a mere boy who does not swim. Down you went. I have always wanted to ask you what you saw when you went under. Dark water and silt? The many rocks we'd thrown with the slips of paper tied around them — our sins and confessions settled in the river's mud? What did you hear when you slid under the dark mantle? I went after you, hauling you up. As I did, you came up glistening, triumphant, and unafraid.

During those wet days, you kept detailed measurements of rainfall and rising water tables here in your Book of Wonder. So, too, in your comments in the margins. The rain never sings a song the same way twice. I think of that spring, that rain, as a second awakening, a second baptism. Can an entire town be baptized at once? Yes, I know it can because I saw it happen. It began that same spring of that history fair. In the mornings I made my rounds: first to Dr. N.'s barn. I could hear the cows lowing well before I spotted Dr. N. sitting in the loft, his head haloed in blue smoke, his pipe in his hand. Below him, the cows stood past their knees in water. Their lowing could in no way be described as cheerful, this in spite of the bright orchestral music blaring from a radio in the loft.

He'd fitted each of the cows with chartreuse-colored hip waders, but this seemed to only increase their distress. Their udders hung low and heavy. Dr. N. switched off the radio, waved his pipe in my direction. "This world is turning to water, you know."

I stacked bales of hay to make a low dry platform and arranged a series of planks to make a ramp. It was slow going coaxing them up the ramp, but as cows are not overly clever and inclined to follow the broad rump in front of them, I managed.

"Yes," he continued. "But I wouldn't want you to think we've been idle."

"Who?"

"Your man, Joels, and I."

I had a cow out of the water and relatively calm. I shoved a bucket under her udders. "I would never think that, Dr. N.," I said, reaching with each hand for a teat.

"I've fastened and yoked planks all around the barn. Sort of like a wooden collar. As the water rises, the planks will rise, too." Dr. N. regarded me from beneath his bushy eyebrows. "We're fashioning rubber pontoons to buoy everything. It would be nice if we could fill them with helium."

The last cow milked, the pails lined up in the loft, I left Dr. N. muttering genius-invention thoughts: How to coax the floatation suits onto the cows? Slick their legs with vegetable oil or sticks of butter?

I headed for the Zetsche manor stuck in that dark hollow of wood. They had a hard enough time managing their water garden. They certainly would not know what to do with all this rain. As I passed the ministallions, they seemed less triumphant. Water licked at their hooves. Crows sat on their heads and made low knocking noises in the backs of their throats. They were laughing.

Mrs. Zetsche met me in the corridor, waved me toward her grand dining room table. We passed Mr. Z.'s study, where financial journals and newspapers had been scattered over his desk. It looked as if he'd taken a stack of those journals and thrown them against the wall. Mrs. Z. reached beneath her chair and produced a brick wrapped in a green sheet of paper. I recognized the slogan blazing across the paper: PATRIOTIC LATVIANS FOR AN ALL-LATVIAN LATVIA.

"Please ignore it, Mrs. Zetsche. It's probably some dumb kid trying to scare you," I said.

"One hundred and twenty years our family has owned property in this region, and we're still treated like foreigners." Mrs. Zetsche touched the brick. "It isn't as if my father wasn't killed in the war. It wasn't as if he, too, was put in prison, beaten." Her gaze lifted to mine.

In her eyes was the look of pain, of a woman wounded. I had to look away. She did not really belong here; she and her husband never would. And she was beginning to understand this.

"Do you know why we moved back?"

"No, Mrs. Z."

"Because Latvia was the homeland, a return to a promise. We reclaimed the family inheritance, the ancestral lands. We weren't making it in Bonn."

Shotgun blasts from the trees punctuated her words.

"We wanted to have children. It took all the money we had to emigrate and pay the lawyers. Everything we had went into investigating whether or not our claims were legitimate. I would have had sons and daughters, many of them by now, and look at us!"

More blasts from the forest.

"I'm sorry, Mrs. Z."

Her little red mouth twisted. "You know, Inara. You're almost like a daughter to me, a distant and strange daughter. I believe that you are sorry for me. Why does that make me feel worse, not better?"

At home I found Father silently regarding the fire in the grate. I sat beside him, placed the brick on the table beside his chair. I did not try to remind him of better times. I was remembering what Mrs. Zetsche had said nearly three years ago when that sudden fire burned the pharmacy to a crisp, that all of our suffering has been the result of our striving against the constraints of time and place and memory, none of which can be moved, changed, broken, or loosened. *Time, place, memory,* she had said. *We need these walls in order to have something to push against, to have something that breaks us.* At the time I thought her words odd — what could she know of pushing, of being broken? Now I wondered how this bit of wisdom had grown teeth, had bitten and drawn blood in the way anything true does. And throbbing behind her words was another, darker truth. We could hate people like the Zetsches, we could love them, but we could not hate them without also hating ourselves. We could not forgive them if we did not first examine ourselves.

This is a puzzle to me: How is it that you have no memory of the history fair? It's only been ten years, after all. You say you don't remember Joels helping you into one of Rudy's old church suits. You say you don't remember your grandmother pulling a tattered coat from a trunk and her telling you, "This belonged to my father; he would want you to wear it."

Under a lowering sky, you and I walked down the lane toward the hall. I could not help noticing that as we passed by the cemetery your head tipped toward the stone markers as if pulled by the murmur of a dream or maybe you were hearing last-minute instructions. A soughing wind, the kind that could tear a mustache off the face of one man and plaster it onto the face of another, tore over the fields and through the lanes. With the wind came water and more water. This weather, coupled with the sad recognition that nothing else happened on Tuesday nights, induced a number of families to brave the elements. The Gepkarses, the Inkises, the Lees, the Lims, and even the widows Sosnovkis and Spassky came. And the almost sure likelihood of a spectacle lured to the hall many of the young men, some of whom I knew had been friends of Rudy's.

At exactly seven p.m. the parents and children arrived, every one of them drenched. The crossbar of the coatrack bowed beneath the weight of so many bloated coats refusing to drip dry. The children ran around in dizzy circles, pretending to be airplanes, horses, anything, while the adults sat on folding chairs lining the walls. Mother was in her element, lining up cups ready for the punch ladle when it was time. After a quick welcome from Miss Dzelz, we rose and sang the anthem, "God Bless Latvia." Father did not sing, but his jaw muscles worked in time to the music and I took this as a good sign.

The anthem finished, we resumed our seats. A quick glance around the room confirmed yet again what an odd mixture of people we were. This stretch of country represented a meeting of contradictions that had, in time, become something like reconciliation. These reconciliations were borne out daily in our small actions, in the buying of bread from the baker, Mr. Tamiroff, who was Ukrainian, but was as Latvian as a body could be; in the handing off of mail from Mrs. Arijisnikov, whose grandfather, through no fault or choice of his own, had been railed from Uzbekistan to Daugavpils and somehow ended up here. There were the Jewish families. And then there were the Zetsches; upstarts, interlopers, some people called them. Curiously absent were the Zetsches. But it was just as well; I could hear the grumbling even now coming from a man who had been let go last week.

The lights dimmed, and slowly a wider circle of light began to assert itself. In the circle stood two microphones on their stands, and behind each microphone, one of the Indrikis twins. One twin wore a business suit and the other wore rags, his face smeared with charcoal.

"I am Mayor Berzins of Sabile. Perhaps you remember how I protected the Gypsies when the Nazi fascists came to our town. I would not let those fascists take my poorer brothers and sisters to the trains that I knew would take them to death camps."

"And I am an unnamed Gypsy," said the other twin, grinning madly. "After the Nazis had been routed by the Soviets, the Soviets tried to take Mayor Berzins away. But my poorer brothers and sisters, remembering his courage and generosity, banded together. With sticks and stones we drove back those soldiers."

The two brothers shook hands, embraced, walked stiffly side by side off the stage. Their mother jumped to her feet. From where I sat, I could not see whether or not tears streamed down her face, but such is the effect of embraceable tales we can feel good about telling and even better about hearing. Best of all, we knew this story was true: a film crew had set up in Sabile a few years ago to make a documentary.

Another child told the story of how his great-grandfather piloted an icebreaker in the Antarctic. Pure fabrication, but we all clapped our hands anyway. One child claimed a distant relative who invented the cadmium loop. The next child told of a grandmother in Balvi who had successfully hidden a Jewish woman in a slim space within a wall. The Jewish woman did not keep a diary cataloging her daily misfortunes, and there had been no tearful reconciliation years later; she'd disappeared after the Germans pulled out. Gone to Estonia was the family's best guess. But the girl's recitation suggested dissatisfaction. What good is a story if we don't know how it ends?

At last it was your and Semyon's turn. The two of you had decided to tell the history of two families at once. Semyon, wearing a long beard made of several balls of steel wool clipped together, stood behind one mic; you stood behind the other.

The two of you began with a *daina,* an old one we all knew.

> *My little wolf rumbles.*
> *My little wolf hums.*
> *My little wolf has a white foot.*
> *If this doesn't make it better,*
> *It won't make it worse.*

A little salt in a wound, it stings, but the hurt makes us stronger. I was proud that the two of you, being only ten years old, understood this already.

"History is a gap-toothed comb," you said, your voice as gruff as you had imagined Grandfather Ferdinands's voice might have sounded. "And we are the teeth in that comb. What I remember is what remains: my wife wrote me letters so that we would not forget. I had been sent to a work camp. She was left behind. She wrote of ordinary events, everyday events, of the dogs whose tails were tied together, set on fire, and turned loose in a field. Of the oxen whose legs were broken so that we could not plough."

Semyon stepped to the microphone and read from his notes. "In 1940 I, too, was sent to a work camp. I, too, wrote letters — to my wife, Anna. She wrote back."

One day a little boy was struck by an army truck. The boy's mother flung her body over the boy while a tank rolled over the top of her. My Anna watched all this. She lit a candle for the boy and his mother. It was all anyone could do.

I stopped smiling. Mrs. Ilmyen pulled at the stitching of her handkerchief. Mr. Ilmyen shifted slightly in his chair.

You retrieved from your pocket a letter. It was the size and shape of those I'd hidden in the piano.

Eight years I had been in a camp. When I returned to my home, I was a husk, a shell. Hollow. But next to my wife's emptiness, my emptiness looked like fullness. The woman who met me on the threshold was not the same woman I'd left. She'd been pregnant with our first child. But it was not an eight-year-old child burying her face in her mother's skirts, but a girl who must have been three maybe four years old. "Where is the other one?" I asked. "There is no other one," she said. "Well, then whose is this?" I asked. "Ours," she said, her voice as flat as a grid iron. "Ours." And not another word offered by way of explanation. And so I took what I had, her letters and my letters, and for six months I read them to her. What we did in camp, making chairs with uneven legs, faulty tables that listed, stretching rubber is what this kind of shoddy work is called. That was one letter. How many days it took the Soviets to pull down the cross on top of the Lutheran church — that was another letter. Her account of the bonfire made of Bibles, yet another letter.

Semyon cleared his throat and read.

In the deep woods of Bierkiniki, old grandfathers with long beards, grandmothers with tired hands, women and children, strong men, weak men, we were gathered. Who needs fairy tales to teach us that bad things happen in dark woods?

This is what my Anna wrote in her diary.

There were shadows flying overhead: crows. There were shadows racing over the ground: wolves. And then the wolves on two legs: men. They gave us shovels and we dug, we dug, we dug. What were we digging? A place to rest. We were digging our own private quiet. We were praying from the psalms, begging a mountain to fall down on us, to cover us.

Semyon paused. That tiny gap between his words you quickly filled with the contents of a letter.

If it had so happened that a woman such as the neighbor woman had been brutalized, then we might tear our hair out in anger, might slit our wrists in shame. As it is, my dear, the birds still sing, and to my ear, the plainer-plumaged wrens sing the sweeter songs.

Mother on one side of me, Father and Joels to my other side. Together we drew our breaths, held, held our air inside of us. These words falling from your lips did not belong to young boys in the third grade, boys who had merely gathered anecdotal family stories and supplied the unknowns with pure imagination. What we heard were the voices of those men: two anguished husbands attempting to piece together all that had happened to their women in the years they'd been at labor camp. I was hearing the difficult passages of Velta's words that she'd fashioned into dark notes, shapes of small birds never meant to

fly, the words on a musical score I'd been too lazy or unwilling to de-
code.

*And the attack on the neighbor woman. Three soldiers ripped her
clothes from her body, bent her over an open windowsill. Afterward,
they left her for dead.*

"My Velta wrote how for several days, unmoored by the attack,
the woman, wandered up and down the lane. So unhinged the woman
was, she did not know to feel shame, did not know she was naked,
bleeding. In her letter, Velta asked me, *How will she live among neighbors and those soldiers? How will she carry on as if nothing has happened? She
will have to throw it all down a well so deep inside of her that these things, the
words used to talk about them, will become irretrievable. They will fall and will
always be falling because there is no bottom to this well.*

"And then I understood, the woman my Velta kept mentioning in
the letters, the silly neighbor woman who had gone insane — she was
describing herself."

As if touched by electricity, I jolted in my chair. I craned my neck
toward the image of Velta on the wall. No wonder her words had been
so few and the ones we did have so strange. How else can a woman
tell the untellable tale to her husband, knowing that every word will
break his heart?

I held my gaze on Velta, aware that around me others were doing the same: Mother, Father, the Tamiroffs, the Arijisnikovs, the In-
drikises, the widows Spassky and Sosnovkis, and the Gepkars and
Inkis families turned and cast furtive glances at that picture of Grandmother Velta. And as they did, a strange alchemy happened. They
were superimposing the figures of their own aunts and grandmothers, sisters and mothers. It was not Velta in that photo now, but every
woman in the village.

And still you pressed on with those letters.

Naked, that silly neighbor woman went to that heap of burned Bibles. She found scraps of paper, scraps of leather. She fashioned a garment of paper, leather, ash. The rain fell. Ink and ash coursed down her back, her arms, her legs — a prophetess, a holy fool, a stained woman, branded in the ink and all the words we'd been taught to hold dear.

Father's face had blanched as white as a turnip. As if hearing fact and atrocity carried in the mouths of these two ten-year-old boys had conveyed him to his own boyhood, a time of metal shovels, hard yellow dirt, coal dust, winter's dark fist.

Semyon's voice lifted, carried by a chanting cadence: "With what words do we describe the three-day torture of a twelve-year-old gypsy girl. Later, her mother found her body, a bullet in the forehead, and she called it a mercy."

You folded the letters, tucked them into your oversize trousers. "Which suffering in particular afflicted my Velta that she could not even after all these years speak of it?"

"Was it the Jews rounded up, locked in a barn, and burned to death? Or the Jews silenced in the forest of Sisenu?" The spotlight on Semyon's glasses turned them into mirrors reflecting a searing light that made us wince.

Through all of this, a low groaning, something like the plaintive lowing of Dr. Netsulis's cows, emanated from the back rows and rolled forward. Stanka wrapped her arms around her sides as if holding her innards in place. Mrs. Ilmyen's mouth wrenched to one side of her face as if it were a seam sewn on crookedly. Miss Dzelz held her head in her hands and muttered, "No, no, no, not at all what I intended."

Yes, we knew, had known, or at least had guessed that these things had happened. The people responsible, people we all knew, were buried in the cemetery. But that didn't diminish the shock of hearing with stinging clarity everything we could not bear to speak.

For as soon as one boy uttered a disturbing question, the next, fighting for supremacy, supplied another unanswerable query.

"Was it the drowning in the slough of the Gypsy family whose name no one will utter?"

"Who wants to know that their grandparents participated in a massacre?"

Oblivious to our groaning, slowly growing in volume, Semyon carried on, his body swaying side to side: "Afterward, we could not speak of these things. Not openly. Why trouble our children with a history that makes them regret living?"

"Who wants to know of a good woman driven by such madness that she drowned her own three-year-old daughter? She called it a baptism for her baby. Who wants to know of the many rapes and the other daughter she didn't want, a product of such a rape. My Velta wrote this and—"

Father jumped to his feet. "For the love of God, dear boy, stop!"

As if of one mind, one body, both Father and Mr. Ilmyen rushed to the podium, each of them tucking each of you under an arm, shuffling both of you off the stage and out the side door.

We trudged home in the rain: Mother and Father in front, Ligita and Stanka behind them, Joels, you, and I bringing up the rear. Father had lapsed into his familiar silence. Joels hummed the coffee-flake jingle; only it sounded more like a dirge. Ligita, as if physically trying to shake off all that she'd heard, lifted her skirt and dashed over the uneven road for home.

I studied Father, his stooped back and pained walk. Mother matched her gait to his, the two of them side by side, carrying this evening between them. You slipped your hand in mine. I squeezed it tightly. Who needs words when we have hands? I wanted you to know that what you had shared—all of it true—could not be helped. Nor were you to be blamed for speaking it aloud. Not your fault that it was difficult to hear.

"That," Mother said to no one in particular, "is why those history texts haven't been updated."

Is there a body beneath that stone? No. Having moved the bodies from the old cemetery to the new, I think your grandfather was the first to figure it out. It's true, Velta drowned her girl the winter after the child was born. A few years later she tried to drown your grandmother. She would have done it, too, had not a neighbor been ice fishing upriver. He watched her chop a hole, saw the ax sink helve-deep in the ice. Heard the little girl crying. He must have known what Velta was about to do, and he carried your grandmother Biruta to the clinic where someone called for the white truck. At least that's how your great-grandmother remembers it. You've read both sets of her letters, you've decoded all her words. You know what I'm saying is true. Your uncle Rudy would like to burn the letters. I can't quite bring myself to do it. We've agreed to let you make the decision.

CHAPTER ELEVEN

S O RIGHT YOU ARE: God gave us two ears, one mouth. The better to listen. So I'll tell you since you've worn me down. The eel recipe.

First, wash him in water and salt then pull off his skin below his vent or navel but not much farther; take the guts as cleanly as you can but don't wash him. Scotch the belly three times with the knife. Then stuff into the belly sweet herbs, nutmeg (grated), butter, and salt. Cut off the head. Pull the skin back onto his body and knot the end. Wrap and roast the eel in a pit or over open coals. Or place him in a pan with butter and water. By the way, you can do all these things and more to lampreys and congers. Kosher? Heavens, no.

I was thinking about visions today. They rarely visit when you want them to. I wanted to sleep, felt myself slipping under, but the sound of wind and wings churning the air outside the window kept tugging at me. A crow flew through the open window. It hovered over the bed. I said, *Well, go on then. Do what it is you've come to do.* So close it hovered, I could see myself reflected in its gimlet eye. Then it darted, pierced my heart with its needle-sharp beak. I bled ink, black and thick, onto the white sheets. The pelican in the wilderness nourishes her own with a freshet of blood. What shall I bleed? What will best nourish? A song, a song from the stone of my heart.

I am the beginner of the song.
I stand in the middle.
If I wasn't the beginner of the song,
I wouldn't stand in the middle.

This is what I'd like you to sing for me when it is my time.

Because people don't have too much patience for those who hear or see things of this world or the next clearly, I kept you close by during those weeks following the history fair. Mother canceled the weekly Ladies Temperance League meeting; there was no combating such forceful, determined consumption — and this with the *kafenica* at half hours.

The rain continued to fall steadily, steadily. Father renewed his old silence as if to say, *What good are mere words against such water, noisy and constant?* Mother, too, maintained a working quiet that seemed like a refuge, a covering, a shield. Only Ligita seemed unperturbed. In the evenings, as a hazed, granular dusk intermingled with the rain, she trotted to and from the cemetery. She'd run with bundles strapped to her back, and I figured this added weight was part of her training. The Amber Girl Dash wasn't long off. I thought she had a sporting chance; her ankles and legs had thickened considerably.

One morning Father awoke and did not get out of bed. By that evening, the time when he'd go to the cemetery to make his quiet repairs, he still had not stirred. Mother and I went to look in on him. Two words he whispered: *I'm tired.*

Over the next few days you sat at your grandfather's bedside and told him about the pigeon races in Samarkand. You provided running commentary on a hockey match in progress three towns away. You did not relate what news you'd been hearing in the graveyard nor did you tell of the most recent spate of vandalism. Nor did you recite passages from Velta's letters. I kept myself busy cleaning, sorting. I discovered Ferdinands's coat, the one you wore at the history fair. It hung on the hook on the back of your door, one side of the coat hanging lower than the other. No. Not a stone in that pocket. Letters. I spread them over your bed, mismatched, disordered. I scanned a panoply of written correspondence, most of which I recognized as belonging to Velta. Such fragility, such potency.

Then I spied Anna's letters. No one had asked after them. It did not occur to me to consider the possibility that the Ilmyens might not want them back.

I pushed my feet into my rubber boots and plowed a slow path through the mud to the Ilmyens' front door. Six weeks had passed since the history fair and our families had not spoken since then. Unlike the silence within our house, this silence held the edged electricity of a deliberateness that hinted at permanence. I knocked on the door. A timid knock. A knock neither insistent nor urgent, my knuckles rapping the wood quietly as if to say, *Should you mistake my summons for the sound of a woodpecker drumming on a tree, should you decide not to answer, I will understand completely. I will go home.* I turned for the lane. Behind me, the door creaked open. Jutta.

"I've got your family letters and, er, things." I pushed the bundle to her chest.

Jutta did not even blink, did not examine the bundle, merely tucked them under her arm and motioned me inside the house as if she'd been waiting there for me all along.

As it was Saturday, the Sabbath, the shades were still drawn from the night before. A menorah anchored a long swath of lace to their dining table, the place where Jutta had tried to teach me chess (*Think, Inara! Think as if life depends upon it!*). Though the lace had yellowed a bit, it still bore an air of nobility. In the corner a hutch built in the Soviet style—that is, with glass doors and a mirror behind the shelves—held the family chess trophies. The top shelf, reserved for Little Semyon's trophies, was nearly full.

Jutta led me past her bedroom through the narrow hallway where there was another glass case full of rare books, an ancient sepia-toned photo of family, and the linen closet where instead of linens I knew they kept even rarer books. In a tiny room compassed about with deep dark oak paneling, something Mother had always wanted in our living room, lay Mr. Ilmyen. He looked like a crumpled piece of paper, like he might flake to bits and blow away if not for the green-and-gray-striped blanket holding him down.

His chess set lay on the nightstand. Mr. Ilmyen followed my gaze to the untouched set. With an outstretched finger, he motioned me closer to the bed. "I feared my whole life I would be more clever than devout. Rather than either of these, I wish now only to be found acceptable to God my maker." Mr. Ilmyen gripped my wrist. "I am dying. I have things I wish to discuss with your father." He released me.

My mouth went dry. "Of course, Mr. I. Of course," I murmured, as Jutta led me from the room to the kitchen.

"Is he really dying?" I had to ask her. Several times already he'd been ill, but each time he'd rallied.

"Oh, yes." Jutta sank into the chair next to the stove. "He's been to the clinic and back. Dr. N. says he's got spots on his lungs."

People with these complaints usually didn't last for long. Mercury poisoning, I figured, the last toxic reminder of what Soviet occupation had done to our soil and water.

"Jutta, if there's anything I can do, anything at all . . ." My words hung in the air, and I waited the obligatory three seconds during which I fully expected and hoped that capable Jutta, who did not need help during childbirth or at any other time in her life, would say, *Oh, no. It's fine.*

Instead, she touched the cuff of my sweater. "I wonder, I know this is an imposition, but our regular girl has left unexpectedly." Color crept up her neck and face. "You know we don't work on the Sabbath." She motioned to the dirty dishes stacked beside the sink and a tub of soiled clothing. Mr. Ilmyen's, I surmised. And then I under-

stood that this is how reparations are made: in the small things like
doing dishes, changing linens. She needed someone to clean and care
for her father, who needed these things on the holy Sabbath as much
as he needed them on the ordinary days. I understood that had I not
knocked on their door first she would never have asked me. But because it was Jutta, who was the sister I always wanted and couldn't
have, I said yes.

I rolled up my sleeves, filled the pots with water for boiling. Jutta
vanished down the corridor, her voice floating behind her.

> Driver ho! Driver ho!
> Let the sled skim gently.
> If it skims gently,
> My sleep is light.

I peered behind the lowered shade and watched the rain fall in silver pins and needles. I listened to the musical sound of water falling
in the eaves, and for a few minutes, I was fifteen again. I plunged my
hands in the scalding water, glad that I was here, glad that I could do
this.

As I finished at the Ilmyens', darkness began to fall. The sun
made a brief, fading appearance before submerging into the clouds.
For twenty glorious minutes every frond of every fern, every blade of
grass, every bud on every tree glistened wet and silver. The puddles
in the lane were not water but platen mercury reflecting light. Aluminum foil wrinkled and glinted at the skyline. Joels had made a fire
in our shed. That evening it seemed to me that he and I — shut up as
tightly as a drum inside our shed, closing our ears to the water outside
and the trouble all around — had all we needed: each other.

Our world was not all right nor were most things in it. But in the
midst of what felt like bewildering change I could not correct or control, I felt a strange calm. Still, my thoughts would kick up like dry
leaves stirred by a wind. Hadn't Velta felt like this before her Ferdi-

nands was taken away? Doesn't every wife and mother imagine and expect that her husband will live long, that her children will remain healthy? Isn't it a shock to every one of these women when their men age before their eyes? "It's like this," Mother had tried to explain to me only a few days ago. "A man's body fails faster than a woman's. They work so hard, and when they start the journey toward the door, they go quickly." I knew that was what Father was hoping for: a quick passage.

I pressed my body next to Joels. His skin smelled of sawdust, both dusky and sweet. He was asleep, lost in the deep slumber of a man who works outdoors. As I so often did these days, I put my ear to his chest to listen to that wet engine working in the dark. How deceptive a man's body is: working and working and then, without a noise, quitting.

"Please don't get tired," I whispered. "Please, please, please don't leave me."

In the darkness, Joels's hand found mine. He squeezed my hand hard. "I won't. I promise."

In the morning I found Father propped up in bed, a blanket tucked around his waist and an open book on the blanket. It was a collection of sermons.

"Mr. Ilmyen is sick," I said.

The news immediately loosened his tongue. "The nerve!" Father said. "I am dying. I had the idea first."

"He'd like to see you. He has things to discuss."

Father danced his fingers over the edge of his blanket. The lining had worked loose where he'd worried the stitching with his restless fingers. He seemed to be tapping out his answer on the edge of the blanket. "All right," he said at last. "I also have things to discuss."

And so the next day in a half-hour halt between rain, Joels carried Father outside. Big Semyon carried out Mr. Ilmyen. They met in the middle of the lane, each man supported by their sons-in-law.

First, they exchanged symptoms.

"Spiders have set up a lace factory inside my eyes," Father said. "Everywhere I look, I see cobwebs and clouds."

"I have swallowed sandpaper," Mr. Ilmyen rasped. "Every breath is a hundred nicks with a hundred nails."

"Inside my legs a sharp-toothed thresher is biting me with its many teeth." Father replied.

I recognized the banter. It was an old game: find a verse of scripture and alter it slightly. It was a game Father loved because he had committed so much of the Bible to memory; it was an easy matter to evoke a verse and distort it for his own purposes.

"My chest is a slab of stone. It pins me to the bed; it crushes me."

"Worms burrow in my teeth."

At last, exhausted by metaphor, Mr. Ilmyen cleared his throat. "I have a confession," he said. "It has taken me seven years to recognize the hatred inside of me. Seven years to forgive those whom I hated, and seven more to ask those whom I hated to forgive me."

"What do you mean?" Father asked.

"For seven years I kicked your brother's stone."

A long look of understanding filled Father's eyes. Then he smiled. "I have always wondered where those scuff marks came from."

Mr. Ilmyen clutched Father's hand. "Forgive me."

"Brother, only if you will forgive me first. For many years I rubbed banana peels on your box of fishing tackle. I have emptied potassium pellets near your most treasured fishing spot."

Mr. Ilmyen's bushy gray eyebrows lifted. "Of course. That explains everything."

"Forgive me," Father implored.

"No, you forgive me first and then I shall forgive you."

"I shall not. It is clear that I am fading fast."

"Yes. But as I am fading faster, you must forgive me first."

This first argument provoked a robust spate of coughing, the signal that they needed Joels and Big Semyon to haul them to their respective beds.

It was cause for relief, this banter. I decided that their energy, their need to argue, meant they were on the mend. Mother was quick to set me straight later as we stood side by side at the sink. We were making soup. In dusk's bend of light Mother's hair looked much grayer than usual. Mother reached for a potato and scrubbed it vigorously with steel wool. She did her best philosophical thinking when she was working, though sometimes this had dire effects on the root vegetables.

"Life," she said, pausing to rub the tendons in her hand, "is a series of entrances and exits. It's just a door that opens and closes. And we are the hinges bearing the weight."

How strange this weight, I thought later as I lay in bed listening to the dogs bark. How quickly the burden shifts from the hard tasks of living to those of dying. As Joels and I drifted into sleep, our separate dark waters, I felt the weight pushing on me. People talk about burdens, about bearing them up for one another, and I used to think of small packages wrapped in butcher paper or bundles slung over the shoulder. But I felt it now, the weight. And it wasn't an object so well defined that it could be hoisted in the arms and handed off. The weight — I knew we all felt it as tangibly as we did sacks of concrete — was worry. And the only way any one of us knows how to carry it is to throw ourselves headlong into a series of tasks: washing, cooking, cleaning, tending, mending. And I was not alone in these tasks, this strategy of coping. Across the lane I knew that Jutta and Mrs. Ilmyen were working just as hard, and even Ligita, who surprised me by doing this, maintained a steady haul of laundry at our house. Which is, I suppose, why we were so shocked when Mrs. Zetsche walked down our lane bright and early one morning. The sight of her in the lane was so odd, like seeing a flamingo in Siberia; that she even knew where we lived was something of a surprise, too.

She was dripping wet, and from our vantage point, it was hard to tell if the water rolling off her face was rain or tears.

Joels hopped to the front porch and held open the door. It was all the permission she needed. She hadn't crossed the threshold before she told us the news: Mr. Zetsche's cast-iron horses had gone missing.

"I am begging you, Inara. You are the only one who understands. My Mr. Z. is not right in the head without the horses. We must get them back." As if to punctuate her plea, we heard the rapid cracks from the trees across the river. It was Mr. Zetsche firing his rifle.

Mother ushered Mrs. Zetsche toward Father's good chair, and Mrs. Zetsche sank deep into the cushion.

From her purse she withdrew a small bundle wrapped in several blue handkerchiefs. With tiny trembling fingers, she unwound the cloth and handed to Mother its shiny metallic contents.

Mother furrowed her brow. "Are these . . ."

"The testicles, yes," said Mrs. Zetsche. "We've received a ransom note. The kidnappers will castrate one stallion for every week we don't meet their demands: five hundred lats per stallion."

Mother pulled her upper lip tight over her front teeth. She was trying hard not to smile. And yet I could only imagine what turmoil Mr. Zetsche was suffering. The cast-iron stallions were his strong, immutable progeny. And now they were in harm's way.

Mrs. Zetsche buried her tiny face in her tiny hands, and small muffled noises commenced.

Mother patted Mrs. Zetsche's shoulder ever so gently. I rewrapped the cast-iron testes in the handkerchiefs.

"The thing is, we've lost our tenants at the Riviera. We've lost most of our savings in the stock exchange. We can't meet these demands; we simply haven't got that kind of money."

Mother and I exchanged glances. That there could be a limit to the Zetsche wealth had never once crossed either of our minds. *Why do people hate us so?* Her words reverberated in my ears as I watched her weeping beyond consolation, as surely as she had lost a child or, in this case, five children.

"There, now," Mother murmured. "It's never quite as bad as it seems. This can be fixed," Mother said, even as the look on her face said, *There's no fixing this. No way.*

Mrs. Zetsche stopped in midsob, wiped her nose with a tissue. "In that case"— Mrs. Zetsche had her hand on her purse, which yawned wide open—"I'll leave these with you." She removed another pair of testicles and, *clunk,* dropped them onto the TV tray.

You say you don't remember your grandmother scolding you. This doesn't surprise me. She rarely had occasion to do so. But the moment Mrs. Z. left, she cornered you in the kitchen.

"Where are those damn horses?" Her fingers, pincerlike, gripped your elbow.

You squirmed; she pinched harder. I didn't stop her.

"It's our jobs on the line, you know. You tell what you know and we might all get to keep working."

You looked sufficiently worried; your ears turned vermilion. "They're somewhere in a barn in Balvi. That's all I know." You would not meet her gaze.

Mother released her grasp on your elbow and folded her arms across her chest. "Balvi. That's not so far away." And I could see her making plans, figuring whom she could conscript into a recovery mission. And if I was honest, I would have to admit that I was glad Mrs. Z. had come to us first. She needed us. Another plus: seeing someone else, namely her, reduced to tears was something like a comfort. Don't the problems belonging to others seem more convivial, more interesting, and possibly more soluble?

That year your grandfather took ill, my rounds became increasingly strange. My first stop: the Zetsche manor house. With a wag of her petite head, Mrs. Z. would greet me. If she held a hankie to her eyes, it meant another stallion had undergone the knife. By this time, she was trusting me with her keys again and she preferred that I clean their many porcelains in their many bathrooms. Ligita, she thought, wasn't scrubbing as well as she ought to. But I divined that Mrs. Zetsche really wanted a captive audience, someone who could radiate sympathy and work at the same time. I did this knowing that Mrs. Z. might not be paying me as much as she paid Ligita and, in fact, might not pay me at all.

Then I'd stop by and see Dr. N., who spent most of his time these days in his barn. He'd encircled the barn with wooden planks. Stanka said his place looked like a gigantic wagon wheel, the planks being both spokes and rim, and the barn anchoring it all in the center.

Inside the barn, a deluge of orchestral, choral, and jazz music fell from rafter speakers to the cows, though Dr. N. and his cows seemed visibly confounded.

"They resist my every effort at cheer," he sometimes complained.

He'd outfitted them in rubber boots, and I thought this had something to do with their lachrymose demeanor. Dr. N.'s funding had been pulled, but that didn't slow him down a bit: the test tubes boiled and burbled, and I had plenty of work inside his manor house and outside. From Miss Dzelz and others, he'd accrued at least fifty barrels of corks and claimed that he was putting them to good use — he'd made buoys out of them and affixed them to the sides of the barn. It was quite possible that his barn could actually float — one end seemed to bob upward ever so slightly from time to time as if it were slowly warming up to the idea.

I kept Mother updated on Dr. N.'s activities. He worked every other day at the clinic, and on his days off, he had the floating barn experiment to work on, and he claimed that he was developing something called the Zambian Space Program, the particulars of which remained very fuzzy. My reports of Dr. N.'s experiments ushered

Mother to an unexpected moment of revelation. She put her hands on my shoulders. "After all these years of hoping and praying that you would be a genius, I can honestly say I'm glad that you're not." And there was not an ounce of malice or sarcasm behind her words.

If you weren't out collecting corks for a school project or playing chess, I'd sit with you.

Having recovered from the history fair and noticing the great quantity of water lying about and falling from the sky, Miss Dzelz, who never liked to let an educational opportunity go by, seized upon our strange weather patterns. She instructed you all to compare this year's rainfall in eastern Latvia to the rainfall of the past one hundred years. You were to measure the width and height of the river daily, which already had risen to the edge of Mr. Z.'s empty Riviera shops. You were to estimate how many days would pass, if the current daily rainfall continued, before all the lower-lying homes and farms would be underwater.

Judging from your reaction — a fervent clambering for tape measures, tin cups, and trips to Dr. N.'s — I gathered that this assignment was met with great enthusiasm by the third grade. Nothing captivates quite like imminent disaster. I thought there was something beautiful about all this water. If the rain stopped — this seemed to happen during the hour that dawn broke and the hour that dusk fell — then the water in the lower fields lay as flat and still as mirrors. And in these hundreds of mirrors, the clouds shone silver and gray. We saw and knew all that we needed and nothing more.

Mr. Ilmyen and Father worked out a schedule for their discussions. At high noon Monday through Friday they met and aired their general and particular complaints. On the Sabbath, which started on Friday night and went through Saturday night for Mr. Ilmyen but started Saturday night and stretched through Sunday for Father, they took a rest

from each other. How they needed it! When they met, and they preferred to do this in the middle of the lane, they went after matters of
theology with hammer and tongs.

"Faith is like a fish that can't be caught," Mr. Ilmyen said on a
Wednesday. A light drizzle fell, nothing serious, and with some canvas stretched between laundry lines, we managed to keep the two pa-
triarchs relatively dry.

Father stretched his mouth into a grimace. "Faith is like a grave
that you can never finish digging."

"Faith is like being on a boat on a river; it is both an individual
experience, the hand at the oars, say. And communal. The boat has
many seats, after all." Mr. Ilmyen turned his gaze to the sky in deep
contemplation. From upriver, we could hear Mr. Z. shooting his ri-
fles, short sharp blasts. "There may be many seats, but not just any idiot gets to pull at the oars," he said.

Father narrowed his eyes at Mr. Ilmyen. "What are you saying?"

"Jews and Baptists can't pull at the oars together," Mr. Ilmyen replied.

"But they can be in the same boat," Father insisted.

"No." Mr. Ilmyen shook his head, and he seemed sorry to have to
say, "They can't even float on the same river."

And that is how the second argument started.

"How can you say this? Your God is my God and my God is
your God."

"Maybe," Mr. Ilmyen said.

Father turned shades of violet. "I suppose we shall never fully
agree. But as you desire God's presence and I desire God's presence,
what we long for is the same."

"Yes." Mr. Ilmyen winced. "But let's not forget that as I am dying
more quickly than you I am closer to the goal than you are."

This polemic would have gone on for hours had Ligita and I not
been hanging laundry. She hung undergarments on the line closest to
our house; I hung towels and sheets on the line closest to the lane. She

was talking to me these days, though I attributed her chatter to sheer boredom; we had a lot of laundry to hang.

Every successful visit to the latrine was a source of great rejoicing for Father; but there were still occasions that Father couldn't make it there in time and I knew this was a source of great embarrassment for him.

It hurt Mother's hands, so bent now that she couldn't hold a book much less turn a page, to wring and hang the bed linens. And I found I was happy to do what needed to be done, happy to be needed and necessary. I reached for a wadded sheet, whipped it into obedience, and held it up, pins in my mouth. The kitchen light had been snapped on. A box of yellow warmth spilled out, a hazy illumined patch of air hung above the yard. Strands of silver rain fell gently. I studied the hazy light, the kitchen window. That's when I saw a dark figure behind the window. Not Mother, not Joels. Certainly not Father.

"Who is that?" I asked Ligita. But she'd gone. Vanished.

I lowered the sheet. There was Rudy at the table sitting in a chair as if he'd never left. I raised the sheet. If I counted to three then lowered the sheet, I'd see my folly exposed, how I was projecting my wishes onto these sheets as if they were movie screens, projecting what I wanted to see because it was what Father wanted to see.

Three, two, one.

I lowered the sheet. Rudy was still there. Now Ligita stood beside him, setting cup and saucer and teapot on the table. Up went the sheet. *Three, two, one.* Down went the sheet. Now you sat at the table, an ear inclined toward your wayward uncle.

By the time I made it to the kitchen, Mother had helped Father from the middle of the lane to the kitchen table. They sat side by side openly studying Rudy.

Also sitting side by side were Rudy and Ligita. They held hands, though one of his hands drifted to her belly. And they gazed at each other as if one were meat and the other salt.

Mother had the oddest look on her face, as if she had solved a difficult problem but the solution was simply impossible to believe. Ligita's midnight training runs were wifely missions laden with food and comfort. Judging from the way Rudy kept patting her stomach all the while gazing at her ankles, the comfort had been reciprocated.

I suppose that's why I didn't notice straightaway that Rudy's face looked different.

His nose had been broken at least twice. It sat like a crooked S in the middle of his face.

You could not take your eyes off of it. This might have been embarrassing, but then Rudy smiled.

"For a while I lost my shadow. Then it found me, punched me. Twice."

"Your shadow?" you asked.

"Yes. It has big hands," Rudy said.

"And apparently big knuckles, too," Father observed.

"God's hands are made of stone," Rudy observed.

Now they were playing that old game: evoke a passage from the Bible. Then twist it.

Father peered at Rudy. He was not looking at his nose but his eyes. "Are you broken?"

"No, Father. I am crushed," Rudy said.

"Where have you been, son?" Mother ventured quietly.

Rudy's gaze lifted from Ligita's thickened ankles to Mother's eyes then dropped again. "Liepaja."

We all knew what that meant. Prison. And I understood why we'd not heard from him, why he kept his gaze lowered. He was ashamed, and I'd never seen him like this before.

Mother drifted to the window and opened it. "What did you do?" Mother's voice floated, spectral and thin.

"Some things and then some other things."

"Well, if you stay, you have to work," Father said.

Rudy's gaze still had not risen from the province of Ligita's ankles. "What shall I do?

Father pointed to the pile of testicles still on the TV tray. "Find the rest of the horses."

And this Rudy did with alarming speed. Because he'd been to prison and back, a fact that we suspected elevated him astronomically in the questionable opinion of his former mates, his word was now law. Not two nights passed and we heard a commotion in our yard. In the morning we discovered the stallions, glistening slick with rain and caught in midprance behind the shed.

We didn't know which of his friends had taken the horses. (*No names! If you love us, son, then don't say a single name,* Mother cautioned.) And it really didn't matter. The fact was we had all five of them back.

What to do next seemed clear. Joels and Rudy and Dr. N. conducted many debates regarding the special difficulties joining cast iron to cast iron presented, the merits of gas welding over electrode and rod. Finally, they settled on a plan. Dr N. had a friend who could be sweet-talked into lending a machine and various electrodes. Many more hours passed, many more arguments, before the men reemerged from the yard: Rudy and Joels in thick work clothes, Dr. N. in his scrubs. The stallions were once again whole and wholly in possession of all their parts.

Mother and I examined their work. It wasn't perfect, their welding, but it would do.

Rudy looked at Father. "So now what?"

"We return them," Father said.

It was just the sort of covert mission Rudy lived for. Father assumed a supervisory role while Joels, Dr. N., and the Merry Afflictions lent their expertise. Dr. N. fashioned a sled out of metal flashing and fabricated a harness and hitch to join the sled to Vanags's stout Pobeda. It was a good omen, the Pobeda, as it meant "victory."

Around three that morning, when the air was as thick and dark as soot, Vanags and Buber brought around the dull gray Pobeda. It took some heavy lifting, some strong bungee cords, before one of the horses was secured to the roof. This gave Vanags some grief. He loved his car like a man loves a beautiful, demanding woman. Seeing how the roof bowed visibly hurt Vanags. But because it was for Rudy and for a fairly good cause, Vanags slid behind the wheel for the slow haul.

We watched the dark slurry of fog incrementally swallow the slowly retreating vehicle. Vanags had to drive this way on account of the many potholes. But this was what made the Pobeda so great: with its high axles, it could negotiate uneven terrain at a glacial pace. Even so, long after we lost sight of the car, we could hear it. The Pobeda was in no way a quiet machine. It spluttered and chortled and wheezed, and this was what made it not so great. This was also why Dr. N. had to build a sled and hitch, and why the noisy car could not be driven directly to the Zetsches' circular drive. The plan: maintain a stealthy crawl in the Pobeda to the edge of the Zetsche property, unload a stallion from the car to the sled, then harness themselves to Dr. N.'s sled and drag the horses to their proper pedestals. All this to avoid waking the Zetsches. "What good is charity, after all," Father reminded everyone, "if you announce it for the whole world to hear?"

You stood with Mother, Ligita, Father, and me, and you watched and listened from the side of the lane: first one horse was carried off, and then the next, and then the next. What we couldn't see you narrated for us: the dismount of the stallion from the roof of the car to the sled, the pull of the sled, the strain on the harness, the triumphant moment when the first, the second, and then the third stallions were placed in their proper spots.

Owing to the great quantity of water standing about in the fields and on the Zetsches' drive, it was tricky convincing the fourth horse to stay upright. It had been sculpted to look as if it were in perpetual flight as none of its hooves actually touched the ground; a stout pole, one end affixed to its belly and the other to a small pedestal set in concrete, held it in place.

And, you told us, they finally arrived with the fifth horse. By this time, the sky had lightened to a slate gray.

We exhaled a collective sigh.

Then, from the direction of the Zetsche property, we all heard a loud blast. It was a sound we knew well: Mr. Zetsche firing his rifle.

You bolted from your seat. "Uncle!" you cried, as you ran out the door.

We heard them before we saw them: Rudy shouting epithets at the top of his lungs, "Bastard! Bastard!" and then Joels and Big Semyon carrying Rudy through the drizzle. Rudy's face was a whitish gray like birch bark. Dr. N. hurried behind, his black medical bag in one hand, a bottle of vodka in the other.

They carried Rudy to the kitchen table and laid him on it. Mother set a pot on the stove to boil. She put her palms on the stove's frame and leaned heavily against it. She couldn't bring herself to look at Rudy, to look at all that blood. Better to keep busy; that was the rule she lived by. And it was a rule I lived by, too. I could not carry his pain; I could not do a thing to bring comfort. But I could locate clean linens, salt, gauze. It was Ligita who patted his hand, whispered tender encouragement while Joels and Big Semyon held him down.

"Drink this," Dr. N. instructed, as Ligita propped Rudy's head up. "It will help with the pain."

It was unusual for this kind of procedure to be done in a home, but as Dr. N. explained, it was either here in the kitchen or at the clinic. As the tools and procedures would be precisely the same, there was really no point in moving Rudy if it wasn't absolutely necessary. And, of course, if he went to the clinic, there'd be paperwork, questions, and a hefty bill.

It took one bottle of vodka for Rudy and one for his leg, but finally Dr. N. dug out the bullet. Rudy gritted his teeth and kept his gaze locked on Ligita through all the sterilizing, digging, and bandaging. "You have beautiful ankles," he murmured at one point, though I noticed his gaze had traveled considerably higher to her bosom.

"It's not perfect," Dr. N. said to Mother, as he washed his hands in the sink. "It would have been better to do this at the clinic, but it will do."

Mother didn't say a word, only leaned against her stove, which clattered and trembled.

Infection set in within nightfall. Rank and putrid, the odor of decay filled the room where Rudy lay. And just as Uncle Maris's leg had turned as black as oxblood so did Rudy's in five days. It was clear, even to him, what had to happen next. "Just do it quickly and cleanly," he said to Mother.

We could not risk the chance of yet another infection. This time Dr. N. insisted on moving Rudy to his lab. As he had before, Vanags lent the use of his car. As Joels and Vanags loaded him in, Rudy could not have been any paler. His hands trembled; his whole body shook. I know that Father wanted to be with his son, but he could not get out of bed. The events of the last five days had beaten him down, and you agreed to stay behind with Father.

"Blood is just so loud," you said.

"Wear your earmuffs," I told you, and without another word, you complied.

Mother, Ligita, and I followed the Pobeda. The sky, that storehouse of water upon water, opened up its floodgates. Rain beat us into the mud. Vanags drove slowly over the lanes so as not to jostle Rudy.

We arrived at Dr. N.'s, and the men carried Rudy inside. Joels would give his blood, and Vanags would lend some of his. We women waited in the corridor. We cleaned windows. We sorted Dr. N.'s laundry. We watched the sky. On her hands and knees, Mother pushed the mud down Dr. N.'s back steps. The water was rising quietly and steadily as the rain fell in an unbroken shower of gray and silver. Needles sewing our world to water. Dr. N. had located morphine and this was a great mercy. No one should have to hear the sound of their own bones being sawn in half. This was why Mother hummed loudly and constantly as she cleaned. A mother shouldn't hear the bones of her son being sawn in half. Nor a wife. Ligita joined in, her humming a rattling buzz in the back of her throat.

When it was over, Rudy lay still. He did not move, did not wake as Vanags and Joels carried him to the car. During the slow drive home through the drizzle, we thought we heard groaning, but Mother kept a tune steady. Through it all, the rain never stopped.

Time slows, stops, moves backward when sickness takes over a family, a room, a body. Rudy babbled. Some of the information was useful. At last we learned which of his friends had thrown that brick at the Zetsches' mansion. Other information, less so. The anecdotal accounts of his days at university, the forays into the forest, how many times and with which girls, who needs to know? And then about prison. This is what put Mother's head in the oven.

"It's enough, son," Father said, passing a palm over his forehead. "Rest."

Father prayed for Rudy; I prayed for Rudy. For two days Dr. N. did not report to the clinic. Instead, he paced in our kitchen, drinking most of the vodka.

Mother wanted to sing. I could see it in her eyes: a silent search for the right words. But what tune do you carry, what song is there, for times like these? We waited, not moving, not talking for a day, then another day. And on the third day we knew: infection. Again. And this I believe is what undid Father. For his own sake, he had run head-on toward death, but death wouldn't take him. Death wanted his son. But Father wouldn't have it. And so he wrestled hour after hour for the life of his son. Father took that infection inside his own blood and fought with it. Rudy's skin burned hot; Father's skin burned hotter. Rudy soaked three sheets; Father soaked four. Rudy kept a steady murmur of strange songs; Father recited passages from First Corinthians. Love bears no record of wrongs. In its weary bones love carries those wrongs, hoists them upon stooped shoulders, and bears them away. Because love can and wants to do it.

On the fifth day heavy silence filled our house. Rudy and Father were sleeping hard. Fighting death had worn Father down; his skin turned white and his face bore long creases deeper than any of those furrows men get from working outside in all kinds of weather.

Toward evening came a knock at the door. Mother went to the door and opened it slowly.

Mr. Zetsche stood on our porch, his felt hat in hand.

Mother remained on the threshold. She did not greet him, did not invite him inside.

"I came by to say how sorry I am. I only meant to frighten, you see, because we've had so much trouble at our place. And I just thought . . ."

"Yes." Mother's voice was as dull as a worn pan.

"And it was still dark and with all that rain . . . I didn't mean, you see." Mr. Z. worked the band of the hat. "Can I speak with him?"

Mother glanced over her shoulder toward the back room. Rudy was murmuring the words to an old song—a dirty one, incidentally—while Father intoned passages from Isaiah.

"It's not the best of times," Mother said.

The hat traveled a slow rotation between Mr. Zetsche's hands. "Oh. I understand," he said at last.

CHAPTER TWELVE

I'M GLAD TO SEE THAT YOU KEPT records of everything Stanka brought during those difficult days: lemons and ginger root for Rudy and sumac berries for Father. I don't believe that she's ever written down any of her home remedies, neither how the herbs and roots and strange lotions were prepared nor in what doses and with what frequency they were to be administered. As you remarked in your Book of Wonder, she delivered her instructions in such a way *(Drink this. Do it! Rub this on your chest. Right now; put this under your tongue, but for God's sake don't swallow it)* that banished any doubt as to their efficacy. And when people are sick, sometimes the best medicine is a strong voice telling them what to do, though I seem to recall your grandfather confiding to Joels that he had liked Stanka better when she had come around only to drink all our milk.

Stanka also brought the latest reports from the river, all of which you verified. I suppose her accounts of the water moving with such force that it gouged small chunks out of the Riviera's exposed foundation convinced me to tuck Velta's letters, your Book of Wonder, and a few photos behind the oven in the hall. It was the highest and driest place I could think of. Dr. N.'s barn was two-thirds underwater. He put a halt to the Joyous Bovines experiment in order to outfit the cows in their buoyancy suits. I know Dr. N. was grateful for your help; not

every ten-year-old can slick a small herd in vegetable oil and wriggle
them into full-body floatation devices.

About this time, Joels carried Mr. Ilmyen to our house. And this
seemed to revive Father a little. His eyes brightened as Joels deposited
Mr. Ilmyen onto the cot next to Father's bed. The chess set was laid
out on the night table wedged in between the cot and the bed.

Mr. Ilmyen moved a pawn. "Faith is like a marriage. It surprises;
it disappoints. Then it surprises again."

"No," Father said. "It is an infection." Father castled his king.

Mr. Ilmyen moved a bishop, putting Father into check. "Then may
we never recover," he said softly.

That night Father called me to his side. You sat on the edge of the
bed, your grandfather's hand in yours. Father pointed to the Bible that
lay open at the foot of his bed.

"Ezekiel. Forty-seven," he rasped. You read: "And he brought me
through the waters; the waters were to the ankles."

Father laid a hand on his chest. "The waters are rising inside. Listen." And you laid your ear to Father's chest. And then Father recited
from Psalms.

> Save me, O God; for the waters are come in unto my soul.
> I sink in deep mire, where there is no standing;
> I am come into deep waters, where the floods overflow me.

I recognized this one not because I had a memory like Father's,
but because it was one of the strange ones that Grandmother Velta had
copied out in her letters. It didn't seem so strange to me now.

You kept your ear to Father's chest. Rain pecked at the roof,
made music in the eaves. "It is raining inside this psalm," Father said.
"And you"—he turned his head toward me—"are a girl made of silver strands. And you." Father turned to Rudy. "You are iron and stone

fitly welded. But your true strength . . ." He lifted his finger in Ligita's direction.

Then he called Mother. It was hard work for him to breathe. He had to rest in between his words. "Have I done enough?"

Mother touched his arm so gently it hurt to watch. "You did enough. Rest."

Again you bent over Father, pressed your ear to his chest.

Your ears burned bright red, glowing as you listened to Father laboring for each breath. "Do not be afraid," you whispered. And then Father was gone.

That night Joels cut the boards while Rudy supervised from a wooden folding chair. Long shearing wails rose from the skill saw. Joels's rich baritone filled the spaces in between the passes of the saw. "When all is in the crapper, think of us." His new jingle for Chem-Do Dry Toilets. By morning, the coffin was ready. Joels and Buber went to the cemetery and dug a hole next to Uncle Maris. They had to work fast. Rain had fallen all night long, and the river had crept up to the edge of our property. When they were done, Joels rang up Vanags, who came around with the Pobeda. They folded down the seats and left the hatch open, and in this way, the car that had previously been an ambulance was now a hearse. Mother, Ligita, you, and I trudged through the mud in our rubber boots. There had not been time enough to chisel a headstone. We'd have to use a simple wooden cross held together with twine.

Though Father had been a quiet man, he'd made many friends over the years. At the cemetery the widows Sosnovskis and Spassky huddled beneath a yellow umbrella shaped like a tulip. The Lee and Lim families, the Arijisnikovs, the Gipsises, and even the families who had argued most bitterly over where their plots lay came to pay their respects. And Mrs. Ilmyen. She stood by Rudy and me. "Your father solved many difficult mysteries." Her voice was a low hum, sounding like a wire stretched tightly. "He understood how to live." Mrs. Ilmyen turned and headed back to the cluster of dark shapes standing just beyond the low stone wall: Big Semyon, Jutta, Little Semyon. This is how we learned that Mr. Ilmyen had also passed in the night.

Through all this, Stanka watched quietly. I think she was in a state of disbelief. None of her tinctures and lotions had beaten back death. She walked backward around the mound. Three times she did this. Then she took a breath, held it. Then let it out. As she did, her breath was not a sigh but a song.

> *Sweet does the wind blow,*
> *So sweet,*
> *So sweet,*
> *From the garden rows.*

It was a Gypsy tune, and Stanka, whose voice usually sounded like gravel being raked with a stick, managed to turn it as soft as a gentle break in the rain. After Stanka had finished, we sang *dainas,* the old ones we hadn't sung in years. We knew these words by heart. They were water over rocks. They were breath in the lungs. We sang our love through time and light and momentary trouble. The clouds hung low, bending to our voices. The water rose to our songs. Our songs carried our tears, and our tears unlocked the quiet ruminations of the fields and stones and soil, and of those who lay beneath stone and soil.

If ever one of us flagged, Rudy raised his crutch, urging us on. You were the only one who did not sing. You were listening. At one point Ligita motioned you over to where she stood. She pointed to her belly. You placed a furry ear on the swell of her stomach; a smile spread across your face.

"She's singing," you said.

The rain fell flat and heavy. One by one our friends and neighbors dispersed. I did not want to go home. I knew that the mud would be to the top step and the shed was already one meter underwater. Minutes passed. An hour. I did not go to the river; it came to me. I had stood on its banks in sorrow. I had stood on its banks in joy. Now, as it swelled far beyond its banks, it lapped at my feet and I felt divided, confused. We had just sung and it had felt good and right. Now I felt empty, small, and defeated. Over the surface of the floodwater, the storks flew upside down, their reflections shadows wobbling behind them. From the low hills, the dogs barked, but it sounded as if they were swallowing yawns. Only the water from the sky moved as it usually did, rain falling drop by drop, point of proof each. The sky was closing in on us, one liquid bit of pressure at a time.

Mother joined us, one arm around you, her other arm around my waist. With help from Ligita and Joels, Rudy hobbled through the mud toward the stand of birch. "Our world is so small," Mother said. "Too small and we are so small in it."

"But we're not invisible," I said.

"No. We're not invisible, just small. Broken but not crushed. So it would be foolish to cry, wouldn't it?" She pitched her voice toward you, but she was looking at me. A question too burdensome to carry alone. "I have always thought I could draw strength from the river as if I were dipping a bucket in it." Mother's gray eyes and the river water one and the same color. "I used to believe that strength would rise and fill me. I'm not sure if I believe that anymore."

She gripped me tightly. We were all feeling broken, but the exact shapes of our ragged edges were in no way alike. This is the peculiar thing about sorrow: it is carried differently from person to person. It is unique and therefore uniquely painful.

The water lapped at our boots; mud crept into my shoes. I was about to suggest we head for higher ground, the hall maybe, when a colossal amount of noise came from upriver. Geese honking, dogs barking, and what sounded like every cow in Latvia bellowing.

"Ahoy there!" Dr. N., about one hundred meters upriver, waved his arms. He stood on the detached roof of his barn, now a barge held afloat by a thick bottom made of hundreds upon hundreds of wine corks. Beside him, Miss Dzelz held an oar. The barge approached: fifty meters, then twenty-five. He'd tethered his cows to the front and rear. Wearing their bright flotation suits, they bobbed beside the roof like enormous yellow buoys. They seemed to understand how ridiculous their situation was, as their chuffing and snorting tipped from simple confusion to bellows of outrage. The barge gently nuzzled the alders. Then it became wedged tightly against the trees.

"Be so kind!" Dr. N. called out. "A little push, please. And then hop aboard."

The cows tethered to the front of Dr. N.'s floating barn roof lowed and grunted. Ditto for the cows tethered to the back. I looked at Mother. She looked at me. We had two choices: stay where we were and huddle and cling. Or we could step onto the barn roof and head for high ground.

Mother placed a foot gingerly onto a plank, testing it. "It appears something wonderful can come of lavish drinking," Mother said, as she stepped aboard. The rest of us followed, the rear brought up by the Ilmyens. Joels and Dr. N. pushed against the alders with their oars and the roof broke free. I'd never seen Dr. N. so jubilant. At last—an experiment with tangible, useful results. We were floating, no doubt about it. And the cows, too. Carried along by the river's current, they kicked listlessly from time to time with their hooves as they surveyed the passing landscape.

Dr. N. nudged Joels. "Who would have guessed they'd be such good swimmers?"

Beside him, Miss Dzelz grinned. Had it not been for the two of them bathing each other in long looks of love, the situation on the barn roof would have been nothing short of awkward. For there, sitting side by side looking small and forlorn, were the Zetsches. Mr. Zetsche was not wearing his elevated shoes. Mrs. Zetsche did not have her many fine things beside her. It was just the two of them. We could not escape them and they could not escape us.

Mr. Zetsche's gaze slid over us, paused at Rudy, then dropped. He adjusted his hat so that the brim shielded him from our presence. He hadn't been with us at Father's grave; he knew that he wouldn't have been welcome. It pained me to see how clearly he understood this.

Carefully, Mother crossed the roof. She made her way to Mrs. Zetsche and sat beside her. For a long moment, neither woman spoke. In the distance we could see the blue and green and red roofs of barns and houses. A flat land of flattened geometries. Small squares of yellow, the light from within the school and the hall, wobbled downriver.

"Ruined," Mrs. Zetsche said quietly. "Everything is ruined. The manor house—it's gone." Mrs. Zetsche was shivering.

"I know," Mother said, as she took off her own coat and gently draped it around Mrs. Zetsche. How quickly this river erased that great rift between those whom we presumed had too much and those whom we presumed were worthy of having more. We were losing everything together, watching it float and bump and knock along the water. Disaster rendering us equal in our losses. We could not look at them or anyone else with envy. And maybe this was the biggest loss of all: who could we blame now for our troubles?

We drifted past the Arijisnikovs, who sat on their chimney and cheered us on. By this time, the rain had stopped, the clouds had lifted. The darkness above smeared with the dark water. Then lights. Stars. Stars wobbled in the sky; stars wobbled on the inky surface of the water. I had something like a vision then, or maybe it was just a glimpse of insight beyond my ordinary understanding. For a glorious three and a half minutes I apprehended what this all meant. We were collectively being baptized. We were floating above and beyond our ordinary longings, our ugly mistakes, our complicated history. It was all for this moment. And I would be the woman I had always wanted to be: wise beyond my years, sturdy and useful in a way that far surpassed the mere physical limits of my body. Mother would not be weary. Rudy would not be angry. And Ligita. She would have her child, who would be healthy, who would call her mother, who would look upon her with the eyes of love. And you would, at last, have a world worth listening to.

As though you could hear my thoughts, my deepest hopes, you dipped an ear into the water. Could you hear Mr. Zetsche's stallions thundering along the riverbed? Perhaps you were listening to his fine cars, waterlogged and settling into the soft river bottom. Velta's piano played now by pike and eels sliding their bodies over the strings, maybe you heard that, too. Lighter objects—mateless shoes, chessmen, cell phones—they made no noise at all as they swirled merrily downriver.

Ligita sat beside Rudy, her face drawn. She gripped his hand, squeezed it tightly. A contraction. That is when the barge bumped none too gently into the hall. Ligita clutched her stomach. "Uh-oh," she said.

What happened in the hall? It may seem odd to tell you things you witnessed. But sometimes we can look at a thing and not really know what it is we are seeing. Remember the rocks that harbor galaxies of stars? We can participate in their making and not even know it. The cows, as you may recall, clustered outside the hall, pressing their forlorn snouts against the windowpanes, fogging them with their collective snorts and sighs. Their snug chartreuse buoyancy suits, comfortable enough in water, added girth they could not quite account for nor accommodate. With each attempt to sidle alongside one another or squeeze through the narrow hall door, they bounced and toppled ridiculously.

Ligita's water broke. Her shouts, as sharp as corrugated metal, punctured the close air of the hall. Mrs. Ilmyen, Jutta, Big Semyon, and Little Semyon murmured their prayers, a rustling hush from the far end of the hall. Mother and I held Ligita's hand.

Rudy whispered into her ear, "You're doing brilliantly." Her pain amplified his; he pounded his fist into his thigh in a series of dull thuds that sounded, you wrote, like a weaver's shuttle thudding across a loom. Every thud was another beat to that measure of his tuneless song.

Mr. Zetsche, who had not said a word all this time, approached Rudy cautiously. In his hand he held an unlit cigar. He cut the nib. "It's not much, but believe me when I say this: it is all I have." Mr. Zetsche offered Rudy the cigar. With a trembling hand, Rudy took it while Mr. Zetsche struck a match and held the light as Rudy coaxed the flame, his cheeks working like the leathery folds of a fireside bellows.

Around hour eleven we grew restless. Joels had gone out and milked the cows, no easy feat as they were still fitted in their flotation suits. The Zetsches had drunk their way through an entire tureen of coffee. We had memorized one another's faces. There was no electricity, just the carbide lamps and their sharp smell and garish light.

"What will we do if the water keeps rising?" Mrs. Ilmyen wondered aloud.

"We'll sing," Joels murmured, and Stanka concurred with a bobbing of her head.

"We sang already," Big Semyon reminded us.

"We could pray," Jutta said.

"It can't hurt." This from Miss Dzelz.

"All right," Mother sighed. "But please—none of those long-winded Lutheran prayers."

And through it all, Velta watched in silence. Sky hanging over her head, clouds at her breast: milk of heaven. Her mouth pressed tightly. Not from anger. Not from resignation. But from recognition. *When your life has been as full as mine, who needs words?* Father had said this and she was saying it now. We needed this new life, loud and boisterous and messy, as much as we needed our old lives set in tidy words, written on musical scores, and etched on our faces. *See how quickly this all changes,* her eyes said. *See what a little water can do.*

A cry. Low and long. And then another cry. High and jagged. The baby was here.

· · ·

The river shrank, leaving behind a thick layer of marl, river mud, grass, and ruined heirlooms. You helped the men dredge the river and wrote of their curious retrievals: Mother's typewriter, a wooden spinning wheel, two of Mr. Z.'s stallions. The other three had sunk to their withers in the soft river bottom and there they would have to stay. Mr. Zetsche, it turned out, wasn't kidding when he said all was lost. Their mansion, once so grand and stately, sat reeking and gutted. And this made an occasion for a sort of healing. You heard Mrs. Z.'s almost imperceptible sniffles; you suggested we build their house first. Joels agreed, and he and Rudy went door-to-door collecting volunteer labor.

Young men, old men. Rudy's mates, the Merry Afflictions. Little Semyon. They gathered on a plot behind the hall, the highest elevation in town. One wheelbarrow of concrete at a time — mixed by hand and wheeled by hand amid dew, rain, and dusk — the new minimansion took shape. Smaller than their previous home, this newer one did not have as many shiny porcelains. But it was what we could build and it was what they needed.

Were some of those young men the same ones who'd thrown bricks through the windows, set fire to the Riviera's shops? No one asked; no one needed to ask. This was the water's reckoning, calling us to account. This was forgiveness worked out one stone at a time.

This generosity did not go unnoticed. Mrs. Zetsche stood beside Stanka for long stretches of time during those weeks as slab by slab, beam by beam, a new mansion emerged. It did not escape our notice when, from time to time, Mrs. Zetsche wiped at her eyes — genuine tears. Stanka often stood next to Mrs. Z., offering her dark sunflower seeds and spare tissues. *How many generous people live in this town?* Mrs. Z. was asking herself this, I imagined. I knew the answer: like the little stones at the river's edge, too many to count.

The river moved differently, slower in places where it had once been swift, surging over rocks where once had been still pockets for sleeping eels. We couldn't catch them to save our lives that next year. "Water has its own will," you said one day, as you twirled a fuzzy gun-barrel cleaner into first one ear canal then the other. The barrel cleaner a gift from Mr. Zetsche. "That's why it is a sin against nature to try to contain it or control it."

And like the river, you had changed. In the three years following the flood, you grew taller than Rudy and we had to stop calling you Little Maris. You became simply Maris. The muscles in your back and neck thickened, as did the downy fuzz on your ears. Thinking you were the Bear Slayer incarnate, a PR firm lobbied hard to make you the national hockey team's mascot. You were even profiled in a magazine that heralded you as the next presidential hopeful. Joels and I discussed the situation; we'd endured other legends that could not be stifled. We'd saddle this rumor — and many more — and ride it.

You tell me that it was during this time your powers of hearing changed. That broad pallet of sound that had for so many years kept you awake at night narrowed considerably. Regarding certain sounds, you were almost deaf; you could not hear the political goings-on in Riga and did not care to. When Mr. Z. enquired about the economic outlook and the news of Hong Kong markets, you reported an unusual trending toward Arthurian reenactments in Canada and shifts in the polar ice whose groaning and cracks sometimes kept you up at night. Quieter noise, too, interrupted your sleep.

You could hear different bodies of water, could hear what color their beds were, how fast they moved over their beds; you heard the fish dreaming in the rivers: the Daugava, the Neva, and even the Amazon. But it was the Aiviekste you listened to most. In autumn, the height of eel season, we could not manage to hook a single one. It was the eels, you declared, pounding the side of your head with your open palm. They were in distress, you said, prevented from making free passage in the river by a heavy solid object. Upon further investigation, we learned what that solid object was: the steel plate of Velta's piano. Wedged in a tight bottleneck of the river, it took all of the

men working and a hydraulic winch whining and ratcheting to pull it
out. And this, too, worked a shift inside the way some of us thought
about eels. They were not so different from us in their desires. All
they wanted was to live their lives unobstructed and unobserved. It
seemed wrong to catch and eat them somehow.

I can see texture in the air, weight to the light. I can measure the
strength of a shadow by its crisp edges. I'll never hear as well as you
do, but I can discern a sweetness to breath and cricket song and the
yelps and rumbles of dogs down the lane, noises that used to annoy
me. And Uncle. His voice is a faint rasp, but I can distinguish it from
that of the cicada and the cricket. It's an incessant rattling, the sound
of vitamins shaken in a bottle. And I understand he has things to tell
me. A score to settle.

"A mirror is not, I repeat, not a miracle." Uncle's voice is a scratch
at the window. I understand now that I have prevented his passage; I
have been his haunting.

I have worn the white gloves and scoured Oskars's Bible forward
and back. I am no theologian, only a shabby practitioner of faith. But
I have to believe the answer is yes. I am in need of forgiveness. It has
taken me some time to realize it, but my anger toward Uncle has
pinned him to me, and for this, I need his forgiveness and he is in need
of mine. Our mutual ire has kept us bound together. About burying
him with the Bible, I will confess — just between you and me — that
I am guilty but unrepentant. Though it became his condemnation, a
curse, it is also his blessing. He has been steadily wounded on account
of those psalms boring holes in his hips. But, you've written in your
Book of Wonder, isn't a blessing a thrash in the wound, isn't this the
pain of redemption, isn't this how we are gloriously healed?

Time moves in one direction, our bodies catalog its passing. After
the flood, you recorded every change in the river's movements, every
shift of mud, snag, deepening pocket of dark water. It took two years,

but your uncle Rudy learned to operate a backhoe with one leg. Your auntie Ligita achieved the fame she so desired; working as a hand model, she often rode the bus to Riga for photo shoots.

You have been such a good cousin to their Little Biruta. She tugs on your ears and you never lose your patience. They named her after your grandmother, and I think nothing could have brought her more joy: hearing the sound of small feet pattering up and down the hallway.

Though Little Biruta was far too young at the time to really understand, your grandmother told her the importance of the potato and the correct way to shred beets. That's how I knew your grandmother was ill: she was releasing the family recipes.

She said she was tired, that's all, but a call to Dr. N., some tests at the clinic, and we had our answer: she'd been suffering a series of small to large heart attacks. "But didn't you feel them?" I asked incredulously. "How could you not know?" And she smiled, as she did so often in those last days, a tired, helpless smile. "I thought I'd swallowed a stone. Ha."

Mrs. Ilmyen brought over her prized pair of heels and insisted your grandmother at least try them on. Never in her life had she been fussed over. Never once in her life had she allowed it. And now our clumsy excess of attention — Rudy carrying in a tea tray! — only alerted her to the gravity of her situation. "I really am dying," she said to me. "Yes," I said.

One evening in July when the light through the window painted her bedroom walls in swaths of lilac, Mother lay in bed. I sat with her, my rough, cracked hands on hers. "I'm afraid," she murmured. "I know I shouldn't be. Every good thing is on the other side. Why am I so afraid of the good things?"

I did not know how to answer her then. I'm not sure I will ever know the answer to that question. I sang for her instead, my voice reedy and thin and unsure.

I am the beginner of the song.
I stand in the middle.
If I wasn't the beginner
Of the song,
I wouldn't stand in the middle.

I hummed the song to Mother, the beginner of my song, the one who stands in the middle.

Mother put a hand on my hand. "Something is changing inside of me. Before all this, I could not see God anywhere. Now I see God everywhere I look." Her gaze had drifted to a corner of pooling shadow.

I squinted, wanting to see what she could divine in that burgeoning darkness.

She died that night. We lit a candle, kept it at the bedside. You guarded the flame while Rudy and Joels brought in the coffin, lifted Mother's small body, and tenderly set her inside. For the wake, we made *rasols,* this time using ham, onion, and potatoes. All the while, I heard Mother's voice. *Don't even think of serving it without crushed dill!* Stanka gave us a down pillow, a traditional Roma gift at funerals. If we were Roma, we'd have ended up with twenty-seven pillows. Why twenty-seven and not twenty-eight or twenty-six Stanka could not say. But the down was genuine—she plucked the geese herself.

I know you remember the walk to the cemetery. How we picked up the coffin, walked a little way, set it down. This is how we carry burdens together. We shift the weight; we allow the hands to breathe; we change positions. Together we stoop, grab the straps, lift, and shuffle forward.

At the cemetery we walked to the hole in the ground beside Father. You and Little Semyon and Rudy and Joels lowered the coffin with ropes. Then Rudy and Joels shoveled the dirt into the hole, heaping the dirt into a mound. We piled high the oak boughs, the red roses. We piled high the *dainas: I will open a casket of songs and engender joy.*

Spring's green witchery has returned. Yellow light climbs the wall. Sets the green on the birch shivering. The light through the leaves casts a fine gold on the floor. I hear humming. The bees have returned. The bees have made a nest inside my head. How they work, tirelessly reeving a home within my loosely woven thoughts. They dart like needles, knitting light and sound. Stanka tells me that God needs no light in heaven, no sun, no lamp, for the bees hum light and clover all about heaven. We shall drip with honey. She says this as she sits beside me, her long knitting needles clicking and clacking.

I am of two minds about the noise of knitting. On the one side, I like the sound of rhythmic ticking. On the other side, I can't help but hear the tick and sweep of a hand over a clock's face. Each tick says, *Now.* I'm hearing my last breaths being counted.

I was thinking this and wishing you were in the blue chair. I wanted you to remind me that asteroids are built of the leftover scraps of planets or to recount for me the patience and humility with which for thirty years an Arab astronomer, your hero, observed the tranquil wanderings of a distant star. Or to tell me the theory that globular clusters of stars contain at their centers black holes. Knots and lace. I wanted to hear something, anything, when Stanka nodded to the corner of the room. The long mirror set in the leather ox harness stood there, returning to us our astonished images. Who had put it there? I can't even imagine. A puddle of darkness gathered beneath the mirror. The glass turned to liquid and hummed. Did Stanka see a long white hand beckoning me? Did she see what I saw: a claw wanting to catch me by what's left of my hair and pull me through? I don't know. But she leaped up from the chair and lunged with her needles for the glass. She skewered that mirror and it shattered in a delicate tinkling of glass. As those pieces fell to the floor, they caught the last light and multiplied it exponentially. I sat on the edge of the bed, bathed in light.

What is it I dream of during my fevered sleeps? White gloves, the hall oven, Mother's dark hair, Uncle's lopsided smile. I do think of David from time to time. Sleep ushers unbidden, extravagant, expansive memories. In sleep I am a different woman, as light as air, buoyed up by better, wiser water. Crazy talk, I know, but I have committed myself to telling the truth, odd as it may be. So I'll tell you. In my dream a crow perched in my open hand. *Speak,* I said, *your servant is listening.* As sharp as a quill, as quick as thought, it pierced my heart. I heard my name called across water. I cannot stop what will happen next. Death is a baptism in a river that rushes swift and cool. I have one foot in the river and one in the mud. I have no regrets. I am not afraid.

I do miss them all terribly. Father, Mother, Joels. Joels went quickly, and for his sake and yours, I was glad. You're right. Life isn't fair, but it is just. We will all die, some of us sooner than others, and no one knows that better than our family. I'll never forget how, as we dug Joels's grave, you muttered, *I never want to dig another grave again.* And here you are, in the chair, your palms cracked, fingers curling. On account of my grave. You could be bitter. Hate God. Hate this life. But you've always maintained a capacious vision, a vigilant belief in all possible possibility, an unashamed pursuit of wonder, which in itself is a rare kind of grace.

You are reading from your Book of Wonder: tar water and brake dust will seal out the dead. If you stand in a river, you will never feel the same water touch you twice. A story is never told exactly the same way. Though the words are knots anchoring and calling forth shape from emptiness, no two shapes evoked are precisely alike. The words work on us differently each time we hear them. I suppose this is why we sing the *dainas* and say the psalms. As familiar as they are, they will never grow old. We stand in those familiar waters and feel ourselves transformed anew.

This is the power of word worked through the body. This is why we must tell our stories, sing our songs. This is how we forgive and are forgiven. *Is this enough?* you ask me often. Of what use are our lives, our stories? What use to tell them in a world going deaf? Well, I've always believed you are a prophet. So shout. Tell the untellable tale. You stand in the middle, singer and song. You hold the sash binding us together, binding up our wounds.

So much more I wanted to tell you. All the aches our flesh is heir to. Don't be afraid of sorrow. It is the making of many. I want to tell you why we eat crunchy yellow peas in a bowl on New Year's or count fish scales. Why some people throw old shoes and broken things out a window. Why we jump fire on Jani Day.

You have asked for advice and this is it. Let us weave our dark parables; let us bury them deeply and firmly, pushing them down to an unshakable foundation, a bedrock of truth. Let us build upon that. Let us tell our stories and sing our songs. Let us baptize our world in words.

ACKNOWLEDGMENTS

Deepest gratitude to my parents who told me all their stories and encouraged me to tell mine. I thank my husband and children for their unswerving faith in me. I thank Julie Barer for guiding the ship to shore and Jenna Johnson and Pilar Garcia-Brown for their keen vision and kind hearts.

Many thanks to the many friends and readers who gave countless hours reading the manuscript in all its incarnations. Specifically, I wish to thank William Boggess, Don Comfort, Adrianne Harun, Colleen Jefferey, David Mehler, Bernie Meyer, Lynn Otto, Melissa Pritchard, Geronimo Tagatac, Colette Tennant, the members of the Chrysostom Society, and colleagues at Corban University and Seattle Pacific University's Low Residency MFA program.

For their help with research, I wish to thank the good folks at the YWAM base in Talsi, Al and Carolyn Akimoff, Judite Dzelzs, Ilga, Lev, Inara, Kristina and Ivo, and Peter and Emma Samoylich. For their guidance and aid in research, I wish to thank everyone with Bridge Builders International, specifically Charles and Nancy Kelley, Inete Zale, Katie and Dan Roth, Dustin and Kristine Peterson, and Paula Hewitt. Special thanks to Ilze Gulens, Juris Kronbergs, and Knuts Skujenieks for their help.

Research for this novel was made possible through the generous assistance of the Howard Foundation and Oregon Literary Arts, Inc.

Reading Group Guide

1. Discuss the importance of *dainas* to young Maris, his family, and his community. What role do these songs play in their lives? Would you say *dainas* bring people together?

2. This novel follows a family of grave diggers and revolves around themes of secrets, memory, and the relationship between the living and the dead. What does grave digging lend to these ideas? How do our central characters view the dead and their legacies?

3. Maris has very large, fuzzy ears that allow him to hear the secrets of the dead. Discuss elements of magic in the book. How do they serve the story?

4. "And now this: your Book of Wonder. You opened the thick cloth-bound cover and out of a cloud of dust rose a moth, its wings transparent yellow, fluttering, up, up. I took it as a sign that this book of unraveling thread and flaking binder's glue still held life, sudden flight, and subtle possibility" (page 23). What does Inara mean by this? In what ways does Maris's Book of Wonder hold life, flight, and possibility?

5. On page 51, Inara says to Maris: "Why am I telling you in such detail about what might seem like irrelevant conversations that happened before you were born? The short answer: it's a way to keep our loved ones alive, if only in our embroidered fictions." Discuss the ways in which stories and memories are transmitted throughout the novel. Who does the telling? Who does the listening? Does it matter that many of these memories are "embroidered fictions"? Can truth telling happen through fiction?

6. Would you call this novel a love story? If so, why? If not, why not? Who are the lovers in this book? And what types of love does the author explore?

7. "Every creature carries within itself an internal clock, an unerring sense of when it is the precise time to do or not do something" (page

196). Inara begins to perceive the "order and design" (page 197) in every creature. What does this realization mean to her and how does it affect her outlook? How does her realization of this "internal clock" tie into the larger themes of the novel?

8. Many of these characters have endured so much sorrow, yet humor manages to assert itself. Discuss the role of humor in the novel and in the lives of its characters.

9. What advice does Inara hope to impart on her son? What does she mean when she says, "Let us baptize our world in words" (page 299)?

Q&A with Gina Ochsner

How did the idea for the book originate? Why did you choose to set it in Latvia?

One day I stumbled across the book *A Woman in Amber* by Agate Nesaule. In it she described how as a child she had endured multiple occupations in Latvia. I marveled at the courage it took for her to write such a moving account of what was a very dark time. I marveled, too, at my complete ignorance regarding historical events that occurred during those years in the Baltic countries. In fact, I did not even know where Latvia was. By coincidence, around that same time I signed up for a Russian language class at a local community college. On the first day we were asked by the instructor to work in pairs. My partner turned out to be a young man of about eighteen years of age. We exchanged greetings in English, then Russian, and launched into our scripted dialogue. I noticed he had no trouble whatsoever with Russian grammar, conversation, or pronunciation.

"What in the world are you doing in this beginner-level class?" I asked him.

"Well," he said, "I needed an easy A."

"But how do you know Russian so well? Are you Russian?" I asked.

He looked at me with horror. "God, no! I'm Latvian!" I looked at him with a blank expression. He grimaced. "Everybody in Latvia was forced to speak Russian. But I hate Russian. I hate Russians." We finished our scripted grammar dialogue and on the drive home I replayed our conversation. Where, I wondered, did his rancor come from? At eighteen years old, he seemed a little young to be so bitter. What was it like to live in Soviet-occupied Latvia in the 1970s and 1980s? I decided I should try to find out. I would begin with history and then would find more work written by Latvians.

I went to a local independent bookstore and walked straight up to the help desk. "How hard would it be to find books about Latvia written by

Latvians? Also, how hard is it to find a good Latvian-English dictionary?" I asked the woman working there.

The woman's eyes lit up. "It's not hard—not too terribly hard. Just expensive," she said. "But, may I ask, *why* do you want these things?"

I had been bitten by the Latvian bug. It was like falling in love, it just happened.

She pointed to her name tag, which read "Dace."

"I'm Latvian," she said. "And nobody comes in here asking for anything about Latvia. This is so exciting!"

By the end of that week, Dace had combed through her personal library and loaded me up with her family's history books.

The more I read the more I realized how little I knew. And I sensed there was so much more than what history books could tell me. I wanted to know what Latvia looked like in different seasons, how Latvians ring in a new year or celebrate a new birth, which kind of beer would be voted best in an informal poll. I knew that I needed to see Latvia for myself.

My family was dubious about my plan. I had a long and thoroughly established tradition of getting lost. "You don't speak Latvian and the Russian you speak is *so* bad!" My mother said. "How will you get along?"

Another impossible question. I answered the only way I knew how: with a smile and a shrug. Ten years and five trips to Latvia later, my journey has resulted in many beautiful friendships and now this, a book.

Did you find it challenging to write from the perspective of a Latvian?

One of the biggest hurdles for me was grappling with the questions: What right do I have to try to tell a story about people living in a country I have never lived in? And what gives me permission to try to show and explore Latvian history? These were huge concerns for me and I consulted my Latvian friends often, begging them to be frank. "Well, Latvians as a rule are almost always frank," one friend said. "So I'll tell you. Some Latvians will never forgive you for writing about Latvia. On the other hand, if you don't, I'll never forgive you."

Even though I had the blessing of one friend, I knew it would be important for me to do as much research as possible. Given my lack of knowledge and language skills, it would be imperative that I find people living both in Latvia and elsewhere who would tell me their stories. I needed to find out what it means to people to "be Latvian." This necessitated several trips to various parts of Latvia. I found myself concentrating my efforts on two smaller towns, Talsi, which is near the west coast of Latvia, and Tilža, which is closer to the eastern border. I wanted to see how country life was different from the city life of the country's capital, Riga. I wanted to hear from people who had lived through the Soviet occupation, about what it meant to be Latvian then and what it means to be Latvian now. I wanted to know how much a loaf of bread cost in 1965. Why do Latvians eat crunchy yellow peas on New Year's Eve? Why do Lithuanians call Latvians "horse heads"? Why do Latvians sometimes joke about the unflappable nature of Estonians? Why are there so many storks in Latvia and what prompts them to migrate each year on precisely the same day in August? Some of my questions were downright silly and some probably seemed irreverent, but I simply wanted to know all that I could from all of the perspectives available to me. What a wonderful journey of discovery!

Can you talk about why it was important for you to explore so deeply familial and community relationships in the book?

At some point during one of my visits to Latvia, while interviewing a man and his father who had been forcibly relocated and had worked several years in a camp, I realized that any story I might try to write would be a story told and carried and remembered by many people. But each of these people might remember different aspects of the same event. Each person might hold radically different interpretations of what happened. And each person's memory, of course, is the "true" rendering of that event. Memory is both privately and collectively constructed. More interviews and more history gathering led me to believe that no story exists outside of relationships.

I hoped to tell a story in which characters are confronted with their own failings, yearnings, misapprehensions, or misinterpretations of people and events. Exploring characters in their relationships and allowing them to have those misunderstandings is another way to allow them to find out who they really are.

You've also penned short stories and essays. Do you prefer a certain medium of storytelling over others?

Time for a confession. I have gone on record as a die-hard short story enthusiast, but something odd and unexpected has happened to me: I think I've fallen in love with the novel. It has been a long courtship, ten and half years, to be exact. But I'm seeing a capaciousness and an expansiveness to the novel that short stories, by definition, don't allow for. This isn't to say that I don't write stories anymore. I do. The short story permits a mischievousness and compression that doesn't always suit a novel.

Both mediums serve stories well, so the question I ask myself is, Which medium is right for the story I want to tell right *now*?

What do you hope readers will take away from the book?

This may sound ridiculously sentimental, but so be it: I hope readers leave the last page carrying with them a sense of delight and wonder in the simplest acts of existence. Life, chaotic and maddening as it can be at times, is far too fleeting, too fragile to ignore. I hope readers leave the narrative with a renewed sense of awe and reverence for the natural world and our place in it. And I hope readers feel a renewed curiosity about this world and their own tangle of relationships. As I was wrestling with the last few chapters, I was feeling a sadness that the process of actual writing was drawing to a close, but I was also invigorated. My characters' curiosities have become my curiosities.

For more from Gina Ochsner, please visit her website:
www.ginaochsner.com.